Iron Ties

Also by Ann Parker

Silver Lies

Iron Ties

Ann Parker

Poisoned Pen
PRESS

Sourcebooks, Poisoned Pen Press and the colophon are registered trademarks of
Sourcebooks, Inc.

Published by Poisoned Pen Press, an imprint of Sourcebooks
P.O. Box 4410, Naperville, Illinois 60567-4410
(630) 961-3900
sourcebooks.com

Library of Congress Cataloging-in-Publication data is on file with the publisher.

Printed and bound in The United States of America.
POD 10 9 8 7 6 5 4 3 2

For Aunt Dorothy,
who preserved the family history and introduced me to
the pleasures of researching the past.

For female relatives, who went west (or east)
in search of adventure: Corinne, Bette, Frances, Elsie,
great-grandmother Mary, great-great aunts Pauline and
Caroline. And for Granny, Inez Stannert Parker,
who came to Colorado and stayed.

For Bill, who walks the present with me.

For Devyn and Ian, who carry the future.

Acknowledgments

The road for *Iron Ties* was a long one. Not quite as long as building the transcontinental railroad or fighting the Civil War, but nearly. Thanks are due to a battalion of people who lent their support, expertise, and readers' sensibilities.

First of all, my family. Bill, for everything. Ian, for a good critical read and suggestions for keeping my fictional teenager from being too "hokey." Devyn, for her inspiring drawings and her spirit. It ain't easy to have a partner or parent who time-travels into the 19th century, often without warning, and I'm grateful to them all for hanging in there. Thanks to my parents, Don and Corinne, and to my sibs and their partners, for moral support. I'm particularly in debt to the Colorado contingent—Dave and Elly, Bette, Joel, Kim, and Jake—for encouragement, lodgings, the warmth of extended family.

I am indebted to an army of experts who were most gracious with their time and expertise. Regarding railroads: Kenton Forrest at the Colorado Railroad Museum library kindly answered my barrage of questions. Lisa Hayes and John Ainslie were generous with their time and expertise, and I thank them for the a lively, informative, and much-needed "what if" conversation. Ann Thomsen provided great leads for the future. Mary Reed and Eric Mayer shared a fascinating document on attitudes towards railroads. Dani Greer offered enticing tidbits on General Palmer, founder of the Denver & Rio Grande Railroad. For information on the Civil War and related topics: Roy Marcot shared his knowledge of Berdan's Sharpshooters and Remington firearms, for which I am most grateful. Steven Crain deserves a twenty-one gun salute for lending me a goodly fraction of his Civil War library collection and answering endless queries with grace and good humor. I'm also much obliged to the 69th New York Volunteer Infantry, Company A reenactors for a firsthand look at Civil War life and armaments. As for the rest, I want to thank Laurie Powers, members of Women Writing the West, and Ellen Hedges for horse-related information, Kathleen York for sidesaddle insights, Dr. Doug Lyle (the doctor is always in!) for medical advice, and John Karachewski for a quick geological consult. All flights of fancy, errors, and falls off factual cliffs are my responsibility.

For critique of the draft(s) and parts thereof, I'm indebted to: Camille Minichino, Penny Warner, Kathleen Antrim, Colleen Casey, Mike Cooper, Amy and Steven Crain, Margaret Dumas, Janet Finsilver, Dani and Michael Greer, Kim Hansen, Fred Hoffman, Jonnie Jacobs, Claire Johnson, Rena Leith, Henie Lentz, Peggy Lucke, Staci McLaughlin, Carole Price, Priscilla Royal, Catherine Sketchley, and Gordon Yano, as well as Jane Staehle for that last, fast read. A special thanks goes to those "on the ground" in Leadville who graciously read and commented on the draft: Carol and Bob Elder, Nancy and Jeff McCain, and Janice Fox.

Leadville and its denizens, past and present, deserve special mention. Especially Bob Elder, for answering frantic queries from afar and for sharing the amazing letters of his grandfather, George Elder, who came to Leadville in its heyday to start a new life. Thanks to Elizabeth Bush of Apple Blossom Inn for making my Leadville stays enjoyable and to Hillery and Bruce McAllister for their kindness and insights into Leadville—past and present. And to those who keep hold of history: the staff of the Lake County Public Library (with a special tip of the hat to historian Nancy Manly), the National Mining Hall of Fame & Museum, and the Leadville Historical Society.

I'm indebted to the Colorado Historical Society and the Denver Public Library for their collections, where I never cease to find historical treasures, and for their always helpful staff.

Thanks also to Colorado's Helen Dawson for coming up with the title, and Terry McLaughlin for anteing up at Left Coast Crime, El Paso, for a role in *Iron Ties*.

And to my web designer, Kate Reed…where would I be in cyberspace without you? Thank you, Kate.

Finally, the great folks at Poisoned Pen Press have my heartfelt gratitude. You probably wouldn't be holding this book and reading this if not for them. Special thanks goes to editor Barbara Peters, for her insightful comments and for steering me back on track when I wandered off on side spurs. And thanks to all the rest of the Press-ers—Rob, Marilyn, Nan, Jessica, Geetha, Monty, and Jen (PPP-U.K.)—for helping make *Iron Ties* a reality.

"The great questions of the time are not decided by speeches and majority decisions…but by iron and blood."

—Otto von Bismarck

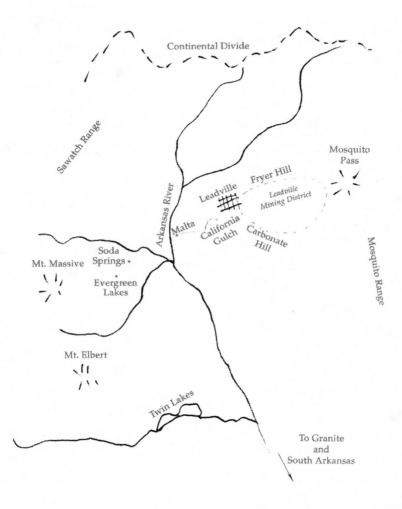

Downtown Leadville

Prologue

June 1880

If there's a heaven on earth, I've found it here, in Colorado.

Standing at the edge of a snow-pocked rocky slope, Susan Carothers set down the canvas-covered box holding her small view camera, three glass plates, and black hood, and topped it with the folded tripod. She examined the landscape and let out her breath in a long, contented sigh.

High-mountain grasses rippled alongside the Arkansas River. A few spindly aspen and fir that had escaped the axes of prospectors and loggers hugged the riverbanks. Meadows beyond raced across wide spaces to bow at the toes of Massive and Elbert, the tallest peaks in Colorado.

The new train track glinted below. Silent. Untraveled. It paced the base of the slope at a cautious distance and sent out a splinter of a side track where two railroad cars waited their turns to travel on. A trestle carried the main line across the gulch and river, from east to west. Several miles up the valley, out of sight beyond the bend of the ridgeline, laborers toiled over wood ties and steel rails. Foot by foot, they were building the road of the iron horse, bringing it ever closer to Leadville.

Susan turned to the north, squinting at a cluster of abandoned charcoal kilns nestled at the mouth of the gulch. The morning sun cast their elongated beehive-shaped shadows toward the river.

With a professional photographer's eye, Susan translated the scenery's greens, blues, and browns into the blacks, whites, and grays of a photograph.

Perfect!

She turned her back on the kilns and trestle, eyeing an abandoned shack and mining portal situated on a ledge halfway across the steep terrain. The ledge would yield panoramic views of the mountains. Views that would sell well at her studio in Leadville.

She scowled, thinking of the saddle horse and burro she'd hired, now tied off on the brushy bench behind her and sheltered in a copse of scraggly firs. All the coaxing and tugging in the world hadn't convinced the burro, burdened down with photographic equipment, to take so much as a step onto the talus. Where the loose rubble ended and the slope steepened to near vertical, she could see a well-defined trail, cut into the rock, leading to the shelf and cabin.

She brushed at the knee-length skirt covering the bloomers of her Reform dress and pondered her next move. *I'll cross the slope and set up the camera in the cabin so that it looks out the window. If it rains, the equipment will stay dry.*

Susan glanced up at wispy clouds. A year and a half of living and working in Leadville had impressed upon her how fickle weather could be in the Rocky Mountains. Over the course of an hour, the innocent blue sky might transform into a thunderstorm of Wagnerian intensity.

She bent down, gripped the tripod and the handle of the heavy camera box with firm resolve, and stepped forward, trying not to think what would happen if she lost her footing on the loose rocks.

By the time Susan arrived at her destination, she was out of breath in the thin mountain air.

The shack squatted on the dusty bench, facing a mine portal shored up with timber. She wondered if the former occupants had had any luck or whether Disappointment Gulch had lived up to its name. *Ah well. I'm prospecting for scenery, not ore.*

She entered the shack and looked around. Hard-packed dirt floor. Rough timbered shelves along one wall. A window, long emptied of glass, framed a mountain vista that echoed her vision. Susan smiled and lowered tripod and box to the floor. Eager to get to work, she removed her coat and hung it on a crooked nail in the wall.

It took an hour to set up the camera at the window. Satisfied at last with the placement and the light, Susan knelt on the dirt floor, rustling through the box for a replacement to a plate holder's stripped screw. The wind paused, and the river's whisper was broken by the sharp clip-clop of a horse.

Resting a hand on the rough timbered window frame, Susan looked down at the railroad track, nearly a hundred feet below. A man dismounted and, reins in hand, glanced up and down the track. Susan noted his ramrod straight bearing, and his military-style cap and greatcoat—*faded blue? Or gray? A soldier?*

He walked to the siding and the cars, examining the rolling stock. He then headed away toward the trestle and the kiln field. Susan considered, then shrugged, deciding that he was probably on railroad business.

She turned her attention back to her camera, removed the lens cap, made the exposure, and replaced the cap. Before she could remove the plate, the soldier reappeared without his horse, cradling a box in his arms.

He crossed to the siding. Susan debated whether to call out and make her presence known. He opened the box and extracted a tube, the length of a man's forearm. And red as danger. Susan sucked in her breath and retreated a step into the shadows.

She'd lived long enough in the mining town of Leadville to know what that tube held.

Giant powder.

More powerful than black powder, by far. So dangerous that the railway companies refused to transport it, leaving muleskin-ners to haul it by freight wagons over the high mountain passes to Leadville and the other mining towns.

The soldier methodically placed two, four, six cartridges beneath the railroad cars and attached blasting caps and long fuses. Susan watched in horror.

He's going to blow up the cars!

She ran to the shack's entrance and stopped. There was no way to retrace her steps across the slope without being visible from below. The best course of action, she told herself, was to wait until the fuses were lit and then to run for the mine portal. When the giant powder exploded, there was no guarantee the shack would survive the flying debris. Heart pounding, Susan returned to the window to see another rider approaching from the north, from the direction of Leadville.

The soldier must have seen or heard the rider as well. He stepped between the two cars, hidden from the rider's view, but still visible to Susan. After some scrutiny of the approaching horse and rider, he looked up in Susan's direction, removed his cap, and waved it.

He's seen me! Panic curdled in her stomach.

She shrank against the cabin wall before logic whispered that the friendly wave was not meant for her. *For whom, then?* A vision of the ridge above her rose in her mind like an image materializing on a photo plate—steep slope topped by a jagged assembly of outcrops, protrusions. Many places to hide.

Feeling trapped between the men below and possibly more above, she peered around the window frame to see horse and rider ease into a trot, finally stopping by the soldier. The soldier replaced his cap and stepped out from between the cars. He sketched a perfunctory salute to the newcomer, who nodded back and leaned forward over the saddle, examining the half-full box and the fuses snaking across the dirt.

The wide brim of the rider's slouch hat flapped in the breeze like the wings of a buzzard trying to take leave of the ground. His nondescript clothes and horse were dirt-brown. Man and mount seemed nearly invisible, calculated to blend into the landscape.

The two men talked. Distance and the river's murmur hid their words.

The soldier turned away, gesturing at the train cars.

The rider pulled his revolver, aimed it at the soldier.

Susan stifled a gasp.

The soldier turned back to the rider. Froze. Holding one hand up in surrender or supplication, he reached slowly to the inside pocket of his jacket, pulled something out. He held it out, wadded in his fist, as his voice rose in anger, vying with the river's relentless song. "Damn you, Eli! The oath…years ago. Kill the general…for this!" The cloth in his hand unfurled into a long strip.

The rider, Eli, shouted back, "…turn you in or kill you, your choice!"

The soldier's ramrod posture dissolved. He slumped, lowered his hands as if defeated. The cloth fell from his grasp in a rippling wave to the ground and he crouched, the flicker of sun on metal, a revolver now in his grip.

The two guns fired, nearly simultaneous.

Eli fell from his saddle in a scuffle of dust.

His horse turned tail.

The soldier also crumpled to the ground. Eli shot him again and again, until the twitching stilled.

The soldier's dropped cloth, pushed by the wind, tumbled along the siding into the grass, colors flashing red, blue, white.

Eli sat up slowly, holding his leg, attempting to stop the flow of blood.

Another gunshot boomed through the shushing wind.

Not from below, but from the ridgeline above.

Eli clutched his jacket, the brown cloth blooming with red. His shout rang clear: "I won't tell, I swear! Don't—"

His yell was cut off by a second report from the ridge, a thread snapping under a scissors' blades.

Susan sank to the dirt floor, hand to mouth, fighting nausea and fear. The wind briefly gained the upper hand, rattling the shack, mingling in her ears with her terrified sobs and the staccato pounding of her heart.

Suddenly, a new voice sounded from the direction of the tracks. "Je-sus! What happened?"

The response floated down from above her, full of anguished rage. "You were on lookout, dammit! He died because of you!"

Again, from the ground: "I was tryin' to catch his horse. Fool animal got away. Je-sus. This is Eli, from town!"

"We gotta finish the job! The way he planned!"

"Finish it? There's no reason now—"

"He'd've wanted us to!"

"Wait! Wait! I've got to move them. We can't let anyone tie this to us."

Susan rose, trembling. *I'll stick to my plan. Should I peek out the window—?*

"On three!" shouted the man below.

Her breath caught.

"One!" His voice was moving away.

There's no more time! The certainty of it chilled her in the dank cabin air.

"Two!" His voice had retreated further still.

She moved to the door, gathered herself for the last-second sprint.

"Three!"

The explosion from the tracks, she expected.

But not the one from above.

The ridge top ruptured with a roar.

The sound buried Susan's scream as she raced for the mine portal. Rocks and dirt thundered down around her. Mere steps from the portal, pain—instant, intense—blasted through her head. She fell. Crawled the last few feet into the mine entrance. Collapsed into darkness.

Below, the dead men's horses, wandering by the river, bolted and ran.

Chapter One

Inez Stannert rested a gloved hand on the rifle stock behind her saddle and contemplated murder.

Her grip tightened while she watched Reverend Justice B. Sands and Miss Birdie Snow converse by a half-framed building on the outskirts of Leadville. Inez's mare shifted uneasily beneath her, as if reading her thoughts. Inez smoothed the black mane. "Whoa, Lucy. Shhh."

The reverend and Miss Snow stood slightly apart from the handful of men who had laid hammers and saws aside to cluster around a large food hamper. Inez's gaze narrowed on the pale blue bow perched on the back of Birdie Snow's long ruffled skirts. The same blue washed the feather fluttering on Miss Snow's straw summer hat and her fringed parasol.

An ensemble straight out of Godey's Lady's Book. *And I'll bet she wears blue knickers to boot.*

Miss Snow held out a covered picnic basket, a small companion to the one being plundered by the construction crew. Reverend Sands cradled his hat in the crook of his arm and accepted the basket. Inez saw him smile before he offered his arm to Birdie. They picked their way around a pile of lumber to the private carriage blocking the rutted road.

The bow twitched like the tail of an eager bluebird. Inez indulged in mental target practice.

Touching the heels of her worn boots to Lucy's sides, Inez approached the carriage.

Miss Snow lifted china blue eyes—wide as a doll's—to the horse and rider that suddenly loomed beside her. "Oh!" she chirped, then addressed Sands. "Another volunteer for your efforts, Reverend. How wonderful that so many of the church's menfolk came to build the mission. I hope I brought enough chicken and lemonade to go around." Her voice faltered under Inez's glare.

Reverend Sands shaded his eyes, his gaze on Inez as warm as the sun. "Mrs. Stannert! What a surprise and a pleasure! One moment while I help Miss Snow on her way." He opened the carriage door.

Birdie's gaze snapped into focus as she took in Inez's male attire—dusty boots, worn trousers, faded corduroy jacket and waistcoat—and, finally, Inez's face. Recognition dawned. "Mrs. Stannert?"

"Miss Snow." Inez's voice dripped ice.

Birdie flushed, bright as a robin's breast. "Pardon. I, I didn't recognize you in the, um, hat."

She fiddled with her hat ribbons, with the cameo at her lace collar, looking everywhere but at Inez astride her horse. Birdie cleared her throat. "I should be going. Papa's expecting me. See you at services tomorrow, Reverend."

She picked up her skirts to step into the carriage. The reverend's gaze flickered to the blue flash of a silk-stockinged ankle.

Inez sucked in a breath through clenched teeth.

Sands shut the door, and, as the carriage rattled off, settled his broad-brimmed black hat back on his head. He turned toward Inez.

Inez pulled the reins around. "You're busy, it seems."

Sands grasped her stirrup. "I'm never too busy for you, Inez. You should know that by now." His voice covered her anger, gentle as a blanket. He turned to the men sprawled on the ground, backs against the plank wall, feasting on chicken and biscuits. "Jake!"

A pale boy with sunburned cheeks advanced, chicken leg in hand. Sands bequeathed him the basket. "Reinforcements for the troops."

Inez said, "You'll miss your chance at supper."

"This is more important. There's something I want to show you." Sands took Lucy's bridle and steered horse and rider around the unroofed building. He stopped in the rear of the two-story structure, among the piles of rough cut lumber. "Jump down."

No sooner had her feet touched the ground than Inez felt his hands on her waist. Sands spun her around and kissed her hard.

Her slouch hat fell to the ground. The wind tumbled it through the short grass and struggling mountain daisies as he whispered in her ear, "Have I ever told you how irresistible you are in trousers?"

She pushed him away. "Really? I thought your weakness was silk stockings."

He retrieved her hat. "Only when they're on a certain woman." He watched as she brushed the dust from the brim. "You're rather prickly today, Inez. Is this about Miss Snow?"

"She's all of, what? Nineteen?" Inez jammed the hat back on her head. "A mere child."

"Very young," he agreed.

"Brassy blonde hair."

"I prefer brown. Dark brown."

"And those baby-doll blue eyes."

"My tastes run toward," he squinted at her, "green? Or is that brown?"

"Hazel," she said stiffly. "As I understand it, Miss Snow came straight from finishing school in Philadelphia to spend the summer romping about the Rocky Mountains, batting her eyes at all eligible bachelors approved by her father. Who happens to be a lawyer for the Denver and Rio Grande Railway."

Reverend Sands pulled Inez close. "I prefer a certain strong-willed woman with hair cropped short." He pushed a strand from her forehead. "Who can beat the devil at poker, play piano fine enough to make angels cry, and is smart enough to run her own saloon."

The next kiss was long and reciprocal. The faint crackling of paper in her breast pocket finally reminded Inez why she'd detoured to see Sands on her way out of town. She pulled back and said quietly, "My discomfiture isn't entirely due to Miss Snow and her well-turned ankles. My sister's letter arrived."

"She's bringing your boy to Denver, isn't she?" His gray-blue eyes quizzed her.

"No." Inez swallowed with difficulty. Her sister Harmony's careful script rose like words of fire in her mind's eye:

> *The family doctor insists that William's summer is better spent by the seaside than in the West, particularly since he is so young and his lungs still weak from his first winter in the Rocky Mountains. By the time you read this, we'll be in Newport with Mama and Papa. Rest assured, dear sister, your little son will be spoilt endlessly by his grandparents.*

"I should never have sent him back east last summer with Harmony," she whispered. "But I was at my wit's end. Mark had disappeared. There I was, with William not even a year old and a missing husband. I couldn't leave town, couldn't leave the business. I kept hoping Mark would return. But William couldn't stay. Another Leadville winter would have killed him."

The reverend's arms tightened around her. "Under the circumstances, it's a blessing you had a sister able and willing to care for him."

"But I'm afraid—" Inez hesitated, then rushed on— "that I'll never get him back. Oh, that's rubbish, I know. Harmony has William's best interests at heart. And, if the doctor says he shouldn't come west because of his health, then he shouldn't. I just have this feeling...."

His face softened with concern. "Maybe you should go east then. See your son. And your sister. Set your mind at rest."

She stepped away from his embrace, turning to smooth Lucy's mane. "I can't go now. Abe and I have one month to finish the second floor of the saloon before the railroad comes to town. If we can find the money. The money. Now that's another thing. The miner's strike nearly ruined us."

The iron taste of bitterness, tinged with fear, filled her mouth. "First Mooney told the strikers to stay away from the saloons." She remembered the disbelief she'd felt—the near betrayal—when she'd heard of the pronouncement from the strikers' spokesman, Michael Mooney. "He didn't warn them away from the brothels. Or the dance halls. And then, if that wasn't enough, the governor sends in the state troops to keep order and shuts us all down for a week."

Inez gripped Lucy's bridle fiercely and turned to the reverend, trying to bring normality back to her voice. "In any case, Abe and I have to watch every cent. We've got two men pounding nails and laying boards this week, and then that's it until more cash comes in. Abe may be a gem of a business partner, but he isn't one to crack the whip. I've got to stay and see it through."

Sands pulled out the hammer holstered at his belt and tossed it up in a lazy circle, catching the handle on the down spin. "You haven't seen William in over a year. Whenever the topic's come up, the timing for going east is never right. What's keeping you from going back? Something from the past?"

"Pah! The past is over and done. My sights are set on the future. And my son." She watched him toss the hammer again. "And you don't exactly practice what you preach when it comes to facing the past. When talk turns to the war, you always change the subject. The war, and your life after."

"What do you want me to say? The war was a dark time. I don't dwell on it. As for afterward, most of it was a blur. The liquor saw to that." He paused. "In all those years, I didn't have many sober days."

"You're very handy with that hammer. Is that another part of your past you don't wish to discuss?"

The reverend smiled. "Our Lord was a carpenter. Pounding nails clears the mind, opens the soul. You should try it sometime, Inez."

She waved a hand dismissively, then adjusted her reins and wiggled one boot into the stirrup, preparing to mount. "Enough. If I'm to meet Susan I'd best be going. She planned to leave Twin Lakes early this morning to capture paradise on those glass plates of hers on the way back to Leadville. I told her I'd meet up with her by Braun's charcoal kilns, in Disappointment Gulch." From her perch on the saddle, Inez studied the clouds. "I hope her choice of venue isn't prophetic. It looks like rain or possibly snow later today."

Sands shook his head. "Snow. And it's nearly July. When does summer come?"

"Ah, but this *is* summer at ten thousand feet in the Rockies. Sun. Wind. Rain. Snow. And dust, of course. Enjoy it, Reverend."

"And I was hoping you and I could ride out to some mountain meadow Sunday afternoon. Gather wildflowers." He ran a hand over Lucy's shining black coat, then, "What's this?" He pulled the rifle from its scabbard.

"A Sharps. Single-shot breechloader. Rather like the one you keep hidden behind the door in the rectory."

He examined it. "Well maintained. Where'd you get this?"

"Evan's mercantile. The clerk who sold it to me said some Johnny-come-lately who was giving up and leaving town traded it for a song and some supplies. It even came with its own case."

Sands snugged the gun back into its resting place. "A firearm for distance. Not a gun for a woman."

"Oh really." Inez arched her eyebrows. "Well, I took a fancy to it. Thought I'd do a little target shooting. And I brought my revolver, as well." She patted a pocket as Lucy shifted, impatient with standing. "I'm hoping to convince Susan to try it out while I take a potshot or two with the Sharps."

"I didn't think Miss Carothers put much stock in firearms."

Inez frowned. "She insisted on traveling back from Twin Lakes without an escort and unarmed. Said she didn't want anyone dithering around while she took her photographs and that she hates guns. Foolhardy. I may travel alone, but I always go prepared. Better to have a gun and not need it, than not have it and need it, I say. Weather permitting, after she shoots the scenery and we shoot some tree stumps, we'll head back, double quick. I've got to spell Abe at the bar and get ready for tonight. It'll be the usual game in the usual place with the usual people.

Probably the usual winners. Plan on dropping by?" She smiled down at him.

"You can count on it." He took a step back and extracted a handful of nails from his pocket. "I'll be there to walk you home. As usual."

Chapter Two

It took an hour for Inez to navigate Chestnut Street's two miles.

The main thoroughfare into and out of Leadville was a seething mass of human and equine energy. Freight wagons pulled by mule teams hauled out silver-rich ore from the mines east of town and brought in building materials, food, and supplies—everything from steel drill bits forged in St. Louis to satin evening gowns designed in Paris. Carriages vied with stagecoaches and prairie schooners for right-of-way. Inez, like the others on horseback, wove past pack trains and delivery vans while pedestrians dodged hooves and wheels. Dust hung in the air, obscuring wooden false fronts, brick buildings, and boardwalks.

Even more pervasive than the dust was the silver fever that lodged in the nook and cranny of every soul in Leadville. Jammed streets, packed saloons and mercantiles, busy bordellos and crib houses—all were testament to how the passion to get rich quick could shake a man down to his boot soles and grip a woman's heart tighter than true love.

East of town, silver mines with names like Little Chief, Chrysolite, and Robert E. Lee fueled fortunes in return for the sweat and lives of hardrock miners who toiled in the underground drifts. Leadville's rich carbonates of silver and lead sang a siren song to the mines' stockholders and owners, and drew thousands of people from the four corners of the earth. Miners and merchants, con men and moneymen, soiled doves and seamstresses—all began their search for fortune by journeying up Chestnut Street.

Inez reined in her mare by the ever-growing mountains of mine tailings that marked the city's limits. She yanked off the kerchief that filtered dust from her nose and used it to wipe the grit from her face. The crush of vehicles, she noted, didn't stop at the edge of town.

Inez urged Lucy onto a side trail that cut to the east side of the Arkansas River and wound back and away from the main road. The noise and dust subsided, the summer sun warmed her face. Still, something in the breeze—a coolness, a pale ghost of winter's chill—warned Inez that the sun would not linger through the afternoon.

The sun had traveled some distance into the west when she paused by a small spring and loosened the reins. As Lucy drank, Inez heard the clash of metal on metal and the shouts of men drifting from the other side of the ridge. Lucy lifted her head with a snort, bit jangling. Inez patted her neck.

"It's the birthing of the iron horse, Lucy. No cousin to you. Let's take a look."

With a touch of her heels, Inez directed Lucy up to the crest of a ridge paralleling river, road, and track.

Below, half a hundred men labored to bring the Denver and Rio Grande Railroad's line to Leadville. Inez leaned forward, hands resting on the saddle horn, and observed. Low-bedded carts piled high with wood ties advanced to the fore and, once emptied, retreated to the rear for new loads. Guided by the graded path, track layers advanced with hand-hewn ties of untreated timber, dropping the ties at regular intervals, like the same note measured out again and again on a drum. Hard on their heels, teams of men placed pairs of twenty-foot rails of narrow gauge iron, three feet apart: the twin lines of Manifest Destiny. Behind them came the spike drivers, their picks and spike mauls rising and falling to marry the rails to the ties. Finally, workers shoveled in loose dirt to fill the gaps between ties.

A symphony of men and tools, metal, wood, and earth.

Inhaling the thin mountain air, Inez admired the forms of the men—some stripped to undervests, others with shirtsleeves rolled to their shoulders.

Inez barely registered the nervous swivel of Lucy's ears. But she could not miss the voice behind her, deliberate as the click of a gun being cocked:

"Got business with the Denver and Rio Grande, stranger?"

Startled, Inez turned, one hand instinctively reaching for the Sharps.

A man sat easy on a huge bay, rifle pointing not at her, but close enough. The first thing that struck her was the size of the hand holding the gun—oversized even for his rangy large-boned frame. The brass buttons of a military-style single-breasted jacket were undone, revealing a worn blue wool twill shirt. He had the look of someone who had long ago accepted that the cuffs of his ready-mades would always be two inches too short to cover his wrists.

He spoke again, in calm, measured tones. "As I said, mister, state your business." The rifle nodded in her direction.

"I've no business with or interest in the railroad. Just stopped to admire the view."

At the sound of her voice, he removed his dusty hat, revealing shoulder-length hair the color of dried grass and streaked with gray. A neat trimmed beard framed a long, strong-boned face. "Pardon my rough words, ma'am. Preston Holt, at your service. Payroll guard with the Denver and Rio Grande. Hired to protect the payroll and stop trouble before it starts. Riders on the ridges draw suspicion, ma'am. Specially on payday. It's safer on the main road. Some of the guards are a tad more trigger-happy than I am." He nudged his enormous horse closer and said, "Path's down yonder. I'll follow you."

There was no choice but to give way gracefully, particularly since his horse blocked the path she'd taken up. Inez started Lucy along the crest.

The silence was broken only by the click of shod hooves striking loose rocks until Inez ventured, "So, Mr. Holt, you're looking for trouble? I thought the Rio Grande and Santa Fe railroads settled their differences months ago with the Supreme Court decision. Not to mention that agreement signed back east."

"You're talking the Boston Accord." The amusement in his voice was plain. "The high muck-a-mucks have their Philadelphia lawyers draw up a paper saying the Rio Grande gets first line to Leadville, the Santa Fe turns south to New Mexico territory. Carved up the West like a pie. Well, what's signed in Boston don't mean beans out here."

As they started down the front of the ridge, Holt continued. "Last summer, bullets flew, skulls got broken, all for right-of-way through the Royal Gorge to Leadville. Those who were there haven't forgotten, some are still hankerin' to get even. And there's others who find the word 'agreement' painful. Smacks too much of 'truce' or 'surrender.' And it's not just the Santa Fe railway. Hear tell there are those with the Denver, South Park and Pacific road who wouldn't mind seeing us lose time, face, or money in reaching Leadville. So we watch for trouble when riding in with the payroll."

"Thought I was scouting to blow up the train?" Inez laughed.

Holt didn't.

"I'm paid to watch for strangers who seem a mite too interested in the goings-on. And to keep an eye on things." He nodded toward the sweating, dust-covered workers below. "That tracklaying gang's got two unfrocked clergy, a bonafide professor, two Yale men, and forty Irishmen. Not a one qualifies for sainthood. The closer we get to town, the more chances for trouble. I hear the Rio Grande wasn't the horse most Leadville folks were backing. But you might know more about that than I do. Ma'am."

"Mrs. Stannert," she said belatedly.

"Well, Mrs. Stannert, the railroad never knows where trouble'll blow in from, far away or up close. That's why I'm here. How about you? Out gathering wildflowers?" His eyes flicked over her unconventional riding habit of men's trousers and shirt, and lingered on the rifle.

"I was on my way to meet a friend, who was riding up from Twin Lakes this morning. Perhaps you saw her earlier, if you rode up from the south. A young woman riding a horse and leading a burro weighted down with photographic equipment—cameras, boxes, and such."

"No, ma'am." As their horses hit level ground, Holt pulled up alongside Inez. "I've been on the side trails. Your friend probably took the main road." He looked over the stooped backs of the men and the flash of picks and mauls rising and falling in the sun's glare. "There's someone yonder who might've seen her."

He stowed the rifle, much to Inez's relief, cupped his mouth, and shouted, "Reuben!"

A horse and rider on the far side of the rails swerved around the work group and approached. Inez noticed the boy at the reins sported the same out-sized hands as Preston Holt. Only, on the youngster, those hands reminded her of the giant paws of a puppy still growing into its size. The boy's face was scarred from smallpox, and Inez thought she could detect a faint fuzz masquerading as a beard along his jawline. *Hard to tell his age— could be anywhere from sixteen to nineteen.*

But the rifle at his side hinted that he was old enough for a man's job.

Holt did the introductions, slow and deliberate. "Reuben Holt, Mrs. Stannert. Reuben, the lady here has a question for you."

Reuben's gaze settled on her trousered legs.

Holt reached over, pulled Reuben's hat off, and slapped it against the boy's too-large shirt. "Hats off for ladies."

Reuben's pockmarked face flamed cherry red, and Inez revised her estimate of his age downward. He glared sullenly at Holt before fixing his eyes on the knobby knuckled hand clenching the crown of his hat. Even the part in his pale hair was red with embarrassment.

"No offense taken, Mr. Holt," Inez said quickly. "Pleased to meet you, Reuben. Did you by chance see a young woman riding up the road near the Twin Lakes junction earlier this morning? She would have been trailing a burro."

"Naw."

The bay swayed as Holt shifted in his saddle, and Reuben modified his statement hastily. "No, ma'am."

Preston Holt scanned the road as if Susan might suddenly appear on the horizon. "Probably still south of here, then. Unless she changed her mind and rode by earlier."

"Miss Carothers change her mind? Not likely."

Holt nodded. "Could be she took the main road while you were behind the ridge. If I see her, I'll tell her you rode by. And Mrs. Stannert, stay to the main road coming back. It's safer."

"Thanks for the advice, Mr. Holt. Next time you're in Leadville, stop by the Silver Queen Saloon, corner of Harrison and State. I'll see you a free drink."

"You work in the saloon?" He appraised her again. Eyes sharper this time.

She gave him a faint smile. "I *own* the saloon."

Preston Holt touched his hat in farewell, with a ghost of a returning smile. "I'll keep your offer in mind, Mrs. Stannert."

With a final nod to the two Holts, Inez turned Lucy toward the road. Behind her, she heard Reuben say, "How was I supposed to know? She don't *dress* like a lady!"

Holt's reply was lost as Lucy mounted the graded bank to the road.

Inez urged Lucy to a canter. At her back, she could sense storm clouds building, pushing her apprehension on the wind. Time flowed past.

Rounding a bend in the road, Inez yanked on the reins. Lucy slid to a stop.

On the other side of the river, beyond the gulch, boulders and debris buried the tracks and spilled out across the access path at the foot of the steep slope. Halfway up the slope, Inez could make out what might have once been a building, destroyed by rubble. Something metallic winked from the wreckage. Looking higher, Inez saw black winged shapes, circling.

Chapter Three

Inez cupped her hands around her mouth and shouted, "Susan!"

The wind snatched the word away.

Dread curled around Inez's spine, icy as the air.

Inez left the main road and crossed the river, urging Lucy up switchbacks on the side of the gulch as fast as she dared, finally arriving atop a small plateau covered with dusty sagebrush and firs. She looked around, and her heart fell at the sight of a horse and burdened-down burro tied off under the trees. The burro had dislodged a box of glass photographic plates from its panniers. Glass slivers glittered in the dirt and spare grass. The horse's eyes were wide and wild, its reins thoroughly tangled in the brush, its coat caked with dried sweat.

Inez wound Lucy's reins around the trunk of an anemic evergreen and gazed across the slope to the broad ledge.

The temperature had dropped throughout the afternoon, and dark clouds now loomed. A snowflake fell. Another. The wind picked up, blowing dust and desultory bits of snow over the ground.

Taking a deep breath, Inez plunged onto the narrow trail faint across the talus slope. Where the slope steepened into a cliff, she stepped onto the path. With the ledge only ten feet away, she stopped. The rock avalanche that had destroyed the cabin, littered the ledge with boulders, and sent rock and dirt hurtling to the tracks below had brushed the last of the path as well, covering it with loose rubble. Inez gazed at the ledge. So close.

She bit her bottom lip hard and scrutinized the rocks concealing the path ahead. *I'll keep a firm hand on the rock face and stay away from the edge.* Three steps in, her boot slipped on loose rubble.

Inez screamed, leaped forward, and grabbed a sharp-edged outcropping.

Her scream rang in her ears, mixed with the clacking of stones as they fell to the ground far below. Blood pounding, Inez waited until the small avalanche ceased, then she steeled herself and bounded the last few steps to firmer footing.

Once on the large shelf, Inez sprinted across the stone-littered area to the shack. Jagged boulders and slabs blanketed what was left of the cabin. Inez's breath caught when she spotted a glint of metal that resolved into a mangled, half-buried camera.

"No," she whispered. "Please, don't let it be."

She glanced around. The only spot that offered even a modicum of protection was the mine itself. *If she had time to get there.* The portal gaped, its entrance partially blocked by debris.

Angling around a massive boulder, Inez spotted a dust-covered lump of rags just inside the mining entrance.

"Susan!"

She was curled into an unresponsive ball, face buried in her arms. Her green skirts and bloomers were streaked with red rock dust—at least, Inez hoped it was only dust.

Inez hurried forward and knelt at her friend's side. She touched Susan's shoulder and, when there was no reaction, rolled her onto her back. Susan's hat was knocked askew, ribbons still tied tight, her face streaked with dirt and blood. A nasty purple bruise swelled at the hairline.

"Jesus," Inez whispered. Then louder, "Can you hear me?"

No response.

Inez ripped off a riding glove, cupped her hand close to Susan's nose, and was relieved to feel the stir of breath.

Inez pulled a flask from her jacket and soaked her kerchief liberally. She gingerly dabbed at her friend's face.

Susan's eyes fluttered open, confused, then wild with fear. She screamed.

Inez jumped. The contents of the flask sloshed. "Susan! It's me!"

Susan struggled to focus. "Inez? I thought you were...."

"Who?"

She took a shaky breath. "The killer."

"What?"

"Dead men...on the track. Shot."

"Men on the...." Inez thought of the enormous pile of debris covering the rails.

A clatter sounded high above them. Inez ducked instinctively. Fist-sized rocks bounced onto the terrace, accompanied by blowing dirt.

Inez stood, trying to force strength back into knees gone rubbery. "We've got to get off this ledge. The slope above us isn't stable."

"My camera."

"It's smashed up. We'll end up the same way if we linger." Inez grasped Susan's arm. "Can you walk?"

Susan shakily stood. "Ow!" She lurched. "My ankle!"

Inez winced in sympathy and thrust the flask at her. "Drink this. It'll dull the pain. You have to walk. At least to the horses. I can help, but I can't carry you. The first few steps are the worst. We'll need to move fast."

Susan took a small sip and spat. "Ugh!"

"That's my best brandy!"

Another rock clattered down.

"We've got to go. Here, lean on me."

Inez wrapped an arm around Susan's waist, taking some of her weight. Together they lurched to the path. Inez half-carried, half-dragged her friend across the rubble, propelled forward by a harrowing vision of the two of them tumbling down the slope and landing like crumpled dolls at the bottom.

They finally reached stable terrain and picked their way back across the talus field. Susan moved like one half awake. Inez felt as if her arm would pull from the socket with the strain of holding her friend upright.

At the horses, Susan collapsed on the ground. Inez checked the animals, wondering whether her friend would be able to ride at all. She turned to ask and saw a fresh trickle of blood ooze down Susan's cheek. Susan brushed at her cheek, then stared at the wet smear on her glove.

Inez pulled out her flask, took a sip to burn the dust from her mouth, and thrust it at Susan. "Finish this. Now, I want to have a look at your head."

She untied hat ribbons, peeled off the blood-soaked felt, and parted Susan's sleek brown hair. The gash, she was relieved to see, didn't go to the bone. But the swelling and Susan's hazy state of mind concerned her. Nonetheless, she pushed her worries aside and spoke in a matter-of-fact tone. "Looks like you might need some stitches in your scalp. Now, what's this about men on the track and a killer?"

Her friend began shivering. Inez stripped off her own jacket and vest and snugged them around Susan, silently cursing herself for not bringing a waterproof coat or at least a blanket against inclement weather.

Susan forced out words between chattering teeth. "T-two men were below. They argued about...killing generals? There was a s-strip of colored cloth. Red, blue, and white. Important, I think." She covered her face. "Someone above me, I didn't see who, shot at them. What happened to me? I can't remember."

Someone above.

The back of Inez's neck prickled with apprehension. She rose from a crouch and examined the landscape. Nothing stirred in Disappointment Gulch, on its slopes, or in the kiln field. The only sound was the hiss and roar of the river. The ridgeline above the gulch looked empty. A thumb of rock capping the cliff thrust skyward toward the threatening clouds as if to emphasize the need to get off the hill and back to the main road.

An inhuman screech drew her attention to the entombed rails. The carrion birds had landed. One flapped its wings and screeched again as if staking a claim on what was buried beneath.

Chapter Four

When the railroad camp came into view through the mist of rain, Inez felt like singing hallelujah. She'd been riding double on Lucy for what felt like hours, holding Susan in front of her and trailing a pack string of riderless mounts—Susan's rented horse and burro plus two other horses Inez had found by the river, reins dragging on the ground. Mindful of Susan's story, Inez had spent precious minutes calming the animals and adding them to her string.

Canvas tents drooped in a field next to new-laid tracks and railroad cars. Some of the cars were two stories high and looked like frame shacks on wheels, complete with doors, windows, and stovepipes. A limp line of wash sagged along a rooftop. Inez spotted a long line of men waiting by what she guessed was a payroll car.

A huge bay horse stood patiently by one of the two-story cars while its rider, shrouded in waterproof, conversed with someone inside. For a moment, Inez forgot her frozen hands and aching arms. She half-stood in the stirrups, shouting "Mr. Holt!"

Preston Holt turned.

Inez closed the distance. "My friend, Miss Carothers, needs a doctor. She was caught in a rockslide by Disappointment Gulch. It buried your rails and perhaps a couple of men as well."

As Holt dismounted and headed toward the women, a figure swayed into view through the open doorway: shirttails out, waistcoat unbuttoned, near empty bottle hanging loosely from one hand. Pencil-thin black mustache and inkwell eyes to match. "What the divvil's this about?" he slurred. "Rockslides? Buried men?"

He pointed the bottle at Preston Holt. "Dammit, Holt! You're hired t' keep trouble from happening! The general doesn't pay you and your kind t'—"

Susan struggled to alertness. "They talked about a general...." Her voice drifted off.

Holt took in Susan's condition in a glance, then addressed the drunk in the car. "It'll wait, Delaney. An injured woman needs help."

Delaney squinted at Susan and Inez. "Woman?"

"Mrs. Stannert and Miss Carothers are from Leadville," Holt said, emphasizing the words Mrs., Miss, and Leadville.

Delaney passed a hand over his face. "Christ. Women. From town." When he looked up, he appeared almost sober. "Get a wagon and get them out of here. See t' the rockslide. Get the men t' clear it out tonight. With lanterns, if necessary. McMurtrie can't hear about this." Delaney retreated to the dark interior, muttering.

Holt gazed after Delaney and shook his head. He addressed a driver lingering nearby with an empty wagon. "Fetch Reuben. Leave the wagon here." He turned a somber gaze to Inez. "Steady, Mrs. Stannert. We'll get you and your friend back to town."

Inez nodded and held Susan tighter.

Holt disappeared inside the nearest shack-on-wheels and reappeared moments later with several blankets. After arranging them in the empty wagon, he lifted Susan from Inez's saddle as if she weighed no more than a sack of flour and carried her to the wagon bed. He was rigging a canvas cover against the rain when Reuben rode up, looking like a half-drowned pup that had been rolling in mud. Close on his heels and no drier was a short, wiry man also wearing a waterproof coat and sporting a soaked derby, dripping spectacles, and a Lincolnesque beard. He clutched a briefcase tight as if afraid someone might take it from him.

"Mr. Holt!" the short man called. "I was by the payroll car when your message was delivered to the young man here. I thought, if a hand was needed helping folks to town, I'm heading that way with papers for Snow from Palmer and the board."

Holt nodded. "Much obliged." He made the introduction. "Mrs. Stannert, this is Mr. Duncan. Works for the Rio Grande lawyers and such."

The short fellow removed his hat in courtesy, hastily replacing it as the rain pattered on his already plastered hair. "Most call me Professor."

Reuben stood stock-still, eyes glued about a foot south of Inez's face. Glancing down, she saw her flannel shirt was plastered to her breasts like a second skin.

Inez grimaced and plucked at the soaked shirt. It pulled away with a sucking sound.

"Reuben!" Holt's voice held an edge. Reuben tore his gaze away from Inez's chest. "Fetch my jacket. In the saddlebag."

Face flushed, Reuben brought the jacket to Holt.

Holt handed it to Inez. "It's a fair piece to go in the rain." As she gratefully thrust her hands through sleeves the size of tunnels, he continued, "I'd take you myself, but sounds like I've got marching orders from Delaney. Professor and Reuben will see you safe to town." He spared a sharp glance at the boy, before turning to her string of horses. "Where'd you find these?"

"The gray and the burro are Miss Carothers'. The other two were wandering loose by the river, about half a mile this side of the gulch."

Holt put a calming hand on the pinto and examined its markings. He grunted. "This one's ours." He stood, hand on the horse, head bowed in thought. Finally, he looked at Reuben. "You stay here."

"But—"

Holt cut him off. "Rockslide might've buried some men. Professor's fixin' to go to town as it is."

Reuben's face darkened, taking on the aspect of the clouds overhead.

Holt walked to the wagon for a last look at Susan. "When your friend's feeling better, I've got some questions for her." He squinted up at Inez. "And for you, Mrs. Stannert."

Her heart skittered at his steady gaze. "Certainly, Mr. Holt. I believe you know where to find me." Inez said the words with a distant politeness she didn't feel. It was the heavy wool of the oversized jacket, she decided, that was causing her to perspire.

The professor hopped into the wagon and picked up the reins. As Inez turned Lucy toward the road, she heard Holt say to Reuben, low but pointed, "…questions for you, too."

Chapter Five

Inez rode close to the wagon, one eye on Susan, the other on the muddy road.

After some time, the professor cleared his throat. "Poor lassie. I heard about her accident. Did she say what happened?"

Inez sighed. "Miss Carothers gave me some garbled story about men arguing on the tracks below her. I'm worried about her head injury, she's not very clear in what happened. Apparently there was a rockslide afterward onto the tracks. She thinks the men may be buried there."

He seemed to ponder her words, then nodded somberly. "Cliffs can be treacherous by the tracks. The surveyors and engineers, they do their best picking routes and blasting them out, but afterward the slopes can be unstable."

The terrain flashed briefly in Inez's mind: near vertical above the shelf, sloping to tracks and river below. "It didn't look like the route had to be blasted," she ventured. "And my impression is the rockslide came from above her."

"Ah well. I'm no engineer." He shrugged. "I dinnae think the crews'll be seeing a day off until the track's cleared."

Inez pulled Holt's jacket closer about her. The damp wool collar brushed her lips. "That Mr. Delaney. Will he truly make the crews work all night?"

"Delaney." The professor weighed the name in some invisible balance. "He's a section boss. Supervises a portion of the crew and the layin' of the track. But fact is, he's only some poor and distant cousin of the chief construction engineer, J.A. McMurtrie. When Delaney's in his cups—which is often, I hear—others step in and take charge. Or sometimes he just promotes the nearest body to do his job."

"Such as Preston Holt?" Inez raised her eyebrows. "He's a payroll guard, true?"

The professor grimaced, as if caught out. "Holt is a man of many parts. I don't pretend to know the half of them, even though I'm privy to meetings of the Rio Grande's board and its lawyers. But I believe Holt's charter is somewhat wider than just guardin' the payroll." A drop rolled off the tip of his nose. "A straight-shooter, Holt is, by all accounts. A company man. With Delaney as he is today, Holt might even lend a hand in takin' the men back to where the trouble is. Look over the scene."

"A payroll guard running a construction crew and a professor working for lawyers." Inez shook her head.

"Degree from University of Edinburgh. Did some teachin', here and there. Even took a spin as an inkslinger not too many years back, when I was a sprout of twenty."

At this, Inez took a closer look at him. She'd pegged him first at about forty. But the dust that had settled into the creases of his face and muddied his aspect had fooled her. She now realized he was closer to her own age, about thirty. "You were a member of the fourth estate?"

"I've a way with words. Won't deny it." He deflated. "Ah well. Dinnae last."

"A newspaperman." She rolled the possibilities around in her mind like a smooth marble in her hand. "Did you like the work?"

"'Twas far more satisfying than taking notes at meetings and delivering files from Denver and the Springs to the end of the track and beyond." He sighed. "America. Land of opportunity. Seems everywhere I've gone, opportunities have vanished. Glorified errand boy is what I am now. Things have not turned out like I was expecting at all."

"Hmmm." She eyed him. "Not to downplay the seriousness of the circumstances that brought us together, but this could be your lucky day, Professor. If you're interested in returning to your previous profession."

"Some silver baron needing a tutor for his bairns?" He grimaced. "I gave up teaching for good."

"No, no. I was thinking along the line of journalism. You know the railroad *and* the newspaper business. Those are the more interesting parts of the equation." She allowed herself the briefest of smiles. "Give me a week, Professor. Then, if you're interested in slinging ink in Leadville, come see me at the Silver Queen Saloon."

"And why would you bother with a poor soul such as myself?"

"I see a way to help a friend and make a friend. Easy as that."

For the balance of the trip to town, Inez thought on Jed Elliston—publisher, editor, and sole reporter of *The Independent*—and resolved to say no more until she'd had a chance to sound him out. *Could be useful to have a newspaperman or two in my debt.*

She spied the tailings at the town limits shadowing into view through the misty rain and growing dusk. Inez led the professor through Leadville's back streets, which had liquefied into rivers of mud, to St. Vincent's Hospital at the north end of town. A nun whose determined expression whitewashed a face lined with exhaustion and years met Inez on the porch. At Inez's request, a small boy was sent to fetch Doctor Cramer. Inez and the professor helped Susan from the wagon, while the nun, who introduced herself as Sister Mary Bernard, took quick measure of Susan's condition and told one of the other good Sisters of Charity to prepare a private sickroom on the second floor.

Once Susan was settled, the professor melted away, with many apologies of errands to run and papers to deliver and well wishes for Susan's speedy recovery. Inez pulled a chair up to her bed and took Susan's hand, keeping an eye on the doorway for Doc's appearance.

The minor key murmurs and moans of the hospital's residents were rent by a chilling scream, seemingly on the other side of the wall from Susan's iron bedstead. Inez saw two Sisters of Charity sweep by, a rush of black shadows.

Sister Mary came in and shut the door firmly behind her. "Doctor Cramer is on his way. He'll be here shortly, Mrs. Stannert."

The door flew open, and another sister, who looked barely old enough to be out of school, nearly collided with Sister Mary.

"Yes, Sister?" the older nun said with a touch of irritation.

The younger woman's face was taut with fear beneath her wimple. She held out an envelope with a shaking hand. "Another anonymous note, Sister Mary. They said they'll set the place afire this time, if we don't sell the land—"

Sister Mary cut her off. "Let's not burden visitors with hospital matters." She glanced at Inez.

Footsteps approached, echoing down the hall. Inez recognized Doc Cramer's limping gait, counterpoint to the thump of his cane.

Inez, stood, hastily brushed the front of her trousers and shirt, feeling out of place in men's garb, and hurried toward the door. Sister Mary was out in the hallway with the young nun, and Inez heard her say, "Deliver the note to Father Robinson, he'll handle the situation. It's not the first threat the hospital has received from lot jumpers."

"Mrs. Stannert!" boomed Doc Cramer, his face a map of wrinkles and concerns. He stopped before Inez and the sisters, set his medical bag on the floor, and removed his stovepipe hat, glistening with rain. "I came as soon as I heard about Miss Carothers. Good evening, Sisters." He added a little bow. "I'm glad you had room for a female patient tonight. As soon as I've seen to Miss Carothers, I might as well attend to those pneumonia cases I've been following in the ward."

A scream followed by a stream of curses at top volume emanated from the room next door. Doc's shaggy eyebrows shot up nearly to his hairline. "Perhaps, Sister Mary, I should attend to that fellow first."

"I think that's best, thank you, Doctor. Room Sixteen."

Doc retrieved his medical bag and hurried to Room Sixteen.

Inez returned to Susan's bedside and examined her friend's face in the light from the coal oil lamp. The sisters had cleaned

Susan's face, and the bruises looked nearly black against her pale skin.

Sister Mary joined Inez in observing Susan, her head tilted critically to one side. "I believe Miss Carothers will be fine, given time to rest and recover." She bestowed the smallest of smiles upon Inez. "Your friend is in good hands. There's no need to stay. I'll keep her company if you must leave."

Inez nodded reluctantly, thinking of the horses waiting outside and Abe at the saloon, no doubt wondering what had happened to her. "Thank you. Would you please tell Doctor Cramer to come see me when he's done?"

"Certainly." Sister Mary claimed Inez's vacated chair.

Inez cleared her throat. "Sister, if I may ask?"

The sister looked up, eyes dark and calm as the sky at midnight.

"The note. I thought lot jumping was confined to downtown and the mining areas. Why would anyone want to seize the hospital's land? You're on the very edge of town."

Sister Mary folded her hands in her lap. "After the railroad purchased lots a few blocks north, we began getting letters insisting that we move our hospital to another location. Ridiculous, of course. We have absolutely no intention of doing so. Lately, the letters have become more threatening. But we trust that the Lord and Father Robinson will take care of the situation." She bestowed another tiny smile on Inez. "Not to mention the local parishioners, who have no qualms about reinforcing the Lord's will with their own considerable firepower. Whoever wrote the note will find we give no quarter to land thieves."

Chapter Six

Back outside the hospital, Inez buttoned up the borrowed jacket and looked around. The professor had left the string of Susan's hired horse and burro, the chestnut she'd found by the river, and her own black mare. Inez laid a soothing hand on Susan's hired animals and the unknown horse, and examined the brands in the dying light.

All of them had come from the nearby C&H livery. The very place she boarded Lucy. She wrinkled her nose, hoping she'd not have to deal with its newest owner and partner. *I've no great desire to tangle with Bart Hollis. Luckily, he's seldom around.* She cheered up a bit. *Most likely, Jack or Mr. Carter will be there. Maybe I can find out from them who rented this other horse.* She stroked the chestnut gelding, noting the distinctive fur saddlebags on either side and wondering if they might hold a clue to the rider's identity.

Rolling back the cuffs that engulfed her hands, Inez reflected that presenting a name to Preston Holt might go a ways to repaying him for his help. She examined the saddlebag fastenings. The buckles were straightforward, but the bags had been further secured with rawhide lashings. The knots looked like they'd require much time or a sharp knife to undo. *And I've neither right now.*

It was but a few blocks to the false-fronted building labeled prominently "C&H Livery—Feed and Sale, Stable, Transfer and Ore Hauling a Specialty."

"Hello! Mr. Carter! Jack!" she shouted at the entrance as she dismounted and shook the rain from the borrowed coat. A shadowy form moved deep inside the barnlike structure. A moment later Bart Hollis sauntered out of the gloom.

If Inez had to choose one word to sum up the bits and pieces of ex-marshal Hollis, it would have been "narrow." Hollis' long face held squinty eyes and a droopy mustache that followed the curves of his downturned mouth. A torso thin as a rail sported a pair of dirty red braces that prevented his trousers from sliding off nonexistent hips and puddling around his mud-covered boots. Narrow also summed up Hollis' views on "wimmin," "niggers," "micks," "bohunks," "injuns," and "yanks." Orientals escaped his scorn only because those who dared venture into the Rockies avoided Leadville like the plague.

"Waaall, look what the cat drug in." Texas stretched long in his vowels, almost as long as the contempt in his tone. He lounged against the splintered jamb. "That Old Harry you leadin' around by the nose, Miz Stannert?" He spat a brown stream of tobacco juice into the mud. "Cain't say I'm surprised."

Inez resisted the impulse to lash back at his taunt. After being forced to turn in his badge, Hollis had bought a partnership in the livery, now called C&H, and named every animal in it after those who'd wronged him. It must've given him great glee, Inez thought, to name a gelded mount after Harry Gallagher, one of the most influential silver barons in Leadville and the man who'd engineered first his appointment as marshal and then his dismissal. Rumor had it, Hollis also had a pair of jackasses answering to Inez and Abe. She had no desire to check the veracity of that story.

Inez gestured at the two livery horses and burro. "These are all yours. I see you gave Miss Carothers the most obstinate horse in Leadville."

Hollis hitched up his pants. "An' I'll bet you gave her lessons on how to ride Old Harry like an expert an' keep him happy. Right, Miz Stannert?"

Inez and Hollis eyed each other with intense mutual dislike. Inez was sorely tempted to slap Old Harry's rump and set him galloping down the street and let Hollis chase after him. Then, she remembered why she was determined to stay civil to this man whom she considered lower than a snake—and took a deep breath instead. "Miss Carothers was hurt in a rockfall near Disappointment Gulch. Your other customer," she indicated the chestnut, "was less lucky. It appears he's buried under a ton of rubble on the Rio Grande tracks."

Hollis finally moved out into the rain, lifting his boots fastidiously over mucky puddles. He gathered up the leads and examined Old Harry's companion closely. Anger and puzzlement chased across his normally sour visage.

He looked up, caught Inez watching him, and affected a nonchalant air, remarking, "Not a scratch. Horace, you're one lucky son of a bitch."

Horace, she knew, referred to Horace Tabor, one of the richest men in Colorado, thanks to Leadville's silver-heavy carbonates of lead and his own good timing. Tabor was affable, easy-going, and would probably laugh and wink at anyone who told him of Hollis' pique. Harry Gallagher, though, was a different matter and a different man.

Inez led Lucy into the livery. Hollis followed, trailing the hired horses and burro and hollering, "Jack! Put down that bottle and get on up here! Got three horses and a burro, all in need of a rub-down."

"So," Inez said, "who took Horace out?"

He eyeballed her shrewdly. "Cain't say as I 'member."

"Maybe those saddlebags hold something that would indicate who the rider was."

He glanced indifferently at the bags. "Those knots'd take time t' undo. Cain't say as I've got the time or inclination right now."

She exhaled fiercely, trying to stay calm. *I should have just borrowed a knife at the hospital and cut the straps when I had the chance.* "Maybe a shot of Red Dog, on the house, would jolt your memory."

"Mebbe. Might need two shots. One fer the first name, 'nother fer the last."

She hesitated.

"Longer we dicker the more whiskey I'm gonna need to recollect."

"All right, all right!"

Hollis smirked and led the animals further into the livery, the elusive saddlebags receding with them into the dim interior. Hollis' voice drifted back to her: "See ya t'night. Save a bottle for me."

Chapter Seven

Inez pushed open the back door of the Silver Queen Saloon. Abe Jackson, her business partner, glanced up. His white shirtsleeves were rolled up and captured by his sleeve garters, the dark skin of his forearms showing a fine sheen of sweat from working in the humid kitchen. He was halfway through decanting a barrel of potent spirits into the row of bottles on the kitchen table. The label on the barrel depicted a dog, which appeared to be in the advanced stages of hydrophobia, inked in gruesome red. The accompanying words could be taken as a warning or an invitation, depending on one's thirst and state of mind: "Red Dog—Strong enough to make a dog go mad."

Abe looked Inez over critically. A drop of rain rolled down her forehead, and she used a soggy sleeve to wipe the tickle away.

"Lord amighty, Inez. You and Miss Carothers get lost in that storm?"

Inez recounted the afternoon's events, finishing with, "Susan is at St. Vincent's under Doc's care. I expect to wring more information from him later tonight."

Abe banged the bung into the whiskey barrel. "Damn shame. You let me know if there's somethin' Angel and I can do to help out." He eyed Inez's outfit. "I don't recall seein' that coat before."

"Courtesy of Preston Holt, a payroll guard for the Denver and Rio Grande Railroad. I'll return it tomorrow when I let him know about Susan's condition. Holt wants to talk with her.

About the deaths, I imagine. I think one of the fellows worked for the Rio Grande."

Abe glanced at the jacket hem, hanging below her knees. "Railroad men have a bad reputation. Don't think I'd want a man of that size comin' into the bar and gettin' rowdy. Bet he'd be a hard one to toss out the door."

A vision of Preston Holt flashed, not unpleasantly, across her mind. "He was courteous. Quite the gentleman in fact."

"Uh-oh. Honeymoon's over."

She stripped off her wet riding gloves and jammed them in a pocket. "Just what do you mean by that remark?"

Abe began loading the bottles into the crate. "You can bluff with the best over a hand of cards, but when it comes to men, you wear your heart on your sleeve. Your face, when you mentioned that payroll guard, got me thinking. The reverend and you been sparkin' for nigh on five months. Guess I'm wonderin' if you're gettin' tired of him, gettin' ready to give him the heave-ho. Five months. That's a long time for you, Inez."

"How presumptuous!" she sputtered, her face growing hotter by the moment. She started to unbutton the coat hastily, as if to shed herself of anything that had had contact with Preston Holt. "I was married for more than ten years to Mark. Still am married to him." The pair of silver and gold bands on her ring finger glinted in confirmation. "Not that Mark and I didn't have our ups and downs, as you well know, what with the three of us traveling together the whole time. But through the good and the bad, I stuck by the marriage. It was Mark who walked out last spring, not me—"

"Don't get your dander up, Inez." Abe smoothed his salt-and-pepper hair, the coarse kink invigorated by the humid air despite the brilliantine. "I'm just thinkin' over the past year. First there was Harry Gallagher for—couldn't've been more'n three months—then the reverend came t' town around Christmas…lessee…Bat Masterson wandered through and looked a strong contender 'til he headed back to Kansas. So it's been you and Sands for four, maybe five months. Dependin' how you count."

"What nonsense!"

He shrugged. "Don't bother me none, Inez. I just figure for you, it's like spring cleanin'. Some women hang out the rugs and give them a good beatin', you throw out the old beaus and find new ones." He squinted at her. "I got just one request: When you take on a new sweetheart this time—specially if it's this railroad man—point him out to me so I don't rile him by mistake."

"Reverend Sands and I are just fine."

"You're sure a fool for sweet-talkin' men, Inez."

Before she could form a retort, Abe picked up the crate and said, "I'd put the jacket back on if I was you. Unless you're looking to start a riot when you walk into the saloon proper."

Inez glanced down and was reminded of the revealing properties of wet flannel. She blushed, reshrugged into the jacket, and held it tight to her neck as she followed Abe into the barroom.

"Honestly, Abe. You get married and all of a sudden you've got a holier-than-thou attitude that won't quit." She also thought, but didn't say, that Abe had gotten considerably testier since he'd announced earlier that spring that Angel was expecting. When Abe had first informed her of Angel's condition, Inez had burst out, too startled to hold her tongue, "But Abe! Who's to say the child is even yours!"

He'd glared at her in a way to freeze her feet to the floor. It was a stare she'd seen him direct at serious troublemakers who were heading for serious trouble. After a long pause, he'd said, "Angel's my wife." He said the words as if they were straight off the holy tablets of the Israelites, words penned by God himself. "Any child born to Angel is a child of mine. And I don't want to ever hear you say different."

Abe set the crate on the near end of the bar and began unloading the bottles. Struggling for a less confrontational tone, Inez continued, "Furthermore, I find it strange that you continue to defend Mark to the bitter end—he was the smoothest talker of all. Why, Mark could charm the aces to the top of a deck, we both know that. But you won't give Reverend Sands a chance."

Abe shrugged. "Sands handles trouble and a gun like he was born to it. Then, he turns around with the Good Book and preaches 'bout the heavenly spirit. I don't believe your reverend quite knows his own self. Either that, or he does know and he's foolin' everyone, includin' you. You're damn right I don't trust him."

"Yet he saved your life last winter as much as Angel or I did." She glanced around the room. "Is Angel still here?"

"I was waitin' on you before takin' her home. Didn't want to leave King Solomon alone." Abe nodded toward their recently hired bartender, Solomon Isaacs. Sol's red hair shone like a copper-colored beacon behind the bar.

Inez spotted Angel crossing the room, heading toward a crowded table. Clothed in a dark skirt and gray shirtwaist and further armored with a white bib apron, Angel looked the proper young matron. However, no proper Leadville matron, no matter what the age, would be using the swell of her pregnant belly to balance a tray of whiskey bottles and shot glasses.

A booming voice at the table caused Inez to pause. "Is that…."

"Yep. Chet Donnelly's back from the hills," Abe said shortly. "He and some boys've been playin' cards for drinks since we opened. Angel don't cotton much to him and neither do I. So soon's you're ready, I'm takin' her home."

Inez nodded and started toward the stairs leading to the second floor. She inclined her head at their piano player, Taps, who was warming up on the upright at the foot of the stairs.

He tipped his hat, grinned, "Evening, Mrs. Stannert," took a good look at her attire, and swung into an upbeat version of "Buffalo Gals."

Patrons turned and stared. Regulars called out greetings. The expressions of strangers ranged from curious to shocked to lascivious. Inez decided to take the high road and waved with dignity as she mounted the stairs, feeling like a frontier version of the Queen of England. The cacophony faded as she slammed and locked the office door behind her and dulled to an indistinguishable roar as she entered her private dressing room behind the office.

Once in her inner sanctum, she shucked off the damp clothes and splashed water into a washbasin. *Although why I bother after the soaking I got.*

After a quick cleanup and a dash of rosewater, she layered on clean undergarments, fingers flying through the laces and ties. Inez opened the door to her seven-foot wardrobe, inhaling the cedar scent as she confronted her better dresses alongside her husband's abandoned frock coats, waistcoats, and trousers.

She touched one of Mark's waistcoats, tracing a pattern of gold threads weaving through silver and black, then smoothed one of her watered-silk dresses. The outfits hanging side by side reminded her of the day she and Mark had exchanged hasty vows in upstate New York. Only later had she realized that the silk dress—with its French lace, satin ribbons, and Paris cut—paired with her guilty defiance had betrayed her for what she really was: the runaway daughter of a wealthy man. Mark, handsome as could be with his laughing eyes and fast-talking charm, had wrapped his arm around her waist as if he owned her. No wonder the justice of the peace had balked until Mark doubled his fee. *He knew we were eloping. Probably guessed that Mark was a sporting man, gambling on making his fortune by marrying me.*

Yet even as she thought this, another inner voice insisted: *Nonsense! We loved each other. Through all the hard times, all that conspired to part us, we stayed together. There was no reason for him to walk out last year. We were planning to sell the saloon and move to California, for William's health. Something took him from me. Maybe he was bushwhacked by cutthroats and his body tossed down a mineshaft.*

Inez shook her head and dismissed the tired argument. It rose regularly like a spirit, summoned whenever she thought of the day Mark had left the house to talk to a prospective buyer for the saloon and never returned. Not a whisper of his whereabouts had reached her ears after that, except for a tenuous tale of a sighting in Denver in December. And the teller of that tale, she reminded herself, was not entirely to be trusted in his motives. Yet, ever since January, she'd had a recurring dream in which she was awakened by the metallic sigh of a key in the lock. The front door bolt would slide open, footsteps sound in the hallway, and Mark's silhouette would appear at the threshold to her bedroom.

Recently, the dream had taken a new twist, ending with Reverend Sands rolling away from her in the sheets and reaching for his revolver on the nightstand as Mark drew his gun.

Inez shuddered and pushed the unpleasant vision from her mind.

She pulled out a figure-hugging navy silk polonaise and closed the wardrobe door, shutting her nightmare within. Smoothing her short hair back from her face with practiced fingers, Inez glanced once in the mirror, noting that her hair was growing out from the hasty shearing she'd given it that winter.

Grabbing a clean apron from the hook, Inez covered her dress, thankful that Leadville's chill summer evenings kept her from stifling in her many layers of clothes. Her gaze landed on Preston Holt's damp jacket hanging nearby, and she remembered her riding gloves. She hunted through the jacket's pockets, finally unearthing the crumpled gloves, and laid the damp wad by the washbasin.

She carried the jacket downstairs and into the kitchen, where Abe labored over a second crate of bottles and the dregs of the Red Dog barrel. Inez hung the jacket over a chair, smoothing out the folds before pushing it closer to the large cast-iron stove, still radiating heat from the day's cooking. "You and Angel can leave whenever you're ready," she told Abe as she left the kitchen.

She was halfway across the barroom when she heard Chet say, "Hell, Angel, ya were a sight more friendly when ya worked down the line. Come on over here and bring me some luck."

Inez glanced over at Sol, trapped behind the long mahogany counter, his face draining of color as he fumbled beneath the bar for the shotgun.

Inez shoved her way through the crowd gathered around the back table in time to see Chet, holding a deck of undealt cards, grab Angel and pull her onto his lap. Angel squirmed, moving faster than Inez could shout a warning.

Chet looked down. The handle of a slim knife quivered above the tabletop. The blade nestled between his forefinger and thumb, piercing the deck of cards and the tabletop below.

He slid his hand away tentatively, as if half expecting to leave a finger behind.

Angel bounced off Chet's lap, hissed at him, and yanked out the knife. Ruined playing cards scattered. She slapped the tabletop to get his attention. When he looked up, she held out her hand, thumb crossing her palm.

Inez pushed a gawker out of her path and hastened to Angel's side, adding her own imprecations. "Chet, you fool! While you've been stalking silver in the Rockies these past months, Angel's gotten married. She's Mrs. Abe Jackson now. *Comprende?*"

He blinked in whiskey-induced confusion. "What're you talkin' 'bout, Mrs. Stannert? Why, I think it's great ya hired Angel t' be a waiter gal here at your place. I always said Angel was the purtiest little thing that ever laid on her back an'—"

"Not any more," Inez said coldly. "She's a decent married woman now. And if that doesn't make any difference to you, remember this. The next time you touch her, she says she'll take off your thumb." Inez glanced at Angel to see if she'd interpreted correctly. Angel nodded once, furious. She slapped the table again, then extended her middle finger to Chet and set her knife against the lower knuckle. Inez winced, thinking translation was probably not necessary, but continued, "Furthermore, Mrs. Jackson says, the second time you try anything, she'll cut off your—"

"Won't be no need for that." Abe appeared, and his hands settled on Angel's shoulders. "Next time he touches my wife, this man's a dead man."

Onlookers hastily melted away to the bar. Chet's drinking buddies abandoned their chairs, leaving the prospector alone at the table, pink mouth forming a little "o" through his tangled gray beard. Inez thought that comprehension was, at last, dawning.

Inez said, "I think an apology's in order."

Angel glared at Chet, arms crossed above her swollen belly, foot tapping.

Chet stammered, "No harm meant. Just lookin' for a little fun."

Inez retrieved the empty bottles in front of him. "Time to be on your way, Chet. You know our rules: No drunks served a drink, no married men playing cards. You may not be married, but you surely are drunk. Frisco Flo is running the cathouse on the corner now. If you've got an itch in your trousers and money burning a hole in your pocket, go look for your 'fun' there or any of the other joints up and down State. But not here. Not in my saloon."

Chapter Eight

After Chet staggered out, Inez joined Sol behind the bar. Sol, pale and apologetic, clutched the shotgun in one hand and a bottle in the other as if torn between defending the business and selling a drink. "I'm sorry I didn't get the gun out faster, Mrs. Stannert. Couldn't remember which end of the bar it was under."

"That's all right. Angel can take care of herself. I was more worried that she'd carve up Chet right then and there."

Inez watched Abe and Angel exit through the new door to Harrison Avenue. Satisfaction percolated through her every time she contemplated the entrance. She and Abe had managed to complete the doorway and replace the floor and ceiling before the miners' strike and the subsequent closing of saloons had called a halt to their renovations. With two entrances, clientele had the option of strolling in from Leadville's up-and-coming new business district on Harrison or entering from State Street and the red-light district. Just one of the advantages, she reflected, of a corner property.

The new entrance seemed to draw a better class of men than those coming in from State Street. Even so, those entering from Harrison, once their thirst for liquor was slaked, still tended to exit on State. Not State, but Second, she corrected herself. Leadville's city council had renamed the streets in January, banishing many of the street names reminiscent of Philadelphia—State, Lafayette, Park—and substituting a simple numbering system. Most towns-folk shrugged. The general consensus was that the council could tinker with street names all it wanted, but the red-light district would remain State Street until razed to the ground.

Inez returned her attention to Sol. "You're new to town, so I wouldn't expect you to know this. But just so you're better prepared next time: Chet Donnelly's a wild card, especially when he's tight. Generally, he's more trouble than he's worth, unless he hits the big time with a silver strike. When that happens, he sells his claim to the highest buyer, goes on a spree, and throws money around like there's no tomorrow. I don't mind standing in his path at those times. As my husband used to say, 'We're in Leadville to mine the miners.'"

A voice behind her drawled, "The miners ain't the only ones losing silver here. Seems like the house never loses on those fancy Saturday night poker games you run. So, what is it, Miz Stannert, marked decks?"

Inez pulled a bottle of Red Dog from the backbar and grabbed a heavy-bottomed shot glass before turning to face the ex-marshal. "Sour grapes, Hollis. It's a private game, and I run it straight. None of the players complain. In fact, the only complaints I hear are from you. Which is fairly strange, since I don't recall seeing your face across the table. Now, how's your memory as to who took out the chestnut gelding this morning?" She poured.

Hollis tipped his head back to eye her from under his hat. The smell of the livery—horses, hay, and manure—clung to him along with the tobacco and the sour smell of a man in need of a bath. "You must want that name powerful bad. Wonder why?" He reached for the drink.

She gripped the glass. "Not until I have the name."

"Lessee." Hollis scratched his whiskered jawline. "B'lieve the name started with a…E. Yep. Eli."

She released the glass.

He downed the shot and smacked his lips.

"Last name?"

"I'm havin' trouble recollecting."

She held the bottle up between them. At that proximity, the distinctive fragrance of Red Dog—suspiciously reminiscent of turpentine—stung her nose. Inez said, "I'll pour when you remember."

"And I'll remember when you pour."

Inez stared hard at him. The leathery skin around Hollis' eyes wrinkled with his malicious smile.

Eli. Elias. Elijah. How many men answering to Eli are listed in the city directory, and how many more are passing through? I've no time to sort it out before I return Preston Holt's coat.

She poured.

Hollis snatched up the glass, then grinned, his teeth yellow as a rat's. He raised the whiskey in a toast: "To Elijah Carter, the South, and General Lee. The War for Southern Independence ain't over and never will be." The second drink went down in a swallow, the glass down on the bar with a bang.

"Elijah Carter? He's your business partner!" Inez glared at Hollis, angry at being duped. "You expect me to believe that you forgot that he rode off this morning on that horse?"

Hollis turned his back on her and rested his elbows on the counter, surveying the room leisurely. "Memory's not what it used t' be, I guess."

She took a deep breath to curb a nasty rejoinder and asked, "What was Eli doing south of town?"

Hollis spat and looked down at the resultant glob on the varnished wood planks. "You redid the floors." He glanced up at the stamped tin ceiling, mirror-like in its newness. "The topside too. Heard you're turning the second story into a first-class gambling hall. Wonder where you got all the money to do this. Got your fingers in the reverend's collection plate?"

Inez bristled, but before she could speak, his gaze meandered back to her. "Why're you so interested in Eli and his final hours in Leadville?"

"I'm just curious."

He snorted. "Last time you got curious, I lost my job."

She pushed on, ignoring his barbs in her efforts to draw more information from him. "You don't seem particularly despondent that his horse turned up without him. I thought you two were *compañeros*. That you go back to the war. And you're business partners in that livery. And what do you mean, his 'final hours in Leadville'? Was he leaving for good?"

Hollis scratched his chin. The sandpapery sound of fingernails on whiskers sounded over the clinks of glass on glass, random bits of conversation, the tinkling of Taps playing "Oh, Susanna." Hollis finally said, "Story's a long one. It'll take the rest of the bottle to tell it proper."

Inez retrieved his empty glass. "The next one you pay for."

"The hell I will. Ma'am." He mockingly tipped his hat as he shoved away from the bar. "If it weren't for you, that reverend, and Harry Gallagher, I'd still be city marshal. You owe me more'n a free bottle of rotgut for what you did last winter." He sauntered away.

"The nerve!" Inez banged the bottle on the backbar. *The information is hardly worth the aggravation and the two bits I lost in liquor. So, of those two stray horses, one was Elijah Carter's, the other was ridden by a railroad man. Hollis certainly doesn't seem worried about what happened to his business partner. I wonder what business Eli had with a railroad man. And, if Susan's recollection is right, who killed them and why.*

Chapter Nine

The clock struck eleven in the card room, the evening still young by Inez's reckoning.

She leaned back in her chair, the gathered flounces of her dress smashing up in a knot between her back and the velvet upholstery. She tapped her cards against her bottom lip and regarded Jed Elliston, owner and publisher of *The Independent*, seated across the table from her.

She'd maneuvered the last few rounds of betting toward this moment, driving out all the players except Jed. But now that the time had arrived to stage her own defeat, she felt reluctant to throw away what had become a better-than-average hand. Her queen-high straight would almost certainly outrank whatever Jed had. *If I fold, I'll never know.*

Jed stared down his straight nose at her, cards gathered loosely in one hand. His studied carelessness was one clue to her, among others, that he was bluffing. *If his hand was good, he'd clutch the cards tight and close.*

The gold and silver coins piled on the table glimmered. Without looking at her penciled tabulations of wins and losses, Inez knew the house was ahead. She could afford to be generous, and, more importantly, profit from Jed's ensuing good mood.

With a sigh of resignation, she folded. "It's yours, Jed." She added a slight lift of the shoulders and a small smile of surrender.

His edgy posture relaxed, and he pulled in what she figured must amount to a hundred and fifty dollars. "Poker," he remarked airily, "is a man's game. No offense, Mrs. Stannert. But to play successfully requires the same skills as fighting a battle. One must know one's opponent, and have nerves of steel, a sense of when to strike, when to retreat. Knowledge of tactics, strategy, an ability to calculate the odds. Not part of the feminine sphere."

"Fancy that," she murmured. "And I thought poker was about money."

Bob Evan, owner of Leadville's largest mercantile, adjusted his steel-framed glasses and laced his fingers over his sober brown waistcoat. "Dunno about that, Jed. Some of the so-called weaker sex who come into my store drive the hardest bargains. The kind of ferocity I see displayed over a bolt of calico or a collection of broomsticks is not something I'd want to face on a battlefield."

David Cooper, one of Leadville's most successful lawyers, specializing in claim disputes and mining law, said, "Don't underestimate our hostess, Jed." Always polite, always the gentleman, Cooper handled claim disputes and other mining-related legal matters. Eyeing the new diamond stickpin in his cravat—tasteful, but obviously very expensive—Inez thought that, of all the businesses that had suffered from the miners' strike, Cooper's was not among them.

Cooper continued, "If she threw a hand to you, I'll bet she had good reason."

"The best of reasons. I don't believe in backing a lame horse, a questionable assay, or a busted straight." Inez scooped up the cards lest someone have the bad manners and overwhelming curiosity to turn over her discards.

As she shuffled, Inez's gaze lingered on Jed's shiner. She refrained from adding a pointed comment about the masculine tendency to pugilistic stupidity. His face was not the only aspect bruised. His ego, she knew, would still be smarting from his recent, very public altercation with the Rio Grande's chief engineer, John A. McMurtrie.

For the past year, Jed had regularly lambasted the Rio Grande and its board of directors, including founder and president General William Jackson Palmer, in the editorial pages of *The*

Independent. Not surprising, Inez thought, considering Jed's family fortunes rode the rails of the Atchison, Topeka, and Santa Fe—the competing railroad company. Jed's vendetta had taken a physical turn in an unplanned encounter with McMurtrie in the brass and crystal smoking room of Leadville's Clairmont Hotel. Onlookers maintained that Jed never stood a chance against McMurtrie, who, having successfully faced down the likes of Bat Masterson, was not one to pull his punches.

After the ignoble skirmish, Elliston was *persona non grata* with the Clairmont and the Rio Grande. *The Independent* suffered accordingly. Leadville's other newspapers reported on the railroad's progress, augmented by interviews with McMurtrie and right-of-way lawyer Lowden D. Snow. *The Independent* was reduced to paraphrasing stories from its competitors on one of the most visible and important topics in Leadville.

Inez nodded once to herself, watching Jed count and stack his winnings. *Jed and the professor could profit from each other: the professor could leave off running errands for the railroad's lawyers, Jed could get the inside story on the Rio Grande. Having two such gentlemen beholden to me could prove useful.*

Doc bustled in, hooked his silver-headed cane over the back of his empty chair, and shed his overcoat. "Good evening, good evening all. Apologies for my tardiness. All of my patients at the hospital seemed to need the assistance of a physician at the same time this evening."

Inez rose from her seat and followed him to the burdened coatrack. "We decided something that like must be the case," she said, loud enough for everyone to hear. Then, in a low voice, "Miss Carothers—?"

He searched in vain for an empty hook for his coat. "Miss Carothers will recover with a prescription of rest. Which will be better received away from that hospital, by the way. I've arranged for her to be taken home in the morning."

Inez took his coat from him and pushed the forest of outerwear aside to reveal one bare hook buried beneath. "I worried about the injury to her head—"

"Classic symptoms of a concussed brain. Confusion, headache, sleepiness, inability to remember events prior to the injury—"

"When I found her, she talked about two men who argued and died by the tracks. And I found two riderless horses by the river—"

"Yes, yes." Doc nodded absently, gaze pinned on the sideboard laden with decanters and bottles. "She said something of the sort to me. Anxious as well. Another symptom. Now, don't worry about Miss Carothers, my dear. The vigor of youth is on her side." He switched his gaze to Inez, and the worn and weary creases in his face uplifted into a tired smile. "Don't think me hard-hearted, but with all I saw tonight, Miss Carothers' injuries—a knock on the head, a twisted ankle—could be considered a blessing. One fellow suffered from a most dreadful accident at a prospect hole in Empire Gulch. A premature blast."

He shook his head. "Would you mind getting this old man a brandy, Mrs. Stannert? That old war wound in my leg is reminding me of my age. I'm looking forward to sitting down, playing a few hands of cards, catching up on the news. And I've some news of my own to share with everyone."

Inez moved to the sideboard, relieved, but not entirely removed from worry about Susan.

As she carried a full brandy glass back to Doc, now seated in his usual chair, Doc said, "It's not generally known about town, but…." He paused to sample the brandy and give Inez time to sit, then leaned across the table, taking them all into his circle of confidence. "The Union Veterans Association received word that the 'Hero of Appomattox' is seriously considering our invitation to visit Leadville during his trip to Colorado."

"Ulysses S. Grant?" Jed's counting ceased. "When would that be?"

"Since I was the one who, er-hem, penned the missive, I expect I'll be among the first to know his arrival date."

Jed's expression sharpened, a hungry man scenting a hot meal. "You'll be sure to notify *The Independent* first when you hear, right, Doc?"

"Of course, of course. We know that he's planning on staying with General Palmer in Colorado Springs. I imagine that Palmer, being the generous and honorable fellow that he is, will encourage Grant to add a visit to our city in the clouds to his itinerary."

Jed's expression reminded Inez of a child forced to hear a detested sibling being praised. "If Palmer did something like that, it'd be for the good publicity and to wash off the mud that he accumulated in bullying the Santa Fe."

Doc harrumphed.

Inez inwardly groaned. *Oh Jed, don't.* Lately, every Saturday night, it was the same. Jed would throw a jab at Palmer and the Rio Grande. Doc, a staunch supporter of all things and persons Federalist in the Civil War, would harrumph and rally to Palmer's defense. Inez tolerated the verbal fracas only because the other players seemed to find it entertaining and because the battle of words never transformed into a physical fight.

"How old were you when the War between the States ended, young Elliston?" boomed Doc.

Jed squinted at him. "I was eight. And well schooled in mathematics."

"But not, apparently, well schooled in the great events of your own time. Did you have a brother, father, relative who fought in the war?"

Jed, looking bored, shook his head.

"Well then, I'd wager you have no experience with the courage and valor of men like Palmer. When he was about your age right now, it was '61, and he raised an entire cavalry unit of educated, fine young men like himself from Pennsylvania. Less than a year later, he raised a regiment of twelve hundred men."

Jed sneered. "Palmer's a Philadelphia Friend, right, Doc? So why was such an educated, fine young Quaker in such a rush to spill blood? I'll tell you why. He was after the glory and the power, just like now, with his railroad. And I'd wager he didn't hesitate to pull the trigger in the name of might and right."

Doc, ignoring the verbal bullets whistling about him, charged on. "It was a time of grave and perilous danger to the country and all she stood for. We all struggled with conflicting principles. No one wants to shed blood. But obedience to conscience tipped the scales for many good men, and thank God for that."

"Face it, Doc. Palmer's ambitious, plain and simple, whether it's war or railroads. He once said, and I quote, 'amidst all the hot competition of this American business life there is a great temptation to be a little unscrupulous.'" Jed rubbed his chin meditatively. "I think he was with the Kansas Pacific at the time."

"One can be tempted by ambition and not give in. But in war and business, to succeed, one must have a strong character. And Palmer has that. I've been privileged to hear him talk about how, in the Battle of Chickamauga, he and his men stood brave and drove back fugitives when the line before them broke. He scouted and fought guerrilla bands in the Saquatchie Valley, harassed Longstreet in the French Broad River Valley, raided and camped in the saddle during the long winter—"

"I know what 'raided' means," interrupted Jed. "Burning bridges. Destroying stores. Taking from country folks who don't have two sticks to rub together and leaving them to starve so the army could be fed. You see, I did my homework too, Doc."

"He was trapped behind enemy lines during reconnaissance and thrown into Thunder Castle—"

"He was a spy. Traded his uniform for civilian clothes and gave a false name."

"Chased Jeff Davis into Georgia, captured his supply trains, and drove him into the arms of the Tenth Michigan Cavalry."

Jed rolled his eyes.

Inez, wearying of the argument, said, "Gentlemen, shall we play?"

The door opened. Music spilled into the card room as Sol poked his head tentatively around the corner. "Ma'am? Fellow out here wants a word with you."

Inez raised her eyebrows, annoyed at the interruption.

"Says he's a railroad man. Mr. Hold, Holt, something like that."

She glanced at her watchpin. "A break, gentlemen? Say, ten minutes?"

Once outside the private room, Inez spotted Preston Holt straight away, standing a full head above the crowd.

Sol leaned close and shouted above the noise, "Over there, Mrs. Stannert," and pointed toward Holt.

Crossing the crowded room gave Inez time to compose her opening. "Mr. Holt, what a pleasant surprise! So, are the railroad tracks open tonight?"

Holt tipped his hat in greeting. "Delaney decided tomorrow's soon enough after all."

His words were a sober reminder of the bodies lying beneath the rubble.

He continued, "Came to fetch my jacket. Gave me an excuse to visit sooner rather than later." He glanced around the crowded saloon—the papered walls, varnished wainscoting, new coal oil lamps. His sky blue gaze returned and swept her from the toes of her satin shoes to her hazel eyes. "Nice outfit, Mrs. Stannert."

Her pulse began to throb in her throat. "Thank you." She looked around the room and decided to reply as if he were referring to the establishment. "We're refurbishing the saloon. Leadville's coming up in the world, and we're just trying to keep up with her." She became aware of Abe not five feet away, eyebrows raised. "Mr. Holt, allow me to introduce my business partner, Mr. Jackson."

The two men measured each other over a brief handshake.

She continued, "Mr. Holt, allow us to pour you a drink on the house for your trouble—"

"Next time," Holt interrupted, not unkindly. "The jacket?"

"Of course. It's in the kitchen." Inez led the way. "I do appreciate all your help today," she said over her shoulder as she pushed open the passdoor.

"No problem, ma'am." The door closed behind him, plunging them into the near twilight of the kitchen. A lamp, turned low, hung by the back door as a signal to those seeking the alleyway for relief.

Inez pulled the jacket from the chair and turned, nearly bumping into Holt.

She laughed in surprise, then stopped, feeling ridiculous. "Well, it was much appreciated all the same." She clutched the jacket a moment longer. "By the way, I discovered the name of the man riding the other horse."

Preston Holt nodded once, encouraging her to go on. His eyes in the dim room were nearly invisible in the shadow of his hat.

"Elijah Carter. He owns, ah, owned a livery in town. On the corner of Twelfth and Poplar. North end of town." Thinking of Hollis and his snarly face, she added maliciously, "His partner Hollis could tell you more, I'm certain."

"Much obliged, Mrs. Stannert." He reached for the jacket, his fingers briefly touching hers in the dark.

She felt the wool, worn soft by time and use, slide through her hands as she continued, "I can't help but wonder what business Eli Carter had by the tracks. It's curious. And then, there's the business of the generals."

"Generals?"

"Generals," she repeated, half to herself. "Susan said the two men argued about a general. General Palmer owns the railroad. Hollis mentioned General Lee when he raised a glass in Eli's memory. Now, General Grant may be coming to town. Altogether too many generals."

She stopped. And realized Preston Holt was also motionless.

Inez cleared her throat. "Did you, perchance, discover who'd been riding the Rio Grande horse?"

After a moment, Holt said, "I didn't ride into town just for the coat, Mrs. Stannert. I spoke with McMurtrie and Snow of the railroad about what happened today on the Rio Grande right-of-way. Turns out, a siding and two supply cars were destroyed too. McMurtrie and Snow talked with the federal marshal in these parts. Everyone agrees, this problem—" the last sleeve slid from her clasp— "is railroad business."

"Ah," was all she could think of to say.

The passdoor flew open. Light poured into the kitchen, pinning their overlapping shadows against the stove. Any doubts

Inez had as to the intruder's identity were blown away by Taps' rendition of "I've Got a Friend in Jesus."

Reverend Sands stepped forward, an unreadable silhouette. "Everything all right in here?" The concern in his voice was threaded with the promise of danger. He stepped aside, out of the light. Inez saw him ease his overcoat back from his holstered gun as the door swung shut. Near darkness enclosed them.

Preston Holt stepped away from her, jolting the table and its tin washtub. Dirty glassware rattled, loud as an accusation.

Holt's free hand dropped unobtrusively to the revolver on his left side, out of sight of the reverend.

Chapter Ten

Inez stepped between the two men. Forcing a matter-of-fact tone, she said, "There's no problem, Reverend. I was returning a jacket lent to me during this afternoon's downpour. This is Preston Holt of the Rio Grande railroad. Mr. Holt, this is Reverend—"

"Preston? Preston Holt?" Reverend Sands moved forward, his frown shifting to astonishment.

Holt pushed his hat back and scrutinized the reverend. He said slowly, voice laced with disbelief, "Justice 'Jay' Sands. Well, I'll be."

Sands grinned.

Inez watched in amazement as the two men engaged in an extended bout of handshaking and backslapping. "You know each other?"

Sands turned to her, face shining with boyish enthusiasm. In the half-light of the guttering lamp, he looked younger than his thirty-odd years. "Preston and I were in the same regiment during the war until I...." He paused. Inez thought she saw a shadow, not due to the flickering kitchen light, pass over his face.

He finished with, "Preston saved my life. More than once."

"And more than once I wondered why." Holt's hand engulfed the reverend's. Inez could see he was smiling. "Never followed orders. Cussed arrogant. Should've court-martialed you for refusing to climb that tree—"

"If I'd listened to you, those Georgia boys would've picked me off like a squirrel—"

"Prit'near shot you myself for disobeying a direct order."

"Guess I wasn't cut out for the job," Sands said, sounding regretful.

Holt released his clasp. "You had a sharpshooter's eye and hand, Jay. But not the discipline."

Sharpshooter? Inez raised her eyebrows at that bit of information.

Sands turned toward Inez. "I haven't seen Preston since...." He squinted up at Holt. "It's been seventeen years since the tree, hasn't it. Seems like yesterday, sometimes."

Holt's voice took on a cautious quality. "Hasn't been that long, if you count Nebraska."

Now it was Sands who became cautious. "Nebraska? When was that?"

Holt scratched his beard, watching Sands closely. "I was working for the Burlington and Missouri River Railroad. Makes it '72, thereabouts."

"I...don't recall."

"Yep. Lowell, Nebraska. We stood each other drinks, talked over old times. Before things got ugly."

"Ugly?" Sands sounded mystified.

"Over a—" Holt stopped. He glanced at Inez.

Inez crossed her arms, but kept her expression neutral. *A woman. They fought over a woman.*

"Nebraska," Sands murmured. He touched a thin white scar that ran from his right temple into his wheat-colored hair. Inez saw comprehension dawn. "You were the one—"

"Cracked you on the head and turned you over to the local law."

"Well, Reverend," Inez said dryly. "Another incident from your past brought to light."

Sands winced. "Sounds like an incident that should've stayed in the dark." He turned to Holt, apologetic. "Only thing I remember is waking up in jail. Hung over, covered in blood, my scalp split open, and no idea why." He shook his head. "I was another man back then. It was the whiskey talking. Not me."

Holt considered, and then nodded, as if dismissing the unfortunate episode between them as easily as the high plains wind blows the dust away. "Did I hear right that you're pounding a pulpit now?"

"I've been in the ministry for two years. Last seven months in Leadville."

"Jay Sands. A reverend." Holt seemed to find the idea amusing. "Guess there's no accounting for God's ways."

"What brings you to this part of the country?"

Holt lounged against the table, careful not to rattle the washtub. "Guarding the payroll for the Rio Grande Railroad."

"And you're in town to...." Sands let the sentence hang.

Holt picked it up easily. "Saturday's payday. Those who could find a way came in to see the sights and spend their wages. I'm keeping an eye on things. McMurtrie's request. No hell-on-wheels stuff like the Union Pacific."

Inez noticed he said nothing about the "problem" on the right-of-way.

Sands fingered the silver watch chain that looped across his black waistcoat. "Most likely, they headed straight for State Street."

"Most likely."

Sands lowered his voice, conspirator to conspirator. "Tell you what, old friend. I'm free for a couple of hours. How about I give you the two-dollar tour of State Street, point out the places where your lads're likely to get fleeced and where they'll get a fair shake."

"You know State that well?" Holt sounded amused.

Inez interposed. "He specializes in saving lost souls, abundant in the immediate neighborhood. In fact—" she glanced sidelong at the reverend— "locally, he's known as the Minister of State."

Sands smiled and reached over to extract one of her hands from her tightly folded arms. Doffing his hat with a flourish, he bowed low over her hand, elegant as an Elizabethan courtier, and said, "A minister in service to the Queen."

Her fingers clenched convulsively in his grasp. The open affection in his voice left no room to maneuver or equivocate.

She looked up at Holt, feeling unmasked. Holt locked eyes with Inez for what seemed a very long time indeed. By the time Sands had straightened up and released her, Holt had unobtrusively retreated another pace.

The reverend clapped his hat back on and addressed Holt. "No danger of a repeat of Nebraska. I gave up liquor when I got the call."

Inez thought she heard an undercurrent of warning in his lighthearted tone, but she couldn't be certain.

They all started toward the kitchen door. Holt exited first. Sands pulled Inez aside. "I'll be back before you close."

"Well, don't sample any of the pleasures of State Street while you're gadding about with Mr. Holt."

"The pleasures begin when I walk you home." He stole a quick kiss before opening the passdoor for her. "Don't let Jed end up in the hole tonight. Rumor is, he can ill afford to lose."

"Ha!" said Inez, his kiss still burning on her lips. "Just before you arrived, he won a rather large pot. Most of it from me."

Inez and Sands caught up with Holt, who stood by the card room, surveying the interior and the gentlemen within.

Inez paused on the threshold to explain. "I run a private poker game on Saturday nights. You're welcome anytime, Mr. Holt. Any friend of Reverend Sands is a friend…." She trailed off, as he looked her square in the eyes. "Ante's a quarter eagle. No limit."

"Appreciate the warning, Mrs. Stannert." He glanced into the room once more, then looked down at her, a small smile teasing the corners of his eyes. "Always like knowing the limits and the game. Keeps me from acting the fool." There was a note of finality to his even voice.

She sighed ruefully as Sands and Holt headed for the State Street door.

Watching them make their way through the smoke-filled room, she noticed that the saloon's patrons—even those who verged on their drunken limits—automatically stepped aside to let the two men pass.

They made an intriguing pair, she thought. Holt, a giant of a man, advanced slowly, deliberately, giving others time to move out of his path. Sands, a full head shorter, greeted regulars by name, smiling and nodding to those who addressed him. He moved with easy grace, alert to every nuance in the room.

A Biblical comparison rose in her mind, unwelcome and unwanted.

David and Goliath.

She shivered once, unease tiptoeing up her spine. With a shake of her head, Inez stepped into the smoky glow of the card room.

Soothing strains of Brahms' "Lullaby and Good Night" washed over the saloon as Abe and Sol escorted the last of the evening's clientele out the doors. Abe used the direct approach on the seriously inebriated, grabbing an elbow or collar and propelling them into the night. Sol preferred the talking method, picking up the empty glass or bottle, wiping the ring-marked tabletops with a regretful "Closing time" as if, had he his druthers, they could carouse all night. Inez held the Harrison Avenue door open, wishing the sober ones goodnight.

Jed Elliston strolled up, buttoning his frock coat and looking pleased.

Well he should, after all the money he won tonight. Time to call my favor in.

"Mr. Elliston." She stepped toward the staircase. "A quick word, if you will."

Eyebrows raised, he followed.

She leaned against the balustrade, Brahms flowing around her. "I've met a fellow who's worked in the ink trade. He's interested in taking up the pen again. I believe, given the proper inducement, he'd work for you."

"I'm not hiring," Jed said testily. His hands fiddled with his linen cuffs, adjusting them to protrude a proper half-inch beyond his coat sleeves. Inez thought the cuffs looked a tad shabby.

"I believe he'll work cheap. And he could provide some…
perspective…to your paper on an important topic. You see, he
works for the railroad."

Jed's face darkened. The bruise around his eye became more
pronounced. "He's Palmer's man?" The way he said it implied
that he'd sooner hire a rat catcher.

"Now Jed, don't be hasty. He doesn't sound like he holds to
the party line. He's a clerk or secretary to Lowden Snow and
ferries documents and papers around for the lawyers and the
board. I get the distinct impression he'd be happy to 'tell all'
about the Rio Grande, if you present him with the opportunity."

She could see him wavering, torn between righteous anger
and curiosity. She pushed on. "Tell you what. Why don't I
arrange for you to talk to him next week? Just meet him. You
don't have to make any promises."

"No promises," Jed grumbled.

"No promises," she agreed.

After he left, Inez looked around the room. It was nearly empty.
Sol was guiding a last rubber-legged gent to the State Street door.
Abe was wiping down tables and flipping up chairs. Taps had
finished with Brahms and now sang *sotto voce* behind her:

> I sit within the cellar here,
> Where wine is ever flowing,
> I quaff the best and drink good cheer,
> No care or trouble knowing,
> They swiftly bring the jug to me,
> They know what means my winking.
> The glass is filled and I with glee
> Am drinking, drinking, drinking.

"If that's a bid for a last drink, it won't work. Between your
ardent admirers and Sol's generosity you've had plenty." Inez
removed his empty wine glass from the top of the upright.

He segued into "Moonlight Sonata" with a sigh. "Still a good
three hours until daylight. It'd be a waste of a Saturday night to
retire to an uncertain sleep now." The final phrase died under
his hands, and he closed the keyboard.

She pulled a handful of bills from her apron pocket and counted out his share. "For eight hours." She slid the currency to him on the piano top. "I hope the audience was sufficiently appreciative."

He pulled down the empty beer stein used to collect tips and poured out a double handful of silver and gold coins, with a few stray bills crumpled in the mix, onto the scuffed keyboard cover. "Tolerably so. What with Independence Day coming up, there's a high demand for 'Old Glory,' 'Yankee Doodle,' and 'My Old Kentucky Home.'"

"Well, don't encourage any North/South sympathies. The Fourth can be touch and go. Men drink, start thinking it's '61 and Fort Sumter all over again."

"No need to warn me, Mrs. Stannert. I was there, and I don't want to re-live those times in my dreams or others' delusions."

Taps counted his take into a leather pouch, then pulled out the crutch tucked against the far side of the piano. He hauled himself up and paused, balanced on one foot and his crutch, while buttoning his overcoat with his free hand. His empty trouser leg was pinned up and out of sight below the long overcoat. "Good night, Mrs. Stannert. See you Monday." He swung the crutch around and moved toward the Harrison Avenue exit. A familiar figure entering paused and held the door open for him.

Inez waited until Sands closed the door behind Taps before remarking, "I wasn't certain you'd make it back from your tour."

"I said I'd walk you home, and here I am. Ready to go?"

"I need just a moment upstairs."

Once in her dressing room, Inez shed her outer finery and slipped into a simple gray walking dress, skirts wide enough for a sensible stride and short enough to not sweep up the dust and garbage of the roads, and street shoes. She pulled on her cloak. Glancing around for her gloves, she finally spotted them on the washstand, still crumpled in a damp, wadded lump.

Inez grabbed the gloves, shaking them out. Two objects flew from the creased leather, followed by a sharp rattle and clack—metal on wood. Her eyes focused on a bullet, lying on the washstand. A small copper bit, shaped like a top hat, rolled crazily then hit the china washbasin with a *tink*.

Inez picked up the round to examine it. Unusually long and heavy, hexagonal in shape except for its flat head, the bullet gleamed dully in the lamplight. The whole put her in mind of a strange comet, the lead of it heavy with the potential of speed and violence. She thought it might be .44 or .45 caliber. It was certainly larger than the .32 caliber Short rimfire cartridges she used for her Remington Smoot pocket revolver.

She picked up the copper object. It was a percussion cap for a rifle.

These are not mine. That thought was shattered by a sudden certainty. *They must have been in Preston Holt's pocket and I pulled them out with my gloves.*

She thought back, trying to remember the make of the rifle slung alongside Preston Holt's saddle. A Winchester? Or a Henry? Something fairly standard, she thought, which might use a .44 or .45 caliber. She rolled the bullet between thumb and finger, perplexed. *But the shape and length of this are unusual.*

A knock at the door interrupted her musings. She started to drop the two objects behind the washbasin, and hesitated. Finally, she pulled open the drawer in her washbasin stand, deciding to puzzle it all out later. She pushed the cartridge and cap behind a cake of soap before leaving her dressing room.

Chapter Eleven

Sands hummed "I've Got a Friend in Jesus" while Inez locked the office door behind her. She asked, "You heard what happened to Susan?"

Sands stopped humming, his demeanor sobered. "By Doc's accounts, she's going to be all right. Sounds like she was in the wrong place at the wrong time."

Inez extracted her gloves from her cloak pocket. "Thank goodness it didn't turn out any worse. I'll stop in and see how she is tomorrow. Doc said he's sending her home in the morning."

"Perhaps you and I could call on her together after Sunday services."

Inez turned and started down the stairs of the saloon. A vision of the two of them strolling away arm in arm under the congregation's disapproving gaze flitted through her mind. "Perhaps," she hedged. "Although it might be better if I go on ahead and meet you there. After you escape the clutches of your flock."

She stopped at the bottom of the stairs to fasten her cloak at her throat. "Did you and Mr. Holt enjoy reminiscing about the war?"

Sands winced. "The war isn't something I remember with any pleasure. It may have brought out the hero in a few, but it mostly served to hone men's vices. Right, Mr. Jackson?"

Abe added a refilled bottle of Red Dog to the symphony of shapes and sizes on the backbar. "That's right." He sounded grudging, as if agreeing with Sands didn't sit right. "The war was bad times. No sense dwellin' on it."

Sol, who was upending chairs onto the tables, paused, swinging a chair by its slat. "I missed it entirely. Turned thirteen the day before Appomattox."

Sands settled his hat on his head. "You ought to thank God for that."

Sol shrugged. "My older brother always made it sound downright glorious to be fighting the Rebs." He thunked the chair, seat side down, on the plank table. "When he came home on furlough in '64, I tried to talk our ma into letting me go back with him, but she got hysterical at the notion." He sighed. "Hearing the stories the old-timers tell, I feel I missed out on something grand."

Once outside the saloon, Sands said ruefully to Inez, "So now I'm an 'old-timer.'" He offered her his arm. "I believe those who talk about the war spin a better story at the bar or by the fire to paint themselves heroes or martyrs. They all claim they were fighting for justice, for the one true cause. It's all hurrah for States' Rights or hurrah for the Union."

They began walking, slowly negotiating their way up the crowded boardwalk of Harrison. Sands continued, "The ones who weren't there picture the battles being like that canvas in your card room. Glorious. Bigger than life. But it was more akin to a slaughterhouse. Abe was there, he can tell you."

"I'd rather hear about it from you."

"Perhaps another time."

She tried a different tack. "So, you were a sharpshooter. I wasn't aware that you climbed trees to take potshots at the secessionists."

His mouth tightened. "I didn't. That's why I was removed from the unit."

"Was this before or after you cut telegraph wires and throats?" No sooner were the words out than she realized they were a mistake.

"Before. Now, how was your evening?" His tone said, drop the subject.

Inez shrugged. "The evening went tolerably well," she said, echoing Taps' words. "No Saturday night fights. A minimum of broken glass and crockery. And yours? Did Mr. Holt enjoy the city tour? I hope you didn't abandon him in one of the less desirable areas."

A faint smile creased his face. Inez, her hand sandwiched between his upper arm and his side, sensed the tension ease. His wide-brimmed hat cast his face into deep shadow as they passed under a gas streetlamp. "When I left, he was negotiating prices with Frisco Flo."

"Ah."

"Do I hear disappointment?"

"Of course not," Inez replied, too swiftly.

"Hmmmm." He tucked her hand more firmly into the crook of his arm.

As they approached the Texas House Saloon, a louder than usual array of hoots and hollers sounded from within. The saloon's double doors slammed open, and the building disgorged a three-piece brass band—trombone, trumpet, and cornet. Inez caught a glimpse of crystal chandeliers swinging wildly within while the players lined up by the entrance. They marched in place, feet thundering enough to shake the boardwalk. Settling on a beat, they broke into a jaunty version of "Camptown Races."

A nattily dressed figure appeared at the door, derby hat askew. Inez recognized the casekeeper for the house's faro table as he bellowed, "Big winner at the faro table, and the drinks are on the house! Come try your luck, boys. The moon is right and the cards are generous. Be the next to rake in a Texas-sized fortune here in Leadville! Afore you know it, you'll be counting your silver, smoking cee-gars with Haw Tabor—Colorado's Lieutenant Governor and Leadville's own—and chattin' up the actresses in the opry house."

A petite woman emerged from behind him, short skirts displaying shapely knees. The casekeeper, no doubt awash with inspiration, continued, "Why, the next winner might even coax a kiss from our sweet little waiter-girl here, Molly."

"Name's Camille, dammit!" shrieked the waiter-girl, not so sweetly. With a ferocious swing, she clopped his derby off his head.

Derby, waiter-girl, and casekeeper disappeared from sight as the boardwalk crowd stampeded the saloon. As they waited aside for the crush to pass, Sands asked Inez, "How about it, Mrs. Stannert? Want to try your hand at a game of chance? Gentleman says the moon is right."

She snorted, holding her long skirts close with one hand to keep them from being trampled. "Buck the tiger at the Texas House? Faro's not my game. And particularly not when I'm standing on the far side of the table. Besides, I hear they sand the cards."

"Reverend." A hoarse voice rattled behind her.

Sands dropped her hand and spun around. Heart thudding, Inez whirled to confront a cadaverous face, way too close for comfort. Despite a night temperature close to freezing, he was sweating. Gloveless fingers danced up and down the front of a fashionable but filthy coat as if counting the buttons to be sure they were all there. His eyes were shiny, and the skin around them looked paper-thin and ready to tear. He had the air of a desperate man, preparing himself for desperate measures.

Inez slid her hand into her pocket, and curled it around the comforting grip of her Remington Smoot Number Two revolver.

Cracked lips, surrounded by an ill-kempt beard, parted. A shaky voice emerged. "Sorry if I startled...." His gaze jittered away from Inez's face and he seemed to drift off, lost, until his gaze anchored on Reverend Sands. "Reverend. I, I—" he licked his lips feverishly. "I need help." Tears welled up.

Reverend Sands gripped the man's upper arm, a gesture of support and comfort. "Hold on. Weston Croy? Do I remember your name right?"

He nodded.

Staying in the shadow, Inez drifted to the side to get a clear view of the man. She kept her hand on the revolver in her pocket, watching him for sign of a gun or knife.

Sands was talking low, his words rapid, intense. Inez caught "—Monday. Do you have a place to stay until then?"

Weston shook his head, drying his face on a coat sleeve.

"Go to the Exchange Hotel on Front Street. Tell them I sent you." Sands dug into his coat pocket and thrust a crumpled-up currency note into the man's palm. "This should tide you over."

"How can I repay—"

"You repay me when you get home." He squeezed Weston's arm, which looked to be stick-thin. "Just show up Monday. The office is behind the church."

Weston headed unsteadily toward Front Street, his shoulders hunched as if winter breathed down his soiled collar.

Sands watched until Weston was out of sight, then reached for Inez's hand, still firmly anchored in her pocket. "Thanks for watching my back, but that's one you won't have to shoot." He shook his head. "Mr. Croy came from back east. His story's unclear. He talks about the war as if it was yesterday. Talks about building bridges, finding his wife. Why he thinks she's in Leadville...." Sands shook his head. "More likely he came here thinking to make an easy fortune and tripped over the easy vices in town. Lost his way and any funds he brought with him. An all too common story. Unfortunately."

"I'd venture lack of money's not Weston Croy's only problem," said Inez, remembering his jittery manner and strange shiny eyes.

When Sands didn't respond, Inez examined his expression. Even after nearly six months in his company, it still amazed her how quickly and completely his demeanor could shift to match the circumstances. One minute, the compassionate minister. The next...the warmth in his face was gone, replaced by an expression that was harder, colder. A frown burrowed between his drawn-together eyebrows. Other lines ran down both sides of his nose to guard his mouth. Times like this, he seemed a different person entirely. A stranger.

She shivered.

Sands shrugged, tossing off whatever dark thoughts occupied his mind. He caught her gaze and involuntary shiver. His expression softened. "You look as if you've seen a ghost."

She hugged his arm a little closer. "No ghost. I was thinking, I didn't see you much this week. Last time you walked me home was last Saturday night."

"I've been busy. Near the end of the strike, it looked like touch and go whether it would turn violent. Fool thing for the governor to call out martial law. Could have turned the strike into a bloodbath. I spent a solid day with the men from Silver Mountain, trying to convince them that pulling the trigger was like asking to die. Then, there were the usual rounds. Down to South Arkansas, up to Kokomo, calling around town on those I haven't seen the last few Sundays. Meetings with the other town clergy about the building of the city's poorhouse. Our own efforts to finish the mission at the bottom of State Street. The strike put a crimp in our plans to have it done by the time the railroad arrives. Meetings. More meetings. To say nothing of," he groaned, "an overly long one regarding the pews. A meeting which nearly ended in blows."

"Well, what do you expect? The pews mysteriously start to split and fall to pieces and one lumber dealer accuses the other of selling the church green, inferior wood. The accused cries slander. Before you know it, they're both defending their honor and trying to sell new pews to the church."

They turned from Harrison onto Fourth. The streetlamps, which marched down the main streets of town, quit at the corner. Moon and stars provided the only illumination, touching the nearby mountain range with pale shadows beneath the inked-out sky. Inez's small, one-story house waited near the end of the block.

The reverend's arm slid from Inez's grasp and circled her waist. "Well, I'm not complaining. Any job that keeps me close to you will do."

Inez glanced at the dark windows lining both sides of the streets. Two in the morning, no faces at the windows. Relax, she ordered herself. Yet she only felt safe from prying eyes once they mounted the two short steps to her front door.

As she fiddled with the door key, he moved his hand from her waist to cradle the back of her neck.

"Are you inviting me in tonight?" His voice was as warm as his touch.

Inez pushed the door open and paused at the brink of darkness, turning her head to smile at him. "Don't I always?"

She touched one gloved finger to his lips, pleased to see that the hard lines on his face had melted away.

Inside, she removed her cloak and hat and hung them on the curved branches of the coatrack. In her small parlor left of the entryway, moonlight flowed through lace curtains, silvering the crystal decanter of brandy on the sideboard and the ivory keys of her parlor grand. Inez stripped off her gloves and started toward the piano, thinking of the Bach sonata Taps had played earlier.

Sands grabbed her hand and pulled her close. "No music. Not tonight."

Moving in a pattern reminiscent of a slow waltz, he reversed her course, stepping her out of the parlor and across the hall until her bedroom door was at her back, the brass doorknob pressing against her right hip. As they kissed, Inez slid her left hand from his shoulder, down his chest, to his waistcoat. She began undoing the black buttons, one by one.

He pulled back, gazing at her in a way guaranteed to take her breath away. "I can think of more comfortable places to continue this dance."

Inez pressed against him, taking her weight from the pine panels. She snaked one hand behind to reach the doorknob, grasped it, and turned.

Chapter Twelve

The feather bed lurched beneath Inez, the sudden movement bringing her out of a deep sleep. She flung out an arm, only to have it fall on the empty, still-warm spot beside her.

Inez bolted upright, dizzy from abrupt awakening, and stared around the dim room. Still tangled in a web of dreams, she thought she saw her husband Mark, crouched by the bed, gun trained on the door.

The line between sleeping and waking worlds shifted. Her Leadville bedroom snapped into focus as Reverend Sands rose from his crouch and sat slowly onto the edge of the bed, breathing hard. He laid the Colt on the bedside table with care as if, at the slightest jarring, it might fire without human aid. He lowered his head into his hands with a groan.

A shard of moonlight slipped between the roller shade and window frame, painting a thin stripe along the left side of his back. The muscles along his shoulder blades bunched and stretched as he kneaded his face. The muffled voice that emerged was raw with desperation.

"Christ. I need a drink."

Inez exhaled, trying to calm her jangling nerves. She reached out, gently touched one of the silvered scars that crisscrossed his back, intending comfort. He jerked away. When he twisted to look at her, she had the feeling that, for a moment, he couldn't remember who she was or how he came to be in her bed.

Without a word, he reached to the foot of the bedstead and extracted the woolen drawers looped over the bedpost. Sands pulled them on and buttoned them in a quick, fluid motion then padded silently over to the heating stove in the corner of the room. He hooked the grate open, poked among the ashes, and said irritably, "Cold." He slammed the door shut. "Why are there never the makings of a fire around here?"

She bit back a retort, knowing his distress had nothing to do with the cold ashes and lack of coal.

He padded back across the room and disappeared into the hall.

Inez listened hard, but detected no clink of glass on glass, no rising notes of descending liquid. Sands reappeared in the doorway with one of her brandy snifters and headed for her washstand. Inez could barely make him out in the gloom as he picked up her water pitcher and filled his glass. Clutching the edge of the flannel duvet, she watched as he downed glass after glass of water, tossing them back in a way that, if it were whiskey, she would've been certain he drank to forget.

She finally spoke, her words loud in the silence. "Drowning one's sorrows usually requires something stronger than water."

He refilled the goblet and brought it to the nightstand. "Anything stronger, I might just as well put a bullet in my brain and be done with it." He eased onto the bed and leaned back against the solid wood headboard.

"Bad dream?"

He reached for her hand, entwined his fingers tight with hers. "Worse than bad. It must've been seeing Preston Holt again. All the talk of the war."

She scooted closer, settled her head on his chest. His skin still had the lingering coolness of drying sweat. She rubbed her cheek against the ridge of muscle overlaying his ribs. "Talking it out might help."

She felt his chest rise and fall in a long sigh. Then abruptly, "Judith. Did I ever mention her?"

Inez nodded. Once, he'd shown her an ambrotype of himself and his older sister. Their likenesses, forever captured as children, were framed in his pocketwatch casing. She added, "You said she was everything to you after your parents died. And that she passed away during the war."

His grip tightened on her hand. "When she died, I vowed to kill a thousand Johnny Rebs to even the score. But not even killing Lee himself could have brought me peace."

"I thought she died of a fever."

"Judith was a casualty of war." His voice sounded muffled, sorrowful to her ear. "She was caught spying for the Union. They—" he hesitated, then drew her closer, tighter, "left her where we'd be sure to find her." Sands brushed Inez's hair away from her cheek, an absent caress. "Judith was still alive when I found her. I was there when she…." His voice trailed off. His hand stilled. He finally said, more to himself than to her, "I never could resolve what happened to her with the idea of a just and merciful God."

Inez wondered which way to turn the conversation in the dark, which branch of the suddenly open road to take. Finally she ventured, "Why did she become a spy?"

"Judith had strong beliefs about the war. After our parents died, we were shuffled among relatives on both sides of the Mason-Dixon line. We saw the economics, the realities. Heard talk of states' rights, federalism, abolition, and freethinking. After war was declared, she sat me down in the peach orchard of a Maryland uncle and announced that we were going to help the Union. She'd planned it all out, made the necessary connections in Philadelphia where we'd been living. She was eighteen. I was a boy, fourteen and small for my age. I played the parts she gave me, accompanied her back and forth across the line while she—" He stopped. "Did what she set out to do," he concluded softly.

Inez waited, then ventured, "How old were you when she died?"

"Sixteen."

She stroked his chest with her free hand. This time he didn't flinch. "What happened to you after that?"

"I was ordered to Berdan's Sharpshooters, although I begged to be sent to the front lines. Those in charge must have sensed I was in the mood for suicide. Probably thought keeping me a distance from the enemy would be safer."

"And that's where you met Preston Holt."

"Mmm-hmmm."

"I didn't quite understand. Was he your commanding officer?"

"He taught me to be a soldier. Some of his lessons took. Some didn't."

"What happened after you left the sharpshooters unit?"

Sands stirred. His heartbeat pounded in her ear. "I don't want to talk about it, Inez." He sounded weary. "It only brings the nightmares back."

Inez placed a gentle kiss on his skin and waited to see if more words were forthcoming. She finally snuggled her cheek back against him and asked, "Did you dream of your sister?"

"And others." He released her hand, shifted her head to the pillow. "I'd better go. Morning's coming on."

The dusk outside the window looked the same to her. She reached for him, but he slipped from her grasp and bent to gather his clothes from the floor.

She watched as he dressed. From the nightstand, he gathered his pocketwatch and chain, then picked up his handkerchief and carefully wrapped its contents.

She flicked a finger at the square of linen. "The…French envelope. Now that was a surprise."

"A welcome one, I hope."

"A…surprise," she said, unwilling to let on how uneasy the condom made her feel. It reminded her of Dodge City, the time she found a package of "male safes" in Mark's pocket, the anger and betrayal she felt when reading the claim stamped on the package: For protection from all private diseases. *They were for the actresses, prostitutes. He sure as hell didn't use them with me.* She'd tried to slam the hotel door in his face while screaming every invective she knew and a few she invented. Threatened to leave him, to stay in Dodge. Mark had wedged his foot in the door, worn her down with his pleading: "Inez, darlin', now don't shut the door, I can explain. Darlin', it's not what you think."

Reverend Sands stowed the cloth away in an inner pocket. "It seemed a reasonable alternative to…." He hesitated. "Frankly, I got tired of you halting in the middle of…." He stopped again. "And counting the days until your 'visitor' was due."

She flushed and crossed her arms protectively over her breasts. She'd been unaware that her mental calculations of her monthly cycle had been quite so obvious or that he even knew the discreet terminology used by women. "It's just that they're…not easy to come by." She barely refrained from saying *illegal*. "Where did you buy them?"

"I have my sources." Done with watch and handkerchief, he gathered up his money clip and a handful of coins and stray objects from the table. A small pale shadow escaped and floated to the bed sheet.

Inez reached over and picked it up. Soft, paper-thin. "What's this?" She rubbed it between her fingers. The subdued scent of rose greeted her.

Sands hunted through the objects in his hand, and delivered a small flower, half the length of her finger. Holding it up to the window and the waning moonlight, Inez divined a single aspen leaf with its stem tied around a much-crumpled wild rose.

"Who gave this to you?"

"Miss Snow."

Inez sat up straight, holding the tiny wilted bouquet. "When?"

Sands transferred the remaining objects to various pockets and began buttoning his waistcoat. "She slipped it to me when she came back later."

The scent of roses was overpowering. Inez suddenly realized she was crushing the flower. "She came back?"

"Miss Snow and her father stopped by toward the end of the day."

"Why?" Inez fought to keep her tone neutral, suspicion out.

Sands looked down at her as he fastened the last two waistcoat buttons. "To extend an invitation to accompany them to the church's Fourth of July picnic."

"And you accepted!" She didn't try to hide the accusatory tone.

Sands sat on the bed, rattling his cufflinks in one hand like a pair of dice. "Inez, I asked you to go with me to that picnic nearly a month ago. You declined last week. Said you had to work that day."

"It's a holiday! And, even though it's a Sunday, we've no choice. It's our best opportunity to make up for the miserable two months we've had during the strike. We lost so much money."

"I know. Profits vanished. Work on the renovation stopped. Wholesale liquor prices increased. You've told me often enough. Now tell me this, Inez. What was I supposed to say to Lowden Snow? He's a top lawyer for the Rio Grande, has a lot of pull in town. I couldn't say no. Particularly when I had no other companion engaged."

He cocked his head, regarding her. "Which brings up something I've been wanting to ask you. Why is it that the only time you're available to see me is between midnight and dawn?"

"What do you mean?"

"Don't play coy, Inez. You're many things, but coy isn't one of them." He jabbed a post through the cufflink hole. "Why no to the picnic, no to even a simple after-church stroll to visit a friend. The last time we attended a public function together was…." He paused, thinking. "Was it March?"

"Justice B. Sands." She squeezed her eyes shut in frustration, then opened them. "For the past half year, you've had the congregation, in fact, Leadville in general, eating out of your hand. Particularly the 'polite society' women whose husbands are on the church board."

She turned her back on him, reached under her pillow, fished out her silk knee-length drawers, and flung back the quilt. The cold air hit her bare skin like a splash of glacier water. "Those men listen to their wives. At least, on church matters. And those women draw the line between 'proper' and 'improper' with a firm, unwavering hand."

"My deeds speak for my conduct." He finished with the cuff-links and unlooped his tie from around the bedpost.

Inez twisted around on the bed to face him, holding the silk to her breasts. "The mission, the poorhouse, all your other 'good works' will count for nothing if….Don't you see that Mrs. Terrence, Mrs. Price, Mrs. Johnson, and the others would drop you down the nearest mineshaft if they knew you were committing adultery? And with a saloon owner! Their husbands might not care—most of them frequent the district at least once a week—but if their wives catch wind of us…."

She leaned forward, trying to make him understand. "To them, I'm no different from Frisco Flo, the waiter-girls, the actresses, and all the rest of the women on State Street. All of them, souls you're trying to save. Saving lost souls is acceptable, commendable even. But adultery!" Saying the word was like dynamiting a dam inside her. The words flooded out without consideration. "Didn't that ever cross your mind? Doesn't it bother you in the least that what's going on between us is not only a sin, but illegal as well?"

The reverend pinched the bridge of his nose, eyes closed. He glanced past her to the window, then draped the tie around his neck, snugging it under the stand-up collar. "There's no time to discuss this if I'm to slink away before dawn."

"I'm only thinking of your future!" Inez flapped the drawers. The pant legs snapped out momentarily like pleading arms. She pulled them on and reached for the chemise hanging on the bedpost. "What would happen if you lost your position? What would you do?" Her despair felt dangerously close to tears. She hastily pulled the undershirt on.

"There's law enforcement, carpentry. I could preach and minister without a church. But I can't do without—" he took a deep breath— "you. I want to wake up with you by my side, the sun shining through the window."

"Stop," she whispered.

"To break fast with you in the mornings. To—"

She covered her eyes with one hand. "I said stop." Her throat ached, echoing the pain in her heart.

He stopped. "Then what *is* our future, Inez?" His voice was sharp. "You know what I want. I've made it clear, time and time again. From you, I get smiles and embraces, but no more. So, what do you see as our future? Because sneaking around for a few hours of pleasure once or twice a week…that's not what I had in mind for the long haul."

"I'm not ready for this, Justice."

She felt the mattress sag as he sat beside her. Gently, he pulled her hand away from her eyes. "You still wear these." He rolled the two bands on her ring finger, one gold, one silver. "You're still married, I know. I haven't forgotten. But you're the only one who can change that, who can give us a chance at any kind of real future together. Inez, when are you going to get a divorce?"

She pulled her hand away. "I'm looking into it."

"Looking." The disbelief in his voice rang clear.

"I've asked around." She winced, remembering how she'd cornered Cooper one evening, presented her carefully phrased question. How he'd looked surprised first, then speculative as he'd answered: "My specialty is mining litigation, Mrs. Stannert, not domestic law. But if you wish, I'll see if I can find a reputable divorce lawyer for your…'friend'."

"Well, I've asked around too." Sands reached into a waistcoat pocket and extracted a handful of calling cards. Sorting through them, he handed her one.

There was just enough light for her to make out the name embossed at the top: "William V. Casey, Attorney-At-Law."

"Handles divorce," Sands said. "New to town, so you probably haven't met him. Not the type to frequent State Street."

"That's what they all say."

"Bill Casey's different." Sands faced her squarely. "This is it, Inez. My cards are on the table. I'm a patient man, but no saint, and I want some guarantee that you're serious about us. Two guarantees, in fact. The first being that you'll make an appointment with Casey about getting a divorce."

Inez considered, then nodded, secretly relieved not to have to pursue Cooper any further on the matter. "And the second?"

"When this morning's service is over, I want the pleasure of walking you to Miss Carothers' boardinghouse."

"But the congregation—"

It was light enough to see him raise his eyebrows.

"All right." She glanced nervously toward the covered square of window. "Then it's up to you to handle the rumors, the innuendoes. And if this costs you your church position, don't you ever, ever—even in your dreams—blame me."

"Agreed."

"Now I want a guarantee as well."

His eyebrows rose higher.

She leaned toward him and, with lips a fraction of an inch from his, whispered, "A guarantee that you will not allow yourself to be seduced by Miss Snow." She closed the space between them. After a moment, she felt his hand on her knee. Warm and sensuous on the silk, his touch glided up her thigh, slid beneath the silk undershirt, followed the curve of waist to her breast....

She pressed his hand to her skin and pulled back, staring hard into his eyes. "Do you promise?" Her heart beat rapidly, answering the pressure of his hand. She watched him with the intensity usually reserved for drunks on the verge of violence or cardsharps on a losing streak.

But when he smiled, she saw nothing but tenderness mixed with a touch of sadness. "That you would even ask. Very well. Neither Miss Snow nor any other woman—be she an eighteen-year-old debutante from Philadelphia or the Queen of England herself—will take me from your side."

Chapter Thirteen

Inez listened to the creak of floorboards as Reverend Sands made his way down the hallway and into her small kitchen in the back of the house. The back door squeaked open. Birds trilled, and animal-drawn vehicles clickety-clacked down Harrison, one block away. The steady thump of the stamp mills, crushing ore in the first step to extract the silver, threaded through it all like a heartbeat. The door snapped shut, muting the sounds.

Inez bundled into her flannel wrapper and retrieved several lumps of coal from the kitchen hopper. After coaxing a fire from her bedroom stove, she settled herself at the secretary, unstoppered an inkbottle, and retrieved a sheet of thin writing paper to begin a letter to her sister Harmony.

She sat, tapping the steel nib of her uninked pen on the blotter, staring at the roller shade covering the street-side window. The brown fabric, brightened by the rising sun, was now the color of light caramel. Out on Fourth Street, two carriages squeaked by, their harnesses jingling, heading west.

Several thoughts troubled her and interrupted the formulation of her letter. On the one hand, there was Miss Snow.

"I know you, Birdie Snow," she mused. "I'll wager better than you know yourself."

Set the time fifteen years ago, change the venue to New York and the fashions to hoop skirts, and that'd be me. Flirting with men twice my age.

"Papa would have whipped me black and blue if he'd caught me doing half the things I did," she said aloud. The fire in the stove popped in reply.

And on the other hand, there was Justice Sands. A minister, but admittedly no saint.

I'll bet he's never had to seriously deal with a seductive snip of a high-society girl like Birdie.

She sighed, dipped the pen, and attempted to ink the date at the top of the paper. The "J" in June ended up a big blot. Muttering over the waste, she commenced doodling, drawing out the tail of the J in a long undulating line.

Sands had had romantic liaisons with married women before he took up the ministry; Inez knew that for a fact. She did a quick calculation and concluded that he'd spent his formative social years skulking about the war-torn countryside. She doubted very much he'd had many opportunities to engage in the drawing-room equivalent of hand-to-hand combat with young women of Birdie Snow's inclination and social stature.

And if she's half as bold as I was at her age....

Inez tried to shrug off her misgivings and focus on the letter to Harmony. What words could she muster, what could she say to ensure a space of time with her son William? And once Harmony agreed to a meeting, where could they meet? It had to be accessible by train. Not too far from New York. But not too close either. *Should Papa catch wind of my plans, I wouldn't put it past him to be there. God knows what he'd do. Probably shoot me.* As often happened when she considered her father's extreme displeasure, memories of her elopement with Mark Stannert, the act that had sundered her rocky relationship with her father, crowded all other thoughts aside.

She squinched the paper up in an angry twist and stood to throw it into the stove. As the paper hit the coals, it flashed into a golden light. Gripping her elbows, she glared at the consuming flames.

After Dodge, Leadville was supposed to be their new start. It had begun well enough. Mark had won the Silver Queen Saloon in a poker game, fair and square. Or so he claimed. When he'd slid the silver ring on her finger and snugged it up to the gold wedding band, he'd promised her: they'd settle down, have a family, live a respectable life in Leadville.

"We tried," she said softly to the flames. "We tried."

But Inez was no housewife. She chafed at home, scorched their meals, hated the tasks that never saw conclusion, and suffered from chronic nausea that seemed to last her entire pregnancy. One miserable day blended into the next. Their son, finally brought into the world after a long, hard travail, struggled for life, laboring to gasp the thin mountain air into his weak lungs. Then, shortly after their decision to sell the saloon and move to California with its gentler climate, Mark had vanished.

At first, she'd thought him dead, the victim of foul play. As time went on and no body surfaced, her certainties faltered. She'd heard a slight music of whispers concerning Mark and a blonde actress from The Comique, who had vanished about the same time. Perhaps, with all the responsibilities and burdens, the temptations of State Street had been too much to ignore.

"If I ever find out you ran away with that actress," Inez hissed, "I'll kill you, Mark Stannert."

She dropped back into the chair, a little surprised that so much emotion still seethed below the surface for her errant, and perhaps erring, husband.

And if I get a divorce, what then? Marry Justice Sands?

A vision of herself pouring tea for visiting parishioners—all sitting in a proper parlor stuffed with knickknacks and tatted antimacassars, the legs of chairs and tables modestly covered so as not to give offense—made her want to laugh or cry.

Of course, that's not all there is to marriage.

Her gaze strayed to her bed, its crumpled sheets, the hollow where she and Sands had lain together, fitting like two nested spoons.

She looked away. Would he want children? Most likely. *Men always do. What of William? Would Justice take him in? Would my father give him up?*

The stove's heat bathed one side of her body in unbearable warmth while the other side remained cool. She pushed up a sleeve, thinking irritably how much it was like her life. Hot or cold. Debutantes or drunkards. Tea in the drawing room or rotgut in a red-light saloon. Married or alone. *Yet, while I'm married but unhusbanded, I remain in the middle. Free.*

Her hands stilled as she took in the truth of it, handed up from some place deep inside. *While I wait and wait for Mark—who will probably never return—I'm free to do what I want, order my life as I wish. Why do I hesitate to divorce, to set the wheels in motion for Justice and myself? Is it because I'm waiting for Mark, a fool deluding only herself? Or is it because I prefer to live as I wish, beholden to no man?*

She stared at the empty desk blotter. First things first. She could not go another year, another six months, without William. Come fall, he'd be nearly two years old. Would he even recognize her as his mother? The question pained her.

Slowly centering another sheet, Inez redipped the pen and began again.

Dearest Harmony,

I received your letter of June 15 only yesterday and am, of course, sorely disappointed in the news. My heart aches to see my son before the year is out. If not this summer, then early fall. If we were to meet in Chicago or Philadelphia—

The ink flowed smooth and untroubled.

Chapter Fourteen

The notes of the last hymn shivered and died in the air.

"Please turn and greet your neighbors." Reverend Sands gathered up his notes and stepped down from the pulpit, shaking the hands of the nearest church members.

Inez pressed the satin ribbon in place to mark the last hymn and tucked her pocket hymnal into her bulging reticule. The smell of fresh-baked bread, still warm, wafted up from the bag. Uneasy about appearing at Susan's boardinghouse empty handed, Inez had detoured through the saloon's kitchen before church, looking for something edible and easy to take with her after the service. Bridgette had stopped her chopping and cooking long enough to smooth a sheet of brown paper on the kitchen table and settle a clutch of biscuits in the center. She wrapped those biscuits as efficiently as she'd no doubt diapered the last of her five sons.

All the time, she cluck-clucked over Susan's misfortune. "What's a young woman like her doing out all alone? She should've arranged for an escort from Twin Lakes. It's a mercy she wasn't killed!" Bridgette upended the paper bundle with a thump and whipped a string around it. "If she needs anything else—a poultice for scratches, a good beef broth to bring back her strength—you tell me. I know the widow that runs her boardinghouse. That Mrs. Flynn. She thinks nothing of buying the latest fancy hat, but tight with a penny when it comes to her boarders. She's not likely to part with so much as a fresh bit of marrow to help in Miss Carothers' recovery."

Inez pulled the reticule string tight, cutting off the olfactory memory. She looked up and caught Reverend Sands gazing at her over the head of Mrs. Terrence, the sole proprietor of a candy store on Harrison. Mrs. Terrence had the dubious claim to fame of having stood off a lot jumper twice her size with a pistol. The exploit had been immortalized forever in the town's newspapers.

Mrs. Terrence shook a bony finger under the reverend's nose. His attention snapped back to her. Her reedy, but determined voice reached Inez's ears: "Reverend—you *must* do something about these pews! All splintery and splitting, the whitewash peeling off. It's a disgrace. The church should have mahogany pews, like the ones at St. Anne's Episcopal. St. Anne's has Mr. Tabor to pay for them, but we have Mr. Gallagher, who is surely as rich and who could buy a whole church without batting an eye."

Reverend Sands, nodding in time to her words like a metronome, took advantage of a pause to soothe her. "I understand, Mrs. Terrence, I understand. The church board is looking into it, debating costs of repairs versus replacement. Perhaps you ought to talk with one of the board. Say, Mr. Warner, over there." Sands sidestepped, opening a straight path to Mr. Warner of P.T. Warner Books and Stationery, who stood with a glazed look in his eyes while his wife chatted with two other women. Mrs. Terrence bore down on him unwaveringly, a bullet closing on its target. Unaware of the immediate jeopardy, Mr. Warner smiled and lifted his hat in polite greeting.

Inez smiled as Reverend Sands materialized by her side. "Nicely done, Reverend."

"A good soldier—whether of God's army or otherwise— always knows when to take evasive action." He raised an eyebrow. "Did you enjoy the sermon?"

"Oh, immensely. You were splendid, as always."

"What part did you like best?"

"Ah—" Caught out, she wasn't about to admit that she'd lost total track of his message and floated away on the music of his voice, daydreaming over their previous night together.

From his expression, it appeared no explanation was necessary. "I see." His mouth twitched with a suppressed smile. "I should find ways to encourage your spiritual awareness. We can discuss scripture on our way to see Miss Carothers." He glanced toward the cloakroom. "I'll get your coat."

"Don't you have to close up the church?"

"I found a willing volunteer to take my place." He headed toward the cloakroom, greeting Mrs. Warner and her friends in passing.

The group of women looked from Reverend Sands to Inez, curiosity etched on their faces.

Inez smiled frostily at them and turned away. Brushing the top of the last pew with a gloved hand, she strolled toward the stained-glass windows. The glass threw dazzling patterns of color onto the whitewashed interior. Inez paused at the first window, focusing through a rectangle of clear leaded glass onto the hard-packed dirt path outside. A handful of children streaked up the path, chasing each other in a surfeit of high spirits. A moment later, a toddler in Sunday dress lurched into view, his socks sagging down over the tops of his glossy high-buttoned boots. He was obviously doing his valiant best to mimic the speed of the older children, who had by now disappeared around the side of the church. The child's mother strolled a few feet behind.

With a pang, Inez estimated the youngster at about the age of William. She leaned forward, to keep mother and child in view a moment longer.

A furtive movement caught the corner of her eye. She twisted around to see Mr. Braun, bent over the back of the last pew, hand disappearing into his pocket. He straightened up to find Inez staring at him. Pursing his lips, he tsk-tsked loudly and pulled a neatly folded sheaf of notes from his pocket. "Green wood," he murmured as he passed Inez. "Not well cured. *Eine*

Schande." He hurried up the side aisle toward the meeting room behind the sanctuary.

Curious, Inez returned to where he'd been standing. A good-sized split ran along the top of the pew. The raw wood inside looked shiny, fresh—a wound in the white-painted surface. She frowned and traced the gash with a finger.

Still frowning, she looked up to see Reverend Sands emerging from the cloakroom with her coat over his arm. Taking a deep breath, she approached him, meeting him halfway. They stopped, facing each other at a polite distance. Expectancy pulled against her ribs, the same feeling as before the music began.

He held out the coat. "Mrs. Stannert, if I may?" He circled behind her to settle the coat on her shoulders, leaving her an unimpeded view of several churchwomen—gazes rapt, eyebrows raised. Chin held high, she pushed her arms through the sleeves and fastened the top clasp.

He reappeared at her side. "Shall we go?"

She smiled at him and slid her hand around his proffered arm.

A soft voice piped up behind them. "Reverend, are you leaving?"

Inez turned. Birdie Snow stood with her hands fluttering about her mint green sash. Birdie glanced toward the back of the church. A cluster of men and a few women hovered around the meeting room door. Birdie's father, Lowden Snow, stood in the forefront, tapping his silver-headed cane impatiently on the floor. When he seemed confident of having Inez and the reverend's attention, he pulled out a pocketwatch, sprang open the gold cover, and peered at it from arm's length. Inez's lip curled. *Lawyers. Worse than actors for grandstanding.*

Birdie's voice wavered: "Papa wondered...you looked as if you were leaving, and we thought...Reverend Sands, you called for a board meeting after the service, don't you remember? A meeting to discuss the pews and the picnic social. We, the picnic committee, still want your suggestions on the menu. There are questions about the price of strawberries, the musical entertainment, and whether there are enough carriages and wagons...."

She trailed off as Reverend Sands clapped a hand to his forehead.

He turned to Inez. "It's true. I scheduled that meeting myself, two weeks ago. I plain forgot. I'm sorry."

"Church business, Reverend," Inez said with a tight smile. "I quite understand. No need to apologize."

His expression said she wasn't fooling him in the least. "I'll see you at Miss Carothers' boardinghouse later this afternoon," he said.

"We'll see."

Apparently emboldened by Inez's retreat, Birdie plucked at the reverend's sleeve. He threw a last apologetic glance at Inez before allowing himself to be drawn toward the back of the church.

Steaming, Inez watched them walk away.

"Brazen the way she chases after him. Most unladylike."

Startled to hear her own thoughts spoken out loud, albeit in an undertone, Inez whirled around. Mrs. Warner's two companions lingered by the church entrance, staring with open disapproval.

At her.

Inez had had enough. She headed straight for the women, who hastily sprang apart, leaving her a clear shot out the door and down the steps.

"Good afternoon, *ladies*," Inez snarled. She hurtled past them, head high and back straight. Strangling her reticule with one hand and her coat collar with the other, she headed at a fast and most unladylike pace up the street toward Susan's boardinghouse.

Chapter Fifteen

Inez kept up a rapid clip until her Sunday-tight corset and the altitude forced her to slow down. As she approached the block where Susan lived, she slowed further, contemplating her next move. Inez had not visited Susan at her place of boarding before. The two women most often met over a cup of tea or a meal at the Tontine Restaurant, at Inez's house, at church, or at Susan's portrait studio. Susan had not, of course, ever been to Inez's saloon—such a thing would have been viewed as most improper. For this visit, Inez had fully expected Reverend Sands to pave the way past the boardinghouse door. She'd counted on his credentials as a man of the church to gain them both easy entrance past the formidable Mrs. Flynn. Now, it appeared she would have to negotiate entrance on her own.

Inez stopped two buildings away from the cream-painted boardinghouse. From that angle, she could see it was two stories high, but presented an elaborate three-story false front to the street. Intricately turned porch pillars and an ornate porch railing competed with gingerbread detailings dripping along the eaves like lace on a Sunday collar. Her own lace collar, Inez realized, was in definite need of a starching after her brisk trot. In fact, her entire dress felt wilted, the gray silk sticking to her arms from the summer's warmth.

She looked back up at the house, bristling with architectural minutiae, touched the small knot of hair at the nape of her neck, and squared her shoulders. *What could be more proper than arriving as a representative of the church?*

Inez opened her reticule and pulled out the brown package of biscuits and a calling card. She passed through the hairpin fence guarding the pocket-sized front yard, her long skirts swishing against the pebbled path, and up the three stairs to the porch. She checked the buttons on her gloves to be sure they were all properly fastened and twisted the brass bell turn by the front door. A raspy clatter sounded deep within.

The door was opened by a tall, slender woman wearing an uncannily familiar dress. Inez took an involuntary step back. Same basque bodice, same gray moiré and faille silk combination, same narrow skirt, mid-length banding, and pleated ruffle at the hem. The only difference Inez could detect from her own Sunday outfit was that the woman at the door had opted for a jabot collar, graceful as a lace waterfall down the front of her bodice, in counterpoint to Inez's now-limp collar of ruched ivory threadwork. Inez was willing to bet that once the woman turned around, the same complicated draping, bows, and pleats would appear at the back.

The woman looked young. Too young, in Inez's estimation, to be the boardinghouse proprietor. Based on Bridgette's mutterings, Inez had drawn a mental picture of the penny-pinching Mrs. Flynn as a parsimonious widow with sunken cheeks, gimlet gaze, and steel-gray bun wound tight to her head. This stylishly dressed young woman with blonde hair and limpid brown eyes must, she decided, be one of the half dozen schoolteachers who boarded with Susan.

Smiling in the neutral but polite manner of one well-bred woman to another, Inez said, "Good day. I'm Mrs. Stannert from Miss Carothers' church, come to see how she's doing after her—" Inez swiftly picked from among a number of words— "recent ordeal. Is Mrs. Flynn about?" She held out her card.

"I'm Mrs. Flynn," the elegant young woman replied, smoothing her skirt in a perhaps unconscious effort to wipe the wrinkles from Inez's own outfit. Mrs. Flynn took Inez's card, then glanced toward the interior of the house. Inez became aware of voices decidedly unfeminine in timbre. When Mrs. Flynn looked back, a small frown had creased her otherwise unlined face. "Miss Carothers has visitors with her, but I believe they are finishing up."

"I have no wish to tax her health. Perhaps you might pass on my wishes for her speedy recovery, as well as...." Inez held out the biscuits to the landlady. "To help her recover," she finished lamely.

Mrs. Flynn hesitated, looked down at Inez's card, and moved aside to let Inez enter. "Mrs. Stannert, please come in. A visit from a church representative might be a good idea. Things are so unsettled right now. I don't think the atmosphere is a healthy one for my girls."

Inez couldn't help but find Mrs. Flynn's maternal tone strange, given the landlady was probably younger than many of her "girls."

Mrs. Flynn turned—Inez saw that, yes, the back of the dress was cut exactly the same as her own—and motioned Inez to accompany her.

Lowering her voice Mrs. Flynn said, in obvious displeasure, "I have no idea what possessed Miss Carothers to take such a foolish course yesterday. Miles from town. Unescorted. Not only was it the height of impropriety, but also shows an extreme lack of common sense. And dangerous besides. Why, only two weeks ago, there was that dreadful business north of Granite. Very unfortunate."

Inez nodded politely, recalling the "dreadful business" alluded to: the good citizens of Granite, sixteen miles south of Leadville, had chased, caught, and hung an alleged horse thief. "Alleged" only, since his guilt had been determined in haste, in advance, and without the benefit of a legal trial.

Mrs. Flynn murmured, even softer, "The deputy federal marshal is here. Questioning Miss Carothers. He wouldn't wait until she'd recovered. Said he had to speak with her today, this minute, right here. Appalling, don't you agree?"

Inez murmured in reply, debating whether Mrs. Flynn was appalled at the marshal's insistence on interviewing a recovering invalid or appalled that he'd insisted on conducting that interview on her premises. Mrs. Flynn's next words resolved that question.

"I've never, in all my years of running boardinghouses, had any of my young ladies come to the attention of the legal authorities. It gives such a poor impression. I run a well-respected boardinghouse, none better in Leadville for young, well-bred women. My girls all come from good families that expect me to shelter them and protect them from baser influences." She shook her head. "This dreadful business with Miss Carothers. Very unfortunate."

"Very," murmured Inez. It was not lost on her that Mrs. Flynn had used the same tone and words to describe Susan's hapless situation that she'd used to describe the hanging of a horse thief.

Mrs. Flynn paused at the entrance to the parlor. Inez lingered a proper couple paces behind, out of sight in the hallway. Mrs. Flynn announced to the parlor's interior, "Miss Carothers has a visitor from her church, and she mustn't be tired, on order of the doctor. Perhaps you can talk further when she is recovered and able to come to your office, Marshal?"

Inez heard the creak and shuffle as someone rose from an overburdened chair. "We're finished, ma'am," came a smoke-roughened voice. "Thank you muchly for allowing this intrusion."

Mrs. Flynn proceeded to the front door to let Deputy U.S. Marshal Cy Ayres out. Inez gripped the luckless biscuits tighter as the marshal came into view. Marshal Ayres was no stranger to her, having the good taste to spend a portion of his earnings at the Silver Queen whenever he happened to be in town. She hoped that, under the circumstances, he would not pause to inquire "How's the firewater business, Mrs. Stannert?" or "Cards runnin' lucky this week?" She steeled herself for a quick nod and polite greeting. Marshal Ayres' overgrown eyebrows—gray and tangled like his weedy mustache—shot up at the sight of her. But he merely shifted his dusty brown bowler to his other hand, uttered a perfunctory "Ma'am," and continued toward the front door.

Inez exhaled in relief, turned back to the parlor, and collided with Preston Holt.

He quickly put a hand on her arm to steady her as he stepped back. He let go nearly as soon as he'd taken hold, but the brief touch, to say nothing of a full-body, face-to-face collision, brought the blood rushing to Inez's face.

"Pardon, Mrs. Stannert. Wasn't watching where I was going."

"My fault entirely, Mr. Holt." She was sure the biscuits were nothing but crumbs now.

He'd looked solemn, even a tad grim, when she'd first registered his face, but she thought she detected a twinkle in his eyes as he added, "We keep running into each other."

She hmmmed noncommittally and glanced toward the boardinghouse vestibule. Mrs. Flynn had finished saying goodbye to the marshal and was now watching them, eyes narrowed and questioning. Inez hoped the low-toned conversation had escaped her ears, which were most likely attuned to any hint of "improprieties" on her premises.

Turning her back on Mrs. Flynn, Inez offered Holt a slightly apologetic smile and said with a meaningful tip of her head in the landlady's direction, "Excuse me, sir, but I've business with Miss Carothers, and I've no desire to keep her longer than necessary."

His eyes tracked over her shoulder to Mrs. Flynn, then back to Inez. He seemed to perceive her intentions and offered an appropriately respectful nod before continuing to the front door.

Inez ordered the butterflies in her stomach to stop fluttering as she entered the parlor. The room was just as she suspected it might be, given her admittedly very brief glimpse into Mrs. Flynn's determination to battle the "lower standards" a mining boomtown might try to insinuate into her "young ladies." Several end tables, legs modestly covered with tablecloths, held oil lamps, their chimneys delicately etched, and china statuettes, predominantly angels and shepherdesses. The tables, a small pianoforte, and a display cabinet squeezed in as best they could among several overstuffed chairs, two curved-back rocking chairs, and a single small sofa smothered with antimacassars. Heavy draperies repelled the sun while a modest fire crackled tastefully in the fireplace throwing out unneeded heat in the stuffy parlor. The entire room bristled with decency, respectability, and decorum. Inez began to sweat and despaired of the condition of her clothes.

Susan, seated in a chair by the fire, looked up with dread, as if expecting a lecture on propriety from Mrs. Flynn. She had one leg propped up on an ottoman, a throw blanket covering the limb.

Her bruised face filled with relief. "Oh Inez, I'm so glad you're here!" She motioned Inez forward, her relief sliding into distress. Once Inez was close enough, Susan grabbed her wrist. The wrapped biscuits fell from Inez's grasp and tumbled to Susan's lap. Susan ignored them and pulled Inez closer, whispering frantically, "They don't believe a word about what I saw yesterday. They cleared the railroad tracks…and found nothing!"

Chapter Sixteen

"But surely you found *some*thing." Inez stared down Deputy U.S. Marshal Ayres, as if he was trying to bluff through an exceedingly poor hand. "There must have been some sign of foul play. Maybe the bodies were removed."

Marshal Ayres sighed, leaned his elbows on the battle-scarred desk, and laced his thick fingers together. His firm but doleful expression gave Inez the impression he was praying she would simply acquiesce to his point of view and depart.

"Now, Mrs. Stannert," he began again. "It's like I said. The railroad called me in double quick. I was in South Arkansas, not more than a few hours ride, when the news of the slide came over the telegraph. I got there first thing yesterday morning, talked with the railroad's men, including that feller Mr. Holt, some of the surveyors, and the crew and their boss. The crew was working on the tracks. There was lots of damage, sure. Tracks, siding, two supply cars, pretty well gone. Lots of rocks, dirt, dust, some broken timbers, bits from the cars, and a piñon tree or two. No dead men. No dead nothing, unless you count the trees."

"But I found those two horses, saddles and all, wandering near Disappointment Gulch," she insisted. "Riderless. One was Elijah Carter's, from his own livery. Now why would he abandon his horse by the Arkansas River? That makes no sense."

At Carter's name, Inez saw Ayres' patiently suffering expression alter subtly with a shift of his gaze, a slight frown.

She pounced. "Marshal. Is there something about Mr. Carter?"

The chair squawked as Ayres leaned back, brushing at his moustache as if removing crumbs. "A local constable mentioned this morning that Carter was asking around for me whilst I was out of town."

"When? When was this?"

"Friday late," he said reluctantly.

"That would be just before he left town on Saturday! What did he want?"

"Didn't say. Asked where I was. When I'd be back."

"What business could Mr. Carter have had with—" She looked anew at Ayres. "Could he have been headed to South Arkansas to find you when…?"

The chair squawked again as Ayres leaned forward, replanting his elbows on the desk. "Now, Mrs. Stannert. Carter probably went on a bender in Granite or somewheres. Probably show up next week or two, asking what happened to his horse. I doubt anything nefarious is going on. Much less a shootout on the railroad tracks outside of town."

"Miss Carothers wouldn't have made up such a story," Inez insisted.

"She had a pretty hard knock on the head. She doesn't remember anything about the rockfall and is kinda sketchy about what happened before that. Too," he stopped, looking uncomfortable, then continued, "there's the liquor."

"The *what*?"

Ayres held up a hand as if to forestall a pummeling.

"Now I understand she's a friend of yours, Mrs. Stannert, but there's no use pretending you didn't smell it on her. You found Miss Carothers, after all. And I didn't just go by what the railroad men said. I had a talk with Doc, he noticed it too. He said he didn't think she's the drinking kind, so the liquor probably hit her pretty hard, might've addled her along with that rockfall."

Inez finally caught up to his argument and didn't know whether to be amused or indignant. "Susan was not drunk!"

"Well, according to all, she was pretty well soaked in the stuff."

"Soaked is exactly right. I found her, used my kerchief and the contents of my canteen, which happened to be high-grade brandy, by the way, to clean the scratches on her face. I also had her take a couple sips, to revive her."

The marshal's eyebrows dipped up and down with his nod. "I understand, ma'am," he said in a tone that, to Inez, sounded very much like a dismissal. He pushed back his chair and stood. "We can always talk more about this later. I'm sorry if it seems like I'm rushing you, but I've some other business—"

"And I have no intention of delaying you." Inez pushed her own chair back and, ignoring Ayres' outstretched hand, stood and gathered her parasol. "I know you will be thorough in your investigation. Dead men don't just walk away. Particularly when they've been crushed by a landslide."

Back out on the boardwalk, Inez took a deep breath, then yanked a lace handkerchief from her sleeve and clapped it over her nose. Dust, stirred up by the Monday morning throngs of carts, wagons, coaches, horses, mules, and pedestrians, stung her nose and made her eyes water. The sun cut through the haze with the sharp clarity of light in the high mountains. The still-cool morning air warred with the burning intensity of the sun. Apollo would win this battle, Inez knew, at least until afternoon thunderclouds marched in over the high mountain crests like a well-trained battalion.

And the saloon will fill with men trying to stay dry or wet their whistles.

Anticipating a busy day, Inez walked as fast as her long narrow skirts would allow. Ayres' patent disbelief of Susan's story stung Inez's pride nearly as much as the dust hovering in the air stung her nose. Still, without a body, Inez knew nothing much would be done. Unless Elijah Carter or the unknown railroad man were reported missing. Which seemed unlikely.

She frowned, wondering how carefully the marshal examined the location of the slide. Did he go up to the ridge top? Or just meander along the track? *I ought to go myself.* She glanced at the sun, assessing the time. *But not today. Perhaps tomorrow morning. Perhaps the good reverend might see fit to accompany me.*

Cheered by the thought of having Sands to herself and a pleasant ride the next day, Inez pushed on the door of the Silver Queen Saloon and entered.

She blinked to adjust from the bright outdoors to the subdued interior. A strange tableau greeted her: Abe and Sol, behind the bar, looking gloomy. Bridgette on the other side, arms crossed tightly over her ample bosom, a wicked meat cleaver gripped in one hand. All eyes were pinned on an enormous misshapen mound on the bar.

Inez heard Bridgette say ominously, "Heavens above and the devil below, Mr. Isaacs. Not in *my* kitchen you don't—"

"But we can't put it above the bar," Sol objected. "If it fell down, we'd be brained for sure. Besides, Mr. Jackson says—"

Conversation ceased as the floorboards creaked beneath Inez's boots. The group turned toward Inez.

"What's this?" She tugged off her cloak.

Abe tipped his head at the mysterious object. "Chet." Anger simmered in the terse word.

Inez raised her eyebrows.

"Chet brung it by, half hour ago." Abe looked pointedly at Sol. "I wasn't here yet. If I'd been, I'd've thrown him and that damn—" He glanced at Bridgette. "Pardon." Then he focused back on Inez. "Let's just say he'd be lyin' in the street, and the crows'd be breakfastin' on his innards. There wouldn't've been any speechifyin' or," he pointed with his chin at the lump on the bar, "this."

"Chet was waiting when I unlocked the door this morning," Sol said. "He apologized for his conduct with Mrs. Jackson the other day. Said this was for Mr. and Mrs. Jackson. A late wedding present. A way of saying, uh, sorry."

And a sorry-looking thing it was. Inez finally identified the object as an enormous, somewhat moth-eaten buffalo head, mounted on a polished wood slab. Curved horns glinted wickedly.

Dust—whether picked up from the journey to the saloon or from sitting in some corner, long ignored—powdered the fur.

"He sounded sincere." Sol hunched his shoulders as if afraid of being further berated.

Inez sighed and rubbed her forehead. An ache was forming behind her eyebrows.

Bridgette cleared her throat. "We were just discussing, ma'am, what to do with this—" she pointed the cleaver at the buffalo, as if Inez might not grasp the topic of conversation— "hideous thing. Mr. Jackson said toss it in the alleyway with the trash. Mr. Isaacs said no, hang it in the kitchen. I said it would be a sorry day when I'd allow that in my kitchen. I told Mr. Jackson to take it home."

"I'm inclined to throw it out," said Abe. "Can't say the missus'd welcome it."

Picturing Abe's small and tidy cabin, Inez said, "Of course she wouldn't. My God, it's ugly." A fly crawled over the buffalo's snout and disappeared up one nostril. Inez wrinkled her nose in distaste. "Where on earth did he get this? It's not as if buffalo roam nearby."

"Lookin' at it reminds me of what he said to my wife," grumbled Abe. "I didn't take kindly to his words or actions. Man's a fool, if'n he thinks I'm gonna forget about it."

Inez gingerly touched the tip of one of the horns. She was gratified to find it wasn't quite as sharp as it looked. "I understand, Abe, but perhaps we should hang on to it for a while. After all, Chet didn't know you and Angel were married. It was an honest mistake, given her previous profession."

Abe's frown deepened.

She ratcheted up the persuasiveness. "It's summer. He won't be here long. He'll take off soon, go back to wherever he's prospecting nowadays. But while he's in town, he's bound to be hanging around, and he is certainly free with his money when he's flush. It can't hurt to display his…gift…while he's here. We'll hang it someplace obvious, but away from the bar and more in the shadows, so we don't have to look at it all the time." Inez surveyed the room. The walls were already filled with sporting prints and punctuated by wall sconces. Her gaze traveled upward. *Not over the piano. God forbid, not on the wall leading upstairs.*

"There!" She pointed.

Sol swiveled to look. "Above the door to State Street?"

"Consider. They come in sober from Harrison, leave drunk by State. Maybe they'll look up and reconsider, stay for another drink. In other words, we'll buffalo them into spending a little more money here before they move along." She smiled, then sobered. "We could certainly use every short bit and shinplaster that comes our way. And, it's the only open area not on the ceiling or floor."

She turned back to catch Abe's gaze on her, skeptical.

"Just don't look at it, Abe. We'll take it down as soon as he leaves town." She turned to Sol. "Hammer and nails are in the back. When you get it up there, be sure it's secure." She started toward the kitchen, Sol trailing behind.

"Inez."

She turned at Abe's voice. He came out from behind the bar, heading her way. Something about the way he rolled down his sleeves and straightened his gray waistcoat warned her that he had other business on his mind. *Like he's preparing for battle.*

Bridgette remained where she was, arms crossed, staring at the mounted head as if to make sure the buffalo didn't magically migrate into her kitchen. The cleaver bobbed slightly; the blade glinted.

Abe caught up with her and Sol. "First off, Angel's not goin' t' be workin' here anymore."

Inez nodded. "That's good. She's too close to her time. It isn't proper that she be here in her condition. It's not good for her or for business. Especially with Chet in town. He may've apologized, but I don't trust him to remember that she doesn't work anymore as a—" Inez saw Abe's expression and amended her statement. "That she's a married woman now."

"It wasn't easy convincin' her. She wanted to work until the baby comes."

A vision of Angel giving birth on the kitchen table flashed through her mind. Inez winced. "I'm glad you changed her mind. Home is the proper place for a woman in confinement."

He crossed his arms. "Don't know how much changin' she did. But anyways, speakin' of bits and shinplasters and such, Taps and I worked somethin' out that's a sure thing for bringin' in more revenue."

"Ah?" Inez experienced a tiny twinge of displeasure at having been excluded from a business decision. "What might that be?"

"New act at the Opera House, they're wantin' to drum up business around town. Taps talked with them, then me. I told him we'd be interested." Abe opened the passdoor and held it for Inez and Sol.

"Actors?" Inez felt her displeasure twist sharper and deeper. "You know my thoughts on those in the acting profession."

She entered the kitchen, and heat slapped her face like an open hand. A stew was in the making on the huge cast-iron stove. Liquid roiled in an enormous pot while a large but empty fry pan radiated heat on the rangetop. Sweat formed instantly, pricking her forehead and her neck.

A haunch of pork rested on the trestle table, half carved. Raw chunks and glistening fat were neatly piled to the side. A small cloud of flies rose from the meat, buzzing, then settled again.

Inez took three steps to the table and waved her hand. The flies dispersed briefly. "My God, it's hot in here!" She moved to the back door and threw it open.

Sol and Abe reappeared from the storage room. Sol, carrying a hammer and a box of nails, said, "We're taking on the new act from Tabor's Opera House? I've seen them. They're good. Had the miners from the Adelaide crying in their beers over *Hamlet*." He looked from Abe to Inez, then added hastily, "I'll go see to the buffalo."

As soon as the kitchen door swung shut behind him, Abe leaned against the frame, effectively blocking Inez from retreating to the barroom. "They were going to talk to Pap Wyman about appearin' here. Taps said they should talk to us first."

She raised her eyebrows at the mention of their main competitor, then shook her head. "I'll not have any of the acting trade performing their tricks here."

"This is a bar, not a drawin' room. Tricks are what we need to bring in business. They're comin' round tomorrow. 'Bout four o'clock. We'll talk and strike a deal."

Inez gazed out into the alley and fanned herself with a hand, wishing for a breeze. The sun shone overhead, banishing shadows from the momentarily deserted passageway. The alley's dirt-packed path, a quagmire of mud when it rained or snowed, was hardened into ridges and ruts that could turn an ankle or, in the dark of night, send the inebriated or unwary plunging forward facedown. Broken wooden boxes, some filled with debris, lined the back of the Silver Queen. Garbage piled along the backsides of the other buildings on the block and floated out into the alley. Inez thought she spotted a swollen dog carcass, legs extended stiffly, behind the dance hall two doors down.

Dance halls. Actresses.

Her hand balled into a fist against the doorframe. She said bitterly, almost to herself, "Nothing but trouble." Unwanted, a vision arose of Mark, flush with winning at the Lone Star's faro table. A blonde woman swinging herself onto his lap, stockinged legs flashing under a knee-length skirt, arm curled around his neck. The orchestra on the stage playing a fast version of "Little Brown Jug."

"Inez." Abe's voice cut into her thoughts. "We've got expenses to cover. Bridgette. Sol. Now Taps. I don't want to start buyin' liquor on credit. And if you want to finish that fancy gamin' room of yours upstairs, we gotta think about what's gonna draw in the moneyed crowd this summer."

She looked from the alley to Abe. His arms were crossed, his face tight.

"I'm just sayin' let's try them out, see how it goes. I listen to your ideas, like that buffalo, right? We're partners, half 'n' half."

"Thirds." She walked away from the door and faced him across the table. "It's a partnership of thirds. Mark, me, and you. As Mark's wife—" She stopped at Abe's expression.

He spoke slowly. Deliberately. As if he wanted to be sure she heard every word he said. "I'm gonna let you reconsider playin' that hand. If Mark were here, he'd see the sense of it. If you were thinkin' straight—"

The passdoor flew open, and Bridgette burst into the kitchen.

Abe threw up an arm to keep from getting smacked in the face by the solid wood panel. Staccato hammering echoed from the barroom beyond.

Bridgette looked startled to find the kitchen occupied. Her gaze flitted over Abe and Inez, then zeroed in on the back door. "My lands! Who opened the door? It lets in all the flies!" She bustled to the back door and slammed it shut.

The temperature in the room ratcheted up a degree.

"Sol found a good Samaritan to give him a hand, seeing as there was no other help to be found." She approached the pork and snapped a wave through the air. The flies scattered. "Now, Mrs. Stannert and Mr. Jackson, if we had one of those new doors, with those screens I keep hearing about, why we could get a nice bit of air in here and keep out the vermin." She volleyed a look at the pair of them. "What are you two talking about that has you glowering like a pair of thunderclouds?"

Abe smoothed his mustache. Inez saw his shoulders ease down a bit, the tension flow out of his stance. "The act at the Opera House. We're considerin' havin' them here to drum up business."

"Michael, my eldest boy, says they're very good." Bridgette addressed herself and the cleaver to the pork. "He went to the opera just last Friday after he got off from his job at the smelter, that's a good-paying job, it is. He couldn't stop talking about them, the Mr. and Mrs. Fairplay. If they came here, we'd get quite a crowd." She stopped chopping and looked up brightly. "Maybe Michael could help, if it doesn't interfere with his job. He'd jump at the chance. I believe he has a bit of a case on the missus, the way he keeps talking about her."

Inez threw up her hands. "Very well. We'll talk with them tomorrow." She brushed past Abe and said, "Sorry, Abe. It hasn't been a good morning so far."

He followed her out into the barroom. "You talk with Ayres?"

"I did. He says they cleared the tracks and found no bodies. Ayres thinks Susan was imbibing and not thinking right after that knock in the head. If that particular fabrication makes its way around town...." She shook her head, thinking of the shambles it would make of Susan's reputation, and by extension, her business.

"Hell of a thing." Abe stared at the State Street entrance. Sol's helper had crowded up onto the ladder and now struggled to hold the mounted trophy on the level while Sol pounded nails into the wood frame.

Abe looked back at Inez, bleak. "Here's the deal. Long as that damn thing of Chet's is hanging up there, you're gonna give those actors a fair shake. If we can strike a reasonable deal, we'll do it. And if the lady actors get happy while quotin' Shakespeare and decide to show an ankle or throw a wink or two to the customers, you're gonna just smile and pour the beer."

Inez blinked, taken aback by his intensity. "Abe—"

"I'm not gonna see our business go bust, just because you can't put the past where it belongs." He moved off to steady the ladder for the two men.

Struggling to contain her ire, Inez went behind the bar for her apron. As she tied the strings behind her, she glared at the mounted head. It was, she thought, starting to look more and more like Chet himself. Unkempt, moth-eaten around the ears, glazed eyes, yet, despite its patent silliness, dangerous. *Damn your hide, Chet. You'd better make yourself worth the trouble by bringing all your paying buddies next time you show up and drinking like there's no tomorrow.*

Chapter Seventeen

"So, what are we looking for?" asked Sands. He stood next to Inez at the top of the ridge, gazing out at the view. The Collegiate Peaks marched south, while the Sawatch Range faced them across the river and the valley beyond.

Inez kicked at the dirt, part experiment, part frustration. All she got for her efforts was a puff of dust and another scuff on her worn riding boots. "I'm not certain. I thought perhaps the marshal and the railroad men didn't look up here. Susan insists shots came from above her. This is as above as it gets."

"Unless you want to climb this." Reverend Sands leaned against a jagged finger of rock, nearly twenty feet tall, standing sentinel at the ridgeline.

Inez shook her head, then put a gloved hand on the outcropping, curling her fingers around one of its many stone protuberances and ledges. "No need to hazard life and limb. Whoever was up here would've had a good view of everything going on below, right from this point."

Inez peered down to the ledge, nearly sixty feet below. She could clearly see the rubble that had pounded the hovel and Susan's camera to smithereens the previous week. Looking over toward the train trestle and the gulch, she noted that the shoulder of the gulch, where Susan had tied her horse and burro, was hidden from view.

"He could have watched the tracks, seen the whole episode unfold," she said aloud. "He might not have known Susan was around. You can't see the spot where she left her animals from here. And you certainly wouldn't see it from the back trail to the ridgeline. So Susan would not have been visible until she ran from the shed." Inez thought a moment, then added, "No, probably not even then. With rocks and dust flying everywhere, I'm sure he didn't linger."

Sands leaned forward, examining the debris. "A convenient landslide."

"I thought the same thing. Perhaps we should look around the tracks. I don't believe those dead men got up and walked away. Particularly from under a ton of rock." She paused. "The gunman might have stood right here."

She looked at the ground, willing it to give up some secret, a clue. The dust, stones, and pebbles remained mute. She scuffed the earth again, none too gently. For the first time, a small worm of doubt wiggled its way into her thoughts. *Susan did have quite a dreadful blow to her head. Could she have possibly imagined it? The crack of rockfall transformed into gunfire? A discussion between two men, changed into a deadly argument?*

The reverend's arms snaked around her waist pulling her back against him. Her wide-brimmed hat tipped forward over her face.

"What are you thinking?" His voice sounded close to her ear.

She tugged her hat off and crossed her arms over his. "I'm just trying to see what Susan heard. If that makes sense. It's tempting to think that perhaps the marshal might be partly right. That she remembers some garbled version of what happened. But that doesn't play."

She shook her head, frustrated. "There *were* two horses. One ridden by a railroad man. The other, if Hollis is to be believed, was ridden by his business partner, Elijah Carter. So, if Carter and the railroad man weren't killed, where are they? Why leave the horses? And why isn't anyone looking for them?"

"But when the rockslide was cleared, they found no remains."

"And only Susan, you, and I believe that two men died," added Inez. Suddenly, she stiffened. Remembering. "There's one other. Hollis. He asked why I was so interested in Elijah's 'final hours.' Now, why would he have said that unless he believed Elijah dead? And if that's the case, how did he know?"

She broke away and turned to Sands. A frown of concern, mirroring her own, marked his countenance.

"Oh pshaw." Inez felt irritated, unbalanced. "This just doesn't make sense!"

The wind picked up, loosening the pins in her hair, whipping stray strands into her face. She pulled the hairpins all out and laid them on a stone ledge, nearly at eye level. "I know. I sound ridiculous. What am I thinking…that Hollis had some hand in killing his business partner? They fought in the war together. At least, that's what Hollis claims." She scrunched her hair into an untidy knot and attacked it vigorously with the pins. "I must have said something to him earlier. When I brought back the horse. He is so unpleasant that I just try to wipe my conversations with him from my mind."

Her fingers sought the last pin. It evaded her grasp and fell behind the ledge. "Pah!" Inez stripped off her glove and groped in the crack at the back of the ledge. It was just barely wide enough for her slender fingers. She felt the blunt points of the pin.

And then.

Something more.

"What's this?" She squinched her fingers around it and, unable to hold it properly in the confined space, managed to roll it up the inside wall of the crack and out with her fingertips. Sun glinted on a slender metal tube held between thumb and forefinger. Cylindrical, no longer than a hairpin.

Sands sucked in his breath and took it from her. Carefully.

The identity of the object came to her, just as he spoke the words: "A blasting cap."

Chapter Eighteen

"Many folks carry blasting caps for explosives with them," said Sands, throwing the statement over his shoulder as they rode down Disappointment Gulch to the track. "Miners—"

His gray horse slipped slightly on the steep trail. The summer wind blew the plume of dust into Inez's face just as she opened her mouth to respond.

"Prospectors," he continued.

Fine-grained grit coated her teeth and tongue. Inez pulled a soft, worn handkerchief from the pocket of her long riding skirt and spat into it, letting her horse pick the best way down behind Sands.

"How many people do you think traveled this road in the past six months, coming up from Granite, Canon City, Colorado Springs, Pueblo? There's been prospecting around here and in the gulch. Then there're the railroad surveyors and grading crews. The graders might've used giant or black powder through here to make enough room for the siding and railroad bed. There were crews from the Atchison road here last year, then the Rio Grande—"

"Yes, yes." She tucked the handkerchief into her pocket. "But you said yourself, what a convenient time for a rockfall."

The reverend's horse reached the level at last. "A casual remark. Didn't think you'd take it as gospel, Inez."

They skirted the kiln field and finally arrived at the tracks and siding.

Inez squinted up at the rock wall, spotting Susan's ledge and the scarred section where rocks had peeled off.

"Stop here." She brought Lucy to a halt.

Sands dismounted and approached. "Remind me. What are we looking for?"

"Anything that will verify Susan's story." She took his proffered hand, extracted her left foot from the sidesaddle stirrup, her right leg from around the horn, and slid to the ground. She led Lucy over to the gray while Sands surveyed the landscape.

"The marshal and the railroad crew have been over this ground," he said. "What do you hope to find that they might have missed?"

"I don't know. But I found that blasting cap. My luck seems good, so I'm not about to stop betting on it now. What time is it?"

Sands squinted up at the sun. "I'd guess about ten." He pulled out his gold pocketwatch and flipped open the casing. "Close. Quarter after."

"Good. We have an hour, easy. I need to be back by three, and I know you wanted to stop and see how the county poorhouse was coming along on our way back." She caught the reverend's resigned expression. "What?"

"Thought the plan included a picnic by the river." He glanced toward the streambed beyond the tracks. The sun sparkled off the fast moving water, which did not look muddy for a change.

"All right. Let's take half an hour to look around. You check south, and I'll go north."

It was a futile half hour. Inez walked a good fifty yards of track toward Leadville, exploring the ground on either side, while Sands paced off an equal distance in the opposite direction. Inez spied a jumbled pile of damaged wood ties, off to one side. She walked about the pile and finally clambered up on its lower reaches, hoping to find... *What? Bloodstains on the wood?*

The nearby Arkansas River tumbled ceaselessly over rocks, chuckling at her frustration.

"Inez, those could shift in a minute. Best come down." Sands stood below, horses' reins gathered in one hand.

Swallowing her disappointment, Inez climbed down. "Did you find anything?"

Sands held up a perforated tin can. "A few more like it and the remains of a cooking fire."

"Well, that's more than I found."

Sands threw the can onto the woodpile. "I remember seeing a good place for a picnic close to here."

They took the access path that meandered along a gravel bench by the river. The rock cliffs pulled away from the river as they neared the mouth of the gulch. They passed the trestle bridge that carried the rails across the river and Braun's abandoned beehive-shaped charcoal ovens, the tall timber that had fed them once now gone, replaced by a forest of stumps. A little further on, a small copse of slender trees appeared with a glint of green sward.

Sands had spied it as well. "Over there." He pointed.

Inez unpacked the rolled blanket and carried it to the grass sheltered in the ring of trees and bushes. She shook out the blanket and smoothed it on the ground, then straightened up and looked around. The access path and rock ridge were hidden behind the trees. The ring was broken facing the river, giving her an unobstructed view of the water and the steep bank beyond.

On the other side of the bank ran the main road up and down the Arkansas Valley. The same road that delivered the multitudes hoping for new lives and a lucky break in Leadville, as well as the many who gave up and left, searching for a future a little less hard, a little less cold.

Sands brought the bundled luncheon to the blanket, took Inez's hand, and pulled her down beside him. She sat against a tree and rearranged her riding skirt. Sands removed his hat and lay back, resting his head on Inez's lap. "This is more like it."

Inez rested her hand on the bundle. "Hungry?"

He smiled up at her. The sunlight made his eyes blaze a startling light blue, nearly electric in intensity. "Not for food." He took her hand in his, and held it to his chest. "For your company. And a few quiet moments. 'My soul thirsts for the Lord.' Psalm 23."

She wove her fingers with his, and tipped her head back against the tree trunk. The leaves hissed in the breeze, creating a random pattern of shifting shapes against the sky. She closed her eyes, listening to the river, feeling the weight of the reverend's head, the comfort of their fingers twined together.

Maybe it was the way his eyes had suddenly looked so blue—like Mark's eyes. Maybe it was the sound of the river—a melody and discourse no musical instrument by man could recreate. Whatever it was, the feeling of the moment stirred something in her memory.

A recollection, long discarded, long forgotten, surfaced.

Another river, another stand of trees. Inez's back resting firm against a boulder. Mark, his head in her lap. Their hands entwined, resting on Mark's chest, where she could feel his breath rise and fall. Warmth of sun on her face. Katydids whirring. Abe sat close by, the soft sound of riffling cards almost hidden by the river's speech, as he practiced a particularly complicated false shuffle. Mark looking up at her, his electric blue eyes teasing and warm, then glancing over at Abe. "This is the life. No responsibilities. No worries."

Abe grinned back, teeth flashing as his hands smoothly, automatically, maneuvered the deck. "No worries? Thought those cowboys in that last town were gonna hog-tie and brand you for takin' their wages."

"All's fair in love—" Mark winked at Inez— "war, and poker. Besides, that's why I like havin' a pretty woman sittin' at the table and shuffling the cards. Figured the boys wouldn't get too rambunctious with a lady nearby." He squeezed her hand, and his voice dropped, wrapping about her like a private embrace. "My own queen of diamonds. You did right well at that cowtown back there. Always said you had the magic touch with those hands."

He raised her hand to his lips. His kiss warmed her skin and sent a tingling down to her toes.

Mark murmured, "When we get to San Francisco down the road, I'll see you have a different diamond ring for every day of the week. But to get to San Francisco, we work together." His voice rose in volume to include Abe, and he looked from Inez to Abe, tying the three of them together with his voice and his gaze. "Equal partners, three ways. Taking on new towns, new adventures, whatever waits round the bend."

New adventures.

The memory vanished, the voices from long ago merging into the murmur of the stream.

Inez sighed, opened her eyes, and stared out at the riverbank, unseeing.

Was that why he disappeared last year? He'd had enough of being tied down. Exhausted wife. Sick baby. The business of running the saloon. Saw a chance to move on to greener pastures. No responsibilities. No worries.

She shook her head and tried to banish the twisting ache in her heart, the ache she'd thought she buried so deep that even giant powder couldn't blast it out into the open ever again.

The reverend squeezed her hand. She looked down at him.

His eyes no longer shone brilliant blue, but had faded back to gray. "Penny for your thoughts, Inez."

"They're not worth even half of that." She withdrew her hand and reached for the picnic bundle. "We should dive into the food or we'll be eating from the saddle. It's simple fare. Bread. Cheese. Pickles. Some hardboiled eggs."

"'Man eats the food of angels.' Psalm 78. Simple is good."

He offered her his flask. She paused in her efforts to saw the loaf of bread with his pocketknife, accepted it, took a sip, and grimaced. "Water."

"What? It didn't turn into wine? Must have lost my knack."

She rescued her own flask, lying on the blanket where she'd tossed it earlier. "I know you don't indulge. But since I have no qualms…." The brandy went down smooth, warming her nearly as much as his smile and the sun.

He took his knife back from her and began slicing the cheese. Inez noticed that he was doing a much neater job of it than her ragged slices of bread. He paused, pointing the knife at her flask. "Do you carry liquor in that as a rule?"

"Never know when the weather will turn. Or when it might be needed for medicinal purposes. It came in handy for Susan."

Susan's battered face flashed through her mind, followed by the blasting cap, safely wrapped in a linen napkin and tucked in her saddlebag.

Inez finished a bite of bread and cheese. "I still think that blasting cap indicates the rockfall might have been set off deliberately. Surely those who know about such things could look up at the face and tell whether it was an act of nature or man."

Sands reached for the pickles wrapped in waxed paper. "Have you been to see Casey yet?"

"Who?" Inez was lost for a moment. "Oh! The lawyer. I've had no time."

"No time?"

"I would have gone this morning, but we're here instead."

A rustling overhead exploded into a flurry of chirping and screeching. A large bird arrowed into the sky, chased by two others not even a quarter its size.

"You make time to chase after Susan's ghosts but not to take care of business." His voice was neutral. Flat.

"I will make time. I promise you." Her voice grew hard in return. She picked up a slice of cheese, rolled it between her fingers. It formed a small cylinder, nearly the size of the blasting cap. "What do you mean 'Susan's ghosts'? Her injuries are real. The blasting cap is real. I thought you believed her."

"I'm not saying I disbelieve her. But nothing so far supports her story."

"There are two men missing," Inez persisted. "Elijah Carter and a railroader. And, just before Carter disappeared, he told one of the local constables he was looking for Ayres, but he wouldn't say why."

"I don't know Carter's business with the deputy federal marshal. But if it was confidential, I can see why he'd not confide it to the local law force. Hard to say what's happened with Carter. He might just be out of town for a while, despite Hollis' words. Then again, he might've had enough of Leadville and gone to Denver or points south, west, north, or east. He could've been on his way to see Ayres and met up with road agents and come to harm. At this point, we can only toss guesses into the air. As for the railroad man, Preston and I talked about that. He said since the Rio Grande started laying tracks up the valley, the construction crews lose two or three men a day. Guess they figure prospecting or mining is more profitable than spiking ties or gandy dancing." Sands glanced at the sun. "We'd best get moving if you must be back by three."

Inez rolled the picnic remains into the blanket and Sands loaded the bundle into her saddlebag. He walked Inez's horse over, remarking, "I'm not saying I have all the answers. But I've noticed that you're spending a lot of time on this matter."

"Susan is my friend," Inez rested her right hand on the side-saddle seat and placed her right foot in his laced hands. "It's not as if I've friends in plentiful supply. I stand by the ones I have."

She straightened her right leg; Sands pushed her foot upward. Once Inez was settled in the saddle, Sands mounted his own gray and they rode through the brush to the road by the railroad tracks. Ahead was the bridge that would take them over the river to the main road.

The near white sheen of the bridge's fresh-cut lumber made her think of Mr. Braun, his remark about the church pews, his abandoned charcoal enterprise—now behind them—and his lumber company, still ahead on the way to town. "So has Herr Braun convinced the church board to replace all the pews with wood from his mill?"

"It's not what I entered the ministry for," Sands grumbled, "to referee discussions over—"

A flash of red, trapped against the timbered piling of the bridge, caught Inez's attention. The rest of his comment was lost to her.

She pulled up and hastily slid off Lucy, holding tight to the horn to keep from falling face first to the ground. "One moment," she called out, then half skidded down the embankment to the bridge's trestle at the water's edge. The crumpled rag was caught between wood and gravel bedding. Inez gingerly retrieved it. A strip of cloth, in red, blue, and what she thought might have been white at one time. Neatly bound on one end, unraveled threads on the other.

She turned to Sands, clutching it in her hand, her heart thumping wildly. "It must be! Susan mentioned a piece of colored cloth."

Sands looked at her oddly.

"She said it seemed to be important." Inez examined it. "This is long enough to wrap around a neck, tuck into a shirt. And a star here, near one end."

"Would you like me to go back for the tin can?"

Inez looked up, surprised. "What on earth for?"

"Susan didn't say anything about sharpshooters taking pot shots at cans?"

"That is quite uncalled for. It's entirely possible that this cloth was blown up the track by the wind."

"Throw it away, Inez. You're turning trash into clues. If we were to scour the road into Leadville, I daresay we'd find more rags ground into the dust, a lost hat or two, a glove, thrown horseshoes." He urged the gray onto the bridge. "But if we do that, you'll not get to town by three."

Inez wavered. The end of the rag unfurled from her slackening grip and trailed into the water. The river tugged, eager to claim a new plaything. She snatched it back, dripping, wrung it out, and balled it into her hand.

"Do you want help getting back on the saddle?" His voice drifted down from the bridge.

"I can manage. Go ahead and cross the bridge. I'll be there."

After clambering up the bank to Lucy, Inez stuffed the cloth into her saddlebag. Lucy swiveled an ear in her direction. Inez stepped up onto a nearby rock and mounted with practiced ease. Clicking her tongue, she urged her horse over the bridge and cantered to catch up to Sands.

Chapter Nineteen

Inez and Sands separated at the turnoff to the county poorhouse. The afternoon was racing by, and Inez was determined to arrive back at the time she'd specified to Abe.

She took back streets to avoid the congestion on Chestnut and Harrison. She wondered whether Hollis might be around the livery—and wasn't sure whether she hoped he was or wasn't.

Lucy stepped lively to avoid an empty ore wagon and its team, preparing to head up to the mining district. Inez dismounted and led Lucy through the yawning stable entrance into a world of dust, shadows, and the soft movements and whickerings of horses. The place seemed quiet, deserted—strange for that time of day, she thought. She was walking Lucy to her stall in the back when the sound of a gate squeaking shut drew her attention. One-Eyed Jack, a skinny, dour-faced fellow with a patch over his left eye, limped into view.

"Hello, Jack." She smiled warmly at him.

Jack touched his dented bowler perfunctorily. In addition to his ocular deficiency, two fingers from Jack's left hand, along with his left foot, had long since met his Maker where they waited for the rest of him to arrive.

Inez took in his shabby black greatcoat, bits of straw stuck to it, and his general demeanor. "Why the long face? Has your luck gone bad?"

The one eye rolled expressively in its socket. From somewhere beneath his coal-black beard, a voice croaked out, "Crooked dice."

"Well, I told you that chuck-a-luck isn't a winning game. You want to have a chance of hanging onto your wages, you should stick to faro or poker."

He grunted, reached for the reins, and ran an expert hand over Lucy's withers. "Rode hard. Oats?"

"Extra would be excellent." Inez gave Lucy a fond pat. "We had a good romp south along the Arkansas. She's a trooper."

Lucy twitched an ear and turned an eye to Inez.

"Jack, have you seen Eli around lately?" She picked a stray burr from Lucy's mane, trying to make the inquiry casual.

"Gone. Sold out."

"Sold out? To Hollis?"

"Yup."

"Hollis around?" She tried to keep her dislike for Hollis out of her voice.

"Out. Back soon." He eyed Lucy's coat. "Needs brushing."

"If you would, I'd appreciate it." Inez lifted the saddlebags off Lucy and settled them over her shoulder. "Jack, if I ever find a man who treats me half as well as you treat these horses, I'll grab him up in a flash."

"Horses easier to understand than women," countered Jack.

They traded smiles. Inez dug into the small coin bag in her pocket and handed Jack two bits for his efforts. *It'll no doubt end up in some shark's pocket.*

Jack was the only reason she stabled Lucy at the C&H livery, a fair trek from her home and business. One-Eyed Jack had impressed Inez with his understanding of horses during his occasional visit to the Silver Queen that winter. Upon inquiring and finding out where he worked, Inez had moved Lucy to Carter's Livery at Twelfth and Poplar. All in all, she'd been happy with the care and Eli Carter's polite, businesslike demeanor.

Soon after Inez had resettled her horse, Hollis had become Eli's business partner. Inez had, for the most part, managed to avoid Hollis. But now she had questions, what with Eli nowhere to be found.

She retraced her steps toward the front of the livery, musing. *So, Eli sold his share of the business to Hollis and is now "gone." At least, that's the story.*

Inez turned to the section of the livery that had been partitioned into an office, called out "hello," then walked in. A scarred and battered wood desk faced the entrance, a swivel chair positioned to see the comings and goings of horses, mules, wagons, and men. A few straightback chairs awaited the odd patron or friend. Pieces of tack were tossed in the corners and hanging on the walls. A door to the right, slightly ajar, led back into the stable area.

Or does it?

She'd not thought much about the door before. Her forays into the office area these days were few and to the point. She'd preferred doing business with the soft-spoken Eli and had kept her greetings short to avoid bumping into Hollis. Lately, the office had always seemed occupied by Hollis and his cronies.

She walked farther into the office. The door hung open an inch.

Temptation crooked a finger.

Inez stepped over to the door and tapped on its splintered panels. *If Hollis comes out, I'll just say I want to pay my account.*

Nothing stirred.

Inez glanced around the office, then touched the door, causing it to swing inward with a creak of protest.

A slice of neat, military-style living quarters came into view.

Light filtered through a thin brown curtain into a single room containing two beds catty-corner and a small warming stove next to a hopper of coal. One bed looked recently slept on, the blanket askew, the stained pillow dented. A pair of expensive snakeskin boots stood at the foot. The other bed was stripped down to the striped ticking. A dead lantern sat on a washstand between the two beds. Inez's gaze traveled up to the walls.

A battered tin mirror hung above the washstand, reflecting a broken image of the door and her own half-concealed reflection.

It also reflected something hanging on the wall next to the door. Although the image was poor, she was certain it wasn't a painting. She squinted, tempted to walk into the room, look behind the door, and see what it was. *A quilt, perhaps? Or—*

"What the Sam Hill are *you* doin' here?"

Inez clutched the saddlebags to her and whirled to catch Hollis' furious eyes boring in on her. He stood at the entrance to the office, hand resting on the butt of the six-shooter holstered across his stomach. He looked as if he'd just as soon shoot first, get answers later.

She held up a hand as if to forestall any gunplay. "I've been riding. I know it's nearly the end of June."

The scraggly mustache twitched with his sneer. "I damn well know what month it is."

"I wanted to pay Lucy's stable bill for July." Inez sauntered away from the door and pulled her coin bag out of her pocket. "I thought you might be in the back."

Hollis snorted. "A holler would've told ya no one was here. Or old Jack would've said, if ya'd bothered to ask."

He walked in heavily for such a rail of a man and flung himself into the swivel chair, which squeaked morosely as he rocked in it. "Waaaall, that means I kin tell you to your face. Boardin' cost is goin' up."

"Again? You upped the charge two months ago."

"Expenses." He bit off the word. "It ain't cheap keepin' this place goin'. And with the railroad comin', things are changin' fast. It don't take a genius to see the haulin' and freightin' part of the business is gonna die. The distance to the railhead is shrinkin' every day. Less haulin' distance means less money. And once the damn Rio Grande builds spurs to the mines, that'll be the end of it. Unless I can make a go with just livery and short hauls."

"I understand the business is all yours now." She kept her voice neutral.

Hollis' face pulled in, like he'd been forced to suck on a lemon. "And who've *you* been talkin' to?"

"It seems that your erstwhile partner, the one who left town without so much as a farewell drink and mislaid his horse halfway to Granite, sold the business to you." Her voice seemed to arrive from a great distance, formal and cool. It struck her how much like her mother she sounded.

"Me 'n the bank," Hollis growled. "Place ain't mine by half. So don't lay 'spersions at my door. And weren't you the one babblin' 'bout dead men on the tracks?" He spat, hitting a pail that apparently served as a spittoon with remarkable accuracy. Inez was reminded of how often he spat, and missed, in her saloon.

"So, did he say goodbye for good that morning or did he just take off for a pleasure ride and not return?"

Hollis heaved to his feet. "Don't see that it's any concern of yours. What say you settle up the bill and clear out. I figger we got no more business to conduct here, and Jack and me got a load of shit to shovel."

"It's a lucky thing you're close to the hospital," she snapped. "If the horses have any sense at all, they'll kick you in the head the next time you get close."

"Luck's got nothin' to do with it." He stared out the window in the direction of the hospital. Inez saw his hand ball into a fist on the desktop. "Them bastards are gonna pay for every inch they take from me. It's jest like the damn war. And after. This is what Eli and me fought against. Cain't believe they're back, taking our land. Our rights. Tellin' us what to do."

She blinked. "Who? Surely you don't mean the Sisters of Mercy!"

His gaze wrenched back to her. "Just hand over that gold eagle and go yer way. Don't know why Eli trucked with damn fool wimmin anyhow. You and them whores on State and Fifth—"

"Watch your language. I have nothing to do with those women."

"Wantin' this carriage and that, this horse and that horse." His voice went up in an exaggerated feminine whine. "'Deliver it, I'll ruin my skirts an' shoes walkin' over there an' it wouldn't be proper.' Hell, whores talkin' 'bout proper." He spat. Hard. The tobacco juice from the chaw bulging in one cheek arced and hit the pail without a splash. "They're ridin' all day simperin' around town, don't git the horses back on time. Course," his red-rimmed eyes narrowed in on her like the scope of a rifle, "when it comes to payin' up, they all drag their feet. Like they're not makin' more in a night's ride than I make in a month. Jest like you."

"I'll repeat, since it didn't seem to register the first time. I am not of the same ilk as Frisco Flo, Sallie Purple, and the rest of those…women." She slapped the gold coin on the desktop. Hard. "I want a receipt."

Without sitting down, Hollis yanked a battered receipt book from the desk drawer, dipped a pen in an inkwell and scratched out a furious receipt, tearing a hole in the thin paper in the process. "Take yer receipt and git!"

"If it wasn't for One-Eyed Jack, you'd best believe I'd 'git' permanently!" She mashed the paper into her pocket and escaped out the livery doors.

Once outside on the packed dirt, her heart still racing from the encounter, she stepped quickly down Poplar toward town, stopping only once at Tenth to gaze first toward the livery and then at the nearby hospital. Her scrutiny traveled beyond both to the future location of the railroad yards and depot. Her hand strayed to her throat, and the conversation drifted back to her, overheard from Susan's bedside. The sister's face, serious and taut with fear beneath her wimple: "Another anonymous note. They said they'll set the place afire this time, if we don't sell the land."

"Ah," said Inez softly. She turned east and took in the view of town. The tops of buildings gleamed in the sun. She imagined the thin ribbon of track snaking up, heading to town.

The hospital is sitting on prime real estate, close to the new depot, a tempting target for lot jumpers. And Hollis' property blocks the path the tracks will take to the Rio Grande depot and yards.

A smile curved her lips. *Now I know who the "bastards" are.*

Chapter Twenty

Inez hurried through the doors of the Silver Queen and swiped the back of her gloved hand across her forehead. Sweat and dirt left a dark streak across the worn leather glove. Shifting the saddlebags to her other shoulder, she pulled out her handkerchief. The day's use had given it an unhealthy gray tinge. She dabbed at her face and neck, scanning the room. Miners, off from their shifts at the large mines, ranged along the bar, nursing their beers. They were readily identified by physique—broad shoulders, strong arms—as well as by hands and faces, which, although scrubbed clean, still maintained a tinge not unlike her handkerchief.

A couple of desultory card games progressed without much energy at the tables close by. A handful of malingerers, the day's newspapers spread before them, along with bowls of stew and plates of pickled eggs and Bridgette's biscuits, occupied other tables scattered about.

Could be more, but at least it's not less.

Sol was tapping a beer keg and chatting with a couple of swells who, by the cut of their cloth, were new to town.

In the shadows close to the kitchen, a familiar figure rose from a table.

"Mrs. Stannert. We were wonderin' if you were gonna make it." Abe walked toward her. She quickly took in the figures still at the table—a man and a woman.

Holy mother, am I late?

She hated being late. It gave the advantage to those doing the waiting.

Abe stopped in front of her and handed her a cup of coffee. He was already in his evening working clothes—a starched white shirt, sleeve garters adjusted, waistcoat buttoned. His hair was slicked back as best as it would go, the brilliantine darkening some of the gray. She gulped the coffee. The strong dark taste, buffered by a generous dollop of brandy, seared all the way down, burning a clean path through her dusty throat to her stomach.

She sighed gratefully. "Thank you, Mr. Jackson. I needed that terribly. And I'm so sorry I'm late. I'm a sight, I know."

Abe smiled at her, an expression that warmed her nearly as much as the coffee. She realized, with some surprise, that it had been a long, long time since she'd seen Abe smile like that. Particularly at her. He spoke just loud enough for her to hear. "Mrs. Stannert, you're a sight for sore eyes. I was beginnin' to worry some. Your reverend came through 'bout quarter hour ago, thought you'd be here. I'm glad to see you all in one piece. Now come on over and meet the folks that'll help us mine the miners and get us back on our feet in this town."

He escorted her over to the table. The man had stood immediately when Abe had conferred with her, and held his silk top hat in one gloved hand. *If mother could see him, she would declare him a "fine figure of a man."* That term of approbation had always been saved for men in coats of finest wool, facial hair neatly trimmed, fingernails clean, and of a figure that bespoke wealth and girth. Inez could nearly hear her mother's further comment: *But not too much girth…that would be a sign of the sin of gluttony and, by extension, avarice.*

The scent of bay rum and lavender from the two strangers washed over her, strong enough to make her giddy. She was all too aware of how she must look—dusty, riding skirt creased and stained around the hem where she'd stood in the stream, overlarge panama hat now trailing down her back and her hair no doubt askew. Not to mention the smell that must be emanating from her. *A combination of horse sweat and my own, no doubt.*

Nevertheless, the gentleman smiled widely, exposing teeth of nearly preternatural whiteness, broken only by a large gap between his two front teeth and a diamond winking from an upper incisor. "Charles Ambrose Fairplay, at your service, madam. And such a pleasure we anticipate that service to be." His voice had an underlying drawl that reminded her suddenly of Mark.

Inez mustered her best hostess smile, as if she stood in her parents' reception hall in New York City rather than in a bar in a Rocky Mountain mining town. She held out her hand. "Please pardon me for being late. I can only plead the congestion on Leadville's streets. I should have allowed more time for returning from my afternoon constitutional."

He seized her hand and, as if her fingers were encased in the finest silk from China rather than stained leather, executed a deep bow and kissed her hand.

She resisted the impulse to pull away.

"Ah, a ride in the bracing breezes of the pristine wilderness of the frontiers. Salubrious. Invigorating. Exhilarating, no doubt. Not to mention healthful."

The words rolled out easy and embracing, reminding Inez more and more of her missing husband as he prepared to play a mark for his money.

"You may call me C.A.," the actor continued, "since I look forward to a pleasant, not to mention financially rewarding, relationship with both you and Abraham here." His voice boomed in the confines of the barroom and seemed to echo off the tin ceiling.

Abraham? Inez raised her eyebrows at Abe. *Since when did he revert to all those syllables?* Abe raised his eyebrows a fraction back and smoothed his mustache, perhaps, she thought, to hide a grin.

"My dear, you forget your manners." The cultured voice from across the table sounded amused and gently chiding.

C.A. Fairplay smacked his forehead in comical exaggeration. "My dearest, forgive me."

The seated woman rose, the fabric of her triple-flounced, box-pleated underskirt rustling. "Now *you* must, in turn, forgive C.A. He tends to get lost in the sound of his own voice when pontificating. Which has its good points and bad points when we're on stage together."

Inez smiled faintly back, wishing she were dressed more on a par and had her own fan to flutter in such an animated fashion as the woman before her.

"My wife," C.A. said, a hand going protectively about her waist. "Maude Fairplay. An actress known from San Francisco to New York, and particularly beloved in Cincinnati and Chicago."

Maude smiled. Deep down, Inez experienced a little tweak of satisfaction that Mrs. Fairplay's teeth were not perfect specimens like her husband's. However, the green of her eyes—reminding Inez of the startling green of absinthe—served to draw attention from the fact that her teeth were a tad yellow and incisors crooked.

"You may," she said in a rich contralto, "call me Maude."

Abe spoke up. "Now that Mrs. Stannert's arrived and we're done with the introductions, I suggest we retire to the office upstairs to talk business."

Suggest? Retire? Inez flashed him an amused glance. *Very well, four can play at this etiquette game.*

"Mr. Jackson, why don't you take our visitors to the office, and I'll have coffee sent up," said Inez, as if a fleet of servants were ready to jump at the pull of a cord.

C.A. held out an arm, which Maude, with a graceful twist of her fan, took. Abe gestured toward the stairs. Inez became aware that, sometime during the exchange of introductions, the barroom had gone stone silent, right down to the tink of glassware and knives on plates. As Maude and C.A. began moving toward the stairs, every head swiveled to watch their progress. The actors had nearly reached the stairs when one fellow stepped up to them, broad-brimmed hat clutched to his breast, and said fervently, "Pardon, ma'am. Mrs. Fairplay."

Maude turned.

He cleared his throat. "I seen you in Dodge City, coupla years back. When you sang, I thought you was sent from heaven."

Dodge City. A shock, like an icy mountain waterfall, poured down Inez's back. She stared hard, with new eyes, at Maude Fairplay.

Maude's eyelids fluttered in unison with her fan. "How kind. A few years ago, you say?" She turned to her husband. "We were there about three years ago, isn't that so? On our way to San Francisco?"

"So many places, so many faces. Without my journal at hand, I have a hard time keeping them all straight." C.A. turned to the man. "Well, you'll have an opportunity, my fine fellow, to see Mrs. Fairplay create magic with Shakespeare. Yes, pure magic with the bard at Tabor's Opera House, continuing through the end of July. And perhaps," he laid a finger by his nose and winked, "just perhaps a special performance here at this fine establishment as well." He looked up at Inez, beaming as if their business was a done deal—all perfect teeth, perfect hair, perfect suit.

Perfect scoundrel!

Inez kept the smile on her face until she reached the kitchen.

"It's her, I'm certain!" she hissed, startling Bridgette as she swung through the door and dumped her saddlebags on a kitchen chair.

"Lands, ma'am, her who?" Bridgette clapped a floury hand to her aproned breast and looked around apprehensively. One end of the large wooden kitchen table was covered with rolled-out dough, punctuated where the biscuit cutter had stamped out neat holes.

"You didn't see her? That, that…actress?"

"Here?" Bridgette sounded confused. "In my kitchen?"

"Out there." Inez waved a hand at the saloon proper. "Jesus. I don't believe it. Here in Leadville. In my saloon! She was blonde three years ago. Now, mousy brown. But I'd swear it was her."

Inez stormed into the storeroom and pulled out a key from its hiding spot. She headed for the very back of the room and unlocked the unobtrusive cabinet containing the good silver and crystal she saved for her Saturday night gatherings. "Well, we'll just see about this. I've always said it's a mistake to mess with those in the acting trade. Have you more of that coffee, Bridgette? And something tea-like. Scones or muffins or…."

"There's peach pie in the safe."

"Good enough. Would you please prepare a setting for four and bring it up to the office? And bring this." Inez unlocked the lower door of the cabinet and pulled out a bottle of Napoleon brandy from her private stock.

Inez left Bridgette brandishing a knife at the pie and hurried up to the office. *Please don't let Abe have promised them anything.*

Her hand was on the doorknob when she heard Mrs. Fairplay laugh. The distinctive musical sound—a trill up the scale, then slowly descending—was the last bit of evidence she needed. That laugh was something she'd carry to her grave. It played counterpoint to the memory of the blonde actress, sitting on Mark's lap, arm flung carelessly around his neck. Not much later, the blonde had paused on the stairs to the private second-story rooms and shot a look at Mark full of lust. He had straightened his tie, glanced once toward Inez—who was attempting to keep an eye on Mark while defending herself in a cutthroat game of poker—and headed for the stairs.

"Ma'am?"

Inez started and turned.

Bridgette, coffee, cups, brandy, and pie on the silver tray, was at her elbow looking at her with concern.

Inez realized that she had been standing there, staring at the door panel, her hand slick with sweat, gripping the knob as if she'd strangle it.

She exhaled hard and stripped off her gloves. "'All the world's a stage and we but players in it.' Well, Maude Fairplay most certainly did not play fair back in Dodge." She opened the door, and they went inside.

C.A. and Maude sat on the loveseat, while Abe occupied an overstuffed green velvet chair that had seen better days. All three were smiling, as if they'd just shared a joke. *Or sealed a deal.*

C.A. sprang up as Inez entered. "Ah! Mrs. Stannert! We were just discussing the traveling life. I understand from Abraham that you, too, have some tales from the road. And, I also understand that you are a passionate advocate of Shakespeare and his works. Lovely, just lovely." He beamed.

Inez looked at Abe, who lifted his eyebrows. He lowered and raised them again, their silent signal from the old days: *Don't play your hand yet.*

"So, you're doing Shakespeare at Tabor's?" She accepted a half-full cup of coffee and the bottle of brandy from Bridgette. "What, exactly, are you playing?"

C.A. nearly bounced on the sofa in his enthusiasm. "Our little troupe is here through July. We're finishing *Hamlet* and taking on *The Tempest* next. Perhaps later we'll move on to something more military such as *Henry the Fifth*, provided the rumor be true about the visit of…." He touched the side of his nose again, a gesture, she decided, intended to draw the listener into his confidence. "Perhaps I'm not supposed to say."

He looked at his wife as if for guidance. She described an elegant figure eight with her fan and shook her head slightly.

"You referrin' to General Grant?" asked Abe.

Inez saw the slightest of frowns cross Maude's face, then vanish.

"You see?" C.A. patted Maude's hand reassuringly. "There's naught to worry about, my love. They already know about the general's possible visit." C.A. turned back to them, apologetic. "A fault of mine, nearly unable to keep a secret."

"Ah, but your virtues are legion," said Maude.

Inez leaned back in the chair, wishing she had a whole lot more brandy for the conversation. "I understand you're interested in performing at the Silver Queen," she said more evenly than she felt.

Maude brightened, indeed, twinkled, as she leaned forward, the fan dangling from her wrist. "C.A. has done a brilliant job of rendering *The Tempest*. His Prospero is magnificent."

"And you, I assume, are Miranda?" Inez pictured Maude, her light brown hair loose and flowing, arms dramatically raised, as Prospero's daughter.

Maude picked up the delicate china cup, a border of silver flowers ranging around the rim, and held it primly between thumb and middle finger. "Oh, I play many parts. Sometimes Miranda, sometimes Ariel." She sipped, then clapped a hand to her mouth in a most unladylike fashion.

"Be careful," Inez said demurely. "It's hot."

C.A. blew across the top of his cup, poured a careful bit into the saucer, and squinted at it, looking, Inez thought, like a cat inspecting a dish of cream. Then he announced, "Coffee should be black as hell, strong as death, and," he smiled at his wife, "sweet as love."

Inez swirled the liquid in her own cup. "Shakespeare?"

"A Turkish proverb." C.A. tipped the saucer and sipped.

"Two out of three's not bad. And this," she tipped brandy into her own cup, "may not sweeten it much, but I can assure you, it will smooth the rough edges. And cool it down."

She offered the bottle to Maude, who declined.

"So you played in Dodge three years ago?" Inez inquired, amazed at the steadiness in her tone.

Maude waved a languorous hand. "In our early days. We were just setting out in our careers together. A brief appearance, as I recall."

Inez turned to Abe. "Isn't that a coincidence. I do believe Mr. Jackson and I were in Dodge the same time as you."

It wasn't until the words were out that she realized they implied that she and Abe were more than business partners. Neither C.A. nor Maude batted an eyelash, but Inez quickly added, "My husband was there too. He, alas, passed last year." *Passed out of my life and into another.*

She cut off the condolences she could see forming on their lips. "His name was Mark Stannert. A sporting man, loved the tables. Cards, faro sometimes. And quite a connoisseur of the stage." She watched Maude for signs of recognition. "Just think, our paths may have crossed. Perhaps at the, oh, the Lone Star, say. Wouldn't that be…ironic."

Maude looked back, clear-eyed, no longer laughing. Her mobile face was still and cold as stone. "Indeed. Who's to say? It was, as C.A. says, many towns back. And a long time ago."

Abe cleared his throat. Loudly.

Inez wrenched her gaze away from Maude to find Abe glaring at her. His unspoken message to her required no translation: *Don't push it, Inez.*

Abe turned to C.A. "Well now, what say we talk some dates. Sounds like we've got an understandin'."

"What understanding?" Inez interrupted.

"We can't afford to have you-all come in three times a week. Maybe later in the month, if business picks up."

"Business is fine, we really don't need specialty acts."

"Give us time to promote it. You do some from your end, we'll do some here, maybe put somethin' in the papers. Mrs. Stannert knows the editor of one of the locals. We can try to get somethin' in before the Fourth. If'n you could do somethin' on the holiday, and maybe before then."

C.A. nodded. "The Opera House is closed on the Fourth. We could arrange for an appearance, say, early evening."

"The Fourth," Inez said furiously, "will no doubt be quite busy. Customers come in early, get tight and raise a ruckus—"

A dark hand closed viselike on Inez's arm, choking her off as efficiently as if it'd closed around her neck. Abe stood, dragging her along with him. "Pardon us a moment, while I explain to my business partner here what we've already talked about." His hand tightened even more, warning her not to say anything. "You and the missus could enjoy some of that pie. Mrs. O'Malley knows how to bake them, none better in Leadville. And the brandy's first-rate. Mrs. Stannert always insists on the best."

Abe propelled Inez out of the office and down the short hall to the unfinished gaming room. Once there, she pulled away, rubbing her arm. "That," she said coldly, "will leave bruises."

"You aimed to sink the whole deal from the start."

"Abe. That Maude. She's the woman in Dodge. The one that Mark...." Inez closed her eyes for a moment, pushing the hurt—*How can it still be so sharp after three years?*—back into the dark where it belonged.

"Come on, Inez. You sayin' you recognize someone from that long ago?"

"Oh I do. I do indeed."

Abe shook his head. In disgust. Or maybe, Inez thought, disbelief.

Silence stretched over them, taut as a tightrope. Inez suddenly felt exhausted, alone. She turned her back on Abe and walked across the unvarnished wood floor toward one of the uncovered windows, her footsteps echoing loud in the empty space. Light, bright and ruthless, poured in. It threw dust motes into relief and highlighted the sawdust on the floor and the two sawhorses left from the last foray at finishing the remodel. Inez leaned on the sill, and stared out at the view of town and the mountains beyond. At the end of the block, the second- and third-story windows of Frisco Flo's parlor house stared back, blank-eyed with curtains drawn, over the tops of the intervening buildings.

Inez wished there was a magic spell that could turn the sawhorses into real steeds, so she could just ride away from everything. *Just for a while.*

"Inez, do you want to make this business go or not?" Abe sounded calm, as if he were asking her nothing more than if she preferred her whiskey neat or with a chaser. "This is our chance to strike it rich. These folks—the Fairplays—they're willin' to work with us. They've been courted by a couple of other places, an' they came here. I think Taps had somethin' to do with that. Anyhow, they're even willin' to work without a proper stage, though maybe we'll take some of the lumber up here and throw somethin' together for them. Come July Fourth, and then when the trains come in, we could make a killin' with them. They're askin' a reasonable cut. It'd be just the two of them. Not the whole troupe. They'd do a scene from this Shakespeare play they've been workin' on. He's a real entertainer. She sings, he says. Old Taps could play the tunes."

Inez felt more than saw Abe come up beside her. He rested his hand beside hers on the sill. "Look. I don't know what's got into you lately. You've been ill-tempered as a bobcat. Well, I've been too. Angel, y'know, I worry 'bout her. The strike didn't do us any good, and business hasn't come back real strong since.

But you know what Mark used to say, 'The only thing sure about luck is that it's bound to change.' Well, I can smell change in the air now. Like rain a-comin'. Our luck's gonna change for the better, I'd bet on it. And the Fairplays are the hand we're gonna play to hit pay dirt."

"You're mixing your metaphors," Inez said tiredly. She pushed at the small of her back to relieve a crick from her riding stays. "Do you think they'll play straight with us?"

"Sure. We'll put the deal to paper. And I'll take care of everything, Inez. All you gotta say is yes. That you trust I can do this right."

She closed her eyes, grateful for Abe's words. For his patience with her. For Abe himself. *What would I have done without him these past two years. He stood by William and me through the worst of times and afterward. I'd trust him with my life. I can trust him about this. He's right. We've got to get back on track and tend to business. And if the Fairplays are the bonanza for us he thinks they are....*

"In the words of the local prospectors, if you think it'll assay well, let's stake the claim. But I don't want to talk with them. I'll be polite, but it'll be your deal. Take care of whatever they need, whatever is reasonable. I want the Silver Queen to succeed." She ran a hand along the unfinished sill. "Any profits, our first priority should be fixing up this room so it's ready before the trains arrive, at least." She turned her back on the window. "Agreed?"

Abe's white teeth flashed in a smile. "Agreed. Knew you'd come to your senses, Inez."

"Well, let's go back and put it to paper. And I hope they've left some of Bridgette's pie for us."

Chapter Twenty-One

From the landing, Inez watched the Fairplays exit to Harrison Avenue. She was thinking how good it would feel to change out of her riding clothes when she noticed Sol beckoning from the main floor. *What now?* Inez descended to where Sol was stacking dirty glasses and bowls onto a tray.

"There's a fellow here who says you were expecting him." He nodded down the length of the bar.

To her astonishment, she saw the professor, nursing a tankard of tired beer. "How long has he been here?"

"Long enough for the beer to go flat."

Inez approached the professor, who brightened when he saw her. He doffed his battered derby, which now sported a natty feather in the band. "Mr. Delaney sent me into town to deliver some papers to chief engineer McMurtrie. Delaney's cousin, y'know. Thought I'd take the opportunity to find you. Delaney'll nae remember when I left nor when I return, as long as I'm back with McMurtrie's response by dark. He's a bit too fond of the drop of the pure." The professor looked at his beer sadly as if mourning its condition. "I remembered ye'd promised to intro-duce me to a newspaper man. I hope I'm not inconveniencing ye any, but if there's any chance we could talk with him now...."

Inez turned to Sol. "I'm taking the professor here to meet Jed Elliston. We'll be at *The Independent*, if you need me."

On impulse, she went behind the counter and retrieved an unopened bottle of Kentucky bourbon from the rows lining the backbar.

The professor brightened considerably at the sight.

"To smooth the introductions," she explained.

Inez hurried upstairs to her private changing room and grabbed a cashmere paisley shawl, one of her favorites and long enough to cover all but the lower third of her crumpled riding clothes. She tied on a matching olive-colored straw hat that covered most of her hair and adjusted the bow to sit jauntily below her left ear. Grabbing a pair of gloves, she paused to inspect herself in the mirror above the washbasin and was pleased to see the reflection of a respectable-looking woman peering back.

Then she looked down at her inglorious riding boots. "Rather mars the effect," she said to her reflection. "But if they've sprinkled the streets, it'll be muddy. If not, it'll be dusty. No reason to scuff a pair of perfectly decent shoes in the name of fashion."

A fleeting vision of Maude Fairplay's shoes skimmed through her mind, the toes and the narrow heels under the pleated hem embroidered with a profusion of flowers and leaves. With a tiny spark of malice, she imagined how wilted they would look after crossing Leadville's streets a few times.

Inez flew down the stairs.

Sol said, "He's waiting by the State Street door."

Pulling the shawl snug around herself and the cradled bottle of bourbon, Inez approached the door and paused to gaze at the buffalo above the lintel. The glass eyes stared straight ahead, as if hoping to catch a glimpse of the plains.

She turned to the professor. "Let's see if we can't persuade Mr. Jed Elliston that he could use a hand in reporting about the railroad."

◇◇◇

The office of *The Independent* sat halfway up the second block of East Third in a fairly robust log building, complete with a tent-like half wall above the door. It hadn't changed a bit since Jed had arrived and set up shop in 1878, nearly the same month that Inez,

Mark, and Abe had blown into town, drawn by tales of fortunes made in the mines and lost at the gaming tables.

"If the pickin's are so easy, we might as well be there to pick our allotment," Mark had said. It was after the disaster in Dodge, and Inez had wanted to put as much mileage between that city and them as possible, hoping to obliterate Mark's and her own indiscretions with the dust of time and distance. Leadville, where silver "flowed in the streets," sounded as good a place as any. Then, once Mark won the saloon in a poker game and Inez discovered that she was in a "family way," the decision to settle down and stay was easy. And Abe, as tired of the traveling life as the Stannerts, had agreed to stay and run the business with them.

Approaching the newspaper office, Inez recalled the first time she'd met Jed. It was before she'd become heavy with child and was still doing a turn at the Saturday night poker games that Mark had arranged for the highrollers of Leadville. Jed had strolled in, dressed in his sharp city suit, dark hair slicked back, looking down his long nose at the crowd around the table, heavy-lidded eyes lingering incredulously on Inez before moving on. He'd removed his silk top hat. "Jed Elliston. Owner, publisher, and editor of *The Independent*, the newest newspaper in Leadville. I understand that there's a serious game here?"

Inez looked at Mark. Mark smoothed his mustache and winked, their signal for "pigeon." Then, he turned the charm on, as only Mark could. "Welcome, pilgrim!" He pulled a chair forward to the table and glanced at the other players. "You gents mind one more?"

Yes, Jed was an easy mark at the tables, yet he had stood by her during hard times, in his own way. And he had finally come around to the notion of playing cards with her. Most of the time.

Well Jed, now's time for you to pay up for your recent lucky streak.

She turned to the professor. "I'll make the introductions and start the conversation flowing with...." She revealed the bottle beneath the shawl. "It's probably best if I stay a while, in case Jed gets difficult. When things are running smoothly, I'll leave you gentlemen to your business. I'll warn you, Jed can be insufferable sometimes. Just remember, he's odd man out regarding the Denver and Rio Grande."

"Aye. 'Tis a good thing I'm not a wagerin' man." The professor stared at his reflection in the window of a dry goods store. He removed his derby and dusted it quickly with a forearm, then tugged down on his waistcoat and straightened his wilting celluloid collar.

Inez opened the door of the newspaper office and went in. The professor followed like a shadow.

"Hello, Mr. Elliston," she sang out.

Jed, bent over a typecase, turned around, surprised, a handful of type in his hand, a smudge of ink on his sleeve. "Mrs. Stannert, what an honor." He dropped the type on the top of the cabinet, wiping his hands on an apron. "My typesetter's vamoosed, probably besotted again in some Stringtown gin mill." Jed sounded as if it were a personal affront that the fellow apparently preferred an afternoon's drink to an afternoon's wages.

"You know anyone who'd be interested in a job setting type?" He eyed the professor expectantly, then turned back to Inez. "Here to place an advertisement? Good rates on an eighth of a column. Just the right size for touting any Fourth of July specials."

"Actually, I do need to run something," said Inez, mindful that she needed to get a notice in about the Fairplays. "Maybe half a column's worth."

His eyes, usually half-lidded in that supercilious manner she found so irritating, widened. "Half column, you say? What's going on?"

"We've the Fairplays coming to—" *Not entertain. Not act. What sounds respectable?* "Put on a display of thespian skill. Shakespeare. *The Tempest.*"

Jed's nose fairly twitched in anticipation. "Any chance they'd stand for an interview beforehand?"

"Oh, most likely we could arrange that, but look, I've brought someone to meet you. Mr. Elliston, meet Mr., ah—" She realized she had forgotten the professor's name.

"Duncan, at your service," the professor interposed. Then, extending a hand, he added, "Most call me Professor. My background, y'see."

"I've also brought this." She pulled out the bottle as Jed pumped the professor's hand, and glanced around. "Is there someplace we can talk? And have you any clean glasses?"

Three minutes later, they were all seated around the large table in the middle of the room, papers and notes pushed higgledy-piggledy to one side, the bottle placed reverently in the center.

Inez splashed the bourbon into three chipped enamel mugs, feeling vaguely sacrilegious about not using crystal for such a fine grade of alcohol. She lifted her mug, and the men followed suit.

"'Drink is the feast of reason and the flow of soul.' Alexander Pope," said Inez.

"'Freedom and whisky gang t'gither!' Scotland's own Robbie Burns," added the professor.

They looked at Elliston. He looked from one to the other, then hoisted his mug even higher and pronounced, "'Once to every man and nation comes the moment to decide,/In the strife of Truth with Falsehood, for the good or evil side.'" He added, "James Russell Lowell. Poet. Editor. Abolitionist. Harvard man. Cambridge. Massachusetts, that is." His tone seemed to suggest that his drinking companions might want to refer to an atlas.

They drank.

Inez closed her eyes in delight as the liquor went down fiery as a lover's kiss. She sighed. Then opened her eyes, all business. "Gentlemen, I believe you both may profit from this meeting." She addressed Jed. "The professor is interested in writing for a local newspaper. Right now, he works for the Rio Grande," she added meaningfully.

"I'll be straight with you, Professor." Jed leaned forward. "I've not the highest opinion of the Rio Grande nor those who run it. My stand, and I'm not afraid to say or print it, is that Palmer's a bully and the Rio Grande has played much the 'dog in the manger' with the Atchison road."

The professor turned his mug in his hands and seemed to consider before responding. "Am I to believe that what is said here stays here? 'Twould mean my job, otherwise."

"Of course," said Jed.

Inez said, "We can drink to that," and poured more all around.

The professor drank, then said, "I'll not deny that I've no great love of Palmer and his band. The general's not the gold-plated gentleman he makes himself out to be. When a town doesn't agree to his demands, 'tis Palmer's philosophy to run over it and to hell with those left behind. That's nothing new, to him."

Inez viewed the professor over the rim of her mug. He'd set his hat on the table and was smoothing the feather. His face above his chin whiskers was strained.

"Not from around here?" Jed asked. "Not to pry. But if I hire you to write about the inner workings of the Rio Grande, it's not just your job that's on the line. Could be my neck as well."

"I was born and bred in the States."

Inez raised her eyebrows in surprise. "You were? Where?"

"Here and there. The South, mostly. Father died in the war. 'Twas not our war, and his death meant hard times for my mother and me. I dinnae like to dwell on it. After the war, Mother sent me to relatives in Edinburgh, where I received my education. I returned when she was ailing. She passed on. I came here. And that's probably more'n you wished to know."

Inez and Jed looked at each other. His face echoed her furtive guilt. *At the war's conclusion, I was fifteen, Jed was eight. And neither of us suffered from the war as he apparently did.*

Clearing her throat, Inez topped off the professor's mug. "Mr. Elliston runs a well-regarded newspaper here in town and is currently understaffed."

Jed nudged his half-empty mug across the table to Inez. "So, Professor, what do you do for the Rio Grande?"

"Well, some call me a secretary, some a clerk, some treat me as all-round errand boy. I take notes at the board meetings on behalf of my superior—that'd be Lowden Snow, the lawyer who handles right-of-way issues for the railway. And I deliver papers and orders too sensitive to commit to telegraph at the board's behest." He frowned. "They give me no consideration. I could be deaf as a post for all the heed they pay me as they're talkin' over their grand plans."

"The sorry state of the working man." Jed raised his mug again. "One more toast, if you'll join me. Who said: 'The great questions of the time are not decided by speeches and majority decisions, but by iron and blood.'" He looked at them expectantly.

"Lincoln?" Inez guessed.

The professor shrugged.

"Otto von Bismarck. Appropriate for the Rio Grande and Palmer, don't you think?"

Just as Inez prepared to push back her chair, Jed set down his mug. "Professor, I've a question for you. Mrs. Stannert, maybe you'd add your two cents, since you were there. I heard two supply cars were smashed to smithereens and the rails destroyed by Disappointment Gulch. A real setback for the railroad. What's your take on it? Landslide? Sabotage?"

The professor wet his lips, somewhat nervously, Inez thought. Then he leaned forward, looking earnest. "I'm no expert on such things, but from what I heard and saw, it has the stink of sabotage, sure enough."

"Any idea who?"

The professor shifted in his chair. "Could've been men from the Santa Fe road, still smarting over Palmer and McMurtrie's rough ways and the Rio Grande's victory at the Royal Gorge. Could even be the work of the Denver, South Park and Pacific Railway. The Rio Grande and South Park hammered out an agreement for the South Park to use the Rio Grande's track to Leadville for a fee. But there are always those who harbor bad feelings about such, even after the gentlemen of the boards sign and shake hands all around."

"And it hasn't stopped the Rio Grande and South Park from waging a war over the price of hauling freight," added Jed.

The professor nodded. "I've heard talk that the Rio Grande might construct a line over Marshall Pass to Gunnison. That wouldn't sit well with the South Park. And there's more to tell, should you be wantin' to hear it."

Inez couldn't help but smile. *Jed looks like he'd sell his mother to hear what else the professor has to say.*

"Gentlemen, I leave you to each other. The bourbon goes with me, but I'll keep the rest of the bottle stowed away. When *The Independent* publishes its first 'exclusive' on the machinations of the Rio Grande, we'll toast your mutually beneficial business agreement with another round."

The two men covertly eyed each other as if evaluating the worth of an untested but potentially promising claim.

She stood to leave and was surprised to find she was a bit unsteady. *Oh yes. All that brandy at the picnic. Now this.*

Both men jumped to their feet, and Jed hastened to hold the door open for Inez. She paused at the threshold and murmured, "I expect you can find a way to cut us a deal on a half-page advert in the next issue. Regarding the Fairplays on the Fourth and so on. I trust you and the professor will get on."

"Well, it's all a matter of whether this fellow can deliver," Jed said in a low voice. He squinched his shoulders up in what Inez decided was supposed to be a jaded shrug. "Standard rate per word, and if it's no good, that's that."

Inez waved a hand airily. "That's between you two."

She paused on the dirt street, cradled the bourbon under the shawl, and pulled the soft wool close to her ears and the back of her summer hat.

The fickle weather was changing again.

Gray clouds scuttled across the sun. A puff of wind kicked up a dust devil that swirled around her, snapping the hem of her skirt.

Inez hurried down Third Street, focusing on the worn path rutted in the dirt. *No place to sprain an ankle or end up sprawled in the dust.* Empty ore wagons clattered up East Third heading toward the mines while their full counterparts careened down toward the smelters at the edge of town.

Inez approached a dilapidated saloon and gave it a once over. She'd hardly noticed it on the way to see Jed, but now, walking alone, she registered its seedy appearance. *Little better than a deadfall.* A handful of loungers lurked outside the entrance. She realized with annoyance that she would have to walk between the loiterers and the hitching rack. Walking in the street was out of the question if she didn't want to encounter a mire of liquid horse manure, slops, and decaying vegetable matter, or risk being run over by the wagons.

She ducked her head to avoid the eyes of the men.

She'd hardly taken ten steps past the place when a sudden yank at the back of her shawl nearly ripped it from her body.

A voice behind her said coldly, "I've been looking for you, wife!"

Chapter Twenty-Two

Inez swung around, tearing her shawl from the restraining hand. A man with a countenance as hollow as a burnt-out tree, feral eyes staring not so much at her but through her, stood not three feet away.

The rage in his face drained away. "A-A-Addie?" The name came out in a stutter. "I thought...I thought you were my wife."

Bewilderment slackened his jaw, and in that gap-mouthed expression, Inez put a name to the face.

Weston Croy.

The fellow who'd accosted her and Sands nearly a week before.

She pulled her shawl back around her. "Mr. Croy, isn't it? As you see, you're quite mistaken. I am *not* your wife."

"Addie," he whispered. "She was my sweet Adeline. Until she left me. Took my money. And now, she's here. Somewhere. In Leadville." His tone became accusatory. "She had a wrap. Just like that."

"Excuse me." She cut him off. "Maybe you should discuss your problems with Reverend Sands."

Weston laughed, a sound more like the caw of a crow, and then was beset with a coughing fit. He gasped, "He said go home. What home? She took everything. When I find her, I'll make her pay." He lurched forward and gripped her shoulder, fingers digging in like claws. "Tell Addie. She'll pay."

"Take. Your. Hand. Off." She bit each word off savagely.

Weston yanked his hand away as if it'd been scorched.

She stepped back. Her foot hit a pothole, and she lurched sideways.

Inez cursed herself for not having her pocket pistol.

Whistles and laughter floated from the men by the saloon entrance. A few had spilled out into the narrow dirt walkway to watch the fun. "A hellcat, for sure," called one. "You gonna let her get away with that, Weston?"

Two red spots appeared high on Weston's stubble-covered cheeks.

"I think that you will allow me to go my way. I do not travel unarmed." She turned the bottle of bourbon so the neck pushed against her shawl, hoping it looked enough like the muzzle of a gun to be convincing. *If worse comes to worst, I'll break the bottle over his head. What a waste of fine liquor that would be!*

Weston wiped his mouth on a stained cuff, staring over her shoulder.

"Problem, Mrs. Stannert?" The reverend's voice behind her carried over the street noise. The men who'd been hanging around outside the saloon vanished inside.

Her knees nearly gave way. Sands caught her elbow in a steadying grip.

"Mr. Croy has the problem," said Inez. "A misplaced wife, whom he mistook me for."

Reverend Sands kept a hand on Inez, but turned his gaze to Weston. He looked like he would gladly dispense with praying for Weston's troubled soul and instead send him straight to the Almighty to plead his case in person. "Weston. Wondered where you were. I asked around. The boardinghouse, the mission, the poorhouse. Now I see where you squandered the church's charity." He glanced at the dive.

Weston seemed to shrivel from the outside in. "I…gotta find Addie."

"We've had this talk before. You'll not find her in your condition."

"Addie's sister knew. I made her tell me. Addie's here."

Disgust colored the reverend's face. "When you're ready to leave town, you know where to turn for help."

He propelled Inez toward Harrison Avenue. "Rain's coming. No sense standing here, waiting to get soaked." The hardness around his mouth lingered. "Sol told me you'd gone to see Jed. With a railroad man. What's going on, Inez? I thought you were in a hurry to get back and lend a hand."

"Change of plans," Inez said with careful dignity. "Not that I need you to watchdog me around town. No need for charity, thank you."

He glanced at her sideways from under the hat. With his mouth set and his eyes narrowed, he looked anything but charitable. "Seems like you were in need of a guardian angel just then."

"I can handle drunkards," she retorted.

"Weston's more than drunk. He's obsessed. Trapped in the past. You'd do well to keep away from him."

"Believe me, it was not I who initiated the conversation."

Inez and Reverend Sands walked back to the saloon in silence. At the door, Reverend Sands touched his hat and stood for a moment, looking toward the jagged peaks of the Mosquito Range, looming in the east.

"I've another meeting," he said abruptly. "I'm already late. Now that I know you're safe and back where you belong, I'll be on my way." He looked her over, a peculiar expression on his face that Inez couldn't quite interpret. "Don't go running away again, Inez. At least, not without your pocket pistol."

"How do you know I don't have it with me?"

A faint smile at last. "If you did, you would've had it out and visible."

He touched his hat and opened the door for her. She could feel his eyes on her as she marched across the barroom. *So, what was all that about? He was angry, and not just at Weston. And he certainly was acting proprietary.*

Inez headed for the kitchen, waving at the reflection of Abe, who was straightening out the bottles lining the long backbar mirror. He turned around. "Take your time gettin' ready, Mrs. Stannert. No hurry."

She looked at the few people scattered around the room. *No hurry indeed. We're probably bleeding out money by the hour right now.*

Inside the kitchen at last, Inez took a deep breath. Biscuits were baking, their sweet warmth making her mouth water. Arming herself with a clean bowl from the shelf, she advanced on the stew pot and lifted the lid, earning a face full of savory steam.

The passdoor squeaked open. Bridgette entered, briskly efficient. "Ma'am, sit down, why don't you." She took the bowl from Inez's hands and herded her toward the table.

"No need, Bridgette." Inez sank onto the chair. "You've plenty to do. All I want is a bit to eat and some coffee." She glanced down at her riding skirt, in desperate need of a good scrubbing. "Well, and clean clothes. And a washbowl. And a towel."

Bridgette ladled stew into the bowl. "You're looking peckish. What have you had to eat today?"

"Bread. Cheese. An egg. A pickle." The only other comestibles ingested didn't fit the definition, being liquid. "I don't recall breakfast."

"Well, if you ate breakfast it wasn't mine, because I've been here since five this morning, and I don't recall seeing you." Bridgette set the bowl and a plate of biscuits in front of Inez.

Inez tore a biscuit apart, ate several of the shreds, and sprinkled the rest on her stew.

Bridgette's stern expression relaxed. "Now, let's get you some coffee." She lifted the top of the coffee pot and peered inside. "Heavens, it's nearly boiled away. Thick as syrup. I'll make fresh for you."

Inez took another spoonful of stew and began to feel sober again. She glanced at her saddlebags, still hanging over the other chair, and pulled them onto the table. While eating, she unloaded the blanket, the crumpled paper holding a few bits of leftover bread and cheese, the rag still soaked with river water, and finally the blasting cap wrapped in the linen napkin.

The alley door swung open. A gust of cool air, carrying the damp hint of rain and the scent of sewage, blew in with Sol, who was muffled under a bundle of material. He dumped it on the table in a red-white-and-blue mass. "Mr. Jackson sent me out for bunting for the Fourth. I went to all the dry goods stores on Chestnut and Harrison." He shook his head. "There wasn't much left."

Bridgette pulled out the coffee grinder, retrieved beans from the top of the pie safe, dumped them in, and began to vigorously grind. The smell of fresh ground coffee spread throughout the kitchen.

Inez fingered the fabric, frowning. "Is there enough to go across the front outside?"

"Five yards."

Inez leaned back in her chair. "That's hardly enough to do the outside justice." She brooded a moment. "So, what are Wyman and the Board of Trade doing for the Fourth?"

Sol pushed his hat back, scratching his head distractedly. "Lessee, I walked right past them. They've got bunting all right. Lots of pine boughs. I think I heard one of the livery men talking… nearly every horse, carriage, and wagon's been chartered for the day."

"Hmmph. Everyone's leaving town. That's not good for business here." Inez thrummed her fingers on the table, looking bleakly at the material.

"Ah, but you'll have the actors, and they'll draw quite a crowd," said Bridgette. She dumped all but a small portion of the old coffee out of the pot before adding the fresh ground and water.

Inez turned to Sol. "I've one more errand for you. Go to Braun's lumberyard and see if he has any pine boughs we can use to decorate the exterior. We'll save the bunting for inside, where it can't mysteriously disappear in the night and end up gracing some other business. If things are still slow when you come back, you can start decorating the interior."

Sol picked up the scrap of rag that Inez had saved from the river. "You want me to hang this up too?" He grinned crookedly.

Inez took it from his hand and smoothed it on the table. "It does have a patriotic cast. I found it not far from where Miss Carothers was injured. She'd mentioned something about a multicolored cloth. Seems a long shot, but I thought I'd show this to her."

"And how is the young miss?" asked Bridgette as Inez folded the scrap of material.

"Getting better. We're going to meet for supper tomorrow. She's planning on going to the church picnic." Inez shook her head. "If we weren't open on the Fourth, I might consider it."

Sol settled his hat on his head. "I'll see what I can rustle up for decorations, before it starts raining."

He eased out the back door just as the first large raindrops pattered into the dirt alley.

Inez stood, gathering the blanket, the strip of cloth, and the blasting cap. "I'd best clean up. Thank you, Bridgette."

"Eating properly puts most things right, I believe." Bridgette gave her a critical once-over. "You've got color back in your cheeks and a snap to your eyes. Now that good-looking Reverend Sands won't be so worried about you."

"Worried?" She stopped, hand on the passdoor.

"Well, jealous, more like. When Sol told him you'd left the saloon with a railroad man, oh my, the look on his face." Bridgette plumped the bunting on a chair, put the tin dishpan in its place, and dumped the dirty dishes in with a rattle.

"Jealous of the professor? That little monkey of a man?"

"I never saw the man so didn't have a chance to give a description, did I."

"What other railroader could I possibly—" Preston Holt flashed through her mind's eye. "Ah-ha," she said softly. "I think I understand. The reverend should have more faith in me."

Once in her upstairs office, Inez threw the blanket on her desk, causing a stack of invoices to cascade across the blotter, and hurried to her dressing room in the back. After putting the rag and blasting cap in her washstand drawer, she threw open the doors to her wardrobe and examined her work clothes—fancy and everyday—before pulling out an older dark blue princess polonaise. She slipped out of her riding clothes and underthings and draped them on a chair to deal with later.

Splashing water into the washbasin, she glanced up at the mirror and caught a glimpse of herself in the altogether. Her face and neck were an unfashionable brown against the creamy olive skin below the collarbone. Her mother's voice whispered disapprovingly, an echo of a scolding twenty years past: "Inez, you need to stop running around outside with your skirts pinned up like a young hoyden. It's unbecoming for one of your station. And no hat! You're becoming as brown as an Indian!"

Inez grabbed a sponge, soaked it thoroughly, and scrubbed her face and neck. She wrung it into the basin. The pink rose painted on the bottom faded, as if obscured by a dust cloud. Her face was now of a shade more in line with the rest of her skin, but still nowhere as light.

Leaning forward, she spoke into the mirror. "Hoyden indeed. I shudder to think what Mama would say now, if she knew my circumstances." Inez toweled off and slipped into a clean combination with a sigh of satisfaction.

Postponing the inevitable corset, she pulled the rag out of the drawer and unrolled it, smoothing it out like a runner on the washstand top. A blue bit at the top, surrounding a white star, a thin white diagonal stripe, a sea of red ending with a fray of threads. The weave was loose, like the Fourth of July bunting Sol had brought in.

Fishing around further in the drawer, she extracted the blasting cap and the hexagonal bullet and copper percussion cap she'd inadvertently taken from Holt's pocket, and arranged them on the cloth. She stepped back and stared at the collection of odds and ends. The reverend's words drifted back to her: "You're finding clues in trash."

She said aloud, "Blasting cap for giant powder. A hexagonal bullet for who knows what kind of gun. A percussion cap for nearly any kind of gun. A piece of cloth." *Guns. Explosives. A possible neckerchief, or perhaps a piece of flag or bunting?*

It was a discordant jumble that made no music she could recognize.

She shook her head. *If there's a connection, it's beyond me.*

Chapter Twenty-Three

"Thank you for seeing me on a Saturday at such short notice." Inez perched on the edge of the leather chair, feeling like a schoolgirl confronting the headmistress.

"Not at all, Mrs. Stannert." William V. Casey, Esquire, squared the sheet of legal-sized paper on the blotter blanketing the polished top of his walnut desk. Sunlight from a side window reflected off the waxed surface straight into Inez's eyes. She shifted in her chair to avoid the glare.

Casey removed his half-glasses and continued, "I assume you're searching for representation regarding a domestic issue. That's what I do. Domestic law."

He enunciated clearly, as if she might have mistaken him for one of the more than one hundred Leadville lawyers profiting from claim-jumping disputes and mining litigation.

He laced his fingers on top of the paper and waited for her response. Inez noted his hands were long-fingered, fingernails clean and squared off, with an inkstain alongside one finger.

"Domestic issues. I assume that includes marital issues. Legal ones, I mean."

"You assume correctly."

His eyes, she noted, were kind, drooping at the corners as if in perpetual sympathy with the hapless clients he served on a regular basis. He added, again in the kindly-instructor tone of voice, "Divorces. Separations. Wills. Probate. Child custody. Those sorts of issues."

"I'm investigating the possibility of...." Her gloved hands strangled the satin reticule in her lap. "Divorce. I'd like to know what's involved. The process and so on." Her voice sounded strange, faraway, as if someone else were speaking on her behalf.

He nodded. "I see. And how does your husband stand on this? Does he know you're exploring legal options?"

"I doubt it. He's been missing for over a year. And honestly, I'm not entirely certain he's still alive."

His eyebrows went up, but his gaze remained steady. "Well, we would proceed on the assumption that he is." Casey put on his glasses, picked up one pencil from a neat parallel line of many that marched across the top of his blotter, and wrote three words on the paper before him. Inez wished she could scoot forward, without being obvious, and try to read what he had written.

He looked at her over the top of his glasses. "How long have you lived in Colorado, Mrs. Stannert?"

"About two and a half years."

He made several more careful marks on the paper. "Good. The law requires that the plaintiff be a resident for at least one year." He continued, not unkindly, "The basis for a request of divorce, in a case like yours, is usually on grounds of desertion." His voice walked the line between statement and question, giving her room to respond either way.

"Desertion." Inez broke away from his gaze and stared out the side window. There was not much to see besides the painted boards of the house next door. The boards were so close that, were the window open, she could have reached out and touched them. "Are there other grounds that would apply?"

He spread his hands. "Besides desertion? Habitual drunkenness. Extreme cruelty. Felony." He hesitated, just for a fraction of a minute, before continuing. "Impotency. Adultery."

She shifted in her chair. "How, exactly, is desertion defined, if I may ask?"

"Do you want the exact legal definition?"

"Please."

He smiled, turned his back on her briefly to peruse the shelves of law books lining the back wall. She was treated to a view of the small bald tonsure on the back of his head. He stood and pulled a book down, paged through it, then smoothed it out. "'In any case in which a marriage has been or hereafter may be contracted and solemnized between any two persons....' Let's see. Ah, here it is. 'That either party has willfully deserted and absented himself or herself from the husband or wife without any reasonable cause for the space of one year.'" He glanced up. "I assume he has not provided for you in the interval? You did say you were unsure whether he was alive still."

"True," she said bleakly.

He closed the book and set it to one side. "One thing to consider is what course you would take should he return during the divorce process."

She stared in amazement. "If he hasn't shown up after a year, what would induce him to appear now? Assuming he's still alive."

"Well, for example, he may read the newspaper notice."

"Newspaper notice?" she sat up straighter. "What do you mean?"

He made another short notation on the paper, set the pencil down in its place in the row, and leaned back in his chair. "Apologies, Mrs. Stannert. Let me explain the entire process. Once you decide to retain me or another lawyer as counsel, we notify the district court and a summons is drawn up for the defendant, that is Mr. Stannert, by the court clerk. The summons is usually served by the sheriff or a deputy of the county where Mr. Stannert is. If the summons is served within the county where it is filed—I assume you plan to file in Lake County—he has ten days to answer the complaint. If the summons is served outside of Lake County but in this district, he has twenty days to respond. If outside the district, he has forty days."

"Serve a summons on Mark? It'll be a cold day in...that is, I can't imagine a sheriff, a deputy, or anyone else will find Mr. Stannert. In Lake or any other county."

"Perhaps so. In which case, the clerk of the court may direct us to publish the summons in a public newspaper, published in this state, at least once a week for four consecutive weeks."

The muscles in her neck and back tensed as if in expectation of a knife being stuck between her shoulder blades. "A public paper? Here, in Leadville?"

"Could be. Usually, a paper is chosen that is deemed most likely to give notice to the person being served. When the person's whereabouts are unknown, but if we assume he's in Colorado somewhere, that usually means a paper with a wide distribution, such as the *Denver Tribune, Colorado Springs Gazette*, some such."

"Is all this necessary? I thought, since he's been gone so long, this would be quickly resolved."

Casey chose a different pencil from the row and rolled it between his fingers. "The law is a careful beast, Mrs. Stannert. All parties must have fair process." He smiled wryly. "My previous practice was in Utah. You've heard the term 'divorce mill'? In Utah Territory, judges will even accept collusion—an agreement to divorce between husband and wife. A married couple can appear in court, testify that they agreed to divorce, and receive a decree. All on the same day. Colorado is not Utah. In Colorado, if it appears that the two parties are engaged in collusion—for instance, that they have manufactured a charge of cruelty, simply to obtain a divorce—the judge will throw out the divorce request. Similarly, if both parties have been guilty of adultery, when adultery is the grounds for the complaint, no divorce will be decreed."

He said the last matter-of-factly, as if the statement were nothing more than another tangential point of law. But Inez wondered if the sudden image of the good Reverend Sands that burned through her mind like a white-hot fire did not, in some way, brand her face as well.

Casey laced his fingers on the blotter and continued, "The laws differ state to state, territory to territory. I've handled many cases of desertion by husbands and wives. I can count on one hand the number of times an absent—that is, truly absent—spouse has returned in response to a newspaper notice. But it does happen occasionally, and the law wants to give the other side every opportunity to respond. Divorce is such a final step."

"Let's assume Mr. Stannert will not appear. What then?"

"Then it is an easy matter for the judge, and the divorce proceedings are conducted behind closed doors."

"And that's all?"

"As part of the legal proceedings, it is reported in the newspapers. But amongst all the news of silver prices, the comings and goings of dignitaries, the stock offerings, the latest murder, such notices are not front page news."

Except for those who read every line of type, looking for scandal to dissect.

"If I may inquire, do you and Mr. Stannert have children?"

"One. A son."

He made another notation. "He lives with you?"

"No. He's with my sister back east." Her lips had trouble forming the words. "He left last summer. Our doctor said he'd not last the winter here."

Sympathy filled his soft brown eyes. "I see. Any assets that must be considered?"

Inez cleared her throat. "There's our home. And a business."

Which we own in a three-way split with Abe. She suddenly realized that the particulars of that partnership had never been written down, much less signed and notarized. *My God. There's no proof that I own the Silver Queen in equal part with Abe and Mark. None at all.* It felt as if her personal and financial situation was becoming as tangled and ephemeral as a skein of smoke.

Inez rose abruptly. "I'd like time to think on this. I now see the need to consider this matter carefully. As you said, divorce is such a final thing."

He looked disappointed, then recovered. "Of course. If I can help further—"

"I shall contact you directly. Yes, thank you."

Casey led her to the foyer. At the door he hesitated, hand on the knob, regarded her steadily, then said, "Mrs. Stannert, as you're pondering, keep in mind: There are far worse things in this world than divorce." He smiled ruefully and opened the door for Inez to escape.

Inez paused at the street corner, waiting for a break in the traffic so she could cross. She covered her eyes, trying to shut out the questions and concerns spinning through her mind. *Never mind the business. What of William? Will the judge think less of me for having sent William to live with my sister? Surely, the judge would grant his custody to me. Who else is there, besides my sister. And my parents. I could never, ever let them know about the divorce. Papa would find a way to take William from me, claiming I'm an unfit mother or unbalanced, or mad.*

She dropped her hand and stared west, across the broad, crowded expanse of Harrison Avenue, in the direction of Evergreen Cemetery. Anger at Mark—for being gone, for leaving her to deal with life and its burdens as best she may—boiled up through her. "Damn you, Mark," she whispered fiercely. "Where are you? I wish to God that you were six feet under and I knew exactly where."

Chapter Twenty-Four

The walk to the Tontine Restaurant gave Inez a chance to collect herself. Pausing outside, she checked her lapel watch and was gratified to see she was still "on schedule" despite her extended meeting with Casey.

Don't think of that right now.

Squaring her shoulders, she pushed open the door at 140 West Chestnut. She spotted Susan Carothers straight away, seated at a table with a young woman with strawberry-blonde hair. The woman turned around, giving Inez a view of a bright, hopeful face with a nose that could only be described as "pert."

Inez approached the table and Susan, still seated, indicated an empty chair. A walking cane was hooked over the edge of the table. Inez raised her eyebrows, and Susan explained, "From Doc Cramer. He finally allowed that I could walk from the boardinghouse to my studio and back, provided I use this and stay off my feet as much as possible. Oh!" She turned to her red-haired companion. "Where *are* my manners? Miss Theresa O'Loughlin, this is Mrs. Inez Stannert."

Inez nodded, stripping off her gloves and settling down in the high-backed chair. "How do you do, Miss O'Loughlin."

"Theresa is going to be a schoolteacher here," said Susan. "She's new to Leadville and also boards at Mrs. Flynn's."

Miss O'Loughlin's smile made her freckles glow. "Please, call me Terry."

Inez slid the linen napkin from under the cutlery. "An unusual name."

True to her fair complexion, Terry blushed right up to the roots of her hair. "My father's nickname for me. I thought it has the right sense of adventure for a place like Leadville. I was so excited when this teaching position came up. I was ready to leave home, although my parents would have preferred I stay in Boston."

As Terry chattered about the train trip west, Susan's gaze, which had been taking in the room, froze at a spot over Inez's shoulder and then slowly moved upward as if tracking someone approaching their table.

Terry's voice trailed off.

Inez twisted around in her chair, just as Preston Holt said, "Pardon, ladies. Miss Carothers?"

Preston and Reuben stood nearby. Hats in hand. Preston continued, "Still clear for us to come in for that sittingr?"

"That's right. I'll be back in my studio by one thirty."

Inez raised her eyebrows at Preston. "You're having your portrait taken?"

He nodded. "Reuben's turning sixteen today. Seemed a fitting thing to do."

The boy fiddled with the brim of his hat, staring at Susan. Inez realized that both men had their hair slicked back and the usual dust and grime she associated with working out in the elements was missing from their garb.

Susan added, "Everything is already set up."

"Thanks, ma'am. Much appreciated." Preston turned a smile on Inez, replaced his hat, and began to move away.

"Stop by the Silver Queen, and I'll stand Reuben a birthday drink," Inez said impulsively.

Preston stopped and turned. For a moment, Inez thought he might decline. Instead, he responded, "Thank you, ma'am. We might do that."

"There's a poker game as well," she continued. "Starts about nine in the evening, goes late—or early, depending on how you tell time. Tends to be high stakes, but if you feel lucky...." She realized with some annoyance that her face was coloring up in a way to match Terry's.

The big railroad man gazed at her as if trying to determine what was really on her mind.

She hoped he couldn't tell.

Preston smiled again. Briefly. "Guess we'll see how my luck runs later."

Inez smiled in return, watched Preston and Reuben leave, and turned back to the table to find Terry staring at her, wide eyes and open mouth.

"So." Inez reached for a roll from the silver basket and placed it on her bread plate. "Did Susan perchance explain the business I'm in?"

"Nooooo. You work in a saloon? That sounds," she hesitated, searching for the right word, "dangerous."

"No more dangerous than being a schoolteacher," said Inez, slathering butter on a bit of roll. "I recall an occurrence shortly after we arrived in town—let's see, it must have been about two years ago. Two young ruffians, a boy and girl, decided they didn't like their teacher for some reason or other. They went home at noon, armed themselves with revolvers, and marched up the street to the school, threatening to shoot their teacher on sight."

Seeing Susan and Terry's shocked faces she added quickly, "A student ran and told the school board. They out-maneuvered and captured the desperados, and put an end to the nonsense before the teacher returned from lunch." She waved the butter knife dismissively. "Well, that was Leadville's wild days. I'm certain you'll have no such trouble now."

"Inez, that was just plain mean," Susan said under her breath.

Susan and Inez stood outside the restaurant, preparing to go to Susan's portrait studio. Terry, who was headed in the opposite direction, looked fearfully around at the afternoon crowds walking past her without much more than a glance. She met Susan's gaze. Susan waved goodbye; Terry waved back with a brave smile and hoisted her parasol aloft.

Inez felt a small pang of guilt, seeing the young woman square her shoulders and hurry away. "You're right. It's just....first, she asks if it's possible for her to buy a cheap mine. Then, whether it is true that ministers of the gospel fight in the pulpit. And whether women can be lynched for singing." She rolled her eyes.

Susan hobbled down the boardwalk, leaning on her cane. "I suppose all she had to go by was what newspapers back East report. And they say the most dreadful things about Leadville. As if it's a den of iniquity."

"Well, that all depends on where you go," said Inez, thinking of her brush with Weston the previous day.

"And then, when she asked whether it was safe for women to walk on the streets without a pistol...." Susan paused at the top of a set of rickety stairs leading down to the next section of boardwalk.

Inez took Susan's free elbow to steady her. "As you know, it's my firm belief that a woman who doesn't go armed and alert around here is living in a fool's paradise." Inez glanced at Susan's set expression and added, "I know that's not your opinion. But she did ask me."

"Still, I can't see that there was any need for you to actually take your pocket pistol out and show it to her."

"If the sight of such a small gun makes her faint, then perhaps she needs to reconsider her decision to stay in Leadville," Inez said with finality. "However, I've no desire to scare the wits out of her. She's obviously a young woman with pluck. I can see why you two struck up a friendship. I'll apologize, should I see her again."

The two women moved into the shelter of a bookstore doorway to allow a river of small boys, shouting and laughing, to flow past. Amid the sea of bobbing caps, intent expressions, and scuffed shoes, Inez spotted a firecracker gripped in an urchin's hand.

Susan sighed. "I would appreciate that, Inez. It's important that Terry and the other teachers think well of me and my friends." She commenced walking again, hobbling faster. "Now that my view camera is destroyed and I'm not able to photograph landscapes—I'd hoped to make a name for myself doing those—I need to redouble my efforts to build my portrait business to buy a new one. I put nearly all my savings into that camera. It was the very latest design, used dry plate chemistry, and was small enough for me to handle on my own."

She looked forlorn for a moment, then shook her head as if to clear her thoughts. "Anyway, I'm expanding my portrait clientele. In fact, I talked up my business to the other women at the boardinghouse and have nearly all the teachers scheduled for sittings. Even Mrs. Flynn wants to schedule a session."

"Fancy that!" Inez said, thinking of the proper young matron.

"And," Susan brightened, "I had this other idea. With the railroad crews coming into town on paydays and Sundays, I'm hoping some might want to have their pictures taken, if I price it right. All I need is a few satisfied customers to spread the word."

"Ah. That explains the two Mr. Holts."

Susan flushed and blew a breath upward, fluffing her curly bangs. "The older one, the one who asks questions, showed up at my studio yesterday. He said that nothing more is being done about the...accident. He was nice, but he made it clear the Rio Grande hasn't time to chase after ghosts. He didn't put it quite that way, but close. Anyhow, he asked about portraits and prices. I don't know. Maybe he felt sorry for me. It doesn't matter. It's business."

"Well, if the Holts tell others there's a pretty woman photographer who will take their pictures—"

"I'd rather they be impressed with how the photograph looks than just come to see a photographer in skirts. But whatever brings them in."

"Hundreds of men work for the Rio Grande. Susan, you may have struck pay dirt."

Susan stopped by her front door and dug in her pocket, finally producing a key. She said, "I hope so. And as soon as I get some new images, I'll replace those." She nodded at her display window. A selection of landscape photographs sat front and center, below the stenciled "Carothers' Photographic Portraits: Best Prices and

Quality Work." The Sawatch Range, the Arkansas River with the railroad tracks featured against a sweeping view westward, and a silken waterfall were all positioned artfully on a purple decline of satin.

"It won't do to advertise services I can no longer provide." Susan gazed at the photo of the Arkansas River. "If I had the money, I'd hire a buggy and driver and see if I can find proof that I didn't make it all up." She switched her gaze to Inez. "I think I've convinced Mrs. Flynn I'm not some foolish young woman who dallies alone on public highways, drinks on the sly, and is prone to hallucinations. But I can't quell the rumors entirely."

"Reverend Sands and I went out there and searched the area thoroughly."

Key in lock, she turned to Inez. "Did you find anything?"

"Nothing." The strip of cloth flashed through her mind. "Well, maybe something. I don't want to get your hopes up. A strip of colored cloth."

She shook her head. "I don't remember anything about a piece of cloth. Well, bring it to church tomorrow."

"Can't. Fourth of July. We're going to be open. Early, and all day."

"You're going to miss the church picnic?"

"Most likely. If I manage to escape, it wouldn't be until the afternoon. And then I'd have to ride down by myself. What a bother."

"If you can get away, there's a group of us planning on leaving town later, at about two. We rented a wagon, and there's plenty of room. I don't usually schedule sittings on Sunday, but I have a couple families scheduled right after church. Every dime and dollar counts right now."

"We're hoping some of that silver and gold showers down on us as well."

"Good luck, to all of us, then."

Inez murmured, "Good luck indeed." *Maybe I'd better go to that picnic. I'm not sure I trust luck will keep Birdie from sinking her talons into the good reverend.*

Chapter Twenty-Five

Inez angled around to the backside of the bar, holding the short train of her maroon and black evening dress off the floor, careful to keep a distance from any corner or surface that might mar the watered silk. The lamps were turned high enough to allow the customers to see what they were drinking, but not so high as to destroy the atmosphere of cozy camaraderie. Abe and Sol were busy pouring. On the piano, Taps alternated between light-hearted ditties and soulful ballads. Inez checked her enamel and diamond watch, hanging from a brooch in the shape of a coiled snake. *My Saturday night players should be arriving soon.*

"Nickel buys the latest news." Jed slid a copy of *The Independent* across the bar, nearly under her elbow.

"I think for all the help I've provided, not to mention advertising revenue, you'd spot me the paper." Inez opened the newspaper to page two and was pleased to see an advert about the Fairplays and their July Fourth appearance prominently displayed. "So, did you hire the professor?"

"We came to an agreement. I expect he'll be by to collect on that drink sometime tonight." Jed lazed against the bar. "Did you see the front page?"

Inez folded the paper to the front. The first thing she saw was a modest article captioned "Jumping a Hospital" and, in smaller type beneath, "Trouble on the Sisters' Grounds—One Man Shot."

"Ah, I see they caught the miscreants who threatened to jump St. Vincent's property," Inez said.

"What? Oh yes. That. A couple of ne'er-do-wells sent a note saying they'd set fire to the hospital if the Sisters didn't relinquish the property. It's prime real estate, you know, close to where the Rio Grande depot and freight yards will be. The law caught two of them red-handed last night, tearing down the hospital's fence. But that's not what I wanted you to see."

Jed took the paper from her hands and flipped it, handing it back to her with the section above the fold now prominent. Headlines blared "Citizens Up in Arms Over D&RG's High-Handed Treatment on Right-of-Way Issue!" and "RR Workers Abandon Spikes for Silver in Cloud City!"

"Goodness. What did you do? Chain the poor fellow to a chair in your office until he provided a column's worth of type?"

"More like two." Jed's suppressed smile escaped. "I've sold more papers today than anytime since the news of the strike broke. And that was one of the biggest days ever for *The Independent*. No other Leadville paper got *this* scoop. Think I'll have a drop of that superb bourbon you promised me."

Feeling a little sorry that she'd impulsively offered to give away some of her best liquor, Inez turned to the backbar and lifted the bottle from its place of honor on the top row. She poured, keeping a careful eye on the glass so as to just make the mark. "So, Jed, you're feeling lucky tonight? Perhaps that luck will extend to the cards."

The State Street door flew open with force, slamming into the wall, stirring the red-white-and-blue bunting Sol had draped over the buffalo's horns. Two men stormed in. Inez recognized Lowden Snow, looking apoplectic and red-faced as if he'd just run a race through the city streets and lost. The man with Snow looked vaguely familiar. His round face sported a bushy mustache and a weak chin attempting to hide under a small goatee. His unprepossessing appearance was offset by a steely gaze and an expression suggesting he was not a man to be trifled with.

Abe, beside her, muttered an oath under his breath.

"Who's that with Snow?" she whispered.

"Chief engineer of the Rio Grande."

"McMurtrie?"

"Yep." Abe stood with one hand beneath the bar. Inez saw he held the shotgun out of sight.

She laid her hand over his. "Not yet."

Snow barreled to the center of the room, stopped, and swiveled his head, scanning the crowd. McMurtrie's gaze skewered Jed. He leaned over and said something to Snow.

Snow followed McMurtrie's gaze and, with his silver-headed cane swinging back and forth like a fast-paced metronome, he bore down on Jed. He stopped before the newspaperman, eyes furious and bulging.

"You the scoundrel that printed that libelous doggerel about the Denver and Rio Grande?" roared Snow.

Jed rocked back on his heels. He stuck both hands in his pockets, affecting a casual air. "Jed Elliston. Editor-in-chief of *The Independent*, at your service," he said coolly.

McMurtrie advanced slowly, and, in Inez's opinion, far too menacingly.

"You again." He sounded as if he'd lifted a rock and found a maggot beneath. "Thought we hammered out an agreement at the Clairmont. Guess you've got a short memory."

"Freedom of the press," said Jed with a hint of sarcasm. "Can't stop me from printing the truth, McMurtrie. Unless you're going to say it's a lie. In which case, I welcome letters to the editor."

Snow hit the wood floor once with his cane. The hollow boom sounded like a judge's gavel in a courtroom. "Who is the miserable miscreant who disclosed privileged information to you?" he bellowed. "Company business...not public...jeopardizing on-going legal action...." He was nearly incoherent with rage.

"I'll not divulge my sources," said Jed.

McMurtrie took a step toward Jed, his hands tightening into fists.

Inez, on the other side of the bar, tugged the bottom of her basque bodice with one hand to smooth the contours and tightened her grip on the bottle of bourbon with the other. "Gentlemen!"

She stepped quickly around the end of the bar and advanced upon the three. "Mr. Snow, so good to see you again."

Without waiting for a response, she turned to McMurtrie. "Mr. McMurtrie? I'm Mrs. Stannert, proprietor of the Silver Queen, along with Mr. Jackson, the gentleman in the gray waistcoat behind the bar."

Snow's face froze. "Jackson is your partner?"

Inez was used to the disbelief that crowded folks' faces when they discovered Abe was an equal and not a hireling. She was also used to the speculative looks, the sniggers, the stares. But that didn't mean she let the perpetrators off easy.

She delivered a stare to Snow as icy as Leadville in winter and said in a tone to match, "Yes, Mr. Snow. My. Business. Partner."

She checked McMurtrie's response. His gaze slid from Jed to Abe, and he nodded neutrally. Abe nodded back.

Glad to have shifted attention from Jed, she held out her hand. "So pleased to make your acquaintance at last, Mr. McMurtrie. I'd read that you were in town."

McMurtrie hesitated, then touched his hat politely before shaking her hand.

Inez continued conversationally, "We welcome civilized discussion and debate conducted over fruits of the vine, barley, rye, or hops. However," her voice slid to a more intimate volume to temper her words, "I do not condone fisticuffs or threats of any kind. This is not that sort of establishment." She kept her eyes on McMurtrie, judging him the one who would set the tone for what might follow.

"That said, allow us to stand you and Mr. Snow a drink." She gave him her most seductive smile, and, without taking her gaze from McMurtrie, motioned for Abe to put two clean glasses on the countertop.

The prompt clink of glassware on wood was interrupted by McMurtrie saying, "Another time, Mrs. Stannert. We came here on business." His eyes swept over her shoulder to Jed, who, Inez suspected, still lounged against the bar, smirking.

"What a pity. Well, do drop by again sometime. The offer of a drink still stands." She turned and placed the bottle by Jed, baring her teeth at him in a less cordial manner. "Mr. Elliston, wait here."

Inez stepped between the two railway men, took each man by the arm and moved them toward the Harrison Avenue doors. "Thank you for your forbearance," she said in a low voice. "It's so easy for these things to turn ugly." Her speech was interrupted by the sound of firecrackers popping outside, punctuated by the resonant bang of something far more powerful.

"Some are beginning their celebrations of the Fourth early," she remarked. She released the two men, opened the door onto Harrison's gas-lit boardwalk, and waited until they stepped out before following and shutting the door.

Harrison Avenue was packed. Men and a few women spilled from the boardwalks and filled the broad dirt-packed street, making it slow going for rigs and riders. She could feel the celebratory energy coursing through the crowds. The night's journey from drinking to gambling to whoring had begun.

McMurtrie asked, "You know that inkslinger well?"

"Mr. Elliston? He plays in our regular Saturday night game, which is due to start—" she looked at her watchpin— "in fifteen minutes."

McMurtrie said, "Tell him it's not over."

"Your message will be delivered."

"Tell him—"

Staccato gunshots rang out from around the corner. The volley was followed by loud laughter.

"I thought the discharging of giant powder, guns, and pistols was prohibited in town," grumped Snow.

"It is," said Inez. "But that doesn't stop anyone unless a policeman is facing them square off."

A deep boom sounded from the hills of the mining district.

"Addie!"

Hatless, Weston Croy thrust his sweat-streaked face close to hers.

Inez recoiled.

"They're c-coming!" Weston's teeth chattered so hard she could hardly understand him. "To k-kill us! Hide. Hide in the woods. It's s-so cold. The light draws the snipers. N-no fires. The mud. The cold. I'm so cold. N-need a fire."

He was shaking head to foot. Inez realized that what she thought was sweat streaming down his face was actually tears.

"Stop it!" Inez said loudly, hoping to shock him out of his fit.

McMurtrie grabbed him. "You heard the lady."

Weston tore away from McMurtrie and seized Inez by the shoulders. "We must run! The shells...I hear them. Screaming." Gaslight threw harsh shadows on his face. White shown around his eyes. "Oh, Addie. They hit the caissons. Horses, shrieking. The mud. The cold."

"Unhand me!" Inez tried to push his hands away.

"Get a hold of yourself, soldier." McMurtrie hauled Weston off Inez and shoved him against the side of the saloon.

Another boom. Close enough for Inez to feel it deep inside her chest.

Weston began weeping and moaning, "The bridge...it's gone! The wrong bridge, the wrong bridge. Oh, damn the general! Damn him! Damn him!"

A stream of dark liquid dampened Weston's threadbare trouser cuff, ran over his shoe, and puddled on the walkway.

A stench rose in the cold air.

Inez clamped a hand over her nose and turned away.

In the light of the hissing gas lamps, she saw Doc Cramer, his distinctive stovepipe hat bobbing above the crowd, limping toward her. His smile melted as he took in the scene. "What's this?" He peered at the shivering man crouched against the wall. "Weston Croy?"

"He's crazy," said Inez. "He—" She couldn't finish, pointing instead at the mess on the boardwalk.

Doc Cramer approached him and laid a hand on his shoulder. "Weston. The war is over. It's July 1880, and you're in Leadville, Colorado. You need a quiet place to rest and regain your nerves." He looked at McMurtrie. "The best place for him right now is the jail. I don't believe he's dangerous, but one never knows. If you'll help me get him there, I'll explain to the marshal."

Snow stepped forward, to Inez's surprise, and said, "I'll help. McMurtrie has other business to attend to."

"Let's proceed post-haste." Doc turned to Inez. "I'll be a bit late for tonight's game. A stiff brandy would be much appreciated upon my return."

As they moved away, Weston shuffling between them, Inez heard Doc say to Snow, "Paralytic dementia, possibly acute mania, I've seen it before."

"Good God." Inez stared at the liquefied excrement blotting the plank wall of her saloon and on the walkway by the entrance.

"A bad case," said McMurtrie.

"He thought he was still in the War, didn't he. Every time he sees me, he thinks I'm this woman, Addie. His wife, so he says."

McMurtrie nodded and stroked his mustache. "Some men don't have the moral fiber, the strength to put it in the past."

The saloon door swung open and Abe stepped out, drying his hands on his apron.

"Watch where you step!" Inez called out. Her breath curled out visibly with the words, and the cold at last penetrated her consciousness and the thin silk sleeves. She wrapped her arms around herself, shivering, and turned to McMurtrie. "Thank you for your help."

"No problem, Mrs. Stannert. I've dealt with hardcases tougher than that. If you'd kindly pass my message on to Elliston. And tell him, if he's looking for trouble, the Rio Grande will be more than happy to accommodate."

McMurtrie touched his hat and was gone.

Chapter Twenty-Six

"What happened?" Abe stepped gingerly around the stained walkway.

"A man named Weston. A lunatic. Sol should throw some water on this and get it off the side of the building. Hot water. Something. Whatever's quickest."

Back inside, Inez pulled up a clean glass from the shelf under the bar and splashed bourbon into it while Abe instructed Sol on clean-up procedures. "Quicklime's in the storage room in back," he finished. "Or, if'n there's some strong coffee left, splash that around. It'll kill the smell."

Abe's somber brown eyes lifted to her. "Jed's in the back room with the others. Everyone's there but Doc and you. Think you'd better get ready to do some serious card playin'. 'Specially if you keep drinkin' our most expensive stock." He took the bourbon bottle from her and tipped it back and forth. It was nearly empty. "How much of this've you been drinkin'? Thought you preferred brandy." Abe put it back in its place, last row, center stage, on the backbar.

"Sometimes," she said to Abe's back, "I require a change." She carried her glass to the gaming room.

Doc met her at the door to the private room. "Ah, Mrs. Stannert. I thought you would all be gathered around the table by now." He removed his stovepipe hat and mopped his brow.

"I'm running late. So, you took Weston to jail? Will they keep him there?"

"I had to do some fast talking, but they'll keep him overnight, at least."

They entered to find Jed regaling mercantile owner Bob Evan and lawyer David Cooper with a very different version of his confrontation with McMurtrie and Snow.

Inez looked around the room, remembering the time Mark had spent debating over the details of the décor. They'd invested heavily in the low-hanging chandelier, the bronze lamp sconces that dotted the walls, and the round mahogany table. Mark had said, "Need to make it high class. A place the high rollers'll feel comfortable throwin' their money around." How proud he'd been when it was completed. A vision brought to fruition, glittery and shiny.

But that was then.

Now, the maroon wallpaper had dimmed, its gold flock looking more mustard than metal, muted by the regular haze of cigar smoke and coal oil lamps. The rug, too, had its share of spills and stains lurking among the leafy pattern.

It's time for a change. To finish the room upstairs. But for that, we've got to bring in more cash. I need to play smarter, perhaps encourage new players to join us, some of the moneyed newcomers. And, with luck, the actors will prove to be the bonanza Abe thinks they'll be.

Cooper turned toward her, elegant as usual in a fine-cut suit, looking like he would be right at home in a New York City gentleman's club. "Mrs. Stannert, might I be permitted to say that I've never seen you look finer. The high country summer must be agreeing with you."

"Why, thank you, Mr. Cooper. I'm looking forward to a friendly evening of cards with you gentlemen. At midnight, we can pause and toast the birth of the nation. Let's hope the weather holds for the Fourth, without any unseasonable snow."

She walked toward the sideboard, renewed her bourbon, and prepared a brandy for Doc.

"We were just talking about the railroad," said Bob Evan, the lamplight shining off his steel-rimmed glasses. It was almost as if the light of the sun gleamed from his eyes.

"Indeed," said Inez. Evan talked of little else. As owner of a successful mercantile and a booming mining supply store, he anticipated the arrival of the railroad as some anticipated the Second Coming.

"It will be the best thing that's happened to Leadville since Tabor developed the Matchless Mine, mark my words." Evan adjusted his glasses. The reflection from the lamps vanished and his eyes reappeared. "You should be happy about this as well, Mrs. Stannert. Cheaper goods. Expenses will fall, profits will rise. Just think of all the newcomers that will flood town, thirsty and looking for a fair drink."

"And looking for pickaxes, shovels, and drills," added Inez, mindful of Evan's stock-in-trade in hopeful prospectors who, even now, arrived in Leadville, hoping for the next big strike.

She handed Doc the snifter and pulled a fresh deck of cards from the drawer of the side table. Splitting the seal with a fingernail, she said, "Gentlemen, what say you to some poker?"

They settled in their customary seats, with Harry Gallagher's seat, to Inez's right, vacant.

Doc said, "Harry should be back soon from that extended business trip."

Inez made a noncommittal sound. *The longer he's away the better.* It'd been more than six months since she'd last seen the silver baron. A shudder traveled down her back and lodged at the base of her spine at the memory of their heated confrontation. He'd predicted Inez and Sands would not last through summer.

We proved him wrong on that.

The first hour played out uneventfully, but to Inez's modest benefit. Jed, perhaps because of the success of his latest issue, had loosened his purse strings and was playing more freely than he had in quite a while.

Evan, always the cautious type, also seemed more relaxed and willing to take a chance or two. Doc played well, actually improving his situation. Cooper, who as a player was impulsive—surprising, given his very orderly and strategic approach to matters of the law—was enhancing Inez's takings nicely.

For the first time in over a month, Inez began to relax and feel the flow of the game run through her again.

The door creaked open, and the outside sounds of the busy saloon washed over her as she debated the wisdom of drawing to an outside straight.

Sol's voice interrupted her deliberations. "Ma'am?"

Inez set her hand facedown and twisted in her chair.

Sol stood, barring the door somewhat ineffectually. Towering behind him was Preston Holt. Inez saw Reuben hovering to one side, a small slice of his highly flushed face appearing between Sol's gartered sleeve and the doorframe.

"These fellows here say you invited them to come play a round or two." He looked dubious, as if he thought they might be trying to pull his leg.

"Thank you, Sol. Yes, let them in." Inez turned back to her regular players. "Mr. Preston Holt and Reuben. Mr. Holt is the Rio Grande payroll guard who rescued Miss Carothers and me after her unfortunate accident by Disappointment Gulch."

Jed's expression soured at mention of the Rio Grande. Cooper and Evan looked mildly curious. Doc nodded cordially.

She smiled at the two railroad men, noting that Reuben was looking a great deal more rumpled than earlier that day at the Tontine Restaurant. "I understand it is the younger Mr. Holt's birthday tomorrow. Or perhaps," she glanced at her lapel watch, "I should say today."

She waved at the empty chair next to her. "Have a seat. Ante is a quarter eagle."

Preston started forward as if to take the seat. Reuben grabbed his sleeve.

Preston glanced at him. "You sure you want to do this, son?"

"Heck, it's my birthday. You bet." He slid into the chair and squirmed around a bit on the velvet cushion.

She turned toward the bartender, who was still hovering by the door. "Sol, would you bring that chair by the stove over for Mr. Holt?"

"No need, ma'am. Reckon we'll lose a little less if only one of us plays." He looked at Reuben. "One hand, Reuben. That's all."

Reuben was busy taking in the room. His eyes lingered on the prints of Civil War battles, and then moved to the sideboard with its collection of bottles and crystal decanters.

"You're welcome to a drink on the house while we finish this hand," Inez offered.

Preston's hand landed on Reuben's shoulder, keeping him down in the chair. "I'll fetch us beers from the bar. Thanks, ma'am."

After he left the room, the round finished up quickly, Jed the winner.

"So, you're Rio Grande men," said Evan as Jed counted his take. "General Palmer keeping you busy?"

"Hell yeah." Reuben looked at Inez, suddenly abashed. "That's…yeah. Yessir. I ride for the payroll, but lookin' at the crews' progress and what-all, we figure it won't be long afore they're layin' track through town."

"Speaking of the crews and such," Jed said. "You've all heard about the graders that struck pay dirt outside of Malta? They were doing some prospecting on the side, found a promising hole, and jumped ship from the Rio Grande. They aren't the only ones. The Rio Grande is bleeding men. No sooner are they brought in from Utah and Canadian territories, than they take off, thinking to strike silver."

"Palmer and McMurtrie are putting all they've got into reaching town proper by mid-July," said Evan.

"An unlikely timetable." Jed sounded triumphant. "There are Leadville landowners who're not interested in selling out on Rio Grande's terms."

"It'll all come to an end soon, one way or another," Cooper remarked, removing a cigar from a slim silver case. "Snow, their attorney, is working on it. Once eminent domain is declared, the holdouts'll have no choice. Their property will be condemned and that will be the end of the line for them."

"Typical high-handed Rio Grande behavior." Jed snorted. "Palmer's little more than a bully in the schoolyard."

Doc harrumphed.

Oh no. I cannot take more talk of the war. Not after Weston.

She leaned toward Doc and said under her breath, "Doc, this has been a trying evening. Can we all just play cards and—"

Doc held up a hand. "My dear, I've been thinking long and hard about how to pound some sense into this young fellow about Palmer. I told him of the general's courage at Chickamauga. I've expounded on his strength of character at Castle Thunder. Alluded to his amazing exploits in the mountains of Tennessee and the Saquatchie Valley and more. All to no avail. Please allow one last story from this old man."

"You promise it's the last?" Jed sounded supremely bored.

"I heard this not from Palmer himself, who is far too modest to relate such a tale, but from one who was there and knew him well. After Lee's surrender, Palmer and his cavalry were riding back into Tennessee when a bushwhacker shot at Palmer from the roadside. A very near miss, could have ended his career and more right then and there. The gunman was captured and turned out to be a boy no older than Reuben here. In a lesser man's hands, the boy would have been shot or hung on the spot. But when the boy's mother came and pleaded for his life, General Palmer told her to take him home and keep a better watch over his actions. I believe that story sums up the man, his principles, and his honor."

Looking as triumphant as if he'd stormed the hill and planted the flag, Doc leaned back in his chair. He gazed around at the gathered company as if he'd forgotten they were all there. "All that reminiscing has made this old man thirsty. Is there any more of that most excellent brandy, Mrs. Stannert?"

Inez picked up Doc's goblet and rose to fill it. She turned to Reuben to ask if he wouldn't like a whiskey chaser to go with his yet-to-arrive beer. Reuben was glaring at Doc with such fury that Inez took a step backward.

"Palmer's a blue-belly, right? If he'd rode through Missouri back then, he'd've been dead. Missouri shooters don't miss."

It was the way he said it: Muh-zur-ah. The cadence and inflection a stronger rendition of what she heard in Preston's voice. *So, the Holts are from Missouri. But why is Reuben so angry? He was just a babe when the war was over. What has Palmer ever done to him?*

Doc gaped at Reuben, obviously taken aback at his outburst.

Inez slid her hand into the pocket sewn into the seam of her evening dress and curled her fingers around the grip of her pocket revolver. She hoped she wouldn't have to give Reuben a tongue-lashing and toss him out on his ear.

Cooper was looking at Reuben kindly. "A Missouri man, are you? Missouri had it hard during the war. But you're far too young to remember that."

Reuben switched his pugnacious stare from Doc to Cooper. "Don't have to remember. 'Cause I *know*." He pounded the table with his fist. The coins jumped and clinked. "It was the Yankees' fault what happened in Missouri. Yankees. Jayhawkers. Republicans. Radicals. It was *their* fault the railroads came. It was *their* fault the freight rates got so high Pa couldn't hold onto the farm—"

At each "their," he hit the table. Liquor shivered in the glasses, cards sloughed off the neatly stacked deck. Inez narrowed her eyes, thinking that if his rant didn't cease soon, she'd be forced to take him down a peg.

"It was *their* fault Ma died—"

The door opened again, letting in the muted roar of men's voices. Preston entered, holding two tankards. Reuben stopped talking, guilt and shame flooding his face. Preston set a beer on the table by Reuben and stepped back to lean against the wall.

The men shifted in their chairs, not knowing quite where to look or how to proceed.

*So, the Holts lost their farm. And Preston's wife....*Her throat closed. *Enough. I'll bet this isn't how Reuben pictured his birthday evening. Best to carry on as if he never said anything. To call attention to him would only make it worse.*

She cast a smile about the table. "Everyone set on drinks? Here Doc, I'll take care of your brandy." She filled it and set the glass before him. "Now, let's play, shall we?" Inez sat down and slid the cards to Jed.

Reuben reached into his pocket, and pulled out a worn photocase. He laid it on the table, one large chafed hand covering it, as if to protect it from view.

Jed shuffled for a long time, smirking at Reuben. Inez was sorely tempted to kick Jed under the table to wipe the smile off his lips.

Evan cleared his throat and picked up the conversational thread from before Reuben's outburst. "Well, I'm not normally a church-going man, but I tell you, I got down on my knees and sang hallelujah when I heard the Rio Grande planned to reach town by mid-July. It's going to be a blessing for businesses that depend on a timely delivery of goods."

"And there are other businesses," drawled Jed, "set to go under, thanks to the ruthless machinations of—"

Inez kicked him in the ankle.

Jed jumped and glared at Inez.

"Is it time for me to cut the cards, Mr. Elliston?" She smiled sweetly at him. "Just set them down, right there, and I'll be most happy to accommodate you. There now. Well, gentlemen, while Mr. Elliston deals, I'd like to propose a toast to young Mr. Holt here." She turned in her chair and held up her glass of bourbon. "Wishing you the best on your birthday and the luck of the draw."

Reuben belatedly raised his beer. Fine crystal tinked against heavy-bottomed glass. The other players, except for Jed, followed suit.

Inez admired the amber color of the liquid in her glass. Her gaze slid over the rim to Preston, who was leaning against the wall, watching the proceedings with what appeared to be amusement. His eyes met hers just as she let the first taste slip between her lips, intense, warm, and smooth, right through the finish, with a hint of cloves lingering on her tongue.

Inez put down her drink. "Ante up, gentlemen."

Coins and paper money formed a small pile in the center of the table.

She picked up her cards. As was her habit, she waited to look at her own hand, preferring to take a reading of the other players as they first viewed what Dame Fortune had blessed—or cursed—them with.

Evan adjusted his glasses. His expression changed not at all, but Inez noted that he took longer than usual examining the cards. *Must be a difficult hand to work with.* Cooper's eyebrows shot up, then quickly returned to normal. *Ah, he must be sitting well.* Jed lifted the merest corner of his cards, leaving them face down on the table. He looked around, his eyes heavy lidded, expressionless. However, Inez could feel, ever so slightly, the vibration of his leg jittering up and down next to hers. *Hmmm. Something's up.* And Reuben—

The boy held his cards close and looked around the table. With a hint of belligerence, he said, "I'm ready. How about you-all?"

Jed sighed and looked at Evan. Evan adjusted his glasses. "Check."

Cooper pursed his lips, then said, "Five," and threw in a half eagle.

"I'll raise you five," Reuben said immediately.

Inez looked at her lackluster hand. Ten high. No chance of a straight. No reason to throw money away.

She shook her head. "Folding, gentlemen." She tossed her cards in, face down, and settled back to watch the scene unfold.

Everyone else called.

Jed stayed pat. Evan exchanged three. Cooper, after some hesitation, exchanged a single card, as did Reuben.

Evan started the round with another five. Cooper matched it. Reuben said, "I'll raise you ten."

Preston stirred by the wall. Inez, preparing to down the last half measure of her drink, paused. Jed's jittering stopped. *Ah, he's going to make his move.*

"I'll raise you twenty," said Jed.

Evan pulled off his glasses and set his cards down. "I'm out."

Cooper hesitated. Inez wondered if he was debating a bluff. *He must not have anything, or he'd not hesitate so long.*

Apparently realizing that his hesitation was a giveaway, Cooper raised a hand in surrender, then threw his cards down. "Fold."

Reuben stared hard at Jed, his left hand squeezing the photocase spasmodically. "You're bluffing, mister. You ain't got nothing."

Jed rocked in the chair, looking smug. "It'll cost you to find out."

Reuben set his cards face down and dug in first one pocket, then the other, pulling out a mash of well-worn bills, a few gold and silver coins. After some silent counting, he pushed them into the middle. "I'll raise ya another five."

Inez raised her eyebrows. Although the amount in total wasn't at all unusual for a Saturday night game, she was certain that, for Reuben, this was definitely high stakes.

Jed was glaring back at him with dislike written all over his face. "Very well. And I'll raise you…ten."

Jed, don't let this get personal.

Reuben looked back at Preston, who was leaning against the wall, arms crossed, beer in hand, and said in a low urgent tone, "Hey, how much money've you got?"

Preston stirred from the wall and came forward. "You plan on paying me back from next week's wages?"

"The whole next month's more like. You got thirty dollars?"

Holt shook his head, then pulled money from his pocket. "You're lucky today's payday, son."

Reuben took the handful of gold coins from Preston and slammed them on the table. Inez winced, thinking of the mahogany finish.

"Raise twenty-five."

Jed looked down at his remaining cash. Inez could almost see him thinking: *The night is young. Reuben's only in for one game. I could be out the rest of the evening, if Reuben does have something better.*

Jed waved a hand in benediction and flung down his cards. "Take it." He looked as if he was about five years old and had been forced to swallow a large dose of cod liver oil.

Reuben let out an ear-splitting whoop. He grabbed up the photocase, kissed the cover fervently, then gathered up the money, cramming it into his pockets. Preston tapped him on the shoulder. "Whoa there. You owe me. And Mrs. Stannert. So what's the rake?"

Inez did a quick mental calculation and said, "Ten dollars."

Preston pulled a gold eagle from Reuben's winnings and set it on the table. "Much obliged."

Reuben drank down the dregs of the beer, his face glazed and shiny with excitement. He turned to Preston. "Reckon I got enough now to go down the street."

Preston settled his hat. "If that's how you want to spend your money."

"Damn straight!" he yelled, then glanced guiltily at Inez. "Sorry, ma'am. Thanks for lettin' me play in your game." He muttered something to the rest that sounded like "a pleasure" and hotfooted it out of the room.

Preston lingered at the door and smiled at Inez. "Don't know if him winning was good or bad, but it'll give him something to talk about 'round the tents later." His gaze caused her cheeks to flush as if brushed by a warm breeze. He nodded to the men around the table, saving a cold stare for Jed, and left, leaving silence like a vacuum behind him.

Inez stared at Reuben's cards, left in a haphazard pile face down on the table.

She looked up at her players. All eyes were locked on Reuben's cards.

"Gentlemen, you did *not* see me do this." She reached over and flipped over Reuben's hidden hand.

A busted straight.

Chapter Twenty-Seven

"How'd the evening go?" Reverend Sands pulled Inez's hand into the crook of his arm as they turned away from the Silver Queen and began making their way up Harrison.

It was two thirty in the morning, but it could have been ten at night for the press of people still out and about. The crackling of firecrackers and stray pops and booms of guns and black powder had lessened considerably. Still, Inez wagered that many folks in Leadville were not getting their full measure of sleep that night, even with nightcaps pulled down around their ears and their heads under feather pillows.

She pulled the collar of her cloak tight to keep the cold from seeping down the back of her neck. "We had a pretty good night, all in all. We pulled in a decent amount from the bar. And the usual game went well." She leaned against him as she walked, feeling the solidness of his arm tight against her side. "Even Jed behaved himself. Well, mostly."

"Mostly?"

She described Doc and Jed's haranguing, Preston and Reuben's short visit to the game room, and Reuben's triumphant departure. "The consensus at the table was that Reuben proceeded to celebrate at Frisco Flo's," she concluded.

"Mmm-hmmn."

She narrowed her eyes at him. "What does that sound mean?"

"I understand Flo's offering special discounts to veterans of the war. A patriotic gesture in honor of the holiday."

"You understand? Does that mean Madam Flo had the poor taste to extend said offer to you?" She heard the snap in her tone, but didn't care. She started to move away.

The reverend covered her gloved hand with his own, holding it in place. "Sometimes, Mrs. Stannert, you're as prickly as a porcupine rattling its quills." He stopped speaking while they walked past the Board of Trade Saloon. Its requisite brass band was braying loud enough to drown out all sound from the streets.

As soon as her ears stopped ringing, Inez said, "Are you going to tell me you went to preach to Flo and the girls on one of their busiest nights of the year? What humbug."

"'O ye of little faith.' Matthew 8:26. Flo and her women haven't been to church for over a month. I stopped by to remind them that the mission will soon be open and that they're also welcome at Sunday services."

"Welcome." Inez gave a short laugh. "I'd say the majority of parishioners are a whole lot less welcoming than you are. So, were the Holts there? Did Reuben celebrate his birthday at the whorehouse?"

"I don't see what it matters, either way."

She twisted her mouth shut. *Truly, what business is it of mine? It's not as if I care.* But the image that flashed through her mind was not of Reuben, lounging in Flo's Turkish-appointed parlor, but of Preston Holt.

She pushed the image away with a guilty mental shove and focused instead on the closeness of the reverend's body to hers as they finished walking the few short blocks to her home.

Taking the two steps up to her little porch, she fished her key out of her pocket. Another low boom echoed from the hills of the mining district. "They'll have nothing left to celebrate with tomorrow, much less fire off at work Monday morning," she remarked, unlocking the door.

"I expect most will be out of town for the Fourth. The races. Picnics. Sure you won't join us?"

"Hard to say." She entered and put the key on the small end table. "Oh, I almost forgot to mention. Weston came by tonight.

He caused quite a scene in front of the saloon. Doc showed up and took him to the jail. Said he'd be safe there."

Sands muttered something under his breath as he shed his hat and coat and hung them on the coatrack.

"What?"

"I said I've got little patience left for Weston Croy. I know that's not right. 'In your patience you will possess your soul.' Luke 21:18. I'll be back in a minute." He headed toward the kitchen. She heard the rear door squeak as he went out.

Inez wandered into her small parlor and turned to the sidebar. She ran a hand over the brandy decanter, still half full, debating, before turning away and advancing on her piano. She picked up the soft gray shawl draped over her piano stool and wrapped it around her shoulders. Sitting on the stool, Inez loosened the laces of her shoes, kicked them off under the piano, and set her stockinged feet upon the cool metal of the foot pedals. Idly, she paged through a stack of sheet music until, about a third of the way down, "La Campanella" surfaced.

Liszt.

Her mother's face swam into memory, looking as it had nearly twenty years ago. Her hazel eyes shone, her face alive with unaccustomed energy as she described watching Franz Liszt play in France. "The God of the piano. That's what they called him in Portugal, Inez. I'll never forget watching him play "La Campanella." It was a highlight of my Grand Tour, before I met your father."

Entranced, Inez had asked her mother to play it for her.

Her mother threw back her head and gave one of her rare laughs. "Oh Inez, my child. It's not a piece I would ever attempt. It's far too difficult."

All of eleven years old, Inez rose to the challenge. "Someday, then, I'll learn to play it, Mama. And I'll play it for you."

Her mother frowned. The animation fled her face, leaving the stern expression so familiar to Inez. "It's not an appropriate piece for a woman—or, in your case, a girl—to play. Liszt composed for the masculine pianist. The intervals, the agility and accuracy required…it's beyond feminine capabilities. Practice your Mendelssohn, Inez. When you're ready for something more difficult, we'll move on to Chopin."

As soon as she could after leaving home, Inez bought Liszt's "Grandes Etudes de Paganini." And no matter what she'd left behind later—possessions, precepts, and principles discarded during the tumultuous decade of traveling with Mark—she'd stayed faithful to Liszt. And Chopin, and Mendelssohn.

In the parlor silvered with moonlight, she set the music on the stand, lifted the keyboard lid, set her fingers on the keys, and flexed her feet on the pedals.

Measures five through thirteen were difficult. The grace notes in measure fourteen made it even worse. She hesitated over the fingering and returned again and again to the quick two-octave jumps, her frustration mounting over each stumbled phrase or clashing note.

The reverend's voice came from behind her. "That doesn't sound like music to relax by." His hands settled on her shoulders.

The tension, which had been mounting up her shoulder blades and into her neck, melted under his touch. She tried the leaps again, slowly, concentrating on delivering the fingers from one chord to the other, like birds taking flight from one tree to another.

"I've not had much time to practice," she said. "No time, actually. And I'll never learn to play this if I don't work on it."

"How long have you been practicing?"

"Nigh on twelve years." She switched mid-measure, leaving Liszt behind, sliding into Beethoven's "Moonlight Sonata."

Slow, liquid notes rippled, waves in a pond.

Sands caressed her neck. She allowed her eyelids to close halfway. The music and his touch washed away the tightness in her stomach, the burning in her eyes, the sadness in her soul. A sweet ache stirred deep inside.

His fingers curled into her hair, taking hold, pulling her head gently back.

He bent over to kiss her throat. Her mouth.

The chords beneath her hands died, the last note drifting into the night.

Chapter Twenty-Eight

"I hope they keep him locked up through the Fourth and beyond." Inez stood at the saloon's Harrison Avenue doors, cup of coffee in hand, and looked north up the street toward the jail.

All manner of four-wheeled conveyances filled the street, carrying families, church and social groups, and every proper young woman in Leadville to day trip destinations like Twin Lakes, Soda Springs, and the Mount Massive Hotel. Parasol fringe fluttered, whips cracked, babies cried, and picnic baskets and blankets jostled on the laps of passengers as wheels bumped over the street's hardened ridges of baked mud. Men on horseback wove through the wagons and buggies, the younger fellows shouting and showing off for the women, who clung to the seats, lace handkerchiefs held to noses to block out the dust.

"My God," she said to herself. "Isn't anyone staying in town?"

"Sure." Abe came and stood beside her, drying his hands on his apron. "When the Fairplays come this afternoon, we'll be jumpin'. None of the theaters are open today, so we'll be the only game in town." He followed Inez's gaze. "Who's in jail?"

"Weston Croy." She went back inside and liberated a bottle of whiskey from the backbar. "Let's go to the office for a moment. I need to talk with you before I start balancing the books."

Upstairs, Inez unlocked the office door. The saloon's cat, a calico that preferred soaking up the sun to hunting rodents, squeezed past her skirts to claim a warm spot on the braided rug.

Inez sat at the desk and brushed the orange and black cat hairs from her dark blue skirts. "The cat is shedding dreadfully. A clear sign that winter's finally over. For a month or two."

Abe lowered himself to the sofa, knees creaking. "That Weston fellow's bothering you some, sounds like."

"More than some."

Abe listened gravely as she related her previous encounters with Weston.

"He thinks, at least sometimes, that he's still in the war," Inez finished.

"Man sounds outta control."

"Reverend Sands tried to help Weston for a while. But it seems now as if he's washed his hands of him."

"That's right. Your reverend was a Union man." Abe leaned back on the settee.

"Like you."

Abe hmmphed. "Partly. At the start of the war, I was wearin' the gray."

Inez stared. "You fought for both sides? But…why? What were you doing on the side of the Confederacy?"

Abe shrugged. "I was a free man, like my pappy. When the call came, I joined the Louisiana Native Guards. Mostly, I was protectin' my home, the home of my family. And protectin' our property too, there was that. There was thinkin' among the colored that everything we had might just get taken away if we didn't step forward. I was defendin' Louisiana, didn't give a hang for the Confederacy. When New Orleans was occupied by Federal troops, they called for free colored to join the Union Army, and—" Abe spread his hands— "plenty of familiar faces from the original Guards started wearin' blue. It was a long time ago, Inez. My point is, lots of men saw hard times. Your reverend, I'm guessin' he prob'ly was in the thick of things. Most, like him, just put it behind them as best they could. Some, like this Weston, just didn't have the spine to see it through."

Inez set her coffee on the ledger. The ledger made her think of the columns of numbers—income one side, charges on the other, and how the charges could deplete, bleed a business dry, until there was nothing left. *If a man saw too much, was too much in the red, maybe there just was no way for him to come back into balance.*

"I wonder what happened that he ended up like this," Inez said to herself.

Abe rested his forearms on his thighs and cracked his knuckles. "He was talkin' 'bout the cold, right? Well, hard marchin' drove some men crazy. The waitin' did too. Almost worse than battle itself."

"Worse." Inez made an irritated gesture. "Everyone mentions the horrors of war, but no one will say. So what was it, Abe? The killing? Seeing others die?"

Abe's mouth tightened. "All right, Inez. Here's a story t' give you a taste, if'n that's what you're askin'. A soldier offered a friend sittin' next to him a drink from his canteen. Was real hot that day. The heat never bothered me too much, but some got sunsick, just plain lost their minds and motivation. Anyhow, this fella'd just reached out to hand him the canteen when a shell hit. Blew his friend's head off, leavin' him sittin' there, canteen held out, and him all covered with blood and brains."

Inez raised a hand to her throat.

"Yep." Abe cracked his knuckles again, then wiped his palms on his black worsted pants. "And that soldier didn't end up pissin' hisself every time a gun went off, like that Weston fella."

"Abe."

He looked up, tension etching his face.

"Did that happen to you?"

"Nope. Happened to Mark Stannert, Inez. Your husband."

Her throat closed. It took a minute to work out the words. "He never told me."

"Reckon not. It's not the kind of story men share with their womenfolk."

She turned and stared out the window, at the hulk that was Mount Massive. "Do you think....Could that have something to do with Mark's disappearance? Maybe some memory set him off. Like what happened to Weston."

Abe shook his head. "I never saw Mark havin' that kind of trouble. But if old Unconditional Surrender Grant comes to town, I'm wonderin' if there won't be a whole lot more men havin' nightmares."

Two hours and a quarter of a bottle later, Inez ran an ink-stained fingertip down the last column of figures, double-checking her addition, then slammed the ledger closed. She leaned back in her chair, staring out the window at the rooftops along State Street and the mountains beyond. A cool breeze slipped in through the half-opened window and shifted a few papers on her desk. She set the ounce of pure silver that served as a paperweight on top, then flexed her fingers absently to work the kinks out of her cramped hand.

The street was nearly deserted.

I surely hope the Fairplays will bring them in. If they're out there.

Discouraged, Inez rested her hand on the recent photo of William her sister had sent, propped open where she could see him while she worked. She traced the contours of his round face, touched the nose in the image. *And what are you doing today for the holiday, little William? Perhaps playing by the ocean. Giving your Grandmere fits with sticky hands, having eaten your fill of ice-creams. And I am so far away.*

Inez grasped the bottle of whiskey and added more to the cup, which by now had lost even the tinge of coffee.

A knock on the door startled her. A splash mottled the leather cover of the ledger. "Yes?" She grabbed a piece of blotting paper to wipe the cover.

Sol opened the door. "Mrs. Stannert, the Fairplays are here. Turns out, the missus needs a place to gussy up. Mr. Jackson said...." He hesitated here, looking over his shoulder as if to determine whether he really needed to continue, then looked back. "Well, he thought she could use your room. In back."

Her grip on the bottle tightened as she stared at the hapless bartender. "Oh. He did, did he?"

"I guess it's the only place with a mirror, and a pitcher and washstand and stuff. Plus it's the only place she could, hmm, change." Sol seemed uncomfortable plowing into these areas of the feminine sphere.

"And I guess Mr. Jackson is too much of a coward to discuss this with me himself."

"Well, he's talking with Mr. Fairplay and—"

"Never mind!" she barked. She shot out of her chair and in a dozen steps was across the office to the door that led to her private room. Once inside, she scanned the area. Her wardrobe stood open, her and Mark's clothes, hanging side by side. She strode to the wardrobe, grabbed a wide-brimmed straw hat from the top shelf, and slammed the twin doors shut, twisting the handles closed with a vicious yank. She picked up the pitcher, saw there was still water in it, and slammed it down.

Grabbing her cloak off the peg, she stormed out of the back room. "Sol, please inform Mr. Jackson that this was *not* part of our bargain. Mrs. Fairplay may use my room. I suppose I have no choice. But she'd better not rifle through my things. I'm off to the church picnic. I believe I'd rather listen to the church women prattle than hear Mrs. Fairplay pontificate about life on the stage and warble her lines." She paused to drain her cup.

Inez turned to go, then stopped, retreated back to the desk, seized the near empty bottle, and slammed down the rolltop to hide the bills and ledger from prying eyes.

"Can't arrive empty-handed," she said tersely.

Sol stared at the bottle in her hand, clearly horrified.

"Oh, stop staring, Sol. I'm not going to bring a bottle of liquor to the church picnic. I'm taking this downstairs so that Maude Fairplay is not tempted to take a little liquid courage on the house before emoting. Please go ask Bridgette to wrap up a cherry pie for the church."

Sol took the stairs down two at a time, whether anxious to fulfill her request or escape her ire, she didn't know.

Inez stepped carefully from tread to tread, the distance seeming to grow and collapse with each step. C.A. stood by the bar, snapping his pocketwatch open and shut, open and shut. Maude was holding forth to a rapt knot of drinkers, who gazed upon her as if she were visiting royalty. Behind Maude, glancing around nervously, a tiny woman with the Orient in her features balanced an enormous valise and two hatboxes, while gripping the handle to a small, wheeled trunk.

Deciding that the missus was otherwise engaged, Inez focused on the mister first. "Mr. Fairplay." She drew out his name in a drawl and held out a hand in greeting. "Soooo sorry I won't be in attendance at your first performance here at the Silver Queen. Alas and alack. I have, however, a church social to attend."

He swept off his pearl-gray derby, and bowed over her hand extravagantly. Inez glared at Abe over the top of Mr. Fairplay's head and continued, "Mr. Jackson and Mr. Isaacs will take excellent care of you and help monitor the crowd that will no doubt be beating down the doors any minute to attend your performance. And here comes Michael O'Malley as well. It appears we have plenty of extra hands this afternoon to handle the adoring throngs."

Bridgette's eldest son was heading toward Inez, a brown-paper-wrapped pie-shaped bundle in his hands, gaze riveted on Maude.

"Thank you, Michael." Inez relieved him of the pie and turned to Maude, who was waving her fan in a dramatic fashion. "Ah, Mrs. Fairplay. The room upstairs is ready for you. I look forward to hearing a review of your performance on my return this evening."

She turned to Abe, adjusting her hat. "You won't miss me at all, I'm sure." Her eyes swept around the half-full room. "Probably no one else will either."

Inez turned and swept through the door, pie held high before her.

Chapter Twenty-Nine

She'd barely rounded the corner to Chestnut when she spied a buckboard rattling her way, holding Susan, Terry O'Loughlin, Mrs. Flynn, a couple of other young women she didn't recognize, and Mr. Braun at the reins.

"What good timing!" Susan's brown eyes were shining under a broad-brimmed hat that was a cousin to Inez's, except for a green ribbon surrounding the crown. "We were just going to drive past your...." Susan looked around at the other women in the wagon. "Well. And here you are! Mr. Braun had offered to see if you could come."

"As you see, I can indeed."

Braun pulled the horses to a stop and set the brake, before stepping from the wagon. "Mrs. Stannert," he said gruffly. "An honor." He took the pie from her, passed it to Miss O'Loughlin, and gave her a hand up into the wagon.

Inez settled next to Susan and said in a low voice, "Your landlady is coming?"

Susan grabbed the wooden seat as the buckboard jerked forward. "I mentioned this picnic to her and she expressed an interest," Susan whispered back. "She said it sounded like a proper event, and even convinced some of the other boarders to come along."

Inez twisted in her perch to see the women seated behind her. Mrs. Flynn sat, parasol upraised, its fringe fluttering. Her pale striped summer dress was hemmed with layers of knife pleats and ruches, looking, Inez thought, more appropriate for a tea in the parlor than a picnic by the springs. Mrs. Flynn was observing the street scene with interest, the ribbons of her bonnet streaming down the back of her neck. She acknowledged Inez with a nod and smile. "Mrs. Stannert, good to see you again. It's been so long since I've been out to a social. It was very kind of Miss Carothers to invite me and the other ladies." She leaned forward and said in a confidential tone to Inez, "I recently completed two years of mourning for my departed husband. Otherwise, I would have declined."

"I brought some lemons." Susan nudged a net bag at her feet. "We can make lemonade at the springs."

"I've not been to Soda Springs before, Mr. Braun." Mrs. Flynn cocked her head and twirled her parasol in a manner that Inez thought positively coquettish. "How far do we have to go?"

"Just five miles. We go on the Boulevard. It is a very smooth ride. Just one steep hill, not so bad." He turned the horses at Third and headed west.

Inez clamped a gloved hand to her flapping straw hat so it wouldn't take flight. As the buckboard left West Third Street proper and approached the toll gate, she marveled at the road— sixty feet wide, smooth, solid, and amazingly free of dust—no longer the crooked "Lunatics Lane" from a year ago. The sun, the gentle breeze, the chattering and laughing of the women around her all conspired to improve her disposition.

Once they arrived, Inez and Mr. Braun positioned several blankets in the shade of some pines. Susan, still relying on her cane, settled on a picnic blanket with Mrs. Flynn nearby. The boarders oohed and aahed over the scenery. Several decided to wander the trails and explore the soda and iron springs.

After shaking out the last blanket, Inez looked up at the forested slopes of Mount Massive. She took a deep breath. The sharp, dusty scent of pine cleared her lungs and her mind.

"Inez, would you take these over to the tables?" Susan indicated the bag of lemons and the cherry pie on the blanket. As

Inez retrieved them, Susan added in a low voice, "And maybe you could find Reverend Sands? I'd like to introduce him to Mrs. Flynn and the teachers from the boardinghouse. I'm hoping they'll eventually join our church."

Inez smiled at Susan. "I've no doubt that, once they meet him, they'll be singing in the choir by next Sunday."

She strolled over to the long tables where Mrs. Warner, presiding over the desserts, was guarding pies, sweets, and melting ice cream from a gaggle of small boys. Inez caught the tail end of what sounded like a lecture in nutrition. "When those plates are clean as a whistle and your mothers say so, then you can have some. And that goes for you too, Bradley." She took an ineffectual swat at a red-headed youngster who made a successful grab-and-run with a handful of candies. The boys scattered.

Inez handed the flustered woman the pie and lemons, inquiring, "Have you seen the reverend?"

Mrs. Warner looked around distractedly, adjusting her bonnet, which was sliding dangerously over one ear. "He was here just a while ago. Oh yes. Miss Snow wanted to talk with him. I think they headed off in that direction." She pointed toward one of the paths leading toward the springs.

Inez nodded her thanks, observing that Bradley and the rest were approaching from the rear, in what looked like an attempt to take the dessert table with a flanking maneuver.

She made her way down the path, enjoying the mountain air and sunshine. Children's voices trilled above the lower pitched notes of the grown-ups. All receded behind her, and the song of birds took up the volume.

Granite slabs—some no bigger than a stepping stone, others the size of a small shed—were scattered among the trees. Inez stopped a moment, listening, trying to determine if what she heard was the murmuring of voices or perhaps a spring nearby or maybe both.

"Oh *please* say yes!"

There was no mistaking Birdie's voice. Inez frowned and looked to the left. About twenty feet away was a large granite boulder.

Inez took a few silent steps, keeping the trees between her and the stone.

The sigh of boughs in the breeze mingled with the susurration of running water beyond the granite.

Birdie's beseeching face came into view, along with the back of the reverend's shoulder and frock coat.

What is he saying? Inez paused behind one of the larger pines and strained to hear, but his voice was too low. From Birdie's face, however, it appeared that his answer was not to her liking.

Inez wavered, trying to decide on a course of action.

Birdie seized his hand, clutching it to her breast. "Don't say that. Oh, you don't know, you just don't know how I feel." Her blue eyes were imploring. Tears began to slide down her cheeks.

Another low murmur.

Inez sensed a subtle shifting of stance between the two figures.

Something giving way.

The reverend extracted his hand from hers, raised it to her face, brushing away a tear.

She lifted her face to his—

Inez's stomach twisted in a sharp somersault. She braced a hand on the tree trunk, the bark rough, sticky with sap.

Turning away, she stared down the path she'd come up. Numb. But knowing that the rage would come.

Lumbering toward her, still a goodly distance away, was Herr Braun, carrying two bowls. The white ceramic flashed hot in the sunlight, a beacon approaching.

Inez retreated hastily from the boulder field, nearly running back down the path as if she'd disturbed a hornet's nest.

Braun held out a bowl of melting ice cream. "Mrs. Stannert. I was looking for you. The bookseller's wife said this way—"

"Mr. Braun." She seized his arm, ignoring the proffered bowl. "I find that I'm not feeling well. Not at all. May I impose on you for a ride back to town?"

"Surely. Surely." He hesitated, then juggled the two bowls into one hand. The metal handle of a spoon caught a sunbeam, reflecting a needle of light sharp as betrayal into her eye.

Inez covered her face, blocking out the stab of light.

"Ach, Mrs. Stannert." His concern sounded genuine. Hesitantly, he took her by the arm. "*Erlauben Sie mich, bitte.* Allow me. Please." He led her back to the picnic grove. They passed a shrieking knot of children, all waiting their turn on a long single-strand rope swing. The girl in possession of the swing had wound the rope up and was now twirling—faster and faster—a clock spring unwinding, speeding up, as time rushed forward furiously. Only to overshoot, wind up in the opposite direction—and unwind again in reverse. Her skirts billowed out behind her, braid stuck straight out, her striped-stockinged legs a blur.

Inez's thoughts careened in the same frenetic fashion. *There's a reasonable explanation. I didn't see what I thought I saw. She's just a girl. He promised me.* Then, reeling the other way…*Don't make excuses for him. Oh I saw plenty enough. It's just like Mark. There was always another explanation. Another apology. And it never stopped. Never.*

"Mrs. Stannert."

Inez blinked. They were standing by the buckboard, the horses twitching their ears and shifting, shivering away the flies that buzzed around them.

Braun let go of her elbow and pulled down the step. "Please." He helped her up into the wagon. "I'll be right back."

He bustled over to the tables, left off the dessert bowls, and stopped to confer with Susan. Susan's eyes widened. She looked at Inez and struggled to stand. Inez shook her head and motioned her back down. Susan settled reluctantly. Braun gestured, and Inez filled in the approximate meaning: to town, back right away. Susan nodded, gave him a glass, and waved at Inez, who gave a half-wave in return.

Braun brought the lemonade to Inez and said simply, "For helping, perhaps," before picking up the reins and attending to the business of getting the wagon back onto the road. The space of silence between them widened as Braun headed the horses back to town. Soda Springs and the noise of cheerful picnickers faded behind them. Suddenly thirsty, Inez drained the lemonade, thankful for the coolness.

"Better?" Braun asked a few minutes later.

"Some. Thank you."

He was quiet for a moment, then said gruffly, "I hoped to talk with you. But maybe this is not the right time."

She looked at him, dazed. "You wished to talk with me?" She could not imagine on what grounds their lives might have a common intersection, aside from the church.

He cleared his throat. "I know you are building in your saloon. It is your saloon, yes?"

She turned to look at him full on.

"I mean, you own the business?"

"I own it with my business partner, Mr. Jackson."

Braun's eyebrows shot up. "*Der Neger?* He is in the business with you?"

"If I interpret your questions correctly, yes, Abe is a colored. And yes, we are business partners, half and half." Inez waited for the coda. *If he says anything that hints of disapproval or condemnation, I will get off this wagon and walk.*

Braun clicked and snapped the reins. "Well then. I propose to make you and Herr Jackson a good deal on lumber."

She relaxed a little, glad that she did not have to fight that battle, at least. "I'll need to discuss it with him."

"Ah, but my terms are good. I can give you a deal. But only for the next two weeks."

"Two weeks....Before the railroad arrives?"

They'd reached the steep hill leading up to town. Braun snapped the reins again, with more vigor. The horses began to labor up the rise. "*Verdammte* railroad!" he muttered. "*Scheisskopf* Palmer." He stopped, looked guiltily at Inez. "Excuse me. I lose my temper when thinking of this. I must close my business. So the stock must go."

"Close your business?" Inez felt as if she'd fallen through a rabbit hole into some crazy world. She'd only wanted to escape from the picnic as quickly as possible, away from the sight of

Birdie Snow and Justice Sands in each other's arms. But now Braun had suddenly metamorphosed from a quiet, rather stiff gentleman to spouting what sounded like Teutonic swear words and announcing he was throwing over his business.

"But, weren't you talking to the church about new pews? I remember you said something about green wood."

"I hoped. I hoped I could persuade the church to buy soon. Ach, it's no use. I cannot hold on any longer. The committee, it is too slow, and now, it's too late. I cannot keep bleeding money. And once the railroad comes, no one will want my lumber, unless I sell at a loss. They bring it in cheaper than I can sell. Already, I cannot cover costs. It's only a matter of time. *Ich werde bankrott sein.*"

She wasn't entirely certain about the last statement, but suspected it had something to do with being bankrupt. The sulfur scent of the smelters grew stronger; the city limits were nearly upon them. "But, don't you own more than the sawmill? I thought you have a charcoal business as well."

"No charcoal," he said bitterly. "The trees are gone in the gulch to make it with. And there is no time to move the business. Also ruined by the railroad. More charcoal, they bring it up from the south. So much of it. If I could have more time, slowed them down." He cut himself off abruptly. "Where do you wish to go?" They had arrived at the corner of Chestnut and Harrison.

"If you wouldn't mind, West Fourth Street, and about one block down."

Braun turned the wagon, forcing the horses to fall in line behind a buggy.

They approached State Street; Inez risked a glance at the Silver Queen. From what she could see through the dusty window, the place looked packed.

She turned and caught Braun staring at the saloon as well. He looked at her with a bitter smile. "Frau Stannert. You are a businesswoman. A good one. I have watched your business since I arrived in Leadville, six months ago. It does well. You make the right decision to expand. I bought my businesses, thinking it would make me rich. But I was wrong. The railroad—*verdammte* Rio Grande. I should have seen what its coming would mean. How it brings in a flood of materials at cheap prices. But I was blind with greed. And hope. Now, I only hope I can escape with enough capital to start over."

He stopped talking, concentrating on turning the horses and wagon across traffic to West Fourth.

When they reached her house, Inez said, "Thank you, Mr. Braun. I appreciate your kindness in bringing me home. And your frankness."

"*Bitte schön*, Mrs. Stannert. You're welcome." He set the brake. "And I would appreciate if you would talk with Herr Jackson about my offer. Soon."

Chapter Thirty

Inez combed out Lucy's black mane, grateful for the dimness of the stall, the patience of her animal. "I'm glad I came to see you," she whispered, working the long-toothed comb through the coarse strands. "I hope you'll forgive me for not bringing a treat nor taking you for a ride."

It was enough to just be in the silent livery, without having to talk to anyone. No sooner had the buckboard and Mr. Braun departed than she'd realized she dreaded going into her home. *To do what? Pound on the piano? Drink more than I should and start throwing things around?*

Going to the saloon also held no appeal. Having to run the gauntlet of customers in festive moods. Watching the Fairplays or, even worse, having to make small talk with Maude upstairs afterward. She did not trust herself to remain civil or sober.

So, she'd fled to the livery and Lucy. It was dark, quiet. All the carriages and most of the horses were gone. Neither Hollis nor Jack was in sight.

Inez stroked Lucy's nose. The horse pushed her muzzle into Inez's hand, perhaps not believing that there wasn't a lump of sugar or an apple yet to appear. Inez dropped the comb onto an upside-down bucket that served as a makeshift table and picked up the currycomb.

She began brushing Lucy's coat in rhythmic circular motions, speaking low and steady. "Well, girl. It's just you and me again.

What is it with men? None have a lick of sense when it comes to women. I swear, if Braun hadn't shown up, I might have pulled the Smoot out of my pocket and shot them both!"

"Horses got way more sense than men 'round women."

Inez whirled around to find One-Eyed Jack draped over the stall door, looking bleary. Straw stuck to the right shoulder and arm of his rusty black sack coat. A strand hung crooked from the brim of his dented derby.

"Jack! I didn't know you were here. Is Hollis around?"

"Gone. Races. Racin' Duke." He gestured with the bottle in his left hand toward the back of the livery, where Hollis' pet stallion, a rich chestnut sorrel, had his stall. Inez noticed that the bottle held in his three-fingered clasp was labeled "Jack Daniels Belle of London."

"Belle of London?" she exclaimed. "You certainly know how to celebrate."

"Yyyyyep." He held out the bottle to her.

She slipped her hand out of the currycomb, took the bottle, wiped the lip off with a sleeve, and took a mouthful. It exploded in her mouth, searing her throat on the way down. She coughed, handed the bottle back.

Jack took a swig, apparently impervious to the firepower of the alcohol.

She ran a hand along Lucy's back and felt Lucy's muscles shiver under her touch. "So where did you come by that libation?"

"A present. From Eli. Afore he left. 'Cause of my name. I was savin' for somethin' shpeshal." Exhausted from stringing so many words together, Jack leaned heavily on the gate and set his chin on the top bar as if searching for a way to hold himself perpendicular.

"Your name? Jack Daniels?"

"Dan-iel." He emphasized the last syllable. "Belle 'cause… my wife was from the North. Like his."

"Eli was a fine man."

Jack held the bottle back out to her. "Real fine."

She took the bottle, but didn't drink. "I thought Eli fought for the South."

Jack hiccupped and slowly nodded.

"Hollis said they fought together."

"Nope. Don't think so. Eli wasn't Texas. Missouri sniper."

"Eli Carter was a sniper for the Confederates? In Missouri?" *Missouri again.*

"Sharpshooter. Ninth Missouri." He waved the bottle desultorily. "In the war."

"Hmmmm." She rested a hand on Lucy's warm flank and pondered how best to profit from Jack's unusual loquaciousness. "Are you saying Eli's no longer a proponent of the Southern cause?"

"Naw. Swore off. Gave up. Got married. Saw her picture once. Be-ooo-ti-ful. Like my Gustine." His long face got even longer. "Eli 'n me. We put the war behind." He looked down at his hand with the missing digits. "Gave it too much t' give it any more."

"But Hollis and Eli got along, yes?"

He looked mournfully at the bottle. "States' rights, yeah, they agreed. Hell, me too, an' I'm no secesher. But they were fightin' all the time. Hollis havin' conniptions 'bout Rio Grande and the big bugs—Palmer, Snow."

"But they were business partners."

Jack sighed. Beneath Inez's hand, Lucy heaved an equine equivalent, as if to share in Jack's pain. "Big mistake. Yellin' all the time." He waved the bottle. "'Bout that flag." The amber liquor sloshed.

"What flag, Jack?" *Maybe Hollis had something to do with Eli leaving.*

"Flag up there." He gestured toward the front of the livery. Toward the office and the living quarters.

Inez remembered the shape on the wall, which she thought a quilt or blanket.

Eli rattled on. "Hollis said, keep it up. Eli said, take it down. Hollis said, damn you son of a bitch." He looked up, attempting to focus on Inez. "Sorry, Mrs. Stannert. Shouldn'ta said that."

"What happened then?"

"Hollis…wouldn't back down."

"So Eli quit the business and left town? Because they didn't get along?"

Jack frowned. "Couldn't agree on railroad right-of-way. But there was more. Got the gun. Got…a letter. Sold the gun. And left. Left real fast."

Foreboding crawled up the back of Inez's neck. "What gun?"

Another sorrowful sigh. "Real fine gun. Sharps rifle."

Inez was silent, trying to digest the possibility that the Sharps she'd bought at the mercantile on a whim might have belonged to Eli Carter. She finally asked, "So, why did Eli leave?"

Jack shrugged eloquently. "Hollis followed."

"Followed Eli?"

"Yep. Saddled up 'n followed when he found out. Hoooooo, he was mad. Eli didn' even tell him he was goin'. Just told," he burped again, "me."

"What did Hollis say when he came back?"

"Nothin'. Came back. Actin' ornery. Horse lathered up. Then later—you. With the horses 'n' burro." The firewater sloshed in the bottle as he gestured. "You left, Hollis cussed a blue streak."

Hollis followed him. Could he have been at Disappointment Gulch? I didn't see him on the road, but I could have missed him while on my way there. Inez found it hard to believe that Hollis would have something to do with Eli's apparent death or disappearance. That Hollis was capable of killing, she had no doubt. But Eli and he had spent time together, had been friends, at one time. *Still, if he was really angry….I can hardly waltz up and ask if he murdered his partner. So why did Eli leave? That might lead me to understand what happened at the gulch.*

An idea began to take shape.

"Jack." She went up to the gate, watching him closely. "You remember when I brought Eli's horse back?"

Jack's head sagged to one side. Inez, noticing the bottle was now empty, decided it might be an attempt to nod. "Do you know what happened to Eli's saddlebags?"

"Eeerrrrmmmb."

Apparently, Jack's conversation was now limited by inebriation. Inez decided to stick to yes or no questions. "Did you give them to Hollis?"

"Hell no."

"Did you take them?"

"Yyyyyep."

"Did you look through them?"

"Nnnnoooope."

"Where are they?"

Jack's arms slipped from the gate. He staggered backward and whammed into the gate of the opposite stall, then, knees melting beneath him, slipped slowly to the ground.

Inez hurried out of the stall, latched it shut, and approached Jack. With much shaking and encouraging, she roused him enough to get him standing back up, and half supported, half dragged him to the back of the livery, across from the empty stall of Hollis' racing horse.

His living quarters were a converted stall of hard-packed dirt and straw, a stool and small rickety table with a washbasin, and a bedroll on a straw tick. She managed to get him to lie down on the crude mattress. She wiggled a hand under the tick. Her fingers bumped against an object. She extracted a long knife, sheathed in leather. *Ah-ha! Could be useful if I find those saddlebags.*

Leaning over him, Inez tried once more. "Jack. Where are Eli's bags?"

Ear-racketing snores were his only answer.

Inez sighed. *I hope the nap sobers him up.* She left the stall, shut the gate behind her, and stood there, thinking.

The saddlebags are not in his room—such as it is. There's no place to hide them, if they're not under the mattress. Where else would Jack hide a set of saddlebags? The office? No, too conspicuous. Besides, that's Hollis' domain. So where does Jack spend his time, besides his room?

The stalls.

She shuddered, contemplating a search of each and every one. The tack room.

Opting for the obvious and far easier area to search, Inez made her way to the tack room, near the front of the livery.

The room smelled of sweated leather, dust, and horse. Not much in the way of equipment was present. A rig with a sprung wheel. A few saddles. A jangle of bits and bridles. A pile of saddle blankets in the corner.

Blankets.

Inez hurried to the corner and began shifting the stack, blanket by blanket. Nearly at the bottom, she struck gold.

The distinctive fur-trimmed panniers. None the worse for wear.

Hastily, with one ear to the entrance for sounds of Hollis or returning riders, Inez undid the buckles. She worried the knots that held the leather lashings tight, then gave up and sliced the thongs with Jack's knife. One saddlebag yielded a shirt, an extra pair of canvas pants, a pair of hose, and long johns. The other held a photocase of cracked leather, its covers bound with a black crepe ribbon, a packet of letters tied with a lavender ribbon and wrapped in a short length of matching purple cloth sprigged with small white flowers, a box of cartridges, and crinkled and nearly invisible in the depths of the leather bag, a much-creased thin envelope.

Inez hesitated over what to do next. Taking the bags flat-out was an iffy proposition, should Hollis come back or see her on the street with them. *But he's at the races, and they're likely to run until dark.* Still, if she should be caught in possession of them, it would be very hard to explain. And if Jack went looking for them and found them gone, she wasn't sure what he'd do. Confront Hollis, perhaps? The results of such a confrontation, she suspected, could be lethal.

She rifled through the pockets of the clothes, feeling a bit like a grave robber, finally shoving the clothes and box of cartridges back into the bag.

Next, Inez untied the black ribbon and opened the photo-case. A woman with dark hair stared out. Firm chin upraised, straightforward gaze. From what little was visible of the dress, it appeared to be made of the same cloth as was wrapped around the packet of letters. A braided lock of jet-black hair was neatly twined around the photo, framing it. Inez closed the photo and rewrapped the black ribbon around the photocase.

She turned her attention to the lone letter. The creased envelope was addressed to Elijah Carter, General Delivery, Leadville, Colorado. No return address. Postmarked June 23, from Colorado Springs. The single thin sheet of paper crinkled loudly as she pulled it out. There were no salutations. Just two lines, scrawled in pencil, in a childlike hand:

The General is coming. And others like him. Remember your oath to your brothers.

Chapter Thirty-One

The General.

Inez dropped the letter to her lap. She stared out at the tack room. Dust motes hung in the air, nearly motionless. Her first thought: *This note could help prove Susan's story, at least the part about men discussing killing a general! I should show it to Justice.*

Her second thought: *Damn Justice Sands! I'll take it to Ayres.*

After that, her thoughts charged in, too fast to number, tumbling in various directions, keying off the few words in the message. *What general are they talking about? No one knew Grant was even considering heading this way until recently. What oath? What brothers?* And finally, more soberly: *Does this really "prove" anything? And will anyone care?*

She looked at the wrapped bundle of letters. *Does Eli have brothers, family somewhere? Hollis said not. Of course, it sounds like Hollis pretty much says whatever he wants about Eli. They were friends. They fought side by side during the war. No family. And Eli's not here to set the record straight.*

She gently slid the photocase back into Eli's saddlebag. *His wife is dead, that much is clear. But maybe there ARE brothers somewhere. In which case, they should be notified of Eli's disappearance. Or death.*

Decision made, she unwound the purple cloth, laid the lone letter on top of the others, and rolled the cloth around the whole bundle of letters. She wrapped the rawhide cords back around the saddlebags, doing one turn less to allow room for quick knot-tying. She set the bags back on the short stack of blankets and piled the rest on top. Feeling fairly certain that things looked as before, she stuffed the bundle containing the letters into the pocket of her cloak, snuck Jack's knife back under his makeshift bed and snoring form, and left the livery.

Stepping through the State Street doors of the saloon, Inez found it hard to believe this wasn't a Saturday night. The bar was nearly hidden beneath elbows and a sea of glassware. The jars that held pickled eggs and crackers were empty. Every chair at every table was taken. Those who couldn't find a seat or a place at the bar held up the walls while working on beers, slices of cherry pie, and other victuals.

Michael O'Malley pushed through the kitchen passdoor, balancing a full tray of bowls, pies, and coffee mugs. His apron was askew, and his blonde hair, so carefully combed that morning, was now an unruly mop.

Behind the bar, Sol tapped a barrel of beer, a row of glasses arrayed before him. As for Abe—she hadn't seen him smiling so broadly since winning big at the races the previous summer. From what Inez could ascertain, he was mixing a handful of Brandy Smashers. The tinkling of the piano, muffled by intervening bodies and conversation, assured her that Taps was still at his post.

She wormed her way past knots of men. Solid, business types, watch chains stretching across ample bellies, off-shift miners readily identifiable by their pasty complexions and broad shoulders, men from the smelters down the road, even some men she pegged as being from the Rio Grande construction crews. A group of men she figured as money men from out of town stood apart—or as apart as they could in such crowded quarters. In their tailored suits, they looked for all the world as if they were in their gentlemen's club in New York or Chicago. Their cold eyes took in the unlikely crowd in the room. Inez could almost imagine them toting up the worth of the town for investment, using this representative slice of its workforce for a guide. A fellow she recognized as keeping company with the local silver barons did the talking. As she passed the group, she heard him say, "Now Tabor, he's got the Midas touch. The Little Pittsburg is almost worked out, no doubt about it, I can't say otherwise. But Leadville's still full of possibility and future. The silver runs here and there. Still much to be found. There's the Matchless, a real winner, going great guns, and the Chrysolite, they incorporated. Solid bankers behind the Chrysolite. Henry Post of New York. Charles Whittier and William Nichols...."

She greeted the men she knew and eventually made her way to behind the bar. She asked Abe, "Has it been this way all afternoon?"

He slid the last Smasher to a serious-faced young banker at the other side of the mahogany counter. "Was even better earlier." He flashed her a wide smile, all teeth. "Damn, but the Fairplays drew in nearly every man passin' by, even at a dollar a head. They all ponied up without a fuss and stayed to drink in the bargain. How was your church picnic?"

A vision of Sands and Birdie rose up, unbidden. Fury boiled up inside Inez like heat rising through a pot of water on a stove.

Abe's eyebrows shot up at her expression. "That good? Hmmph. Guess you should've stayed here. We could've used your help. Right, Sol?"

"Right," he grunted, shifting an empty beer keg under the bar.

"Well, I'll lend a hand now. Just let me run upstairs for a moment."

She headed for the stairs, stopping by Taps as he ended "Little Brown Jug" with an enthusiastic flourish.

He grinned up at her. "Hey, Mrs. Stannert. You sure missed a great show. But maybe they'll do it again next week."

"And what show was that?"

"Well—"

A customer appeared with a beer and handed it to Taps. "For you, fine fella. Good job."

Taps flushed happily and accepted the drink. "Thank you, sir." He took a gulp, then set it on top of the piano next to a stein overflowing with coins and crumpled paper bills. He pulled the music off the stand and handed it to Inez. "You'd like this, Mrs. Stannert. Maude—that is, Mrs. Fairplay—sang while I played these ditties from Shakespeare. Didn't know the Bard wrote songs."

She opened *Cheerful Ayres and Ballads* and scanned the score for "Come unto these yellow sands," "Full fathom five," and "Where the bee sucks."

Inez fanned herself with the music, inspecting the piano player's glowing face. "So, they did bits from *The Tempest*. And Mrs. Fairplay played Ariel? The spirit who sings these songs?"

He clasped his hands like a giddy child. "She enchanted everyone."

"Enchanted them, did she? And how far above the ankle did the enchantment go?"

His grin faded into puzzlement, then he looked abashed. "Oh. Her costume." He cleared his throat and reached for the beer. "It was artistic. Flowing, rather. Parts came up nearly to the," he avoided her eyes, "knee. But only sometimes," he added hastily. "The material...floated. Gauzy, I guess you'd call it."

"Gauzy," said Inez, picturing Maude in a swirl of silk veils and tulle, a-flowing across the floor. "Well, enough of this. I've work to do."

She hurried upstairs and made a quick examination of the office and back room. Her dressing room was neat and tidy... almost too so. The washbowl was empty, the pitcher full of clean water. An unused towel folded to one side. Retreating to the office again, she cast an eye around the room.

All looked proper, in its place.

She went to her desk to deposit Eli's letters. As she pulled up the rolltop, her gaze snagged on William's photo, still on display on top of the desk.

But not quite as she had left it.

The photo was not directly in her line of view as it had been while she worked the ledger but was now angled away. "Damn her!" Inez said fiercely.

She stuffed the bundle of letters into a pigeonhole of her desk and then closed the photocase, tenderly sliding it into another compartment, safe and out of sight.

By common consent, they agreed to close at ten. At quarter to, Jed Elliston sauntered in. Or attempted to. The crowd made sauntering extremely difficult. He finally made his way to the bar and squeezed in between two groups. "Say, Mrs. Stannert, some of your best *spiritus frumenti*, if you would."

Grumbling, she turned to examine the backbar. "You're lucky there's anything left." She rescued a bottle of Old Gideon and a glass that looked at least marginally clean and proceeded to pour.

Jed saluted her with the full glass. "Happy Fourth, Mrs. Stannert. You missed quite the show today in your establishment. Well, you can read all about it in the next issue of *The Independent*." He drank, sighed, and said, "Fine as silk. Seen the good reverend lately?"

Inez stiffened and pulled back. "No."

"Hmm." Jed swirled the liquor in the glass, casually. "Wanted to ask him what he's been up to lately."

The image of Sands and Birdie seared her memory. *So do I.* "Why?"

"Saw him Friday, in the Texas House Saloon. In a back corner with McMurtrie, Snow, Doc, and that big railroad fellow, the one who came to the game last night with the kid, but didn't play. Seemed like an odd set of ducks to be paddling in the waters together. The reverend didn't look happy either. Wondered what would bring the five of them together. Wanted to ask him about it last night, after the game. But you both slipped away before I could catch up."

"Well." She banged the cork into the bottle, a trifle harder than necessary. "Guess you'll have to ask him. Or Doc. Or Snow. Or Holt. Or McMurtrie. Now drink up, we're closing."

She turned to look at Abe, who was busy mopping the counter with a sopping bar rag. "Shall I do last call, Abe?"

"Sure."

On her way to the stairs, Inez stopped and asked Sol, "Would you walk me home tonight? Since Abe will be closing."

Sol looked at her in surprise. "Sure, Mrs. Stannert. But what about—"

"Thank you." She ascended the stairs, leaned on the balcony railing, and let the murmur of men's voices wash over her. Taking a deep breath, she announced, "Last call!"

The sea of hats tipped back, displaying disappointed faces. Someone yelled, "Now, Mrs. Stannert, don't be that way! Where we gonna go for a night cap?"

She put a hand on her hip. "If you find that you've a deeper thirst than a final night cap here can quench, there's Pap Wyman's, right across the street. And for anyone who feels the weight of sinning on a Sunday, be sure to read a few good words from the Bible he has chained next to the entrance and reflect upon their meaning."

Groans, moans, and curses reflected what they thought of that. She went into her office, her smile fading with the light as the door shut behind her.

Inez lit a coal oil lamp and took it with her into the dressing room. She washed her face, feeling the sheen of dust and sweat from the day slide from her. Patting her face dry, she examined her dress in the lamplight and decided against changing. Her linen cuffs and collar, she noted absently, needed a thorough cleaning. She left the dressing room, extinguished the lamp and stood for a moment, looking out the window. Flashes of light here and there showed that celebrating was still in full swing. She felt completely alone in a world intent on throwing one huge party. *Enough.* She left the office, locking the door.

Inez was coming down the staircase, adjusting her gloves, when she sensed a gaze upon her. She looked up to see Reverend Sands across the room by the State Street door, eyes leveled on her.

Chapter Thirty-Two

Blood rushed to her head in a deafening roar, sweeping away her rationalizations and leaving her trembling with a white-hot rage.

Breaking eye contact, she took the last two steps in a single bound. Ignoring Sol's startled "Ma'am?" Inez swung out the Harrison Avenue door and started up the street. Carriages and other conveyances were now straggling back into town, horses and drivers tired and dusty—some of those at the reins more than a little drunk, judging by the blue language flying through the air and the crack of whips. Men in groups, families tugging tired, small children, all pushed to make headway on the boardwalks.

Inez struggled to angle around a mother with a perambulator, only to be grabbed by a familiar hand.

"Whoa, Inez. Didn't you see me?" Sands swung into her line of vision. A string of firecrackers rattled in the street, sounding like rapid rifle fire.

At the sight of his face, she felt something inside her explode with an intensity of gunpowder.

"Oh I saw you. Most definitely. At the picnic." She tried to pull away, but he held tight.

"You came to the picnic?" His eyes searched her face under the street lamps. "I didn't see you."

"I could tell. And neither did Miss Snow."

He frowned.

"I saw you both. Together. Out," she gestured with her free hand, "in the woods."

Understanding dawned. "You think that Birdie and I…." He pulled her closer. "What did you see?"

She pulled back, aware of the whinnying of panicked horses in the street. Aware of the reverend's body close to hers. "Enough. Enough to know that you didn't keep your side of our bargain."

He grabbed her by both shoulders with a sudden violence that stopped her cold. "You're taking this out of context, Inez."

"Tell me about this so-called context."

He paused. "I can't go into that."

"Oh? Afraid of betraying a confidence? A confession?"

"Inez. It wasn't what it appeared to be."

"You're trying to play me for a fool," she shouted. "I won't have it!"

A hole opened in the crowd ahead of her. She ripped away from Sands and darted through.

She'd rounded the corner onto Fourth and was nearly home before he caught up with her.

"I've no time to deal with your foolishness, Inez." He sounded as if he was struggling to contain his anger. "I came tonight to tell you, I'm leaving town—"

She stopped mid-stride.

"—for a couple of weeks," he finished.

"When?"

"Tomorrow."

"Why?"

He sighed and looked up at the cloudless night sky, pricked with stars, the moon bright enough to cast shadows. His expression was grim. Exasperated. "I can't go into that."

She studied him, his strained posture. "This isn't church business."

"No." Irritation whipped through the word. Then his voice softened, became almost pleading. "Inez, trust me. Don't pursue this."

"Not church." She contemplated other possibilities. Jed's remark, less than an hour before, surfaced. "This has to do with Preston Holt, or General Palmer, the railroad, or…."

Something awful reared inside her. A certainty not of her liking twisted tight as a noose around her neck. "Is Mr. Snow involved in this?"

"Drop it, Inez."

She took a step backward. "Tell me this: Is Miss Snow party to your mysterious excursion?"

"I'll not play Twenty Questions with you." His eyes pinned her, warning. "We don't have much time together. In a few hours, I've got to pack, get ready to leave."

She sneered. "Don't forget the French envelopes. They'll come in handy, I imagine."

The shock on his face was immediately swallowed by anger. "Damn it, Inez! Birdie isn't that sort of girl."

"And I *am*?"

She broke away and ran the last few steps to her house. As she struggled to put the key to the lock Sands appeared beside her. "Inez, look at me."

She set the key to the lock and turned it. He stopped her. "Look at me."

She looked straight into his eyes. Everything in that silvered light was either black or white. With the wide brim of his hat casting a dark shadow over most of his face, she couldn't see anything beyond the furious set of his jaw.

Yet his words, when he spoke, were shatteringly gentle. "Who are you so angry at, Inez? Is it just me?"

She pushed the door open. Swung around to block his entrance. "Don't even think about inviting yourself in."

She began to close the door.

He stayed the door with one hand. "Don't shut the door on me, Inez." The words were pleading, but the tone carried a threat.

She contemplated that hand for a moment. Long fingers, square clean nails. Strong, capable. She remembered the first time he'd come to her, searching for information about a murdered man. She'd hesitated, looked first at his hand—the hand of a physical man, unsettling in a supposedly spiritual leader—and then his eyes. She'd let him into her house, and later, into her heart and her bed. She remembered all the slow savoring pleasure his hands, mouth, and body brought to her.

He must have sensed her wavering. He leaned forward, his hold on the door relaxing. "We've got to talk. Let me in. Let me explain."

A wild anger, all out of proportion, erupted within Inez. With a violence that surprised even her, she slammed the door.

Sands snatched his hand away, barely escaping crushed fingers.

Inez locked the door, then, remembering that he had a key, drew the bolt. She leaned her forehead against the wood, willing her blood to slow its ferocious pounding through her temples.

An echo of the reverend's words sprang from her past: "Darlin', darlin', let me in. We've got to talk. Let me explain, Inez." And she'd stand behind the hotel door, shaking with anger and betrayal, as Mark pleaded on the other side. Straight from some woman's bed, her perfume still lingering in his hair.

She pressed the flat of her palms to her eyes. *He's not Mark. He's not Mark.*

The quiet was overwhelming. She'd expected to hear a key in the lock, a pounding on the door.

She rubbed her eyes hard. Then cautiously opened the door.

The porch was empty.

He was gone.

Chapter Thirty-Three

The fact that the Silver Queen was able to make a hefty deposit in the bank on Monday did nothing to improve Inez's foul mood. Nor did Abe's pronouncement that the thespians would perform Friday afternoons at the saloon in addition to Sundays for at least three weeks.

"They're willin' and we're able," said Abe. "That bein' the case, we're gonna ride this train to the end of the track."

The only upside that Inez could see was that the sudden influx of fluid assets allowed her to strike a deal with Mr. Braun as well as order carpets of Axminster and Moquette velvet, in anticipation of good times ahead.

Not that she had time to idle and cogitate over rug patterns and possible new furniture for the upstairs gaming room. Perhaps because of the Silver Queen's heightened visibility, due again, as Abe kept reminding her, to the Fairplays, the saloon was busier throughout the week in general.

Inez and Abe decided to enlist Bridgette's oldest son, Michael, to help with the crowds during the Fairplay events. Bridgette expressed mixed feelings about her eldest spending more time at the saloon. "The extra money will be handy. But that means it'll be more of Mrs. Fairplay this, Mrs. Fairplay that, at the supper table. And after the costume she wore last time. Well."

Inez found herself pouring more than the usual dose of liquor into her coffee. The levels in the bottles she kept aside for her personal consumption dropped at an alarming velocity.

Tuesday afternoon, the city marshal stopped by for his customary drink "on the house," and told Inez that Weston had been released that morning. "That fella—" He tapped the side of his head. "Something's not right. Seemed better once the Fourth of July ruckus subsided. Talked to Doc. There's not much to be done." He shrugged. "It's a free country. Man can do what he wants, long as he doesn't make a public nuisance of himself."

Inez decided to make certain that her pocket pistol was close by at all times after that.

On Wednesday, Jed's newspaper printed another inflammatory article about the Rio Grande, this one on the sabotage allegedly suffered by the railroad. "A 'reliable source' told me that rockslide was no accident. That explosion blew up a couple of cars full of construction supplies," said Jed, sliding the issue toward Inez and Abe. "Spikes, fishplates, bolts and such went flying. Seems like the railroad's having trouble putting the kibosh on things."

"You're lucky McMurtrie and Snow aren't putting the kibosh on you," said Inez, pulling the paper over to read it.

"The real news comes out this weekend," said Jed.

Inez looked up and caught Jed examining himself in the backbar mirror, straightening his tie, which looked brand new.

"And what news would that be?"

Jed glanced around before replying. Even though no one was nearby, he leaned in toward her and whispered, "Grant's arrival date."

"And when's that?"

"July twentieth or thereabouts, according to Doc. But mum's the word until Saturday." He straightened up, gave the tie a last tug, then asked, eyes still on his reflection, "Say, where's Reverend Sands these days? Usually I bump into him sometime during the week. Spreading the word to nonbelievers in the Ten Mile District or Kokomo?"

She pulled back. "I've no idea," she replied tersely.

Jed was now adjusting his hat—a bowler black as ink and apparently new, since it hadn't seen enough Leadville dust to soften it to gray. "When he shows up, tell him I'm looking for him."

◇◇◇

Thursday night, after Sol walked her home, she prowled around her small home, feeling hemmed in. The sound of her shoes, striking the floorboards, echoed and rattled in her head. She sat to play the piano, but nothing came. Her timing was off. She hit the wrong keys. There seemed an emptiness to the room, to the house, that music had no magic to fill. Finally, as the clock ticked toward three in the morning, she surrendered, took the brandy from the sideboard with her to bed, and after several glasses in quick succession, fell into a stupor of a sleep.

Inez awakened a few hours later with the sunrise, feeling not altogether of this world. She dressed and dragged herself into the saloon for breakfast. Bridgette, who was in a flurry of flour, pie crusts, and canned peaches, left off to fuss over Inez and fix her an omelet plain with bread, butter, and fried potatoes. "And black coffee for you, ma'am." Bridgette whisked the eggshells off the surface of the potent brew and handed her a cup.

Abe arrived just as the wagons from Gaw's Brewery rolled up with the beer delivery. "It's gonna be another bang-up day, Mrs. Stannert," he said, checking off the order as the delivery crew brought the barrels in.

The thunderous sound of hundred-pound kegs on the plank floor proved too much for her aching head. "I'll be upstairs, looking over the books and correspondence. Let me know when the Fairplays arrive."

Inez fled to the comparative quiet of her office, pausing first to look in on the new gaming room. The walls and ceiling were finished, along with the trim. The sanded and waxed floors awaited rugs, the new chandelier was in place. The room smelled of sawdust and wax. *Good! We'll have the table and other important furniture in place in time for the railroad and Grant's arrival.*

Once in her office, she settled in her chair, pulled out William's photo, set it before her, and opened the ledger. She reached for a quill pen, then hesitated, hand hovering by the pigeonhole holding Eli Carter's letters. Inez pulled them out, closed the ledger and set it aside. Feeling a bit like a spy, she unwrapped and untied the bundled letters. A few old, faded newspaper clippings fell out, which she put aside for later. After ascertaining the oldest letters were on top, she hooked her reading glasses over her ears and began to read.

An hour and a half later, she stopped, and rubbed her eyes. Only two envelopes, their contents untouched, remained. The letters were all scripted in tiny, neat handwriting that took up every bit of the thin white paper. All of the letters began, "Dearest Husband," making, if anything, the sense of snooping even stronger. The letters were clearly one side of an ongoing conversation between Eli and his wife, Lillian.

Early letters were full of reports on daily life in the small Missouri town. How she really didn't miss the farm now, and how it was nice to have help nearby, what with Eli so far away. Lillian shortened names to mere initials, a shorthand that saved space and that Eli no doubt interpreted with ease, but which left Inez wandering lost in a forest of symbols. Mr. and Mrs. W had invited her for supper on Tuesday. Mr. D was so helpful with taking her letters to the post office on his way to the schoolhouse. How glad she was that Mr. H lived next door now, he had been such help in fixing the leak in the roof. How Mr. K was selling his land, no choice really, and leaving town for good. Repeated assurances that she was well. How she was anxiously awaiting the time when she could join Eli in Leadville. How she missed him so much and cherished the memory of his last visit home to Missouri, five months previous. That the child within her, their first, was growing, "Praise be to God."

One letter that caught her attention in particular appeared to be one side of a tense exchange about "that horrible gun." Lillian's words made Inez sit straighter, a prickle of premonition going up her spine.

"Dearest Husband," that letter began, just as the rest.

Please, no need for your many exclamation points and underlinings of the last letter. I know how you feel about this dreadful weapon and would not sell it without your consent.

I've always known, from the time you explained its origin to me, how it is a part of your past, the past that has molded your very soul. I do not want bickering about it to divide us, like the War that divided your family and mine for so long, the War whose memories take you into your black moods and away from me. But I'll tell you true: I can hardly abide it in the house. I wish it were gone, out of my sight. When Mr. D brought your latest letter from the post office, I had him take it down from its place above the mantel and put it away in its case, for I could not bear to touch it, much less look on it. Every time my gaze crossed it, I thought of the young man, whose body was scarce cold when you took it from him. A trophy of the War, a sharpshooter's rifle, you told me, made for the killing of men. If you refuse to let me sell it now, I only hope that, when I arrive in Leadville hence, with our baby, our future, our hope, our joy, that I will be able to convince you to put the past behind and this weapon with it. With my love always, Lillian.

After that, Lillian's letters became briefer, darker. She feared the smallpox sweeping their town would find her. "But I keep myself apart, as much as possible. Our good neighbors have been kind enough to bring me what I need, so that I can avoid the contagion. Mr. D has been a godsend, helping me and others as well."

Then, the neighbors. "Mrs. H and the boy have been stricken down and are in a bad way. I pray for them both."

Finally, the last two letters. The one on top was addressed in a different hand. Dread and a sense of the inevitable weighted Inez's shoulders. She told herself that it was a story done, that nothing could be done to change its already completed course, for Eli or Lillian.

Inez drained the dregs of her cold coffee, steeled herself, and pulled the letter from the envelope. The pressure of pen on paper was light and the script small and tight, making the words difficult to render. She put her reading glasses on again and squinted to make them out.

After a brief salutation, it continued, "It's my duty and sorrow to inform you that your wife contracted the pox and passed this last week."

Inez pulled off her glasses and closed her eyes. She could imagine the pit of anguish and despair that must have opened beneath Eli, reading the news in a stranger's hand, far from home, far from all that had transpired. Unable to say a final goodbye, to close her eyes, kiss her cheek, even cold, one last time. And the unborn baby....

She took a deep breath. Opened her eyes, replaced the glasses, and scanned the rest hurriedly, rushing past the extended condolences. The word "Colorado" flashed past. She returned to the sentence, hunting down its context.

> *Please advise if I can assist in the selling of your property, shipping of household goods, etc. I may even act as delivery agent myself as I, having heard much of Colorado and her opportunities, have quit my post as schoolmaster and will be heading that way along with fellow travelers, your neighbors, who also are coming West for her opportunities.*

The handwriting, which had become more hurried and tiny as the letter progressed, was nearly unreadable at the signature line. A "B" started the first name and a "D" started the last. But the rest was undecipherable.

The schoolmaster, this Mr. D., he came here? Is here still? She folded the letter and stacked it on top of the others. *Perhaps he brought the Sharps to Leadville. And Eli, perhaps as a last gesture of respect to his wife, because he was sick of it all...the War, its lingering effects...sold the gun to Evan. Next time I'm in Evan's store, I'll have a word with him about this.*

The last letter rested on the blotter before her. She picked up the envelope and knew immediately that it was different. There was no address. Something thick was enclosed, not paper, but something bulkier. And the envelope was sealed. Inez stared at it, loath to violate its confidentiality, but knowing she'd not put it aside unopened. The letter opener slid through the envelope easily, then snagged partway through on the contents. Inez forced it to the end, tearing a ragged rip in the envelope, reached inside and pulled out a length of loosely woven cloth—red, white, and blue.

I've seen this before.

It was a cousin to the one she found by the river.

Chapter Thirty-Four

A knock on the door shattered the moment.

Inez dropped the cloth with a start to the blotter. "Who's there?"

"Mrs. Stannert?" It was Maude Fairplay.

"Just a moment." Inez hurriedly tucked the letters back into the pigeonhole and wound the cloth around her hand like a skein of yarn.

Maude Fairplay eased open the door and strolled in, her maid behind her, struggling to pull the hand trunk over the sill. "No, no, please don't rise. If I might use your back room to prepare?"

"Let me be sure it's ready." Cloth balled in her fist, Inez left her chair and hurried to the door leading to her dressing room. "I won't be a minute."

Once inside with the door shut behind her, she feverishly yanked open the dresser drawer and pulled out the other strip. The cloth pulled from the riverbank was dirty, stained, and worn. The one from Eli's envelope, less so. Yet, it was the same color scheme. The same pattern. Only Eli's was longer, complete, two white stars set in blue, equal distance from the banded narrow ends. "Eli and the railroad man knew each other!" Inez said fiercely to herself. "Rio Grande business or not, I'm going to find out who the man was with Eli!"

Inez wound the two strips of cloth together, put them in the very back of the drawer, and gave the washstand's accoutrements a perfunctory inspection. She opened the door, intending to announce that the room was ready, and found Maude standing by her desk, holding William's photograph. "So." Her voice, usually so melodramatic, was soft, wistful. "Your son?"

Inez walked over, her first inclination to rip the case from Maude's hands and slam it closed. But Maude's tone, combined with the lingering sorrows from Lillian's letters, stopped her. Instead, she held out her hand. "Yes. That's my son, William."

She gave the photocase to Inez. "So like his father."

Inez snapped the case shut, still looking at Maude. "Dodge City."

Maude backed up a step. "So you knew. All along." Her face twisted. "You look as if you wish to stab me through the heart. But truly, since we are both here, through some horrible trick of fate....'The wheel is come full circle.' Edmund, from *King Lear*. Fathers and their children. Oh, Lear had his. You have yours. But I, I have none. And my heart will never heal from that sorrow."

"That's no excuse for what you and Mark did."

"Of course not." Maude sank onto the loveseat. "I cannot dissemble. The name Stannert...I thought, it's possible there are many Stannerts. What are the chances that it would be him and you? When you said he was dead, I thought, maybe I could avoid you, since you seemed intent on avoiding me. But it isn't possible to avoid the past." Maude's eyes were tired, haunted. "Well, we're alone now, Mrs. Stannert."

The maid by the door stood still as a statue, frozen with an expression of dread etched on her features.

"So I suppose this is the proper moment to say I'm sorry. That what occurred between your husband and me was—" Maude fluttered her fingers. "A dalliance, on his part. Clearly, he'd no intention of it being more than a single encounter. My reasons were, alas, complicated, and far from noble. I hoped that, by clearing the air, we might make peace between us. If you wish, Mr. Fairplay and I will cancel the rest of our appearances here at your saloon. I've no desire to put you through an excess of pain. The decision, Mrs. Stannert, is yours." Maude settled back into the curve of the small sofa.

Inez had crossed her arms fiercely during Maude's speech, holding herself together by sheer will.

But in the silence that prevailed after Maude's words, something curious happened. The knife of anger, which had twisted its point into Inez's heart, melted, and left a sensation that Inez had trouble identifying at first.

Rather like sorrow. Tinged with fatigue, and a lingering sense of loss.

Forgiveness.

Inez finally released a sigh. "Oh heavens, Mrs. Fairplay. All that was long ago. It probably would be no surprise to you that Dodge wasn't the first or last time my not-so-sainted husband strayed. Please, no dramatics in my office. Save your energy for your performance." She held out her hand.

Maude said, "Thank you, Mrs. Stannert," took Inez's hand, and stood.

"There now," Inez said briskly. "Much better. You seem a bit unsteady. I have a special stock of brandy that should settle your nerves. Send your maid downstairs if you'd like some, and I'll arrange it."

With a tremulous smile, Maude murmured her thanks again and moved to the back room, her beribboned skirts swishing softly over the floorboards.

Chapter Thirty-Five

The bell tinkled over the front door of Susan's studio as Inez entered. The studio appeared empty—not, Inez hoped, an indication of the current state of Susan's business.

Susan popped her head out of the back room, looking expectant, then surprised. "Hello Inez! I'll be there in just a minute."

She disappeared into the back.

Inez sat down in the waiting area, set a pine gun case on the floor, and flexed her aching fingers. She'd lugged the heavy case from her home to the post office, where she'd mailed a letter addressed to "Postmaster" at Eli and Lillian's small Missouri town. Inez had included information of Eli's almost-certain demise—at least, she felt, deep down, that Eli was dead, no matter what others said—and asked about the identities of the mysterious Mr. D and Mr. H of Lillian's letters. *If I can get a name, perhaps I can move another step forward in all this. Or maybe not.*

Anxious for a distraction from Eli and the mystery of his life and death, Inez picked up a copy of E. Butterick and Company's summer catalogue. She flipped through it, pausing to examine the walking skirts.

Susan reappeared, wiping her hands on her stained apron. "I was just gluing some prints to their mounts. I expect the customers will be around for them later today."

Inez nodded, then frowned at the catalogue. Rows upon rows of tiny engravings of skirts bedecked with tucks, horizontal folds, pleats, shirring, flounces, and other draperies marched across the page. "The skirts are narrower every season. It's beyond me how we're to walk around in skirts so tight they don't allow one to take a decent step."

Susan crooked her head to see what Inez was looking at. "Oh yes. A customer recently arrived from New York brought that in. I thought some of the ladies would like looking through it while waiting."

Inez tossed the catalogue onto a nearby low table. It slid across the surface, coming to rest at the farthermost edge. "How nice it would be if there was a single catalogue that would allow one to buy all kinds of things—clothes, rugs, cabinets, watches, stoves— all from the comfort of one's home and deliver them as well!"

"Are you thinking of buying a new stove, Inez?" Susan dropped into a nearby chair.

"Eventually. Certainly before winter. We're finishing the gaming room upstairs in the saloon. Besides the warming stove, I'd like a new sideboard. And a cabinet. I was lucky enough to find suitable rugs at Daniels, Fisher and Company. A mine manager had placed an order and then left town after the strike, so I was able to buy them on the spot. But ordering furniture is likely to take quite a while. Although the railroad's arrival will speed the delivery."

Susan half rose. "Would you like some tea?"

"No, no. I'm just making my rounds. I need to stop at Evan's store next. But I have something to show you."

She pulled the vaguely ominous missive to Eli from her pocket. "This came to Eli Carter, who owns the C&H Livery with our own ex-marshal, Bart Hollis. Eli was probably one of the fellows you saw on the track. He rode the horse from his own stable and was apparently leaving town for good that day."

Susan read the scrawled note and frowned. She handed it back. "An oath. What kind of oath?"

"I'm not certain. But I do think it's significant that it mentions a general. Particularly given the 'kill the generals' statement you heard before your accident. Had you ever met Eli?"

Susan shook her head. "When I hired the horse and burro, I spoke with Mr. Hollis."

"So you wouldn't have recognized him if you saw him on the track," Inez said, more or less to herself.

Susan played with one of the curls fringing her forehead, pulled it straight and allowed it to spring back into shape. "I can't remember what they looked like anyway, so it wouldn't help even if you described him. Sorry, Inez. Are you going to show the note to Marshal Ayres?"

"I'm afraid he'd just pooh-pooh it all. As he reminded me, without a body, there is no crime. And I don't think he's in town at present."

"How about the city marshal? Or someone at the railroad?"

"The city marshal could care less since this whole business happened outside city limits. But the railroad. Now that's a thought. I wonder who would be the right person to notify. Mr. McMurtrie? He's chief engineer. The lawyer, Mr. Snow? He's out of town, I gather. Maybe the professor—he works for the lawyers. Hmmm. Mr. Holt." She perked up. "He's a payroll guard, but I get the definite impression that's not all he does. In any case, he might know who would care about this note. If anyone would, that is."

"Oh!" Susan jumped up. "Speaking of the railroad. Let me show you something before you go." She hobbled into the back room and returned, holding a stack of cardboard-mounted cabinet cards. "It's my latest work. Here are a couple of the boarders."

Inez recognized Terry O'Loughlin next to an urn set on a pedestal. She rested an elbow on the urn, which trailed ivy and held a plant with spiky fronds.

"Mrs. Flynn had her sitting recently." Susan half smiled. "She brought a half dozen outfits, all very up-to-date and proper, and wanted photographs of herself in each and every one. It took nearly an entire day to do them all and paid for a good portion of a week's room and board. I haven't mounted those photographs yet, but I think I'll put a couple in my display window when they're done. They should be a good draw for the genteel women in town. Mrs. Flynn's very photogenic, what with those dark eyes and brows, and her light hair….Oh! Speaking of very proper, you'll never guess who's been at the boardinghouse 'to call' twice this week. With calling cards flying back and forth and all."

"Who?"

"Mr. Braun. And guess who he was calling on."

Inez thought back. On Widow Flynn's smiles and sidelong glances in the wagon and as she settled herself on the blanket at the picnic. "Your landlady?"

"None other! Now, here's one of the men from the railroad." Susan passed another cabinet card to Inez.

"Why, that's the professor!" exclaimed Inez.

"You know him?"

Inez looked at her curiously. "He drove the wagon that brought you to the hospital."

"Yes, that's what he said."

"You don't remember?"

Susan shook her head. "The first thing I recall is waking up in the hospital. It was night, but one of the Sisters was there, keeping me company. Anyhow, I eventually had to confess I didn't remember him at all. I don't think he quite believed me. He was nice, though. All the time I was setting things up, he kept inquiring about my health." She handed Inez the last card. "And here are the Holts. You can certainly tell they're related, don't you think?"

Preston and Reuben Holt—jackets buttoned up, collars straight, hair slicked back—sat in matching chairs, the spiky plant and urn between them. Each held a rifle, muzzle up, butt to the floor, the long lines of the barrels forming a vertical frame. The plant, its fronds reaching for the sky, looked for all the world like a hostage. Preston was to the left, Reuben to the right.

Inez examined the photo closely, remembering the kitchen episode, with Preston reaching for his pistol on his left. Then, Reuben at the poker table, reaching for the cards with his right hand. "They're differently handed."

"Ah. That explains it. I originally had the elder Mr. Holt on the right, but they wanted to switch sides so they could hold the guns like that. Makes them look rather formidable."

Inez privately thought that Reuben's fierce scowl was over-done. *At sixteen, it's probably more important to look tough and threatening than civilized.* Preston stared into the camera, face impassive, gaze steady. His eyes seemed to look straight through her. A small thrill trickled down her back.

Inez shook herself. "Very nice, Susan." She handed the cards back. "When do you expect they'll return?"

"They were in town last Saturday, so I suppose they'll be in town tomorrow." She looked up from her handiwork. "Would you like me to show Mr. Holt or the professor that letter?"

Inez hesitated, then said, "Maybe just let them know I'd like to talk with them." She stood and tucked the letter away. "The other horse belonged to a railroad man. I would like to know who." She reached down and retrieved the long pine case. "That man must have known Elijah Carter. The letter was posted from Colorado Springs, where Palmer's headquarters are. So there might be a connection. One never knows."

Inez stopped in at Evan's mercantile, only to learn that the store-owner was in his mining supply store next door. Business had been so good over the past year for him that he had bought the building next to his original store and split the business into general merchandise and mining-related goods. She found him in deep discussion over the relative merits of pack animals. "No question about it," he was saying. "If you're headed to the Ten Mile District, with the amount of supplies you're handling, a burro is the way to go."

After the customer left, Inez stepped forward and set the pine case on the display case. "I need you to tell me about this gun."

Evan grunted as Inez unlatched and opened the lid. "Oh yes. The Sharps rifle. My newest clerk mentioned that no sooner had we put it up for display than a woman came in and bought it." He looked at her soberly. "I didn't realize that woman was you,

Mrs. Stannert. It's not a gun for a woman, you know. It was made specifically for Berdan's Sharpshooters, a Union regiment in the war. This is an excellent rifle for long distances, but no good for the situations you'd encounter here in Leadville. Your Smoot pocket revolver is practical up close, your husband's old Navy Colt for intermediate distance, and your shotgun or a standard rifle for distance. Should that be necessary."

"So I've been told. Did you buy this from Elijah Carter? The clerk had no idea of its provenance. He thought the owner had been a prospector, trying to raise a grubstake."

Evan adjusted his spectacles. "That new hire of mine isn't the brightest star in the sky. Recent to town, and I think he's got a bit of the itch to stake a claim himself. But you're right. I bought this from Eli Carter. He left town recently. I've heard there's a suspicion of foul play." He shook his head. "His horse was found riderless south of town. I'm betting road agents had a hand in that."

"Did he say where he was going? Or why he wanted to sell this gun?"

Evan picked up the rifle, hefted it, as if testing the weight. "Breechloader. Uses .52 caliber linen cartridges." He opened the breech, checked it, and sent a sharp glance over the top of his glasses. "Did you get the cartridge tins?"

"Oh yes, your clerk sold me the whole kit and caboodle, including the case. So, Eli didn't say anything about where he was headed or why?"

Evan shook his head. "I was surprised. Thought he had a going business and was planning to bring his wife up here. He talked about it once. But, I suppose the coming of the Rio Grande changed that. The railroad is all good news for me, but for Eli and the others in the livery, hauling, or staging services, it's a different matter. Too, there's the business of the right-of-way."

A-ha! "What business, exactly?" She tried to sound merely curious.

"The railway's lawyers—Lowden Snow and the rest—are still having trouble clearing the ownership titles to some privately held city lots. I think the livery's one of those that's holding things up. Can't be making Snow very happy."

"I heard Eli sold the business to Hollis. One wouldn't think he needed the money from selling the gun. Did he seem happy to be leaving?"

Evan set the rifle down gently in the case. "Now that you mention it, he was kind of low. I didn't know he'd sold the business to Hollis. At any rate, he didn't haggle over the price. Almost seemed glad—or at least, indifferent—to get rid of it. He mentioned he had one last bit of business to set right. Once that was done, he said, it would be time to move on."

Time to move on.

"Thank you." She began to close the case lid.

Evan stopped the lid. "Do you want to sell that rifle back to me? I'll give you what you paid for it. Can't see what good it'll do you."

She looked down at the gun. The metal had a dull sheen, the walnut wood of the stock shone as if it had been polished regularly, not neglected. A deep scratch and nick along the edge of the stock-mounted patch box had been partially filled in as well. The double-set triggers reminded her, incongruously, of lovers spooning front to back. Of Eli and Lillian. Of her and Sands.

"Perhaps later." She closed the lid.

Chapter Thirty-Six

Saturday evening, Doc was late to the game. Inez wondered whether one of his patients had taken a turn for the worse and half expected to see him arrive, brow furrowed, mouth downturned. But when he finally limped in, he was beaming and flourishing a copy of *The Independent*. "Masterful article, my dear Elliston. Now the town knows that The Citizen is on his way, as promised. General Grant in Leadville. 'Twill be a visit to remember."

"Well, Grant's going to have to walk from the Boulevard," said Jed. "Snow's not having any luck clearing ownership titles to those lots north of town. I understand the grading and track-laying crews have come to a dead halt."

Doc harrumphed.

Inez tensed.

"Snow's doing all he can," said Doc. "A sorry state, when a few can hold the city and railway hostage. Not a good showing for our guests."

"That means more decorations," Inez cut in, seeing Jed bristle. "Mr. Evan, have you any more bunting?" The only piece left in the saloon was still hanging over the buffalo, the rest having disappeared long ago, along with the dried and brittle pine boughs.

Evan sucked in his upper lip. Inez could almost see him mentally scanning his inventory. "I did order extra, Mrs. Stannert, knowing that Grant's visit was a possibility. A gamble, but I believe it's paying off now. I'll save some for you. I'll bet anything in red, white, and blue will be worth its weight in silver over the next couple of weeks."

"How long will Grant be staying?" Cooper asked.

"About five days." Doc headed for the sideboard. "We've got a full plate for him. Events and tours from morning to the wee hours. And Mrs. Grant as well. A sterling company is arriving with him. Governor Routt, Governor Hunt, Governor Smith of Wisconsin, General Palmer, and others. The Union Veteran Association will be handling the hospitality. And as I have some small voice in organizing the schedule…well, Mrs. Stannert, I can't promise, but I will do my best to see that you have the opportunity to meet the Great Man yourself."

"Me?" Inez nearly dropped her cards.

"Don't forget your local press, Doc," Jed interjected.

"Of course not, of course not." Doc brought over a brandy for himself and set a second in front of Inez. "For our lovely hostess." He raised his own glass to the table. "To General Ulysses S. Grant, commander in chief of the Union army during the war and former president of these United States."

Inez hoisted her snifter with the rest. Her goblet and Doc's met, ringing with crystal clarity.

"Seen the good reverend of late, Mrs. Stannert?" Doc settled in his chair.

She pursed her lips and made to study her hand intently. "I believe he's out of town."

"So soon?" Doc appeared to catch himself, then looked around at the table. "Well, since you're deep into this hand already, I'll just wait until the next."

Soooo, does Doc know something about this mysterious trip? I'll need to find a time to pull him aside and ask him a few questions.

It was good that the saloon was doing well of late and didn't require Inez's winning that night to pay the bills. Her mood turned blacker and blacker and her attention wandered, with the expected results that she lost more than she made in the house rake.

"I'm afraid we must end for tonight, gentlemen," she remarked at one thirty. "And, I have good news for you. In one week, well before General Grant's scheduled arrival, our room upstairs should be ready for us."

"Excellent." Evan peered at her over the top of his glasses. "It's been a long time coming, for you and Abe."

"And I do hope that, those of you who are not otherwise engaged, might drop in tomorrow—or should I say later today— and see the Fairplays. They'll be doing something special from *Henry the Fifth* at three in the afternoon, a sort of salute to the military man I gather, to honor Grant's impending visit. You can come and spend a little of that money you all won from me tonight."

"I'll be here, without a doubt." Doc ran a hand over his hair. "Assuming, of course, there's no sudden crisis that demands my attention."

Sunday afternoon, Inez paused from her bartending duties to wipe the perspiration from her forehead and look around. If she didn't know better, she would have said that the Silver Queen was the only saloon open that day, for it seemed that a goodly percentage of the male population of Leadville was crammed into the large room.

Mindful of last week's successes with the Fairplays, Abe and Sol had banged together rough benches and a makeshift stage that could be brought into position between the kitchen pass-door and the piano. "Y'know," Abe had said, jingling a handful of nails in one hand. "We might think about doin' this sort of thing on a regular basis. When the upstairs opens, we could knock out the wall of your gamin' room down here and put up a stage. Get the acts comin' through town. Musicians and such."

Inez held up a hand. "Whoa, Abe. You're going too fast for me. Let's get through July and see how things stand."

Still, looking around, she had to admit that Abe had a point. On the days that the Fairplays performed, the crowds came early, waiting impatiently for them to open at noon, and lingered afterward. They drank and ate more. And, there was the dollar a head charged at the door for the performance, which, even when split with the Fairplays, made a tidy sum indeed.

"Ma'am, ma'am." A small voice at the end of the bar caught Inez's attention. Maude Fairplay's maid was standing by the bottom of the stairs, looking frightened, but determined.

A couple of the drinkers nearby looked at her askance.

"A Chinee in Leadville," muttered one. "Thought we ran 'em all out of town last year."

"Gentlemen, you are talking about Mrs. Fairplay's private maid," said Inez haughtily, sweeping around to place a protective arm around the tiny woman's shoulders. "I'll thank you to be civil."

The maid whispered, "The missus, she has need of a...." She blushed. "Lacing, if you please. Broken. No extras."

Inez turned to Abe and shouted to be heard above the noise, "I'll be back shortly." She headed upstairs with the maid.

Maude was in the dressing room, staring at her reflection in the mirror, high tragedy written on her features.

She swung around, holding her black-satin-trimmed corset up to her torso, giving an excellent view of the swell of her breasts. "Thank you for coming to our aid. The extra laces are somewhere, who knows where, and I will never fit into my dress without some tight lacing."

Inez flung open her wardrobe, pulled out a drawer and hunted through extra shoelaces, a spare buttonhook, various ribbons, and lace cuffs.

She heard Maude's gasp and turned around to see her staring into the wardrobe. Inez followed her gaze and realized she was staring at Mark's clothes, all hung neatly. Waiting.

"You kept his clothes," she said faintly.

Inez reached out and touched the silver-and-gold threaded waistcoat, his favorite. "I suppose, in the back of my mind, I keep expecting him to return. But it's been a long time now, and I no longer know if I really want him." She froze, realizing what she'd just said, and looked back at Maude.

Maude's face was frozen as well. "So. He's not dead."

Inez, cursing herself for the slip of the tongue, closed the wardrobe doors firmly, and handed the lace to the maid. "He may as well be. He walked out, more than a year ago, and I've not heard a thing from him since. Left me and our son to fend for ourselves."

Maude looked as if she might faint. "You mean, he may be out there, somewhere? That might explain…." She stopped.

The maid laced the slender cord and began pulling it tight.

"Explain what?" Inez felt an uneasy dread.

"I…hesitate…to say," gasped Maude. Her waist contracted, her breasts plumped up above the frilly edging topping the corset as her maid jerked and pulled. "Oh…Mrs. Stannert…I don't… wish…to fuel any hopes…or fears…on your part, but…."

"Tell me!" Inez gripped the handle of the wardrobe, willing Maude to spit it out.

"It…was…Central City. Two…months ago? C.A. thinks…I… was having an…attack of the…vapors. A bit of female…hysteria."

The maid tied the cord and backed away to the trunk.

Maude took a shallow breath, then a slightly deeper one. "I need to be able to breathe, if I'm to project my voice." She stopped, seeing Inez's expression.

"All I can tell you is, I'd only seen him once that time in Dodge, several years ago. But there, in Central City, in the first row, was a man who…well, I thought…although he was thinner in the face than I remembered. I nearly fainted dead away on the stage. But I'm a professional, and I'm proud to say I carried on and no one knew. Except for C.A. He sensed something was wrong. We talked about it later."

"Central City." Inez stared at the sunburst carved on the wardrobe panel, its lines burning into her mind as if she gazed on the actual sun itself. "Less than two days' journey from Leadville."

She wrenched open the door of the wardrobe and began yanking Mark's clothes off the hangers, pitching them with venomous energy into the corner of the room.

"Mrs. Stannert!" Maude rushed forward and grasped her arm. "Please. Don't listen to a silly woman's babbling. One face, among so many. The focus of the stage, my imagination—"

"Oh, you're not the first to report a possible sighting." Inez ceased her flinging and stared stonily at the heap of trousers and fancy dress shirts, piled higgledy-piggledy in the shadows.

"Please, talk to C.A. I'm sorry to have said anything at all. C.A. and I, we talk about everything, there are no secrets between us." Her face softened from despair to a sad smile. "He knows about all my…peccadillos. My weaknesses. He will tell you, it was no doubt a phantom of my imagination."

Inez closed the closet door firmly and said, "You need to finish getting ready. The audience will be getting restless, and when men get restless in a bar, it means nothing but trouble."

And trouble is what my life seems to breed these days. Nothing but.

Chapter Thirty-Seven

Inez stood by Abe, elbows on the bar, as C.A. Fairplay strode onto the makeshift stage in Elizabethan hose and garter, his barrel-chested torso covered in clanking armor. He looked every inch a king with his iron-gray hair styled and his mustache waxed to a fare-thee-well. He turned his face up to the second-floor landing and intoned "Fair Katharine, and most fair!/Will you vouchsafe to teach a soldier terms/Such as will enter at a lady's ear,/And plead his love-suit to her gentle heart?"

Maude, who had made her entrance from the office above, paused at the railing, looked down with queenly majesty, and said in a halting French accent, "Your majesty shall mock at me; I cannot speak your England."

There was no resisting the magic that flowed between the two, the passion that lifted C.A.'s speech from memorized words to an outpouring of the heart.

Hardly a rustle was heard from the audience from beginning to end. Maude turned to the audience for her final words as Queen Katharine: "God, the best maker of all marriages,/ Combine your hearts in one, your realms in one! As man and wife, being two, are one in love,/ So be there 'twixt your kingdoms such a spousal/That never may ill office or fell jealousy—"

Jealousy.

"Which troubles oft the bed of blessed marriage,/Thrust in between the paction of these kingdoms,/To make divorce of their incorporate league—"

Divorce.

"That English may as French, French Englishman,/Receive each other. God speak this Amen!"

The audience broke into wild applause.

"Damn, they're good," said Abe, applauding with the rest. "They oughta do somethin' like that for Grant."

Inez grunted.

Abe's gaze shifted from the Fairplays to her. "Somethin' wrong?"

"Later," she said and began clapping as well.

There was a general stir throughout the audience as C.A. and Maude took their bows. Inez looked about, counting off those she knew by name or by sight. Everyone from her Saturday night poker game was there. Chet Donnelly was also present, clapping and hollering louder than the rest, keeping company with a group of like men. With hair bleached white by the sun, faces burned leather-brown, and clothes that needed a good dunk in the river, they all looked as if they'd just hauled in from the Ten Mile District. They made a studied contrast sitting shoulder to shoulder with an assembly of company miners, all in their sober Sunday best, faces pale from spending daylight hours underground.

Clustered just inside the Harrison Avenue door, Preston, Reuben, and the professor stood with men who, she guessed, were part of the rail construction crew. Standing a bit separate from them, the railroad section boss, Delaney, leaned against the wall by the door, looking drunk and sour. Michael O'Malley blocked the door, making sure that those who didn't pay the cover charge waited outside until the show was over. She caught her breath, sighting Weston Croy, partially blocked by Michael's shoulder, craning his neck to see inside.

Standing just inside the State Street door, similarly guarded by Sol with his baseball bat near at hand, she spotted Hollis and—

"Jack!" she said in surprise.

One-Eyed Jack had his hat in his hands and was staring about in puzzlement, as if he'd wandered in for a drink and found himself in the opera house instead. Jack's gaze traveled over the audience to the men by the Harrison Avenue door. He suddenly stiffened and stepped back, trodding on Sol's toes.

C.A. was saying, "Now, Mrs. Fairplay will entertain suggestions for songs from the audience, performed by herself and this fine young man at the piano."

Doc cupped his hands around his mouth and called out, "A song to celebrate the impending visit of General Ulysses S. Grant, eighteenth president of these great United States, to this wonderful city of Leadville on July twentieth."

Maude frowned a little and looked a question at C.A. He nodded, so she conferred with Taps. Taps sounded a chord and they swung into "The Girl I Left Behind Me."

She finished and someone else yelled, "How about another song?"

"A good ol' Union tramping song!" yelled another. There was a general murmur of approbation under which Inez thought she detected a rumble of disapproval. Maude bent her head to Taps to deliberate.

Inez felt Abe shift next to her, uneasy.

Maude turned to the audience. Taps did a toe-tapping intro and Maude began to sing: "Yes, we'll rally round the flag, boys,/ We'll rally once again,/Sounding out the battle cry of Freedom."

Most of the crowd joined in.

Inez and Abe locked eyes.

"We need to call a halt to this," she said in a low voice.

He nodded.

The song ended to thunderous applause and cheering.

Before Inez could announce that the act was over and invite those outside to enter, Delaney, who was standing by the stairs, took two quick steps to the piano.

His gun pointed at the piano player's head.

"You know the Southron version, piano man?" he inquired with a drunken slur.

Taps shook his head, hands frozen on the keyboard.

Delaney set the muzzle against his temple. "It's easy. Just play it again. Mrs. Fairplay, d'you know the words?" Maude's hands were up at her throat. Looking like she was ready to faint, she shook her head.

"Then I'll sing it! Play, you bastard."

Taps began playing haltingly. Delaney sang, "Our flag is proudly floating/On the land and on the main,/Shout, shout the battle cry of Freedom!"

A dangerous growl mounted throughout the room. Much to Inez's horror, other voices scattered around the room began to chime in, gaining strength at the chorus: "Our Dixie forever!/ She's never at a loss!/Down with the eagle/And up with the cross!"

She saw Reuben singing along with defiant enthusiasm. From either side, Preston and the professor clamped a hand on his shoulders, shutting him down. Other men around the room glared at the singers.

"Jesus Christ! Abe, get the gun!" Inez hissed. She began to sidle to the end of the bar closest to the piano.

Someone spat at the man singing next to him. A stir like a wave rolled through the room.

Delaney broke off. "No one move!" he roared. "I'll splatter this fella's brains all over the floor, and that'll be an end to the music!"

Abe froze. One hand below the counter.

Sol slowly hid the bat behind his back.

Yanking his arms from Preston and the professor's grips, Reuben shouted, "Sing 'Bright Missouri, Land of the West'!"

Inez heard Abe curse below his breath.

The professor hissed into Reuben's ear.

Reuben glared at him.

Delaney smiled lopsidedly, sweat streaming down his face. "Good call, boy." He then addressed Taps. "You know the tune?"

There was a slight pause. Inez held her breath.

The muzzle pressed against the piano player's head moved with his nod.

Delaney's grip on the revolver stayed tight. "Play."

Inez glimpsed Weston, pushing against Michael O'Malley's outstretched arm. Michael seemed panicked, but determined to keep him out. Weston stared at Delaney with manic loathing etched deep into his face.

Attention divided between the piano player's fumbling finger work and the audience, Delaney commenced singing:

"They forced you to join in their unholy fight,/With fire and with sword, with power and with might./'Gainst father and brother, and loved ones so near,/'Gainst women, and children, and all you hold dear;/They've o'er run your soil, insulted your press,/They've murdered your citizens—shown no redress—/So swear by your honor your chains shall be riven,/And add your bright star to our flag of eleven!"

On the last beat of "eleven," he slammed the keyboard cover down on the piano player's hands.

Taps and Maude screamed.

The room exploded.

Men lunged at each other. Benches overturned. Someone yelled—more in anger, Inez judged, than pain.

Yanking her pocket pistol out, Inez tried to push her way to the piano. She saw Preston grab Delaney by the neck, rip the gun from his grip, and throw him to the ground.

Weston broke past Michael, hurled toward Preston's back, pulled a gun from his tattered coat pocket—

"No!" she shouted.

Preston whirled around and caught Weston's wrist. Using Delaney's gun, he pistol-whipped Weston across the face.

Weston howled and dropped his gun. He staggered back, nose erupting with blood, and shouted, "The Rebs are attacking! Setting fire to the town! Blow the bridge, don't let them cross!" Weaponless, he threw himself past the professor and out the door into the street.

Appalled, Inez looked around. Sol was now in the thick of the crowd, swinging his bat, trying to break up the fray. Abe had the shotgun and was standing where she knew the cashbox resided under the bar. He looked grim, undecided. She understood his hesitation. Shoot? And maybe encourage others to do the same? Wade out into the mess and leave their considerable cash undefended and chance having someone tear the gun from his hands?

A voice, louder than the rest, drew her attention: C.A. straddled Delaney, who was supine and struggling on the floor. C.A. had him by the ears and was pounding Delaney's face into the boards of the makeshift stage, roaring: "Frothy flap-mouthed foot-licker! Jarring unwash'd horn-beast! Surly ill-nurtured measle! You bottle-ale rascal, you filthy bung, puny sheep-biting lout!"

Maude crouched by Taps, who was doubled over on the piano stool.

The professor stood motionless, an arm's length from Inez, next to the Harrison Avenue entrance. Arms crossed, he watched the battle rage with something akin to disgust on his face. His immobile posture enraged her more than all the fighting around her.

"Do something!" she screamed at him.

He turned his head slowly toward her. "It's not my war," he said coldly, without a trace of a heavy burr to his words.

She stared at him, feeling like she was surely going crazy. "For God's sake! I'm not asking you to fight! Just...go! Find a policeman! The marshal! The law! Bring them here!"

He disappeared out the door.

She turned back to the room. Everywhere, moveable furniture was being used as weaponry. Fists, feet, elbows, and teeth were being applied randomly to whoever came within reach, and not a few pistols and knives were being brandished. It was only a matter of time before someone decided to pull a trigger or drive in a blade.

A sudden commotion at the other end of the room drew her attention. Someone had hold of one end of the red-white-and-blue bunting draped over the buffalo's horns and was tugging—hard.

Seeing there was no way she could push her way across the chaotic room in time to stop the buffalo head's descent, Inez dashed out the saloon's Harrison Avenue door. Moving as fast as her long skirts allowed, she raced around the corner of the building to the State Street entrance. She arrived just in time to see the buffalo head come crashing down, flattening three unfortunate patrons beneath it and breaking off its heavy wood mount.

As one of the flattened heaved the enormous head off his legs, someone yelled "Gold!"—a pronouncement followed by the sound Inez had been dreading to hear: the sharp report of a revolver.

The answering heavy crash of the shotgun blast announced that Abe had made up his mind to pull the trigger.

Chapter Thirty-Eight

Whether it was the mention of the magic metal or the sound of serious firepower, nearly everyone paused. Taking hold of the delicate balance, Inez stepped forward and shouted, "That's *enough!*"

Sol hit a final home run into the shoulder of a man attempting to eye-gouge another. Abe held the shotgun on the company at large.

At the center of the disordered room, Doc stared, shock plain on his face, at the bullet-sized hole in the planks at his feet, and then looked up at Reuben. Preston Holt had a struggling Reuben by the collar. There was a short tussle, and a gun clattered to the floor, forced from Reuben's hand.

In the suddenly silent room, Inez heard Preston say, "Control yourself, son."

Reuben screamed, "I ain't your son!" and tore away from Preston.

Preston grabbed him by the front of the shirt and dragged him over to Inez. Breathing heavily, Preston gave Reuben a rough shake, saying to Inez, "This boy'll make restitution on a share of the damage and face the music for tryin' to shoot the doctor, there. McMurtrie'll hear of Delaney and the rest."

Reuben shouted, "I ain't no boy!" and tried to pull away.

She hardly heard them, distracted as she was by two men, on their hands and knees, scrabbling about the buffalo head, grabbing gold coins and stuffing them into their pockets. Two quick steps and she was by the nearest, who groped inside the open neck of the buffalo. The muzzle of her Remington Smoot was digging into his neck before he had time to twist his head around to see who had him by the collar.

"That," she said, twisting his collar, "is not yours. Put it down."

He dropped the money to the floor.

"Empty your pockets."

More gold coins followed.

She raised her voice. "None of you leaves until the money goes to its rightful owner. Who happens to be—"

"Mr. Jackson," bellowed Chet, his scuffed boots inches away from Inez.

She looked up. At that unusual angle, Chet's enormous belly swelled overhead, the scraggly ends of his beard straying over the bulge. He stepped back, and Inez saw his furious ruddy face and popping blue eyes far above. He also had his gun drawn and pointed at the other man, still on his knees in a prayerful stance.

"'Tarnation, that's why that damn buffalo was so heavy. Flapjacks, my long deceased partner, alwus did say it was worth a fortune. He died up mountain three years ago. Well, ain't no nevermind now." He added, loud enough for all to hear, "I gave that there fine trophy to Mr. and Mrs. Jackson as a weddin' present. So, boys," his voice dropped to a dangerous snarl, "this here claim 'taint yours for the staking, if you get my drift."

They did.

Men picked themselves up off the floor, some attending to bloody noses and other superficial injuries. Most began to slip out the doors.

Doc approached Inez, his face sagging in dismay. "I'd no idea that my suggestions would lead to such a volatile situation."

She took his hand and rose, dusting off smudges on her skirt where she'd knelt by the buffalo. "Well, Doc, neither did we. Would you help us with the wounded? Especially Taps. You saw what happened to his hands. I hope they aren't broken. I expect the law or some version of it to be here shortly."

No sooner spoken than McMurtrie and Snow came striding into the saloon, the professor shadowing them. Inez stared at Snow. *What's he doing here? I thought he was out of town.*

McMurtrie, who still had a starched linen napkin tucked into his collar, looked around, removed his napkin and hat, and shook his head. Inez made her way through the rubble.

Without preamble, Inez pointed to Delaney, who was sitting up on the stage, a bloody handkerchief held to his battered face. "I understand, Mr. McMurtrie, this…thug, who, by the way, started all the trouble, is a relative of yours? In addition to being an employee of the Denver and Rio Grande."

McMurtrie stared at Delaney, who in turn stared at Inez with pure hate. Sol, guarding him, the bat hovering menacingly, took a step closer.

McMurtrie removed the toothpick he was chewing and said, "Can't do anything about the blood tie, but I can guarantee that, if it's up to me, he's not going to work for the railway much longer."

Snow shoved his way between them. "You cannot lay blame on the Rio Grande for this," he said loudly and with great fervor, as if orating before a jury. "His actions, and those of any of the other men who participated in the brawl, are not the responsibility of the company."

Inez realized she still gripped her pistol and quickly pocketed it, lest she be tempted to use it on Snow.

"Of course I'm not blaming the railroad," she snapped. "However, there are certain employees," her gaze targeted Delaney and Reuben, still in Preston's grip, "who will no longer be welcome here."

She turned to Doc, who stood at her shoulder. "Are you going to press charges against Reuben? He tried to kill you!"

Reuben flushed beneath the blood smeared across his face and shouted, "He's bringin' Grant to town! The man who butchered those just tryin' to stay free! Who destroyed the South! Who—"

Preston shook him again, a controlled fury in the motion. "Boy. Stop now. You're in enough trouble."

"I ain't no boy! Quit callin' me that! I'm as old as you were when you went to fight—" His words cut off as Preston twisted Reuben's shirt in his fist.

Doc shook his head vehemently, still pale. "No, no. No charges. He missed, after all. He's still young. I don't see the good that would come of pressing charges." He looked at Preston. "Take him home and keep a better watch over his actions."

Inez heard a strangled gasp. The professor, standing behind McMurtrie, stared at Doc as though he'd seen a phantom. He ripped his gaze from Doc to catch Inez staring at him. Fear and disbelief scraped his face bare, stripped years from him, so it seemed that a frightened boy stared back at her. He quickly broke eye contact and began searching his pockets.

Doc broke from the group. "I'd best see to the piano player."

McMurtrie nodded and, without taking his eyes from Delaney, said, "The law on its way, Professor?"

"What?" The professor had pulled out a handkerchief.

"The law."

"Oh, aye, I believe so, sir." The cadence of Caledonia was back in his voice. He commenced dabbing the sweat from his forehead. "Pardon me. I'm…not used t' such violence. In the courtroom and boardroom, the violence is more of a…verbal nature. As you gentlemen know."

Inez narrowed her eyes at him. He avoided her suspicious gaze.

"Right. When the law arrives, have them take this sorry piece of—" McMurtrie glanced at Inez and amended, "Delaney here and lock him up. I'll deal with him in the morning."

Ignoring Preston's somber gaze, Inez left the group and hurried to Taps.

Taps cradled his hands to his chest, rocking back and forth. Doc twisted the cap back onto a small flask, which he slipped inside his waistcoat. "The brandy will help," he said in a low and soothing rumble. "Once you're home, we'll get you something stronger for the pain."

"Are his hands broken?" Inez asked.

Doc's face looked pouched and tired. "The left most likely is, but in any case, they're both badly injured. He'll need help getting home." Doc glanced at the empty pant leg, and the crutch leaning against the piano.

Sol, still standing guard over Delaney, said, "I'll get him home, Doc. Soon's I'm done here." Bootsteps echoed across the room behind Inez, and Sol added, "The law's arrived, so I can leave whenever he's ready."

Inez twisted around, for once glad to see one of Leadville's police officers. A brief explanation from McMurtrie and Inez was all it took for him to haul Delaney to his feet with a rough "You'll be lodging at the jail tonight."

As Delaney passed Inez, he spat. The bloody glob landed on the floor by her skirts. "Damn Yankee whore!"

Fist on hip, she stared him down until the policeman jerked him away.

Turning her back on the departing Delaney, Inez crouched by Taps. "He should have his nose cut off his face for what he did. Don't worry about anything but recovering. We'll hold your place open here and see that Doc takes care of you until you heal. How much is your room and board? Can you cover it?"

"I've got some saved." Tears flowed down his face. "Jesus. I thought I was dead for sure. Those songs. They reminded me."

Doc shot a warning glance at Inez and patted Taps on the shoulder. "There, there. Plenty of soldiers here. We remember, as you do."

"The war's over," whispered Taps. "Fifteen years ago. It's bad enough I hear the drums and songs in my dreams. When he asked if I knew 'Bright Missouri'...." He tried to wipe his eyes with his cuff, holding his red and swollen hand away from contact or pressure.

Inez pulled a lace handkerchief from her sleeve and gently wiped his face. "I always thought for some reason that you'd fought for the North."

"I don't see what difference it makes, one side or the other, now."

"Absolutely right, young fellow." Doc grasped him under one arm, Sol the other. "We need to set all those differences of the past behind and focus on the future."

Inez followed them to the door and said quietly to Doc, "Be sure you send the bills to us."

Chapter Thirty-Nine

Inez sat at one of the tables, brandy in hand, waiting for the Fairplays to change and leave. Abe approached, a key dangling from one hand, a leather pouch from the other.

"All locked up, Inez. No one's gonna be comin' in the doors."

She propped her chin on one hand. "What a God-awful day."

"Worst part was Taps." He sat across from her.

"I hope he heals. To be a musician and have someone do that to your hands." She shuddered.

Abe set the pouch on the table between them with a clink. "There's about seven hundred dollars in here from that buffalo head."

"Good Lord! Well, that will make a nice nest egg for you and Angel."

"I already took out some for us." He pushed the bag toward her. "This here's for you. I kept out some for Taps, too, t' keep him afloat 'til he comes back."

"Are you certain, Abe?"

His eyes squinched in a smile. "Way I see it, the money's part yours anyhow. If you hadn't been so damn stubborn 'bout keepin' that buffalo head around, I would've thrown it out with the trash."

"You've got a point." She picked up the bag. "I'll put it upstairs in the safe after the Fairplays leave."

Abe stood. "Guess I'll be headin' home unless you want me to wait."

"I've no fear about walking home in broad daylight."

"Suit yourself. See you tomorrow, then."

Inez absently picked up the bag and set it down with a rhythmic "clink," staring at the piano, thinking how close Taps had come to playing his last song. Delaney's bizarre performance haunted her, as did Reuben's fierce loyalty to a cause defeated before he was born.

"I'll never understand," she said aloud.

"Understand what, if I might ask?" C.A. came down the stairs, bloodied breastplate tucked under one arm, overstuffed valise in one hand.

"The war. How it lives on, even though it's long over."

C.A. approached and pulled out the chair opposite her. "May I?"

She waved her hand, then held up the bottle. "May I offer you…?"

"No, thank you. Quite enough excitement for today. I've no wish to add liquor on top of it." He sat and asked, "Did you have family in the war? Brothers? A father? Or did you live somewhere touched by battle?"

She shook her head, thinking of her very sheltered life in New York. "To me, the War between the States meant that suitable escorts were in short supply, all being in uniform and generally far away."

He sat back. "Suffice to say, it left no one untouched. Not even you, I daresay. Shakespeare had it right, particularly in *Julius Caesar* with 'Cry havoc! and let loose the dogs of war, that this foul deed shall smell above the earth with carrion men, groaning for burial.'" The soft intonation of the South increased in his voice as he added, "I still see the carrion men and hear their groaning in my dreams."

He shot a glance at Inez. "The last is editorial comment. Not the bard." He looked at the bottle in her hand. "Perhaps, a drop, if you wouldn't mind, Mrs. Stannert. Since you offered."

She went to the bar and brought back a clean snifter, filled it partway, and pushed it across the table to C.A.

He thanked her, squinted at it appreciatively, and took a sip.

Setting the glass down, he said, "I understand you and Mrs. Fairplay spoke of your common history."

"Frankly, I'm tired and don't see what use it would be to discuss it right now."

C.A. twisted one end of his mustache, pondering, then said, "I understand your reluctance to revisit the subject. However, this may be the only time you and I have to chat, so forgive me if I declaim a moment. Pretend I'm talking to myself, if you prefer. First, every day, I tell Mrs. Fairplay: 'Doubt that the stars are fire, doubt that the sun doth move, doubt truth to be a liar, but never doubt I love.' Nothing she could do or has done changes that. Nothing."

He turned the glass in his hand. "When I wooed Maude, I said, did, anything to win her. She wanted children. I swore by the sun and stars that I did as well. But I did not tell her," he cleared his throat, "that such a desire would only be a dream, should we marry. Afterward, when we became man and wife, the truth willed out, as the truth always does. In Dodge, I finally told her that we would never be able to have a family. Due to...a very unfortunate war injury."

He sighed. "I don't remember your husband. I do remember Dodge, for it was nearly our Waterloo, mine and Maude's. This confluence of circumstances, of meeting you in Leadville, so soon after her spell in Central City, has me concerned. I do not believe she saw your husband there. She's prone to fits of female hysteria. It took considerable persuasion on my part and a goodly dose of nostrum for her to recover from that episode. Forgive me for sounding selfish, but I hope that being here, facing her delusions, will drive the poison from her, once and for all."

The door upstairs squeaked open, and Maude appeared at the railing, dressed in a stylish walking suit. "Are you ready, Mr. Fairplay?"

He sprang to his feet. "Never more than when you are, my love. I believe we should go straight away to the hotel where you can rest."

Maude descended; her maid followed, the rubber wheels of the traveling trunk thumping at each step. "I do feel the need to lie down."

Inez rose to unlock the door for them. "In the future, no more requests for songs from the audience."

"I think your suggestion a good one," said C.A.

Maude paused at the door, eyes wide, hand to bosom. "Without a pianist, I think no songs at all. I cannot sing unaccompanied."

Inez debated, then said, "I believe I could take over duty at the keyboard."

"Oh!" Maude clasped her hands. "That would be most excellent." She sobered. "I do hope the young man…Taps?…will recover."

"As we all do." Inez closed the door behind them. *Yet, if what C.A. says is true, the afflictions he suffers in spirit are not so easily cured by time and rest.*

Chapter Forty

Inez arrived early the next morning, hoping to get a head start in determining the previous day's profits and losses. Abe and Sol planned to come in early as well to deal with the broken benches and makeshift stage.

She knocked on the kitchen door to avoid startling Bridgette and looked around at the alley. Rotting debris and broken crates lined the back of the building. Inez wrinkled her nose at the sweet cloying scent, haunted by a fetid undertone of decomposition. *Two weeks until Grant arrives. No doubt Leadville will be in a frenzy of cleaning and sprucing up. We should probably pay someone to haul all this away and dump it north of town.*

The kitchen door opened, revealing Bridgette looking as if she were being forced to stand in a midden. "Ma'am," she said without preamble, "someone wants to talk to you. And she won't leave until you do!"

That said, she swung the door open wide. Inez stepped in and with a jolt recognized Frisco Flo, owner of the high-toned brothel at the other end of the block, sitting at the kitchen table, idly stirring a cup of coffee.

"I'll be in the other room. Call me when you're done. Don't take too long or the biscuits will burn." Bridgette fled the kitchen to the barroom.

Inez leaned against the doorjamb, peeling off her gloves. "Miss Flo."

"Mrs. Stannert." Flo covered a yawn. "I should be a-bed, but thought if I was going to talk with you, I'd best head over early rather than later on. Goodness me, your cook acts as if I've the pox or some such. Well, to business, so I can repair to my beauty sleep." She fished around in a silk purse and placed a small leather case on the table. "I understand you know the boy this belongs to. I'm hoping you can return it to him."

Inez recognized the photocase Reuben had clutched to himself during the poker game on the evening of the third of July.

Flo tapped the case with a fingernail. "One of my girls had this hidden in her room. He must have left it Saturday night. I imagine she was hoping he'd come back for it. Or for her." She wrinkled her powdered nose. "It's not good for business when the girls start thinking like that. Well, most likely we'll not see him again. It's not as if those railroaders are made of money." Her baby-blue eyes drilled into Inez with frank curiosity. "He boasted your poker game funded him. Fancy that. From your table to my beds."

She fluffed her curls languidly. "Speaking of business…aren't you going to join me for a cup of coffee?"

Inez remained standing, gloves in hand. "I think not."

Flo's penciled-in dark eyebrows lifted. "No? To the point, then. I'm going to leave State Street. The clientele is taking a downward turn and we're getting more of the rough element." She eyed Inez with an expression Inez couldn't quite identify. "There's an elegant building on West Fifth, close to Harrison. Close to the big hotels. Close to the mining district—and all that money. A good neighborhood. Not far from Winnie Purdy's and Sallie Purple's places. And they both do a handsome business. I heard about your…windfall yesterday."

Inez smoothed her gloves. "News travels fast."

"From your saloon to my house. A hop, skip, and a jump. Anyway, I'm wondering if you might want to throw in with me." She held up a white hand. "Now, don't be hasty in your decision. Think about it. Probably would be one of the best investments you'd ever make. And, we could be partners." She smiled sweetly, then stood. "Ta-ta for now. You know where to find me. At least until I head uptown."

Frisco Flo left by the kitchen door, but Inez would have bet her bottom dollar that she didn't creep down the filth-laden alley to the back of her house of ill-repute. More likely, she thought, Frisco Flo had merely straightened her beribboned bonnet and sashayed the few steps up the alley to Harrison and thence to State. *She certainly didn't get all gussied up to come visit me. No doubt she's strolling down the boardwalk, doing a little advertising on the return.*

The case sat on the table, waiting for Inez's curiosity to get the better of her.

It didn't take long.

Inez moved the cup aside, a rouged mark on the rim where Flo's painted lips had rested, and drew the photocase forward. The cover was worn, showing an intricate design of interlocking diamond shapes framed by swirls of vegetative flourishes.

I'll bet Flo didn't hesitate to peek inside.

She released the small metal catch and opened it.

The first thing that caught her eye was the panel on the left. Instead of red velvet lining or a facing image, the panel held a worn fabric wedged into the case's gold frame—white star on blue background.

She turned her attention to the image.

The tintype was of two men in military uniforms, sitting side by side, each holding a rifle to the outside. It was an uncanny echo of the photo Susan had just taken of the Holts, minus the plant. Right down to....

Inez squinted, not sure she believed what she was seeing. She patted her pockets, found her reading glasses, and put them on.

One of the men was a younger Preston Holt. She'd stake her life on it.

The other person also looked familiar.

She focused on his face, trying to age the man in the frame by fifteen years. Lengthen his beard. Whiten his hair.

A shock of recognition blew through her.

Elijah Carter.

The next thing that penetrated her bewilderment was their uniforms. Military, yes. However....

She couldn't swear to it.

But the uniforms and markings looked Confederate.

Both of them.

"So you're askin' what, exactly?" Abe poured himself some coffee. He had arrived at the back door just as Inez had snapped the case shut.

Inez tapped the photocase. "Take a look at the tintype inside. Tell me if the men look familiar. Also, the uniforms. Are they from the war? What side?"

"You sure have a mighty interest in the war these days." Abe set his mug of coffee on the table across from her and lowered himself into the chair.

"Well, it didn't have much to do with my life before now. Seems like, with Grant coming, nearly everything that happens has some tie to those times."

Abe opened the case, peered at it, then looked up at Inez. "The one on the left, he bears a passin' resemblance to Eli Carter. If'n you were to bring him in here, trim his beard close-like and take off some years, I think it'd be him. Man on the right looks like that railroad man you fancy. The one with the firecracker of a son from last night."

Inez realized her hands were clenched into fists on the table. She opened them and laid them flat on the wood. "I don't fancy the railroad man. Well, not seriously. But all that aside, your observations are the same as mine."

"Hmmm." Abe studied the photo. "No surprise 'bout the boy's leanin' to the South, then." He closed the case and slid it back across the table to her. "Both wearin' the gray, I'd say."

Inez stared down at the case. "That can't be."

"Why's that?"

"Preston Holt fought for the Union. He and Reverend Sands were sharpshooters together. They talked about it once, while I was present."

Abe pulled the case back again and opened it, taking another long look. "Well, sometimes clothes don't mean much. Folks wore whatever they could get ahold of. Especially the Rebs. But most didn't wear coats from the other side. Too much danger of gettin' shot by your own. Holt and Sands were sharpshooters?"

"Yes. In Berdan's unit. I remember that part of the conversation."

"Well, like I said, clothes don't make the man. But these two are dressed up for the picture, jackets and all. Thought Berdan's men wore fancy green coats. Your reverend'd be the one to ask. And I believe Holt's holdin' a gun for distance. It's not a Sharps like Berdan's shooters had, though."

"No? How on earth can you tell?"

"I got a good look at that Sharps rifle you bought the other day. Double-set triggers, a breechloader. Fine piece of work. This one here ain't the same gun a-tall. Got a single trigger. And it's a muzzleloader. If you look close, you can see the ramrod there, under the barrel. What Eli's holdin'—if that's him—looks like your Sharps."

She held out her hand.

He gave the case back to her.

Inez put her glasses back on and squinted at the tiny rifles, details sharp in the tin surface. "You can see all that? Well, I'll take your word for it. I can tell though, neither is wearing a dark jacket." She took off her glasses and stared at Abe. "Preston Holt and Elijah Carter. They knew each other. Fought together? Is it possible Holt could have been a sharpshooter for the Confederacy early in the war before switching and fighting for the Union?"

"Men changed sides sometimes. I did." Abe gazed at the small window high above the stove, overlooking the alley. The diffuse light accentuated the lines in his face, heightened the gray in his hair, bleached his dark skin.

"Are those biscuits I smell burnin'?" He rose and started toward the oven.

The passdoor swung open and Bridgette advanced, her expression making it clear that she was ready to do battle with any harlots lingering in her dominion. The asperity faded into consternation. "Jesus, Mary, and Joseph, the biscuits! Ma'am, I thought you were going to call me when that...woman left." Bridgette seized potholders and threw open the oven door. She heaved the tin cooking sheet onto the range top with a clang. "Lands alive." She fanned the smoke away and tipped one biscuit up to inspect the bottom. "I'll scrape them, yes, I believe so. What a waste it'd be to toss them all."

"Abe, do you think it's possible that he fought on both sides?" Inez persisted.

Abe turned back to her, arms crossed. "Anything's possible. But what makes you think it didn't happen the other way—he started a Yank and switched to a Johnny Reb?"

Chapter Forty-One

All week, Inez felt Eli's ghost hovering nearby, peering over her shoulder, asking her what she intended to do. Questions gnawed at her: What was the connection between Eli and Preston Holt? Was Preston one of the men at Disappointment Gulch, maybe Susan's mysterious shooter on the ridge top? Inez couldn't reconcile that cold-blooded kill with Preston's reaction when she brought Susan into camp after the accident. And the reverend trusted him—that much was clear. Inez felt certain that Sands would have sensed if something were amiss with Preston Holt.

But that being the case, who had the shooter been?

And who was the man Eli argued with on the tracks? What were they arguing about, exactly, and who killed whom?

An uneasy possibility stole past her questions and encamped in her mind. A possibility she couldn't expel. Could Eli and the railroad man have been involved in a plot to assassinate Grant or Palmer? It seemed farfetched, yet there was the comment about "killing generals" and the note she'd found in Eli's saddlebags.

Did the note precipitate Eli's departure from Leadville or was it something he'd been planning all along?

And what, if anything, did Hollis have to do with this?

Hollis stood to profit from Eli's departure by taking over the entire business, Inez thought. Although, with the coming of the Rio Grande, the freighting and livery business didn't look like such a sure bet anymore. Too, Hollis made no secret of his Southern sympathies.

She half expected Preston Holt to visit the saloon that week, but days rolled by without his appearance. *Since I declared the Silver Queen off limits to his son, maybe he's not going to come around. In which case, I'll have to go to him.*

The note to Eli remained in her desk, with Reuben's photocase serving duty as a paperweight.

The Holts aside, Inez heard more about the railroad and its men as the week progressed. The graders and track-laying crew proceeded steadily up to Leadville from Malta, closing in on the city limits. Inez heard many wagers made as to whether the Rio Grande would wrest right-of-way from the last remaining holdouts between the approaching line and the depot site at Twelfth and Poplar, before Grant's arrival.

"What will the railroad do if they can't negotiate right-of-way in time?" she asked Cooper, who strolled in one afternoon after presenting a case at the courthouse.

Cooper raised his glass of bourbon. "They'll condemn the property. But, knowing McMurtrie, Snow, and some of the rest of those Rio Grande fellows, I can well imagine that late some night a crew will be ordered to push on through by moonlight. Those residents involved will wake up in the morning to find a line of track running through the backs of their lots." He pulled out a cigar and added reflectively, "I'd not care to be in Snow's boots right now. Good thing the railhead's so close to town. He's been in court a lot lately. I've no doubt he's getting a lot of pressure from those in charge to resolve the issue."

Snow did not reappear after that night in the saloon. Inez could just imagine him roaring, his face turning purple, as Hollis and the few others stood firm, refusing to give way. *And in that case, if he's spending time here in Leadville and NOT in Denver or the Springs, is Birdie out flitting around on the good reverend's arm?* The possibility only increased her ire.

True to his word, Evan saved bunting for the Silver Queen to decorate for Grant's visit. Inez sent Sol to pick it up, not trusting Evan's delivery boy to defend the precious cargo against other patriotic and desperate merchants. Discussion of Grant's impending visit flowed freely with the liquor. Flags and streamers disappeared from dry goods inventories faster than summer snow from the rooftops. Inez heard rumors that the "Palace of Fashion" planned to obtain a statue of the Goddess of Liberty and display her by their front door. Others prepared banners and garlands of pine and spruce enough to fill a forest. Talk was that, at the corner of Chestnut Street and Harrison Avenue, the city would erect a grand arch, thirty feet high and sixty feet wide, entirely surmounted with pine boughs.

As the weekend of July seventeenth approached, Inez began to calculate how and when to intercept Preston Holt. Finally, she told Abe that she needed a few hours on Saturday to settle some business. "I won't leave until after the Fairplays' afternoon performance. And I'll be quick. The out-of-town press will be about, and Jed's promised to bring a contingent of them by."

Saturday afternoon's performance proved just as crowded as the previous shows. The Fairplays worked their magic with a scene from *Romeo and Juliet*. Maude's enthusiastic singing more than compensated for Inez's unpracticed sight-reading of the popular tunes chosen with care by C.A.

After the show was over, Inez excused herself, preceded Maude up the stairs, and dressed hurriedly in some of Mark's castoff clothes. Worsted wool pants, worn and baggy at the knees, a faded shirt and black suspenders, and a nondescript heavy brown waistcoat—all rumpled and dusty from having been thrown in the corner nearly a week ago. Viewing herself in the mirror, Inez decided the nondescript clothes made her, if anything, more invisible. "Just passin' through," she said to the mirror, and pulled down on her hat brim.

She picked up the photocase and opened it one last time, running a finger over the fabric lining. The loose weave and white star stirred a tactile memory.

There was a knock on the door, Maude's voice calling, "Mrs. Stannert? May I come in?"

"Just a moment, Mrs. Fairplay."

Opening her washstand drawer, Inez pulled out the strip of fabric she'd rescued from the river and ran its length between thumb and fingers. She then rubbed the fabric critically, like a dressmaker testing the quality of a velvet. Although much the worse from wear, the rescued fabric had the same feel. She held it alongside the photocase, comparing it to the photocase lining. Stains and dirt aside, the star on the river cloth and the star in the case looked the same.

Cut from the same cloth?

"But how could that be?" she said aloud. "I found this in the river two weeks ago. I'd wager this other has been in the case a long, long time."

"Mrs. Stannert?"

Maude's voice from the other side of the door broke her musings. Inez tucked the photocase into an inner pocket of the waistcoat, the long strip of fabric into a trouser pocket.

Perhaps Preston Holt will have some answers.

Inez was glad to be out of the dust and sulfur smell of the town, even as the late afternoon spread long shadows over the ground. Her mare seemed happy to stretch her legs as well. Lucy had several prancing fits while heading out past Malta and into the flats where the construction camp had taken root.

The railroad camp was a couple of sidings and a sea of tents. She paused near the outskirts of the camp, wondering which way to turn, then decided to press on along the perimeter in hopes of meeting someone who might know Preston Holt's whereabouts. She angled toward the cars at the sidings, figuring that a payroll guard would probably be close to the payroll car, which, by definition, would be on a track.

A man on horseback approached and queried about her business. Pitching her voice low and soft, Inez stated she was looking for Preston Holt, who rode for the payroll.

"Oh sure." He scratched his jaw, his fingernails making a rasping noise against his whiskers. "Everyone's paid today. Most've gone up to Malta or Leadville. You might find him in the car on the back siding, behind that two-story bunker." he nodded at the sidings, the first and foremost holding a two-story railcar dotted with windows. "I believe though, he might've gone to Malta."

She thanked him and headed toward the sidings.

When the two-story bunk car loomed, she dismounted, tied Lucy off to one side, and circled around back.

Sure enough, a single-story car with windows and a door faced her. She knocked. Hearing nothing, she debated, then turned the knob. The door swung open.

"Hello?" she called.

She pulled out the photocase—her excuse for entering, should someone come by demanding to know what she was doing—and stepped up into the car.

Directly behind the door was a heating stove, just big enough to hold a coffee pot. Pairs of bunks lined either end. Coal oil lamps sat tight in holders along the plank wall. A table, built out from the wall, and another platform with a set of small doors underneath to hold storage gave the bunks at the far end some privacy. All of the beds were covered with identical gray blankets. A few personal odds and ends lay on the table. She wandered over, looking at the straight-edged razor, the cup of water, soap scum and bristles floating on top, and the small tin mirror nailed to the wall. On one of the upper bunks, someone had laid out a shirt. Too small for Preston Holt. Folded neat on the bunk below were a pair of socks. Likewise, too small.

Not exactly sure what she was looking for, if anything, she wandered to the other end of the car, careful to step lightly so as to not make much noise.

Aha!

Hanging on a nearby peg were two overcoats—the larger being the coat Preston had loaned her the day she'd rescued Susan.

She reached out to touch it, the memory of the heavy wool still with her.

Whispering voices. Outside the back wall.

She froze.

Not exactly whispering, she corrected herself. More like voices attempting to be quiet, but rising out of the whisper range in frustration or insistence.

"You sure it's there?" said one.

"I knowed that's where he put it."

"I'll be takin' a chance going in. What's to keep someone from showing up when I'm inside or when we're walking away? Did you think of that?"

"Don't matter! I need that gun! And the cartridges."

"All right! All right! But we need a signal. You stand beside the cars and be on lookout. When it's clear, whistle once. Then, if someone heads this direction, you start whistling 'Dixie' or any other damn tune you please. If I hear music, then I'm high-tailing out of there."

A murmur of assent.

A sigh. Then, "I'm headin' to the door. But remember, I'm not going in until I hear you whistle, sharp and short."

The door!

Frantic, she scanned the room.

There was only the one door.

No other way out, unless....

The windows!

But they were high off the ground.

She'd need time.

And there was no time.

Footsteps circled the near end of the car, approached the door.

Inez threw herself down and, belly to the floor, crawled under the bunk she'd surmised was Preston's.

Her elbow smashed into a hard object.

She snaked over it. Something pointed raked across her ribs. She wormed herself up tight against the farthest wall, positioning herself so she faced out. The blanket hung over the side of the bed, forming a small gray curtain and blocking much of her view.

The smell of dust, leather, and neatsfoot oil assaulted her senses. A pair of gigantic overboots was within reach. She dragged them to her, using them as a partial blockade, leaving just enough space between them to peer out. Lying there, sweating despite the cool air, waiting for a whistle or a tune, she reached for the long object she'd crawled over, thinking to use it as another barrier between her and whoever might enter the car. Her eyes and hand finally took in the object that had given her arm and ribs such grief.

A gun.

Or, more precisely, a rifle.

Fear surged through her.

Is this what they're after?

She could see the barrel poking out from the oilcloth wrap. And in the dim light that filtered under the bed, she could see something more.

She squinted and then, just to be sure, gently touched the end of the uncovered muzzle.

The hexagonal shape of the bore matched what her eyes had seen.

Hexagonal. Like the bullet lying in the darkness of her washstand drawer.

Further down, she saw the sharp-angled metal of a telescopic sight.

Her gaze traveled the length of the gun, which disappeared into the wrappings disturbed by her frantic wiggle into hiding.

A box lay on its side, long white oblong objects spilled out.

In a panic, she realized that she'd probably kicked over the box of long cartridges in her frantic bid to hide. She jack-knifed downward and scooped the cartridges back into the box, hoping she'd have another minute before—

A piercing whistle.

She slid the cartridge box nearly out in plain view and pushed the gun so it lay between the boots and the cartridge box.

The door swung open. Dying afternoon light stabbed into the car.

If he spots the rifle and cartridge box right off, he might just lean down, grab them, and go.

Carefully, silently, she slid her small revolver out of her pocket and covered it with her gloved hands to dowse any stray shine from its metal barrel.

A pair of dusty boots rounded the corner of the open door. And stopped. She imagined the intruder looking from side to side.

She was scrunched against the wall, partially curled up, lying amidst dust and dirt.

The boots turned and approached. The planks shook with each step, each tread sounding a hollow boom.

The boots stopped in front of the cartridge box.

Every detail about the boots seemed etched as fine as a steel-engraved print: the dark brown leather, new-looking but dusty, a deep gouge on the toe box of the right boot, still fresh.

The man exhaled in a heavy grunt. Leather creaked, cloth rustled as he bent a knee to the ground.

She squinched her eyes shut. Then forced herself to open them. *As if closing my eyes will make me invisible!*

A muttered note of triumph.

A gloved hand grabbed the cartridge box and withdrew.

Inez held her breath, trembling.

The hand appeared again and grabbed the muzzle of the rifle. The gun and its oilcloth cover slid out and away from her.

Feeling exposed, Inez tried to still the trembling that wracked her body.

The hand reappeared, sweeping back and forth, knocking into the boots. She heard a hissed oath, then "Two boxes, he said, two boxes."

Casting a desperate eye around, Inez spotted the second box of cartridges, far up by the head of the bed.

The hand began pulling the boots out—

A lilting version of "Dixie" rent the air.

Inez had never in her life been so happy to hear the anthem of the South.

The hand disappeared, the man grabbed the rifle and the one box of cartridges, straightened up, and pounded out the door. The door shut with a protesting squeak.

The tune continued for a few seconds more, before coming to an abrupt halt.

Setting the Smoot down beside her, she rested her forehead on her fist, fighting the waves of relief that threatened to overwhelm her and leave her less able to act than fear had.

Minutes passed. No one entered. No sound other than the faraway noises of the camp, buffered by distance and the intervening bunkhouse cars.

I can't lie under this bed forever.

She dragged herself out on elbows and knees. Stood up on shaky legs. Then went back down on her knees to retrieve her hat, which had ended up smashed between her and the wall and was now cobwebby in the extreme.

As an afterthought, she pulled out the box of cartridges still under the bed and pocketed one. *To compare with the one I found in Preston's coat pocket that day.*

She shoved the box back under the bed, pocketed her pistol, dusted off her clothes and hat as best she could. With a deep breath to settle herself, she headed to the door and opened it. Her feet had barely touched the ground when—

"Stop right there!"

Delaney stood at the end of the bunkhouse, carbine trained on her.

"Wait!" Her hands flew into the air, then she pulled off her hat. "It's me. Mrs. Stannert."

His eyes widened.

Revealing her identity did not have the desired effect. The gun stayed trained on her torso.

"I was looking for the Holts. Reuben left something in town that I was trying to return. If I may?" One hand inched down to the top button of her waistcoat and hovered there.

Delaney scowled. The muzzle of the rifle made an abrupt circle, which she took for assent to continue.

She cautiously extracted the photocase and held it up, talking all the while. "I asked one of the guards on patrol—that's what you call it, on patrol?—where I might find Preston Holt. Although, I suppose I could have asked for Reuben. To return this case. The guard directed me here."

Delaney's eyes narrowed as she talked.

She wondered, with part of her mind, how sober he was. Then, suddenly remembering what McMurtrie had said about Delaney not being with the Rio Grande much longer, she wondered what he was doing there at all.

His eyes were mere slits now, and he seemed to read her mind. "Bet you thought you'd not see me again."

She pocketed the case. "Not necessarily. I merely banned you from the Silver Queen. I have no power to persuade you to leave the state."

"Ha! Even that piss-poor distant cousin of mine McMurtrie couldn't get rid of me entirely. Though pullin' guard duty on Saturday night's not my idea of—" He stopped. Then, suspiciously, "Wait a minute. Why are you dressed like...." The muzzle of his rifle described another arc, encompassing her outfit. "You're up to something. You've got that guilty look. Just like those two I just caught hanging around here. Them. Now you. Too much of a coincidence, I'm thinking."

"What two?" *Say the names. Please say the names.*

"Hey Delaney, what's the problem?" The guard that Inez had first spoken with was walking down the siding, rifle resting in the crook of his arm. He stopped, stared at Inez. "Oh, it's you. No luck finding Holt?" He turned to Delaney. "Put up your weapon. He talked with me first. Came looking for Holt."

The "he" threw Inez for a second, until she realized the guard was still taking her at face value—trousers, waistcoat, and all. She gave Delaney a triumphant "so there" look, which she wiped off her face when the guard turned back to her. She hastily donned her hat, as the guard continued, "No luck in the bunk car? Well, Holt's probably at Malta. Heard a bunch of them talking about going to the Red Garter, so you might start there." The guard looked back at Delaney, who hadn't moved. "Hey, Delaney. I said, lower it."

Delaney lowered the rifle about two inches, looking as if he'd prefer to ram it down Inez's throat.

The guard pushed his hat back. "My name's Sketch, stranger. Yours?"

"Stannert."

He nodded. "That your horse back there? The black beauty? Fine looking horse. I'd better escort you off the camp. Some trigger-happy folks around here. Delaney, you're supposed to be checking the perimeter. Heard that mountain lion's been sniffing around the cook car again, so step lively. Shift's up in half an hour."

Without waiting for an answer, Sketch gestured to Inez to follow, and walked away. As they rounded the two-story bunkhouses, he said conversationally, "As they say in the army, that soldier just got broke down to private. Used to be section boss. Surprised he's still here. But I'll tell you, Stannert, it gives me great pleasure to order him around."

Glad enough to let Sketch chatter on, Inez gathered Lucy's reins and started to the camp's nearby perimeter, the talkative guard keeping pace. His ultimate objective in striking up a friendly banter became clear to her when he asked, "You from around these parts?"

"Yep," said Inez, surprised by the question.

"I heard that all you have to do to strike silver is stick a shovel in the ground. Is that true? I've been looking around while on duty. And wondered. What kind of signs should I be looking for?"

Inez hesitated, reluctant to say anything that might cause him to remember her, but finally answered, "From what I hear, your best bet these days is around the Ten Mile District. That's where the new strikes are being made."

"Ten Mile." He scratched his chin. "Hmm. Bet that's where Holt went."

She stopped. Lucy's nose bumped against her shoulder blade. "Who?"

"Oh, sorry. Hiram Holt. Too many of those Holt fellows around."

Inez, confused, felt the same. "So Hiram's ah, related—"

"Yeah, kin to Preston and the kid. Wasn't never too crazy about working here. No surprise, I suppose, that he'd strike out on his own. So, Ten Mile, huh? We'll be building in that direction, if General Palmer gets his way. And he usually does. So maybe I oughta just wait until we get there. Unless you think all the good territory'll be staked out by summer's end."

Inez gave in to Sketch's one-track monologue. "Waiting until you can get the lay of the land is a good idea. It's never a sure bet, finding a mother lode."

"Well, guess those fellas that struck outside Malta were just lucky." He sighed. "A couple of graders. Had an assay done, then up and quit."

"Everyone's hoping to get rich," Inez said, swinging into the saddle. "Thanks for the help. Might've ended up a sorry mess if you hadn't shown up."

"Ah, Delaney," he said dismissively. "More bluster than anything. No one listens to him anymore."

Inez touched her hat and rode away, feeling a tickle between her shoulder blades as she imagined Delaney's rifle trained on her back.

Chapter Forty-Two

The first stars emerged overhead and the clouds blazed orange rimmed with gold when Inez rode into Malta.

Malta's one main street straggled up California Gulch to Leadville proper. Its businesses catered to those "on the road"— saloons, smithies, liveries, and a couple of hotels of varying degree. The smell of sulfur from the nearby smelters tinged the air and the street was crowded with off-shift workers from the smelters, wheeled vehicles, and travelers. Inez reminded herself that Malta had captured the train traffic, for the time being, as the last stop on the Denver and Rio Grande line to Leadville.

Thinking of the train, Inez remembered that the Colorado State Press Association was on a daylong jaunt to Leadville and would be visiting her saloon later that evening.

I hope I can find Preston, return the photocase, and find out who Hiram is. Another son? A cousin? No matter what, though, I mustn't be late getting back to town. No doubt the newsmen will only show up for the novelty of playing cards with a woman, but as long as they spend their money.

The Red Garter proved easy to find. Not only for the legion of horses crammed flank to flank along the hitching rail, but also for the rousing polka that blared out from within its double front doors.

A barker dressed in fancy eveningwear was working the boardwalk in front of the dance hall, sweat stains set in dust showing in the armpits of his shabby cutaway. "Come on in, lads! We've got some of the prettiest ladies this side of Chicago just chompin' at the bit to sashay around the floor at only a dime a dance. These beauties know the galop, the polka, the waltz, the schottische, and all the latest eastern ballroom steps and quadrille changes!"

Somehow, I doubt that.

The barker's eyes settled on Inez in the gathering dusk. "Hey you, young feller! C'mon in and hang your hat a while. Let's make some room for your noble steed." He removed his top hat and swatted the horse at the end of the hitching rail. "Move over y' lazy galoot!"

The horse jumped sideways.

"There. Plenty of room!"

Inez touched Lucy with her heels and brought her to the rail.

"You'll not regret it," the barker chortled, and made fast work of tying Lucy to the rail. "Payday on the Rio Grande, and the place is jumping!" He practically pushed Inez through the entrance.

Once inside, Inez's eyes began to water. The air was close, choked with the smell of bad whiskey, tobacco fumes, and sweat, tempered with the scent of perfume—over-applied and tired. It matched the women she could manage to make out through the haze and the dim coal-oil lighting—haggard women, dressed in too-short skirts that showed off ankles and calves and short sleeves that bared arms to the shoulder.

Inez was willing to bet that most of them were mothers and wives, driven to desperate measures while their husbands, sons, or lovers, dreaming of riches, chased the elusive silver spirit up and down the Leadville district and beyond.

All the available women were dancing, although not nearly as enthusiastically as their partners. Many of the men were doing a vigorous polka, nearly carrying their partners in their gusto.

Some of the men were not waiting for a female partner to become available—a wait, she surmised, that could be very long, given the paucity of women and the overabundance of men.

Pairs of men also hoofed about the floor, handkerchiefs tied to the arms of those taking the female role.

She squeezed past the crowd lining the dance floor and took up a post at the bar, pulling off her heavy leather riding gloves.

The bartender, a woman dressed in the same scanty wear as the dancers but a great deal older, came over and said, "If you're gonna stay, you gotta buy."

Inez ordered a beer, figuring it would be the least vile of the possibilities.

Bottle in hand, she examined the room, looking for Preston Holt. Or Reuben. Or the professor. Any of the railroad men she knew.

The polka ended with a mighty blat from a trumpet and a flourish from the piano.

The pianist, wearing the reddest waistcoat Inez had ever seen, stood and bellowed, "Brass and pianner are takin' a break. But Stringbean here," he waved at the portly fiddle player, instrument firmly clamped under triple chins, "will lead ya through a square dance. So, gents, grab a partner and form squares."

As the horn and keyboard section rushed the bar, there was a general heaving and pushing from the sidelines into the dance area. Men who'd been watching rushed forward, coins in hand, attempting to steal a partner from those who were now digging frantically in their pockets for yet another coin.

A touch on her elbow made Inez whirl around, nearly sloshing beer from her bottle.

Preston Holt stood a hairbreadth away, grinning down at her, eyes crinkling at the corners.

Some bit of her inner anatomy—not her heart, she fiercely argued—leapt into her throat at the sight of him. She smiled back and set the bottle on the ring-scarred surface of the counter. "So, you saw through my disguise."

"I've seen it before."

She cleared her throat, trying to sound noncommittal—and manly, in case there were any eavesdroppers in the close space. "I'd rather hoped to see you earlier this week."

He leaned one elbow on the bar. Picked up her beer, then set it down again. A bull's eye in the stained wood. "Thought I was barred from your saloon."

"Not at all." She found it hard to make the words sound casual and leaned on the bar in kind, facing him.

He raised his eyebrows, then looked to the fiddle player, who was yelling, "Need two couples, right over he-yar," and waving his bow at a half-filled square in front of him.

Querying Inez with his eyes, Preston pulled a handkerchief from his neck.

Feeling her blood pounding in time to the impatient stamp of dancers, Inez held out her arm. He tied the kerchief above her elbow, and they pushed through the watchers to the dance floor.

When they reached their spot, the fiddle player did a lightning-fast run up the strings, then proceeded to call out a rapid set of figures while playing a blistering rendition of "Turkey in the Straw."

There followed the most energetic dancing in Inez's experience. Between do-si-dos, forward-and-backs, allemande lefts and allemande rights, she found it hard to keep in mind she was dressed in men's clothing. Every time their hands met, arms brushed, an electric pulse seemed to shoot to the base of her spine.

Sweat streamed down her face, soaked her back, as she strove to keep up with the calls. She trod on the toes of a dance hall woman, whose face also showed the tracks of extreme exertion, and who swore at her in terms she'd only heard previously from some of the miners—and only when they thought she wasn't listening. More dancers fell behind, and there was a general disintegration of the squares amidst hoots and catcalls to the fiddler to play "somethin' slower, dammit!"

The fiddler ceased his calling with a "home to your partners!" and completed a blur of finger work designed to elicit applause. Inez, standing by Holt, obliged with the rest.

"All righty," the fiddle player said. "Let's take it easy on the ladies this time around."

The ladies were indeed shooting nasty glances at the fiddle player even as they mopped their faces with their aprons or, to the delight of on-lookers, with their skirt hems.

The music eased into a waltz. Inez looked at Preston, sorely tempted to invite him to dance.

He turned to her. "Took you from that beer. How about I buy you another?"

She swallowed her disappointment. "If you'll allow me to buy the round after that."

They drifted from the floor to the bar.

"So you were looking for me?" he asked, as they waited for the bartender to come their way.

"Oh, yes. I was asked to return this to your son." She fished the photocase out of her waistcoat pocket and handed it to him.

"My son?" He frowned and popped open the case. His brow cleared. "Thanks." He closed it and set it on the counter. "But Reuben's not my son."

"He's not?" This news gave Inez pause. She focused on untying the kerchief from her arm to hide her consternation. "But, I thought you were kin." She dropped the cloth on a clean spot on the counter.

"We are. He's my brother's son."

The bartender finally whipped by. "What'll it be, gents?" she snarled.

Preston ordered, while Inez digested that bit of information. When the bartender had delivered the bottles, Inez said, "So, that picture isn't you."

Preston opened the case again. "Nope. My brother. Folks always did say we looked alike."

"Your brother." The words were like a lamp shining in the darkness. "Hiram."

He looked at her curiously and nodded.

"I heard he worked with you and Reuben on the railroad. For a while."

"Yep." A shadow crossed his face. "Workin' for the Rio Grande didn't agree with him."

She exhaled in relief. "I'll admit, I thought the likeness you. But I couldn't see how you came to wear a Rebel outfit when you fought for the North."

"We fought on different sides, Hiram and me. Happened in plenty of families." He started to close the case.

She laid a hand on top of his, to stop him. "Do you know the other man in the photograph?"

Preston was not looking at the image but at her. She withdrew her hand.

He glanced at the photograph. "Nope." He shut the case and tucked it away in a pocket. "I'll see this gets back to Reuben."

He took a swallow from the bottle before asking, "Where's Jay Sands these days?"

"He left about a week ago." She turned her back to the bar and stared at the dance floor and the waltzing couples. "He didn't tell me where he was going. And I don't care." The lie came hard, the words bit off like so much tough jerky.

"Hmmmm." Preston grew silent.

The waltz ended, and while couples shuffled and reformed, the brass band and pianist returned to their posts, renewed and recharged. The whole ensemble began a fast version of a song Inez recognized as the "Bluebird Waltz." "Bluebird" brought to mind Birdie Snow. Inez did a slow burn, imagining Birdie and Sands waltzing somewhere.

She turned to Preston, who, like her, was watching the dancers. "Are you working tomorrow?" she asked.

"Nope." He swirled the beer bottle around in one hand, now watching Inez intently.

"Well. I am. But later in the day. I was wondering." She cleared her throat. "I have this Sharps rifle I bought recently. On impulse."

"You were packing that when we met."

"Oh." She colored in a most unmanly manner. "That's right. I was. Well. I've been wanting to try it out. I'm not a bad shot, all in all, but something like the Sharps....So, I wondered if you might be free to accompany me tomorrow morning. Go for a ride. Do some," she took a deep breath, "shooting?" The word almost came out a squeak. "I don't mean to be forward." She shifted her gaze to the door, not wanting to read his expression right then. "It just would be helpful to get some pointers from an expert on handling—"

She stopped.

Entering the Red Garter were Reuben and the professor.

"Sure."

Startled, she looked back at him, momentarily forgetting what she'd asked. "Oh. Excellent. And thank you. The earlier the better, if that's possible."

"I'll ride into town. Meet you. Unless you prefer riding out of town solo like—" He nodded at her, taking in her attire.

"No, no. I only do this when I'm trying not to attract attention." *Well, that didn't come out right!* She hurried on. "And I can bring a sort of picnic." *For God's sake, quit babbling, Inez!* "Is seven too early?"

"Seven's fine."

"Good. Let's meet at the foot of Third. That way you don't have to deal with the traffic getting into town." *And I won't have to deal with anyone who might inadvertently see us on their way to church.* "I should be going. Tonight's the usual game, and I need to get ready."

"I'll ride back with you."

"No need. I'm not afraid of riding to town by myself."

"Seems you're not afraid of much." This was said with a hint of amusement.

"So some say," she replied with a smile, then looked deliberately beyond him. "Ah," she said, as if just seeing them. "What timing! Reuben's here. And the professor. If you get a chance to ask Reuben about the man in the photo, I'd appreciate it. I can explain more on Sunday."

Then, Inez saw Delaney enter. A chill sharp as frost crawled up her back.

Delaney looked around, searching.

She tugged her hat down lower over her face. "I *really* should be going," she said desperately. "Thank you so much for the beer. And the dance. I enjoyed it." She allowed herself a quick sideways glance. "Immensely."

"A pleasure." He doffed his hat, smiling.

She wondered if he had any inkling as to just how much a pleasure it had been for her. And whether the feeling was mutual.

"Leastways, I can walk you to the door," said Preston.

"I think Reuben might require your assistance more than me."

Reuben was having difficulty getting around a contentious threesome. Two men seemed to be arguing over who had the next dance with a certain faded lily-of-the-valley. Each of them had possession of a plump white arm and was trying to hand her a coin. Said lily was swatting their hands and, from all appearances, engaging in verbal abuse in return. Inez judged it a situation that could easily escalate. She didn't want to be inside when it did.

As Reuben tried to squeeze past one of the men, the fellow inadvertently elbowed him in the chest. Inez saw Reuben's face, still bruised from the brouhaha at the Silver Queen, darken in anger. He shoved the man back.

Delaney had caught up with the professor, who was frozen in his tracks. He spoke urgently to the professor, who answered something short. They both looked toward Preston and started scanning the crowd.

I'll bet I know who they're looking for.

As people gathered to watch the row developing between Reuben and the threesome, Inez found an opening and made a break for the exit.

Nearly at the door, she stopped. *Dammit! I should have looked at their boots!*

There was no opportunity now. Feet were well hidden by the shifting mass of humanity crowded around the trio, who were all yelling at Reuben, who was swearing back to beat them all.

Inez dashed out the door and slammed square into the bony frame of ex-marshal and livery owner Bart Hollis. Hollis grabbed her arm, snarling, "Watch it, stranger!" Then, after closer scrutiny, he said, "Oh hell. You." And released her arm as if he'd grabbed a rattlesnake by the tail.

The barker hurried up. "Leaving already? The night's still young."

Screams and shouts erupted from inside. Alarmed, the barker drew his gun and dashed through the entrance.

Inez made a run for the hitching rail.

Hollis caught up as she struggled with the knot. "Hold on. I hear you've been pumping old Jack about Eli Carter. What's your game, Miz Stannert?"

"No game," she snapped, trying to undo the impossibly tangled granny knot and keep an eye on the door at the same time, hoping against hope that Delaney would not suddenly erupt from the saloon. "What's yours?"

"Whaddya mean?"

She abandoned the knot and set her hands on the rail, leaning forward, glaring at him as he stood on the boardwalk looking down at her.

Rather than defend, she determined that the best course of action was to attack. "You say you and Eli fought together. But you did not. You say the two of you were best of friends. Again, you were not. He'd turned away from the war and its aftermath. You did not. You say he had no family, but he had a wife. So. Just how sorry were you really to see Eli go? I know you followed him out of town when he left. Did you have anything to do with his disappearance?"

Hollis retreated a step, face slack in amazement. "You think *I* killed Eli? Hell, I was as surprised as anyone when he packed up and left. I rode out after him, caught up outside Malta. I thought he'd gone crazed, touched in the head, t' up and leave like that. We talked. Well, yelled, more like it. He said, 'Take the damn business. I don't want it, there ain't nothing for me here.' Told me he had something to do, an' I wasn't part of it. Took off down the road. That was the last I saw of him."

Inez put a fist on the rail, furious. "You didn't even try to stop him."

"I wish to hell I had." Hollis' face was uncharacteristically sober in the flickering light spilling from the flyspecked window of the Red Garter.

"So, what are *you* doing here?" She turned back to the knot.

"Trying to set things right. Get some answers. Follow up on a couple things that Eli said to me once, and that Jack said." His eyes narrowed. "What are *you* doin' here?"

The knot gave way. "Leaving."

Tossing the reins over Lucy's head, Inez grabbed the saddle horn and hauled herself up onto the saddle.

A quick touch with one heel and a sideways pull of the reins turned Lucy away from the hellhole of a dance hall. Just before heading out, Inez glanced back. Hollis stood there, staring at her.

But what really caused her to clench the reins tighter was a figure emerging from the entrance and moving into the flickering illumination of the saloon's window.

Delaney.

Half of his face was illuminated, the rest in darkness. But it was clear he was looking directly at her.

He lifted his hand, finger extended like a gun—and pulled the trigger.

She rode away as if the devil were on her heels.

Chapter Forty-Three

As Inez burst through the doors of the saloon, Abe said, "You don't have much time, Mrs. Stannert."

"I'll hurry. I rode straight here, poor Lucy's tied up outside. I probably won't take her to the C&H tonight, since I'll be out early tomorrow. Please ask Sol to take her to the livery around the corner."

"Tomorrow?" Abe wiped his hands on a rag. "We've got the Fairplays comin' in the afternoon. They're countin' on you to supply the music, remember."

"Of course I remember," she said too quickly.

Abe searched her face. "Just it seems you've got your mind on somethin' other than business these days."

"What I do on my own time is irrelevant. I'm here when I'm supposed to be. Plus some. Now, if some of my regulars arrive early, offer them a drink. We're going to use the new room upstairs tonight but have them wait here until I come back down."

Inez hurried up to her dressing room behind the office and stripped. She tossed the filthy clothes into the shadows and filled her washbasin nearly to the brim. She pulled out the oilcloth she used for the floor and stepped onto it. A hunt through the forest of bath and toiletry items on the shelves beneath the stand turned up clean towels and the odd flesh-brush or two before she uncovered the spirits of ammonia. She uncapped the bottle, swirled two teaspoonfuls into the cold wash water, and scrubbed vigorously with the brush, her skin prickling with goose bumps. After drying off with a coarse Turkish towel, she felt raw, but clean. *Now I won't smell of horse, dust, and that wretched whiskey from the Red Garter.*

She returned to the shelves, finally finding the bottle she was searching for. Inez checked that the stopper was tight and shook the bottle to mix the glycerine, alcohol, and rose water. She rubbed the mixture on her hands, arms, throat, and face. Finally, she pulled out the hair dressing that Bridgette had given her: "Olive oil, good bay rum, one dram of oil of almonds. You just shake it up is all. It will bring out the highlights in your beautiful hair."

I just want it to clear me of the smell of that place.

She poured some into her palm, raked it through her hair, whipped a brush through the strands, and used a battalion of pins to fasten it back and up.

Dressing quickly, she pondered over the day's events.

Tomorrow, when Preston and I have no distractions, I shall find out the exact relation between Hiram and Eli. And once and for all, the identification of the railroad man that rode that stray horse.

She was back downstairs in record time to find only Doc, looking lost and forlorn, standing in the middle of the empty gaming room.

He turned, brandy in one hand, his cane in the other. "So, Mrs. Stannert, where are we meeting, if not here?"

"The upstairs room is ready for us." She caught his arm. "Come on up. I'd like to talk with you alone for a moment, in any case. Seems like we don't have any time together anymore." She stopped by the bar to retrieve her brandy and coffee and instructed Sol and Abe to send up the other regulars when they arrived. "Jed's bringing some newspaper men," she added. "So let's do our best to entertain them."

As they ascended the stairs, Inez asked, "Doc, I've wondered all week. Why didn't you press charges against Reuben when he shot at you during the fracas last Saturday?"

"I suppose we can thank General Palmer." He gripped the banister with one hand, his cane in the other. "What came to mind at the time was Palmer's brush with the young bushwhacker, and the good general's response. I thought, if he could be magnanimous in war and absolve the youngster who shot at him, well, I could do the same for an act of passion committed during a brawl."

"That was very noble of you." Inez thought she herself would not have been so noble, under similar circumstances.

Inez then prepared to play her first bluff of the evening. "Doc, I also wanted to talk to you about Reverend Sands. I'm very worried." She manufactured a low tone, injecting hesitancy and anxiety, and a small note of apology. "He asked me not to speak of his trip to anyone, but I know you're aware of the details. So, I hope I can confide in you. You see, he promised he'd get word to me, let me know that all is well, and I've not heard a thing." She hugged Doc's arm to her side, at the same time helping him up the last five stairs. "This business he's involved in for the railroad and Snow…." She allowed her voice to trail off, throwing a sharp look at Doc from under her half-closed eyes. *Let's see if my hunch is right or wrong.*

Doc looked out of breath, but not surprised. He nodded, lips pursed.

She continued, "I'm concerned about the danger. And now I see Snow around town." *Without his daughter. And where, pray tell, is she? Out gallivanting with Sands?* "I can hardly sleep for worrying." She tried to look distressed, not incensed, as befitted a woman pining for her man.

Her act, while perhaps not of the caliber of Maude Fairplay's, was apparently good enough to convince Doc.

On the landing Doc stopped to catch his breath. "There, there. Don't fret." He patted her hand. "As you know, the good Reverend J. B. Sands is a man who knows his business. And not just the preaching business. Everything he did for the Union, so long ago. Behind enemy lines and so on." Doc's eyebrows jiggled up and down meaningfully.

Of course. All that wretched sneaking and spying.

She murmured encouragingly.

Apparently encouraged, Doc continued, "Snow's only mini-mally involved, so his coming and going is of no consequence. General Palmer knows our good reverend's qualifications. Sands is our eyes and ears, on the lookout for trouble. Can't have trouble now. Even a hint of it. And the sabotage. They're thinking, an inside job. Unacceptable. Palmer needed an outside expert to straighten things out. Palmer and Grant, after all....He told you about the notes?"

What notes? Inez nodded mutely.

"Well, he shouldn't have, really. But then, m' dear, you surely see, it doesn't hurt that—" Doc looked around the empty land-ing and lowered his voice even further— "he's done this sort of thing before. During and after the war. He's capable of handling trouble, in any form."

Unless that form is a woman. She tightened her mouth into a smile.

"Palmer has the utmost faith in our Reverend Sands. All those gentlemen from Philadelphia, they run in the same circles, know each other from the war, from business. The reverend has the confidence of those at the top. Else we'd not have pushed so hard for him to acquiesce to this bit of work. He's perfect for the part, as I said. And with Grant's visit, as point man for the organizing committee, I—" He stopped and looked past her to the stairs. "Ah-ha! Here comes Jed, trailing quite a crowd. The Colorado Press Association, I'd wager. And I see Cooper acting as rearguard. Now, not a word to anyone, right? Wouldn't want Sands and the rest to think I can't keep mum."

Doc stumped over to the staircase, booming, "Evening, Mr. Elliston, and who are your companions?"

Inez's mind churned with questions. *Palmer, the head of the Rio Grande, wanted Sands to investigate the sabotage? Hasn't he his own men to do that? And what's this about Grant and all that business about Philadelphia? What notes? How do Birdie Snow and her father work into this or is Birdie a mere...diversion?*

She plastered a smile on her face and moved toward the assemblage.

Jed looked up from the stairs, with a silly boy grin that seemed to say, "Told you so," and said, "Mrs. Stannert, allow me to introduce you to these gentlemen of the press." The gentlemen, eight in number, came to attention and removed their hats as if called to duty. Jed rattled off the names in a casual roll call: "Mr. Dawson of the *Denver Tribune*, Mr. Wood of the *Colorado Springs Gazette*, Mr. West of the *Golden Transcript*...."

After Mr. West, Inez lost track of the names and publications. Still, she inclined her head and delivered how-do-you-do's and pleased-to-meet-you's down the line. She noticed with satisfaction that they all, to a man, reverted to manners as no doubt taught to them by their mothers—bowing in return and murmuring polite variations of "pleasure to make your acquaintance."

Excellent. They're clear that the Silver Queen is no "Red Garter" establishment. A vision of the aged female bartender in the Garter flew through Inez's mind. She smoothed the skirt of her dark green velvet dress, glad that she'd taken the time to fasten a silver and pearl bracelet to her wrist and matching necklace and earrings.

"Gentlemen, please follow me. You've chosen a good night to visit the Silver Queen as we're just going to christen our new gaming room." She led them to the recently installed doors, still smelling of varnish and new wood, unlocked them, and entered. Jed trailed after her, followed by the rest.

She turned in the middle of the room, gratified to see how the etched glass lamp fixtures sparkled from the flames within, and how the waxed and polished wood floors and paneling, green and gold wallpaper, framed prints and paintings, and two new rugs—with more to come—harmonized into a pleasing whole. The original sideboard, brought up from downstairs, was well stocked, the decanters, bottles, crystalware, and coffee service present and accounted for. *I must remember to tell Sol I approve.* She knew he'd spent the better part of the afternoon preparing the room for the evening.

She waved a hand at the round mahogany table. "We'll eventually replace this with a new one, when we can get it shipped up by train. The coming of the railroad is a blessing in that regard. As for the rest of the furnishings, we're being discriminating in our selection. This is to be a very exclusive section of our establishment."

Several of the pressmen pulled out pencils and notebooks and began scribbling. *Good! The more publicity the better. Who knows? If some of the nobs from Denver and Colorado Springs read about this, they may decide that it's worth their time and money to pay a visit.*

"So Mrs. Stannert," asked one. "Are you the only woman in Leadville running a place like this?"

"Well, gentlemen." She turned and walked to the window, pulling it open to admit some of the sights and sounds of State Street. "I may not be the only woman in the 'entertainment' business, but I wager you'll not find more decorous surroundings elsewhere in town."

A general murmur of approbation heralded her statement.

She bestowed a benign smile on the attentive press, turned back to the window, and looked down the street. Moonlight shone on the mountains, silvering their heights. Lights blazed from the rooms of Frisco Flo's upscale parlor house. Inez could see figures moving about, drawing a curtain closed, pulling it back. An open window here and there. A gentle breeze breathed on her cheek.

A faint boom echoed through the night. A whistle soft and purposeful whished past her ear, accompanied by an odd tug at the side of her neck, like the rake of a fingernail on soft skin.

Glass shattered behind her with an explosive sound.

Chapter Forty-Four

"Jumpin' Jehosephat!" shouted a newsman.

Clapping a hand to her stinging neck, Inez spun around.

One of her newest acquisitions, a painting of Napoleon on a horse with an expanse of French countryside in the background, hung crookedly from its wire, its glass destroyed, a neat hole in the general's hat.

Inez whirled back, taking care to step away from the window's line of sight.

She saw a man, silhouetted, clamber out of one of Flo's second-story windows and jump to the roof of the saloon next door, disappearing into darkness. He carried a stick-like object in one hand.

But Inez knew, it was no stick.

"The bastard!" she snarled. "He nearly killed me!" She took her hand away from her neck. Blood coated her fingers. The stinging increased.

Excited gabbling filled her ears. The newsmen, Jed in the forefront, crowded to the window, jostling for a better look, heedless of their own safety.

"What bastard?" Jed leaned out the window, peering to either side.

"I don't know, but I'm damn well going to find out!"

Doc came forward, distress on his features, handkerchief extended. "Mrs. Stannert! Please, let me look at that."

"Not now!" She snatched the proffered cloth from Doc and ran to the door, holding her skirts up with one hand, the handkerchief to her bleeding neck with the other.

Inez clattered down the stairs, aware of the thunder of feet behind her. She pounded through the dimly lit kitchen and shot out the back door. Anger boiled up and over the commonsensical voice that whispered against venturing out into the dark alley in her good clothes.

She stopped and pulled her small gun out of its secret pocket sewn into the seam of her evening dress. Then, attempting to grip the pistol and hold her skirts out of the filth with the same hand, she moved purposefully through Tiger Alley, eyes to the deep shadows for a lurking gunman.

"Mrs. Stannert, wait!" Jed caught up with her, panting. "Hold on! You can't just go running through the alley like this!"

"Oh no?" She kept moving, forcing him to keep pace.

Before long, she was surrounded by the pressmen, who, she suspected, were looking forward to writing up some sensationalist snappy story for their representative rags.

"Where'd the shot come from?" one asked.

"Frisco Flo's boardinghouse." Inez banged her toe on something hard.

"Boardinghouse?" came another voice, dubious.

"Oh, call it what it is," said a third. "The cathouse down on the corner."

A long, low whistle from the back. "That's some shot. And at night. How far away d'ya think the gunman was?"

Someone began calculating aloud. "Well, the front of the lots are twenty-five feet wide. There're what, nearly thirty lots on the block? That's about...."

Inez stepped into something that squelched nastily into her second-best shoes, cursed, and slowed to a stop behind the Palace Hotel.

"C'mon Mrs. Stannert." Jed headed down the side of the building. "If you want to find out who pulled the trigger, the best thing to do is head for the front door and ask Flo who was in that room."

Grumbling, Inez conceded that Jed's course of action was probably best.

The entire party arrived at Frisco Flo's impressive brick fortress and attempted to crowd up on the tiny porch. A doorman opened the door and bristled at the invasion.

"Someone shot at Mrs. Stannert from one of your upstairs rooms," Jed said accusingly.

Inez pushed to the front of the group and said to the doorman, who was nearly the size and shape of the door he guarded, "Tell Madam Flo that Mrs. Stannert would like to speak to her. Now." The handkerchief, pressed to her wound, was beginning to drip. Her neck felt as if it were on fire.

Behind the doorman, Inez could hear a confusion of squeals and loud exclamations. "Is that the police?" cried a feminine voice. Cries of panic—not all from women—increased in volume.

"Quiet!"

Inez recognized Flo's voice, although it had none of its usual congenial, slightly dizzy cheerfulness.

Flo shouldered past the doorman. "Oh for the love of.…It's not the police, girls. What's this, someone shot you, Mrs. Stannert?"

"From one of your rooms on the second floor."

Flo's ample bosom heaved in a heavy sigh. "And who're all these gents?"

Inez, with difficulty, turned her head. Sure enough, most of them were still taking notes. "The Colorado Press Association."

"Inkslingers." Flo pressed against the doorframe, considering. "Well, our visitors all vanished out the back door. Come on in, fellas. We've a special fondness for newsmen as long as they get the story straight."

They all squeezed into Flo's entrance hall.

Women clustered on the stairs in various states of deshabille, hair tumbling down, piled up, bare feet, shoes without stockings, stockings without shoes.…

Flo turned to them. "I'm going to ask one more time." There was steel to the velvet in her voice. "Who left that window open?"

Not a sound. All the women's eyes were now trained on the men staring up at them.

Flo sighed. "When I took over this place, I had all the bars from the windows removed. Most of you girls remember. I figured, well, in a fire, we all need more than the front and back doors. But—" her voice hardened— "if I discover someone is taking advantage of my good nature, she'll be out on the street servicing johns in the alleys."

She turned back to Inez and the others and crossed her white arms, deepening the cleavage offered by her low-cut gown. "I've no idea who fired that shot. It came from a room that's been vacant for a while now. Evidently, *some*one went in there *some*time this evening, opened the window and….Well, apparently it's an easy matter to get on the rooftop next door and clamber through the window." She sniffed in disgust. "Something I hadn't considered before, but I certainly will now. Who knows *who* has been slipping in a free one now and again. In any case, we heard the shot. Tiny here," she nodded at her doorman, "went up right away, but the door was jammed shut from the inside. Someone had braced a chair against it. By the time we got in…." She shrugged. "Toodle-oo. Gone."

Flo lifted her head high and addressed the newsmen. "This is the first time we've ever had any trouble like this. You all from Denver? Well, you can tell your readers that Frisco Flo runs a tight ship, the girls are clean and well-behaved, and we take kindly to visitors. In fact, I do believe we'll offer a special tonight. Half-off our usual rates for the next couple of hours."

There was a general shuffle of feet behind Inez. She turned to see notebooks snap shut. Some of the men looked hopeful. Others looked discomfited.

The door squeaked open behind them. Inez heard a babble of animated male voices, including: "I been savin' my wages for three weeks for this." Chatter ceased at the tableau of newsmen and Inez in the foyer facing off Flo and the women on the stairs.

Inez saw one of the prostitutes—young, curly dark hair, extremely thin—cover her mouth as if in surprise or to stop a shout. She faded behind the others, wide eyes on the entrance.

Next to Inez, Wood from the *Colorado Springs Gazette* twisted around to eyeball the newcomers, then said in an undertone to a colleague, "Say, isn't that fellow back there the one who gave us the scoop on the railroad trouble?"

Inez turned her head to see whom they were talking about.

A gaggle of Rio Grande men stood uncertainly just inside the door, including Sketch, looking all spiffed up, Delaney, looking pugnacious, the professor, looking aghast, and Reuben, looking sullen and scuffing a muddy boot.

Suddenly, the floor tilted sideways under her feet and threatened to slam her into the wall.

Jed grabbed her arm. "Steady, Mrs. Stannert. Let me walk you back. Doc should take a look at that."

Flo's expression melted into concern. "If I find out who it was—"

"You let me know," Inez said. "And I'll make sure he doesn't do it again."

Jed, holding her steady, pushed through the crowd to the door. Once outside, the cold air revived her enough that she could walk, albeit unsteadily. Jed volunteered his handkerchief, which she pressed over the blood-soaked one.

Back inside the warm confines of the Silver Queen, Inez allowed Abe and Jed to help her to the kitchen, where Doc waited.

"More blood than damage," he announced after cleaning and examining her wound. "Keep it covered. A hot toddy—no stinting on the whiskey—a good night's sleep, and you'll suffer nothing more than a stiff neck. You're very lucky. A major artery lies just below the surface. Why, I remember in the war—"

A knock on the door interrupted Doc's reminiscences. Sol entered, hand clenched into a fist, looking worried, then relieved. "Good to see you're out of surgery, ma'am. Thought you'd like to see what we dug out of that picture."

He opened his hand.

A bullet, sides cut in a hexagon, dull and dark, lay on his palm.

Chapter Forty-Five

At seven the next morning, neck sore and stinging, Inez perched sidesaddle atop Lucy where West Third met the Boulevard. She kept watch south, the early morning sun touching her cheek, twisting Lucy's reins around her fingers.

True to her words, she'd decided to forgo men's trousers that day.

The sidesaddle was courtesy of the livery a block from the saloon. For a fee, they'd been happy to feed and shelter Lucy overnight and supply the gear.

Thank goodness. Don't think I could've managed going all the way back to Hollis' place. She sometimes wondered about the wisdom of keeping her horse so far away—even though she hated the thought of leaving Jack.

She straightened up as the bottom of her riding corset pinched her skin, reminding herself not to slouch, and rearranged the folds of her dark gray overskirt. She didn't own a tailored riding costume like those worn by ladies from Chicago and New York summering in the mountains. Still, her broadcloth skirt was full and long, her boots were stout, her gloves were gauntleted, and her jacket was the same material as the skirt. Beneath the collar of her white shirtwaist, Inez had wound a soft black cloth around her wounded neck.

The only discordant note to her fashionable ensemble was the Sharps rifle, tucked in a scabbard, and her pocket pistol, invisible to all, but a comfort in case of trouble.

Her hand clenched the reins tighter and the fluttering in her stomach turned into a roil when she recognized the figure of Preston Holt on the large bay heading her way.

After greeting each other, Preston said, "Thought about where you want to go?"

"Maybe up Colorado Gulch or past Soda Springs," she said. "It's a nice ride, not too far. We're early enough that we may have the road nearly to ourselves. The after-church crowd won't be out yet."

He nodded. "Think I know a place, if I can find it again." He fell in beside her. Gave her a penetrating glance, then said, "Understand Delaney found you coming out of the bunk car at camp yesterday."

Oh Christ.

"Oh yes." She looked out at the horizon, as if studying the distance to Mount Massive ahead. "Well, it was that photocase I was trying to return to you. I was directed to the bunk car. I knocked at the door, but no one responded."

Think fast.

"At that point, I thought maybe I'd misunderstood, so I tried another car. I finally returned, knocked again, and, yes, I'll admit I was curious." *Slide in some truth.* "So I went in. Shouldn't have, I know. No one was there, and I was on my way out when Delaney showed up. Nearly scared me to death."

He watched steadily, without comment, throughout her performance. She wasn't certain if she'd been successful until she saw the wariness on his face give way to a smile. "Like I said before, can't imagine much scares you, Mrs. Stannert."

"When someone points the business end of a firearm at me, I pay serious attention." She adjusted the loop of rein over her hand. *I hope he doesn't think I took that gun. Time to talk of something else less volatile.*

"That fellow Sketch rescued me from Delaney's wrath. Is he a payroll guard, too? Is that what you've been doing since the war, working for railroads? Why didn't you go back to Missouri, if that's where your family's from?"

He tipped his head back and laughed.

It was the first time she'd heard an all-out laugh from him. It was a warm, uncomplicated sound. Reminded her of a C major chord, played straight out. No dark undertones, all out front.

"Whoa there. That's a lot of questions."

"Oh, I apologize. It isn't really proper of me to ask."

"I don't mind talking some about it." He was quiet for a while, as if deliberating where to start. Finally, "I never had a hankering to farm. That was my brother's road. The only thing Pa taught me that was useful was to shoot."

"So you and your brother fought in the war on different sides."

He pushed back his hat. "Yep. I was for the North. Time came to enlist, I went to Pennsylvania and passed the shooting test to qualify for Berdan's unit. Pa would've turned in his grave to know his lessons went to helpin' the Union. Hiram joined up with a sharpshooting unit on the other side—Pindall's Ninth Missouri. After the war, Hiram stayed in Missouri, I drifted on."

Ninth Missouri. Another clink as an iron link in the broken chain closed. *Jack said that Elijah Carter fought in the Ninth Missouri.*

She spoke cautiously. "The other man in the photocase. With your brother. I believe he was Elijah Carter. He owned a livery in Leadville. His horse was one of the two I found wandering around the day of the rockslide. I've been told that Elijah fought in the Ninth Missouri, like your brother. And, he owned this Sharps." She patted the gun in her scabbard. "Sold it just before leaving town. Apparently, he was leaving for good. I wonder if Elijah was a sharpshooter too."

Preston's brows drew together.

Tread carefully now.

"I don't mean to pry. But I've been trying to find the connections between the two men Miss Carothers saw arguing on the tracks and….Well, you know what she says happened after that. So who was on the Rio Grande horse?"

"You're sure full of questions."

"Well, I thought, once we arrive at our destination, we'll be busy shooting and so on." A blush climbed up her face under the wide-brimmed hat at what "so on" brought to her mind. "I believe Susan's story. And I'm at a loss as to the connection between Elijah and the Rio Grande man he met at the tracks—"

Suddenly, the pieces fell together. Like random notes that, when played as one, form a decidedly minor chord. "Oh no. Was the horse your brother's?"

Inez saw a troubled look flash across Preston's face before he looked up the road. "Gotta preference for where we go from here, Mrs. Stannert?"

The Boulevard had reached the foot of Mount Massive, leaving the wide-open meadow behind. To the left, the smooth road led to Soda Springs and Evergreen Lakes. To the right, a well-traveled but rough thoroughfare wound up Colorado Gulch.

"To the left?" Inez said.

They turned to follow the Boulevard.

Preston finally spoke, his somber tone matching his expression. "Hiram's wife—Reuben's ma—died not long ago. Times were tough back home. So, when I heard, I saw a way to make amends. Hiram and Reuben, they're my only kin now. Told 'em, if they came west, I'd help 'em get on their feet. They took me up on the offer. Shoulda known, though. Hiram didn't like working for the Rio Grande. Didn't like taking orders from anyone, especially Yankees. He always said, if it hadn't been for the Union's iron horse, the North would never've won the war."

"Iron and blood," Inez said to herself, thinking of Elliston's toast to war with the Rio Grande.

"What's that?"

"Someone once said that the important issues of our times are not decided by words and politics, but by iron and blood. Seems appropriate to the railroads as well as the War between the States. So that was Hiram's horse I found?"

His mouth tightened in an unhappy line. "'Fraid so."

She thought of what Jed had said about the explosion by the siding. "I heard the rockslide at the siding was no accident. That it was deliberately set."

"No proof of that." He sounded final. "When you brought the horse back, I talked with Reuben. He wouldn't say anything at first. Finally told me he'd ridden to the railhead with his pa. Hiram took off, headed back to Missouri. Didn't want no more to do with the railroad or the west, Reuben said."

"And he didn't take his horse? Why didn't Reuben go with him?"

"The horse's property of the Rio Grande, so Hiram did the right thing, leaving the horse. Reuben told me he wants to stay out west. That there's nothing in Missouri for him. And I believe him."

Inez thought of Reuben at the poker table, how completely he'd bluffed them all and walked off with the pot.

"But I found the horse—" she started.

"Reuben said the horse got away from him. He searched for a while, then gave up and went back to camp. I got no reason to disbelieve him."

Inez marshaled her arguments, her suspicions, and prepared to march them out, one by one—then took a good look at Preston's face, and changed her mind. She'd seen the same expression on plenty of men across the table and the bar as they struggled to talk themselves into believing something that, deep down, they had doubts about or knew wasn't true.

There's no way I'll convince him while he's arguing with himself. I'll try another time, another way.

"Besides—" said Preston, then stopped.

"Besides?"

He tipped his hat forward. "Hiram and I had what you might call a big disagreement the night previous. Didn't surprise me none that he left. Most folks thought he'd just headed out for the silver fields like the rest, and it seemed easiest to let them think what they were thinking. I'm hopin' now, with Reuben staying on, I'll get to know him better. Straighten him out a tad.

I see a lot of Hiram in Reuben. Hotheaded. Impulsive. Don't like taking orders. And Hiram never did let loose of the war. Course, he had a tougher time than I did."

"Tougher time?"

"As Hiram saw it, he lost the war, lost the farm, lost his wife. Blamed it all pretty much on the Federalists, the Republicans, the Radicals, Grant. Me. Blamed everyone but himself. Didn't help that, when the railroad came on through back home, he and the other farmers thought it'd all make life easier. Instead, the freighting rates just got so high, he had to give it all up."

"Did Reuben say that?"

"Hiram did. Plenty of times. I remember the only time I went to visit after the war. Reuben was real young, must've been ten years or more ago. Anyhow, Hiram held a gun on me 'til I left. He was always the better shot, so, I didn't argue. Especially not with that Whitworth pointed at my chest when I rode up and then at my back as I rode off."

"Whitworth?"

"A rifle used by Confederate sharpshooters. The ones who earned it, that is. Had a hexagonal rifling system. Accurate up to a thousand yards."

"Oh! That's what I found—" Her throat closed on the words that almost jumped from her without thinking.

Under your bunk. The rifle.

He reached for Lucy's bridle, pulled Inez to a halt beside him. "You found what?"

It was clear he wasn't going to let go until she told him.

She cursed herself for the near dead giveaway and said, "When you lent me your coat that day, when it was raining. Well. After I returned it to you, I found a bullet and a percussion cap tangled up in my gloves. I'd put my gloves in your pocket, so I must have pulled it out with them. Anyway, the bullet was hexagonal shape. Very unusual. I kept it, thinking I'd have the opportunity to ask you about it, but kept forgetting. So it was from Hiram's Whitworth?"

He held on. "Hiram gave it to Reuben, afore he left. I've been keeping it with me. It's a valuable gun, and there's been times folks have tried to steal it."

So, it's Reuben's gun.

"I hope you have it under lock and key," she said, knowing full well he didn't. "Someone tried to kill me last night with a Whitworth, or a gun with a similar bore, from Frisco Flo's cathouse a block away." She undid the top button of her high collared shirt and pulled up the black cloth. "They nearly succeeded."

The silence stretched between them several beats. Preston finally looked away.

Inez repositioned the neckband and redid the button. "So you see, I have a vested interest in knowing more about the rifle."

"Someone stole it," said Preston slowly. "'Bout the time Delaney says you were around."

They began riding again.

Inez pressed on. "Did Delaney mention he caught two men lurking around the area before he stopped me?"

"Nope. He didn't."

"You might want to talk to him about that."

"I will." Preston sounded grim.

Inez wavered, uncertain whether to continue with her trail of questions. But there was one more person she hoped to link to the chain that stretched from Missouri to Colorado. "Just one last query, and I'll not talk further of this. Did you ever hear or see anything of a schoolteacher from town, someone with initials B.D.?" A whisper from the schoolteacher's letter, "*...coming out with fellow travelers...,*" seemed to hiss through the trees above them. "I believe he left town about the same time. Maybe even traveled with Reuben and Hiram."

"Nope."

Inez frowned, disappointed. For some reason, she'd felt certain that the schoolteacher who wrote to Elijah would have arrived with the others. *I would dearly love to know who this schoolteacher is. And who the Colorado Springs newsman spotted at Flo's last night.*

Preston was looking off into the woods. "There've been a few fellow Missourians riding in since Reuben and Hiram, looking for jobs. I do what I can to help them out. Have to say, most who signed on with the railroad took off the closer we got to Leadville. Got the itch to get rich, I guess. Here's the place I was thinking of." He veered off the main track, taking a side trail into the woods.

They went in a ways, until the trees opened up into a long meadow, and stopped by common consent. After watering the horses at a small creek nearby, they found a shady place with grass to tether the horses.

"What'll it be, Mrs. Stannert. Shooting first?"

"Sounds good to me. And please, call me Inez."

Preston removed two empty tin cans from his saddlebag, slid the Sharps from her scabbard, and disappeared toward the meadow. Inez lingered by Lucy, picked a stray burr from her forelock, and tickled her nose. Lucy snorted and nudged Inez's hand. "Nothing to give you right now, girl," she said. "Maybe later."

Inez fished out the box of cartridges and walked to the edge of the meadow. Preston was coming back from the other end, pacing the length.

He reached her and asked, "Done much shooting, Mrs. Stannert?"

"A fair amount. Target shooting, when I was younger. Like your father, mine taught me to shoot."

He ran his hands over the Sharps in a familiar fashion. A little shiver caught her unawares.

"Looks maintained, not used much," he commented. "Has it been cleaned and oiled recently?"

"The store I bought it from assured me that it's ready to go."

He nodded. "I'll start at the beginning. Don't know how much of this you might already know. I shoot left-handed, so what I do with my left, you do with your right. This Sharps is a breechloader with a sliding breech-pin. A small block in the gun breech slides up or down in a slot. The trigger guard here is also a lever. When the trigger guard's lowered and pulled forward—" He demonstrated. There was a *snick* sound. "The block slides into position, opening the breech for loading. Got a spare cartridge, Mrs. Stannert?"

She handed him one.

He inserted the glazed linen cartridge into the breech. "When the trigger guard's closed—" he did so— "the mechanism raises the block up, slicing off the rear of the linen cartridge and sealing the breech. Less chance of backflash. Now, it needs a cap or a primer."

Inez handed him a small percussion cap from the packet.

"Pull the hammer back. The pull is strong; you might need to use your whole hand. The cap goes here. There're two triggers. The rear one's a 'set' trigger. Pull it, the one in front's now a hair trigger. Know how to use a sight?"

"Certainly."

"Stand back."

Inez, who had been watching to the side, promptly backed up.

He brought the rifle up.

The two tin cans glinted on a stump at the meadow's far end.

The report echoed loud and long.

Where two cans had been, one now stood.

He lowered the gun. "Been a long time since I fired one of these."

Unspoken stories crowded behind those few words. Stories, she suspected, that he'd never told anyone. Stories that crept in at night. In dreams, in the dark, pulling the past into the present with a stray sight, sound, or smell.

He shook his head as if to clear it, then held the gun out to her. "Want to give it a try?"

"Of course." After a moment's hesitation, she stripped off both gloves and tucked them into the waist of her skirt.

She took a linen cartridge and, copying Preston's movements, loaded the rifle. Before pulling back the hammer, she paused, judging the weight of the gun at about ten pounds. *I can manage this, if I stay steady, don't take overly long to aim, and breathe slow.* She pulled the hammer back with her whole hand, noting the strong resistance, then placed the percussion cap and steadied herself to aim.

"Hold a minute." Preston was suddenly there, behind her. His hands closed over hers. "Hold it more like—"

She could hardly breathe or hear his words, from having him so close.

He moved away, and a vacuum seemed to open up behind her, leaving her shaky.

She deliberately slowed her breath again, then pulled the set trigger and lined the sight up with the tin can, now looking very small and distant. She willed her heart to resume a calm, slow beat. In with a slow breath, gradually out to empty. Set her finger to barely touching the hair trigger. In the pause before the next inhalation, she applied the slightest pressure.

The report deafened her ears, the butt plate slammed into her shoulder with the recoil, heightening the sting in her neck. But all that went nearly unnoticed, with the flush of fierce delight that flooded through her.

The stump stood empty.

Triumphant, she turned to Preston, grinning. "Not bad for a first time, hmm?"

He smiled back, with something else in his eyes. Something that caused her breath to catch.

He moved forward, slowly, giving her time to say the words that would stop him. To make a gesture that would mean "no." To look away.

None of which Inez did. Instead, she held his gaze, although she could feel herself quivering in that familiar prelude to the song of the body's pleasures.

His hand closed over hers. Removed the rifle from her clasp. Leaned it against the tree trunk.

Pushed her broad-brimmed hat back and lowered his face to hers.

One second left.

To deflect the momentum.

But through the welter of hesitation and anticipation that crowded her senses, the only coherent thought that surfaced was—

What harm can one kiss do, after all?

But it didn't take much for one kiss to slide into the next. For his hands to slide up her arms. For her hands to slide around his waist. For the rough pine bark to begin digging into her shoulder blades as he pressed her against the tree. The sharp scent of pine sap filled her senses.

Then, the alarms went off.

She forced her eyes open, put a hand to his chest, and pushed steadily until he broke away.

She kept her hand there, feeling the beat of his heart beneath her spread fingers.

He looked at her from just a foot away.

She compressed her lips and shook her head, increasing the pressure of her hand. It felt as if she were trying to halt a speeding train by standing in the track and holding up her hand.

She hoped that the pressure of her hand would carry greater weight than whatever he might read on her face.

After what seemed an eternity, he moved a space away and turned, staring down the meadow at the empty stump.

The silence stretched long between them.

He finally said, "Guess I read the signals wrong."

No you didn't was what she wanted to say. Instead she said, "I'm sorry."

"I'd best get you back to town." He gave her his hand, pulled her away from the tree. Held her hand for a space of time that whispered at a second chance. If she would but change her mind....

She slid her hand from his grasp. Pulled her gloves from the waistband where they still miraculously lodged. Tucked her shirt back in all around before putting the gloves back on.

The distance between them grew with each step back to the horses. By the time Preston Holt had helped Inez back onto her sidesaddle and slid the Sharps back into the scabbard, it was as if the entire interlude had been an embarrassing situation that had occurred between them long ago, which they were striving, with politeness, to forget.

It was an uncomfortable ride back. Inez tried to think of something to say that would ease the distance between them. A way to apologize. But she found herself uncharacteristically short of words.

The Boulevard became increasingly crowded as they approached the city limits of Leadville. Sunday picnickers and those going out for a pleasurable Sunday ride far outnumbered those heading into town. She was just about to say to Preston that she could manage fine from here, thank you, when she spotted a familiar figure galloping toward them.

The professor pulled to a stop beside Preston. He was covered with dust, his face streaked with muddy rivulets of sweat. With only the quickest tip of a hat to Inez, he turned to Preston. "Ah, Mr. Holt, there's been trouble at the camp. I've been sent to find you." His words tumbled over each other in their haste. "Delaney's dead and Reuben—" He stopped and glanced at Inez, who was wide-eyed. "'Tis not news fit for a lady's ears. You shouldn't be hearing this, ma'am."

"Oh, I should indeed be hearing this," she said, her voice piercing his protests like a spear of winter ice.

The professor glared at her, a burst of anger or annoyance momentarily distorting his features. "'Tis not your business."

"What happened?" said Preston, his voice weary. He took his hat off and passed a sleeve over his forehead.

Inez became aware of how, with the sun in ascendancy, the heat was bearing down on them and the road, raising dust and discomfort. The sweat trickled down from her hairline, and she was tempted to use her sleeve in the same fashion as Preston.

The professor cleared his throat and leaned in closer to Preston. Inez gripped the pommel as firmly as possible and maneuvered Lucy a few steps closer, not daring to deviate from the straight-up, shoulders-back posture required to remain seated in the sidesaddle.

"…head bashed in with a spike maul down by the Disappointment Gulch trestle," she heard him say in a low voice. "The worst of it is, Reuben's missing. Looks bad. We've got to return, right away. Some thought you might be involved, when you couldn't be found."

"I'll head back if you'd take Mrs. Stannert here into town."

Right on top of the professor's "But I'm supposed to bring you back," Inez interposed with, "I'm quite capable of managing the last mile or two."

Preston cut them both off. "All right, then."

Inez suddenly remembered. "Wait."

She dug in her pocket, finally pulled out the envelope with the ominous letter to Elijah Carter, written in the loose, scrawling hand. "I meant to show this to you earlier, but…." *The morning turned out so differently from what I'd imagined.* "This letter came to Elijah Carter. It mentions 'the general' is coming to Leadville. I'm thinking 'the general' refers to Grant or maybe Palmer. A warning or threat, perhaps an invitation to….Oh, I hate to think. Grant and Palmer were generals for the North. Could it refer to a plot of some kind? In any case, I thought you should know about it. So you could take it to the proper authorities. It's unsigned. I suppose it was from someone Eli knew."

She held it out.

The professor looked at her, eyes narrowed. "Sounds like the silly twaddle of a woman."

Preston took the envelope from her. Pulled the single sheet out. He seemed to age before her eyes as he skimmed the letter and its contents.

"Pardon me, Mr. Holt, but we should hurry!" snapped the professor.

Inez, watching Preston closely, could think of only one reason for the pain that washed his countenance. "Do you recognize the writing?"

Preston folded the letter back into the envelope, tucked it inside his jacket, then looked down at Inez somberly. "My brother's hand."

Her mouth opened, but words refused to form.

"I'll get this to the right people. Guess we'll need to talk more about this later, ma'am. And other things. I'll get in touch with you." He touched his hat. "At least we had the morning."

His gaze lingered on her as if he were loath to leave, as if he wanted to etch her face in his memory for some long journey ahead. Then he and the professor turned and joined the river of people heading out for an afternoon's diversion.

Chapter Forty-Six

Monday afternoon, Inez sat in her office alone, her face resting on two balled fists, a single letter before her. The letter had been waiting for her at the post office box shared by the business, her personal mail, and the mail of those that worked in the Silver Queen. "A benefit of working here," she'd told Sol when hiring him, "is that you won't have to wait an hour or two in line to get your mail from home."

When she'd pulled the envelope out of the box, she'd hoped it was from Sands. But it had not borne his familiar hand. Rather, it was addressed in a stranger's script and postmarked Missouri.

Perhaps some answers will come of this and help me lay Elijah's soul to rest. She slit the envelope open with the letter opener and pulled out the single sheet of writing paper crammed with loopy penmanship. Two folded scraps of newspaper tumbled out with it.

The letter began, *"Dear Mrs. Stannert, Thank you for informing us of the untimely demise of Elijah Carter, whose family lived in this town for two generations."*

The postmaster proved to be very forthcoming. She skimmed the contents, noting that Elijah, indeed, had no living kin, as far as the postmaster knew *("and as he was raised here, seems it would be known if that were otherwise.")*. Mr. H was, as she expected, Hiram Holt. About the schoolmaster "Mr. D," the postmaster had this to say:

Brodie Duncan's family was also from these parts, at least his father was. His mother and her kin hailed from Tennessee. And he spent the last part of his childhood there, before going overseas, and then returning here some years ago. After the pox epidemic, Mr. Duncan left for Colorado with Hiram and Reuben Holt. We were sorry to see them go. But it's not unexpected. Our town has never recovered from the ravages of The War and atrocities committed by both sides. All of us bear the scars. The years after have not been easy, and the epidemic was the last straw for many. If you chance to see Mr. Duncan or the Holts, tell them the folks back home are praying for their good fortune in the silver fields of Colorado.

Inez frowned, then picked up one of the newspaper clippings, which described the services for those overcome by the pox including Hiram Holt's wife and Lillian Carter. The second clipping was brief, saying that Brodie Duncan and Hiram and Reuben Holt were leaving for the "fortunes of Colorado" and hoped to find work on the railroads.

Duncan.

She heard it again, the professor, his burr layering over the words, saying to Jed Elliston, "Duncan, at your service. Mostly, I go by Professor. My background, y'see."

Then she heard again, "It's not my war." Words flat, without emotion, almost without meaning. The heavy Scots notes entirely vanished.

Could the professor be Brodie Duncan from Missouri? Inez drummed her fingers on the desktop. *Duncan is not an unusual name. Particularly for a Scotsman. Still. Hiram and Reuben hired on with the Rio Grande, that fits. The professor is also working for the railroad, but with the lawyers. Reuben doesn't act as if he knows the professor overly well. Yet, I've seen how well Reuben can dissemble. But why would they not acknowledge each other? And the professor said, it wasn't his war.*

Her thoughts were a jumble of events, past and present. Inez looked at the Sharps rifle in the corner of her office. *Everything comes back to that damned war.*

Then, she thought of Preston Holt. Delaney's death. Reuben's disappearance. And the hint that, perhaps, there might be an opportunity to revisit, explain, come to terms with what had happened between her and Preston in the meadow.

How he'd said goodbye.

The door squeaked open behind her. She swiveled in her chair.

Abe was there, looking at her with concern. "You feelin' all right?"

"I've been better. How are preparations shaping up for Grant's visit?"

"Not bad. Got a message from Evan. Wants you to drop by his store when you get a chance. Got a new shipment of decorations in, for the big visit. Banners, streamers, and such. He's holdin' some aside for you."

"Guess it pays to play poker with one of the chief merchants in town and let him win once in a while." She got to her feet.

"You look peaked. Is that wound painin' you some?"

It's not the wound that's paining me. "It'll heal. I'll go see Evan. I have some questions for him anyway. About the Sharps rifle. I'm hoping maybe Eli Carter might have mentioned something about its journey from Missouri to Colorado. Someone brought it to him, and I'd like to know who. A long shot I know."

"If that's what you're after, why not talk to Jack?"

Inez lifted her eyebrows. "True. Jack was the one who first mentioned the rifle in connection with Eli. Maybe Jack met the fellow. He might remember his name, what he looked like."

"It's worth a try," said Abe.

Inez followed three women into Evan's crowded mercantile store. They were chatting amongst themselves about the upcoming visit. "I understand Governor Routt is coming and perhaps General Palmer of the railroad as well! They think he'll arrive early evening, but it could be later. I'm bringing the children to see the procession. After all, how often does one get to see a former president and a famous general?"

Inez snagged a clerk. "Where is Mr. Evan, please?"

Evan, it turned out, was in his adjoining mining supplies store. When Inez found him, he was beside a pile that included a pick, ropes, steel drills, a breaking hammer, and other sundry items Inez associated with a would-be miner's "outfit." Evan was talking with someone that, Inez thought, looked familiar from the back, and was closing with his standard lecture on powder and fuse.

"Now, you've got all you need here for prospecting except the blasting powder and fuse, which we keep in the magazine at the head of California Gulch. Take your bill there, and they'll give you what you paid for. They'll also deliver, save you the trouble and caution. I can't say often enough, you've got to be careful of the giant powder. Especially if you haven't used it before. It's tricky, not like black powder. The nitroglycerine is what does it. If the explosive freezes, and it freezes at around fifty-two degrees, it'll crystallize and be very sensitive. While thawing, it becomes highly unstable. I've know men blasted to bits from storing giant under their beds."

The man nodded, obviously impatient to end the lecture. "Aye. Well, we've no beds to store it under. And my partner knows how to handle the explosives, so he says."

"Professor!" cried Inez, surprised.

The professor whirled around, startled, then whipped off his hat. "Mrs. Stannert. Fancy, meeting you here."

"What are you doing? After you stopped us on the road yesterday—"

"Yes, yesterday." He glanced between Inez and Evan, looking trapped between two worlds. "Well, if the truth be known, that incident of yesterday, Mrs. Stannert, is what did it to me. I'm a new man, now, starting on a new venture." He turned to Evan. "I'm thinking that our business is done?"

"Just need your John Hancock right here." Evan pushed a list and a pencil at him. "Just so we both know we agreed to the terms of the trade."

The professor signed, grabbed the ropes and the picks, and said, "I'll be back for the rest, when I've got something to carry it in. Ye'll keep it for me a day or so?"

"A burro, Mr. Duncan. You should look into getting one if you plan to try your luck in the high mountains," Evan called to his retreating back.

"Thankee."

The professor brushed past Inez and moved toward the entrance. Inez hurried after him, throwing over her shoulder, "I'll be back, Mr. Evan."

She caught up with the professor and said, "I've been wanting to talk with you, Mr. Duncan."

"Ah, call me Professor. 'Tis what I prefer." He looked around, distracted. "Yes, ye'd be wonderin' about my change of vocation here. Well, Delaney's death, the sabotage of the line and all is a worry. Ye know, the cars blown to bits where that young woman was, 'twas sabotage, no doubt. And there's been more I daren't write for *The Independent*. Some are already suspicious, wonderin' how Mr. Elliston gets his news."

The professor pulled the door open and went out.

Inez caught it and hurried to keep pace.

He shot her a look of annoyance, then continued, "Snow, McMurtrie, and some top fellows are makin' inquiries. 'Twould be most uncomfortable for me, should they find out. But to the sabotage, there's some thinking it might be malcontents from the other railroads—the Santa Fe, of course, and well, there's the Denver and South Park. They've gotten fed up with Palmer's high and mighty ways, it seems. But now, the business with Delaney. Things are taking a serious turn. So, I've decided to move along. I've been bitten by the bug, you see. Those graders striking it rich in Malta got me thinking I'd try my hand at prospecting."

"Where will you go?"

"Well now." His gaze skittered away from her to the street. "There's a place I'm going to explore further with a partner. An experienced fellow. No sense giving its location away. Could be the next strike, y'know."

"Professor, I have some urgent questions for you. And if you're planning on leaving, I must ask them now."

"Now's not a good time." He reached his horse, dumped the pickaxes and rope on the ground, and looked at the animal, as if trying to figure out how he was going to pack on the equipment.

"It's the only time we have. And remember, I did help you find a job on the newspaper, did I not?"

"Ah well," he grumbled, bending to pick up the rope. "What then?"

"Are you from Missouri?"

He straightened up, staring. "What makes you ask that?"

"A Brodie Duncan left Missouri with Hiram and Reuben Holt, heading for Colorado to work on the railroads. And Hiram Holt is one of the fellows who was killed by the siding."

"Now, there's no proof anyone died, no bodies—"

"Are you indeed Brodie Duncan from Missouri?"

He sighed. Dropped the rope. Looked at the picks miserably. "You're makin' a mistake."

She stepped closer. "What happened yesterday? Do they think Reuben had something to do with Delaney's death? Certainly they can't think Preston, I mean, Mr. Holt, did anything. I can vouch for him. We went riding that morning—"

"Railroad business, Mrs. Stannert," he interrupted. The professor gathered up the rope again, pulled the coils over his head and onto one shoulder, then gathered the pickaxes awkwardly under one arm. "I cannae say more."

"Why not? You've been willing to slander your employer far and wide in the newspaper."

"'Tis not slander!" The professor stopped and looked around as if afraid people were listening. Pedestrians hurried by without giving Inez or the professor a single glance. Nonetheless, he lowered his voice. "But that's not the point now. This business with Delaney. A murderer's about. And I dinnae want any part of it."

"One more question. Did you fight in the war?"

"Mrs. Stannert." He covered his eyes for a moment with his free hand. Then lowered it and looked straight at her. "I was a lad of fifteen in Tennessee when it ended and was straightaway to Edinburgh afterward. Whether I was in the war or no, fought or not, what difference does it make?"

He turned to his horse and awkwardly mounted. As he pulled on the reins, Inez said loudly, "The war seems to make a difference to all but you. And that makes me wonder."

Without a word or a glance, he maneuvered his horse out onto Chestnut Avenue and headed out of town.

Chapter Forty-Seven

Inez headed up Chestnut, thinking that a walk to the livery to talk with Jack, and maybe Hollis, might offer some answers. As she approached Susan's studio, she saw Susan standing outside her door, looking up the street. Then back down in Inez's direction. Her anxious gaze seemed to pass right through Inez as if she was looking for someone else. She began locking her door.

Inez hurried to the studio. "Susan, are you closing? Is something wrong?"

"Oh Inez!" She turned, the "Closed" sign in one hand. In the other, she held her key and a cabinet card. "I'm so glad to see you. I was going to look for a policeman or the marshal. It was such an unsettling experience, and I'd hate for something to happen."

"Wait. What are you talking about?"

Susan took a deep breath. "That strange man. The one that's been bothering you."

"You mean Weston Croy?"

"Yes. The crazy man, who looks like a ghost. He was wandering past my studio just now and burst in, shouting 'Where is she?' I had no idea who he was talking about. I thought he might mean you, actually, since he's been dogging your heels about town. I said, 'Who?' and truly wished I had a gun to brandish around. I think you're right, Inez, I shall have to get something to keep with me here, I wouldn't have to load it, just wave it around."

"Susan! Stop babbling and tell me what happened!"

"He dragged me over to the window, plucked out a cabinet card from the display, and said, 'Where is she?' and I said—it just slipped out, I was so unnerved—I said, 'You mean Mrs. Flynn?' and he shouted 'Flynn! That….' Well, I won't repeat what he said about her. Then he took off. With the card. I have a copy I was going to take to the police." She held out the photograph to Inez.

Inez took it. And was immediately struck by Mrs. Flynn's expression and bearing. "Heavens, we could be sisters," she said, dumbfounded that she hadn't seen the similarity before.

"Yes, you could. Well, except for the color of your hair. But you both have a certain expression, and I believe I caught it here. Mrs. Flynn also carries herself like you, I've noticed. I think it's something to do with good breeding."

The nervous words pouring from Susan hardly registered as Inez took in a second damning detail. "The shawl," she said, dread creeping in despite her efforts to control it. "Mrs. Flynn and I. We even have the same shawl."

The paisley shawl draped over Mrs. Flynn's Sunday best outfit was twin to the one Inez had worn when Weston Croy had accosted her outside the deadfall on Third.

Inez looked at Susan, concerned. "Could Mrs. Flynn be his wife? Addie Croy? But she's a widow."

Susan shook Inez's arm. "Do you think she's in danger? I didn't say where she lives. Oh, Inez."

"I'll head to your boardinghouse and find a lawman on the way." Inez pocketed the photo. Her fingers brushed her revolver. "With luck, it'll take Weston a while to find out where she lives. I can't imagine many folks will come right out and give him directions. Susan, go back inside. If I were you, I'd keep the door locked until this is resolved. He might come back demanding more information." *If he's thinking straight, that is.*

Susan unlocked the door and went inside. "Let me know what happens."

"I'll be back." Inez weighed the odds of running into a patrol on the side streets—faster moving, less foot traffic—versus on

Chestnut and Harrison—slower going, more people. *But if I get there too late....*

Inez started moving at a brisk pace down Chestnut and cut over on Spruce, picking up her skirts to hurry even more. Near the crossing of Fourth, she spotted the familiar uniform of a Leadville officer. She got his attention by hollering an unladylike "Hallo!" He waited while she caught up and listened gravely but, she thought, with a trace of skepticism as she explained her haste.

"We'll see then," he said, setting his police cap at an authoritative angle. He proceeded at a slower pace than Inez would have wished, but at least gripped his blackjack in a firm and ready manner.

They'd nearly reached the corner where they'd need to turn for the boardinghouse when Inez heard the unmistakable crack of a revolver, followed by a bevy of women's screams, and another shot.

The policeman broke into a gallop, abandoning Inez to her own pace. Inez lifted her skirts higher, determining that the situation demanded she overlook the impropriety of flashing boot tops and a bit of stocking, and ran as well. Halfway up the block, she saw the boardinghouse, its ornate cream-painted false front rising above the other two-story and one-story houses on the street. Clustered in front were a handful of young women, a couple with hands to their faces, others pointing up the street toward Harrison.

As she drew closer, Inez heard Mrs. Flynn's voice raised in a strong and fierce timbre. "Yes, I shot him! And I'll do it again, if I have the chance. Weston came here. How he found me, I don't know. I opened the door and he attacked me, saying the most foul things. He hit me, twice, and pulled me outside. Mr. Braun came to my aid and grappled with him. I ran inside and got the pistol I keep by the door. Then, Weston shot Mr. Braun. And I shot Weston. I wish I'd killed him!"

Inez pushed through the knot of boarders to see Braun, crumpled on the sidewalk, hand clutching his side. Blood soaked into the weathered boards. "Ach, Mrs. Flynn, you need not—" he said weakly, and coughed up blood.

Two young women screamed. Mrs. Flynn whirled to them, furious. "Get back in the house!"

They scattered like frightened doves.

Mrs. Flynn turned back, revolver hanging limply from one hand. Her face was beginning to bruise around a weeping gash on one cheek. "Weston is mad. He, he threatened to kill me."

The policeman knelt by Braun, trying to staunch the blood with a handful of lace hankies. He looked up at Inez, desperate. "He needs a doctor."

"Dr. Rice's office is just one block toward Chestnut," Inez said. She knelt by the policeman, pushed him away, and applied pressure to the hankies. "Go!"

The policeman stood, adjusted his hat with a bloodied hand, and ran up the street.

Mrs. Flynn knelt by Inez. "Dear Lord. What have I done?"

Inez said quietly, "Addie Croy?"

She turned a distracted gaze toward Inez.

"What happened?" Inez asked.

Mrs. Flynn gripped the pistol with a lace-gloved hand. "I thought I'd outrun him." Her voice was a whisper. "How did he find me here? In Leadville? I took another name. Dyed my hair—"

Looking closer at Mrs. Flynn's uncovered tresses, mussed and half hanging in her face, Inez detected dark brown roots, betraying the bleached-blonde plaits.

"He often mistook me for you," Inez said.

Mrs. Flynn's blank gaze transferred to Inez.

"Weston followed me around town, called me Addie. He said to me once, something about making your sister tell him where you were."

"Oh no." Mrs. Flynn began to weep silently. "He wasn't like this when we married five years ago. He was an engineer. In Ohio. Built bridges. Never talked about the war. But then…he began acting strangely. And he beat me. He'd have fits, think the war was still raging. Those were the worst times. I tried to divorce him. But he found out, nearly killed me. I should have had him committed. But I was afraid. What if they wouldn't take him in? The beatings. They didn't stop. And he was wild. He'd drag me into the woods, saying the Rebels were after us, that they were going to set our house afire. I was so afraid. I finally decided to take what money there was and disappear, start a new life, pretend he was dead. It seemed the only way out."

Attorney Casey's words came back to her: *There are far worse things in this world than divorce.*

"I understand," Inez said quietly. "Mrs. Croy, you must get free of him. If you pursue a divorce, I know someone who can help."

She looked up the street, away from the weeping Addie Croy. The policeman was returning at a fast clip with Dr. Rice, medical bag in hand. The doctor reached them, said, "I'll take it from here," and knelt by Braun.

"Mrs. Flynn." The policeman's voice was courteous, but firm. "I think you'd best go inside." He looked up and down the street. "So which direction did this Weston fellow go?"

"All the boarders were pointing north," said Inez.

"We'll get a description of him and set a watch here as well. We'll catch him eventually. Although, I've got to be honest, with Grant's upcoming visit, we're stretched pretty thin on the force. Mrs. Stannert, would you mind taking the missus and…." He gestured toward the boardinghouse. The boarders were peering out the windows, horror and fascination painting their gazes.

Inez took Mrs. Flynn by the waist, and led her away from the doctor laboring over Braun, feeling bleakness and the cold sigh of fear enter her soul.

I hope "eventually" is soon enough.

Chapter Forty-Eight

Tuesday morning, Inez hustled Susan to Evan's store as soon as it opened and told him to fix her up with a small pocket pistol. "If you have another like mine, that will do nicely," she said to Evan.

"A Remington Smoot Number Two? Let's see." Evan inspected the gun case. "Ah, here's one." He pulled the shiny nickel-plated pocket revolver from the case and held it out. "A real beaut, Miss Carothers. As Mrs. Stannert will attest."

Susan recoiled. "It looks so…serious."

Inez sighed. "It's supposed to. You want someone to take you seriously when you point it at them."

Susan turned to Evan. "Have you anything smaller? That doesn't hold so many bullets?"

Evan raised his eyebrows but laid the pistol aside. After a moment, he said, "Here's a little Remington derringer. Someone brought it in on a trade. It's clean and ready to go. But you only have two chances to hit your target with this model. Not like the Smoot, which holds five rounds."

"Perfect!" Susan said. "And I'll take two bullets with it, please."

"They're called cartridges before you shoot," Evan said. "Bullets, afterward."

Inez said firmly, "She'll take a box of cartridges."

He packed the tiny gun and the box of cartridges in a brown sack, and Inez accompanied Susan back to her studio.

"I'll give you lessons on how to shoot as soon as possible," said Inez. "In addition, I'll show you how to handle the gun safely, load it, and clean it."

Susan used two fingers to lift the pistol from the bag. "I suppose I should carry this in my pocket. Isn't that what you do?"

"Just be careful not to catch the hammer on a fold of fabric or anything like that. If the hammer's pulled back, it'll be ready to fire."

"Maybe I'll just keep it in the bag." Susan lowered it back into the paper bag and rolled the top down tight.

"I don't know what good it will do you like that."

"It will make me feel more secure. And that's the intention. So, have they caught him yet? Weston Croy?"

"No."

"Poor Mrs. Flynn. Or Mrs. Croy. I hardly know what to call her anymore. She insists she shot him. Mr. Croy, that is. But none of us are sleeping very well in that house. We keep expecting him to appear in a window or pop up at the back door."

"It's a good thing the police are patrolling." Inez couldn't help but feel uneasy, as if the world were holding its breath. *Maybe it's just Grant's impending visit.*

"Thank goodness," Susan continued, "that Mr. Braun is going to recover. How awful if he would have been killed! I do believe Mrs....well, our landlady...is quite fond of him. By the way, have you heard from Reverend Sands?"

Inez jolted to the present. "Oh, yes. I got a short note this morning. He's in...." She pulled the letter out and glanced at the heading. "Colorado Springs. Says he'll be coming into town with Grant's train. Hmmm. I wonder if that means 'on' the train."

"I saw in today's paper that Grant is at the Springs as Palmer's guest," said Susan, trying to fit the rolled-up paper bag in her pocket. "Pshaw! It's too big!"

Inez stared at the letter. The message had been brief, no mention of their tempestuous parting. But just seeing the reverend's handwriting had caused her heart to contract in her chest. Expectation and guilt squeezed tight together.

"You must miss him a great deal." Susan sounded sympathetic.

"Hmmm." Inez stared at the handwriting—firm, precise. *Handwriting.*

"Ah! I've got it!" she exclaimed.

"Got what?"

"A way to find out who he *really* is! Susan, I have to go. I will be back later. You know, you might consider having Miss O'Loughlin come help out until they catch Weston. She's not teaching yet and might enjoy being here with all the pageantry. Aren't the bands and such going to be marching and countermarching on the streets tomorrow, getting ready?"

"Yes! That's true! Thank you, Inez. An excellent idea."

Inez hurried to the saloon and rushed past Abe. "I will be back shortly."

"Well, if you're runnin' around town you might take a look at what the competition is putting up," said Abe, holding a ladder steady for Sol. The bartender was nailing a banner above the Harrison Avenue door that read, "The Silver Queen Welcomes the Citizen of Appomattox!"

Inez dashed upstairs and rummaged through her desk for Eli's letters. She pulled out the one from the schoolmaster and retraced her steps to the mercantile.

Evan was supervising the winding of red-white-and-blue streamers around the columns inside his store. He hastened over to Inez, adjusting his steel-rimmed glasses. "Hello, Mrs. Stannert. Are you in need of more streamers?"

"No, no, nothing like that. Mr. Duncan's bill of trade. Do you still have it?"

"Of course." Giving her a curious look, he disappeared into the back office, reappearing a few minutes later with the paper in hand.

"I just want to see." She put the list with Duncan's signature on the countertop and laid the letter by its side.

Evan craned his neck to see. "Looks like a letter from Duncan."

"I do believe that's the case." Inez was not staring at the signature, identical on both sheets of paper, but at the list of items the professor had traded for his mining outfit. She felt faint. "Is this what he brought in to trade?"

"Yes indeed." Evan turned the list around. "Most of it, not worth much. However that Whitworth rifle, he could've gotten a small fortune for it. Even has the original telescope. But he was in a hurry, not interested in bargaining. I'll probably sell it for several times what I traded for it. The Confederate sharpshooters used them to great advantage in the war. Mrs. Stannert, you look pale." Evan hurried around the counter. "Can I get you a chair? A glass of water?"

"I'll be all right." She scanned the rest of the list. "He sold his boots?"

"Needed something sturdier. Those town shoes weren't going to get him far. I figured I'd take them in trade, polish out the scuffs—"

"Can I see them?"

"See his boots?" Evan wrinkled his brow.

"Yes. Please."

He shrugged. Went into the back of the store, and returned with a pair of boots which he plunked on the counter. "Haven't spiffed them up yet."

The right toe box held a single deep gouge.

The professor. He took the rifle from under Preston's bunk. I didn't notice an accent. But then, it's not always there.

She stuffed the letter back in the envelope. "Thank you. Did Mr. Duncan return for the rest of his outfit?"

"Not yet." Evan picked up the boots and the bill of trade. "But he showed up at the magazine for the giant powder and fuse. I sure hope he's got a place to store it where the temperature is stable. Otherwise, he's going to have fireworks to compete with the ones arranged for the general's arrival."

"The general." She stared at Evan. She thought of the note written to Eli about the coming of the general.

But when that was written, all anyone knew about was General Palmer. Unless. Could Grant and Palmer have been discussing a visit to Colorado? Before Doc or any of the Leadville committee knew about it? And who would have been privy to that information, if not the clerk for the Rio Grande lawyer in charge of right-of-way through Leadville. The clerk who carried correspondence between Rio Grande managers in Leadville and the Rio Grande board. So, Hiram, the professor, and probably Reuben. They knew. But why try to kill me? And what has Delaney's death to do with this, if anything…and did Reuben kill him?

Chapter Forty-Nine

Inez chafed as thirty precious hours slipped by like a rushing mountain stream between Tuesday morning and Wednesday evening.

Newcomers were pouring into town—from out of the mountains, nearby settlements, and even from Denver—brought in by news of Grant's impending arrival. They disembarked at Malta from the twice-daily trains and took carriages or wagons or trusted their own two feet to deliver them to Leadville.

They arrived dusty, thirsty, and hungry to find all hotels full, long waits at the restaurants, and little elbow room at the bars. Business owners realized they had a seller's market and priced goods and services accordingly.

After Inez wrangled a last-minute deal with a local liquor wholesaler, she kept Sol busy all day Wednesday taking inventory on the deliveries and stacking crates and kegs nearly to the storeroom ceiling. He tucked the overflow into the kitchen corners, much to Bridgette's dismay.

The kitchen was hot as Hades on Wednesday, what with Bridgette's non-stop baking and cooking as she attempted to stay ahead of the demand. She flitted around the scorching stove, uncharacteristically flustered. She burned two batches of biscuits and barely salvaged an oven's worth of peach pies.

"Lands, Mrs. Stannert." She wiped the sweat streaming from her face. "My thoughts just keep on wandering. Did you know that my late husband, Mr. O'Malley—God bless him—fought in the war? I'm thinking more on those years now, what with the general coming. We were newlyweds, the two of us. Oh, how Mr. O'Malley would go on about General Grant. He thought the world of him. I hope to get a peek while he's in town."

Inez was also distracted, mainly by all the questions and worries crowding her mind, bubbling away like Bridgette's bottomless stewpot. She poured the wrong liquor more than once throughout the day, and even caught herself providing an inferior grade of bourbon to a visiting toff who had asked, rather snidely, for "the best you have to offer."

She snatched the drink back before he quaffed it and gave him the better brand, snapping, "Wouldn't want you to think that's the best the Silver Queen has in the house."

When they locked up that night, Inez asked Abe if he'd walk her home.

"Sure thing. Seems like you've a powerful lot on your mind, judging by today. And tomorrow's shaping up even busier. The town's bustin' at the seams."

Abe and Inez stood outside the door for a moment, watching the men pass by, many of them with the desperate look of no place to sleep that night.

Abe continued, "We could rent space on the saloon floor, the next few nights. Sol and I could take turns stayin' in. We'd do well at a dollar a head."

"If you think so."

Abe looked at her. "Sounds like your mind's not entirely on business, judgin' by the lukewarm reception of my surefire idea. So what's botherin' you, Mrs. Stannert?"

They started walking up Harrison. Slowly, because of the crush of people.

"I'm feeling more and more uneasy about Grant's visit. There's something afoot, but I can't pin it down. Remember Delaney, the railroad man who held the gun on Taps and started the whole ruckus last week?"

"Not likely to forget that."

"Well, despite all the noises McMurtrie made, Delaney wasn't fired. He's not a section boss for the construction crew anymore, but some kind of camp guard. I bumped into him Saturday night when I went looking for Preston—I mean, Mr. Holt. Then, on Sunday, when I was returning from my outing with Mr. Holt, the professor caught up with us outside of town. He's the railroad clerk I introduced to Jed Elliston, the one working for Lowden Snow, the Rio Grande's right-of-way lawyer. Well, the professor told Mr. Holt that Delaney'd been murdered. And that Reuben—the young fellow, Mr. Holt's nephew, actually— had disappeared. I fear what happened to Eli Carter is tied to all this. Preston—I mean, Mr. Holt—said he'd be back to talk to me about what's going on. But I've yet to see him. It's been two days, and I'd think—"

"Lord, Inez. You lost me on that road somewheres at the start."

"I feel like that too, sometimes. That I'm riding down a road on a cloudy night. Every once in a while, the moon peeks through, and I see a landmark, a glimmer, and I think I know where I'm headed. Then it all goes dark again."

When they reached Fourth Street, Inez sighed. "Would you mind if we walked up Harrison a bit further? If I can better explain what I think is going on, you might have some insights. Oh, I wish Reverend Sands were here!"

"You do?" There was a note of skepticism in Abe's voice.

"I have a sneaking suspicion he's embroiled in this. He's doing something for Palmer and the railroad, I believe. He wasn't very specific." With a twinge, she remembered how she'd cut that conversation short. "He sent me a short letter from Colorado Springs, saying he'd be coming back with Grant and Palmer. I wonder—" She stopped on the boardwalk. Turned to Abe. "Wait. What did you mean by that tone of voice?"

"Yep, you're definitely distracted. Otherwise you'd of snapped back at me a whole lot quicker." Abe took another step, urging her to continue walking.

They had left the gaslights behind and were nearly at the foot of Capitol Hill. The crowds had thinned considerably, and the city noise as well. Inez became aware of the gurgling sound of water in the ditch nearby.

"I'm wonderin', between Preston—I mean, Mr. Holt." He gently mimicked her. "And the reverend, which one you're hopin' to see first."

"That's not…I don't want to talk about it." *Or think about it.*

"Yes. Ma'am." Abe looked down Ninth, little more than a dirt path with a few houses dotted along its length. "Just seems, you're not doin' yourself or them any favors by hedging your bets."

"I am not—"

A gunshot echoed off the nearby hills. Followed by a second. And a third.

A figure was running down Ninth toward them, shouting and waving.

Inez became aware of the sharp smell of acrid wood smoke, just before she heard the dreaded shout, "Fire!"

A cluster of men approaching from Capitol Hill stopped talking. Someone hollered back, "Where?"

The fellow stopped in the intersection, panting, hands on knees. "Twelfth and Poplar! Someone's going for a fire alarm box, but we need all the help we can get. The horses…."

The horses!

Electric fear coursed through Inez. She clutched Abe's arm. "The livery!"

"C&H Livery, that's the one," gasped the runner. "I've got to get more men." He headed down Harrison at a trot, fired his pistol again, shouting, "Fire! Up on Twelfth!"

The central fire bell downtown began to ring an alarm, its clangs echoing over the city, telegraphing the fire's location to the volunteer firemen.

"Lucy!" Inez set out at a dead run up Ninth toward Poplar.

Abe, wheezing, caught up. "Inez! Easy! We'll get there. Won't help if we break our necks doing it."

She could see the strange otherworldly glow cast by unseen flames and the flickering of bright yellow tongues skyward.

They ran on, saving breath for speed. The smell of burning wood, leather, oats, hair, and, most ominously, flesh filled their lungs and the midnight air.

They arrived at the livery, a scene of shouting men, screaming horses, and ghastly orange and yellow flames licking up the back and roof of the structure. Thick smoke roiled up into the dark sky and down into the street.

Men dashed into the livery, emerging with horses, mules, dragging tack and the occasional cart or carriage.

The first of the volunteer fire companies had arrived and were battling the flames as best they could with buckets and hoses. Inez saw shadowy figures with shovels dash behind the structure to dig a firebreak.

Inez pushed through the crowd only to be driven back by a policeman trying to maintain order.

"My horse!" she screamed at him.

"All the ones that are getting out alive are got!" he shouted back. "Over there!" He pointed up Twelfth, away from the fire.

Inez pelted up and around the corner to find a melee of frightened horses and mules. Those with halters or ropes were tied to trees, stumps, fence posts, wagons, whatever was stationary and available. A nearby corral held a few more—but still, the total was much less than the original population. The smell of burnt hair and seared flesh was strong. Men moved among the terrified animals, covering eyes with water-soaked shirts, feed sacks, odd bits of material to keep them from spooking further. Some of the animals had horse blankets and sacks on their backs as protection from flying cinders.

Inez searched the street, staying a careful distance from the hooves of still panicked animals. The light from the flames glossed their coats, highlighted the occasional rolling eye, threw long crazy shadows everywhere.

Then, secured to a picket fence, a familiar shape emerged, a black shadow in the darkness, blanket on her back.

"Lucy!" Inez fell upon her horse.

Lucy started, then calmed, still trembling, at Inez's touch and voice.

"Thank God," Inez whispered fervently. "You're safe!"

Lucy's lathered coat steamed into the cool night air. Inez squeezed her eyes shut to keep the tears in as she stroked Lucy's muzzle, her quivering neck and withers. Inez's hand moved to the blanket on Lucy's back—and stopped.

A tactile memory emerged.

Loose woven cloth, sliding through fingers.

Inez opened her eyes. In the flickering demon light of the burning livery, she saw a flag of the Confederacy spread across Lucy's back. Inez ran her hand over it again, as if in a dream.

"You're damn lucky, Mrs. Stannert," Hollis bellowed in her ear. "You can thank Jack for savin' your horse, when he mighta saved—" He stopped. "So that's where it went!" And tried to yank the flag off Lucy's back.

"No!" Inez grabbed hold of the cloth, prepared for a tug-of-war.

"No? Whaddya mean 'No!'? Goddamned Rio Grande. First they destroy my haulin' business. Then they burn my livery to the ground 'cause of the right-of-way. Oh, mebbe not Snow his-self, but you can bet your ass he gave the order! Bet they think I'll give up now, sell out, and crawl away. Hell, they don't know shit about Texans! Damn 'em t' hell for burnin' my building, killin' my mules and horses that never did no one no harm!"

Stunned, Inez realized that Hollis' face, streaked with soot, was also streaked with tears.

"Bastards! Every one of 'em!" he roared. "If I see Snow, I'll cut off his ears. And you will damn well let go of my flag!"

"Hollis!" she roared back. "I don't want your damn flag! I need to borrow it until tomorrow, to see, to see…Hollis! Did Eli ever talk about a brotherhood? Bound by the flag or pieces of it?"

Hollis stopped pulling. His face, mottled by shadows of the dying flames, went slack with shock. Then, his mouth clamped shut under his singed mustache. His eyes narrowed.

And he said, "Oh. Hell."

Chapter Fifty

"Did the big fire wake you last night, Mrs. Stannert?" Sol greeted Inez as she dragged into the Silver Queen early Thursday morning. "First that, with the alarm and all. Then, the guns early this morning, so everyone could rise and shine to prepare for the big day. Sunrise came awfully fast after last night."

Inez's eyes felt as if river sand had been ground into them. Pebbles and all. She wasn't about to tell Sol that her lack of sleep had nothing to do with Grant's arrival that day, and all to do with the fire, and then with the questions and fears that plagued her. One of the foremost being: *How can I reach Preston Holt if he doesn't come into town? I'll never find him if I go riding about. And I can't do that anyway. Not today.*

She'd been out of the saloon far too much of late and was determined to pull her own weight on this, what was bound to be one of the busiest days of the year. No matter what. She just hoped that her upcoming conversation with Hollis would yield some hard answers and the time to deal with them.

"I counted thirty-eight guns in that salute," Sol said in an unbearably cheerful tone. One for each state in the Union. I heard they're going to fire a thirteen-gun salute at noon, and one hundred and one when he arrives."

Inez pressed a palm against her pounding forehead, wondering how she was going to survive the barrage of salutatory gunfire scheduled for the day.

"Since you and Mr. Jackson are here, I'll get busy outside hanging the last banner over the door and nailing fir boughs around the frame. I could put some bunting above the windows maybe, and—"

"Sol, I know you'll do us proud." She clutched Hollis' folded-up flag in her arms, anxious to get upstairs.

Sol went outside, then popped back in before the door stopped swinging. "That your horse out there at the hitchrack?"

"Yes. She was in the livery that burned last night. I want to keep her nearby for just a while. I'll need to check whether the livery around the corner has room for her. If you'd just keep an eye on her, let me know if she gets nervous. Oh! And the livery owner, Bart Hollis, will be by soon. He's bringing my tack. What's left of it. Please send him up to the office."

"Sure thing."

She poured herself a cup of coffee and told Abe she'd be upstairs. Once in the office, she looked around for a place to unfold the flag. It didn't seem proper to put it on the floor, so she draped it over the office's loveseat. The edging, which could have been tan or a very dirty or faded orange, paraded around the outside of the flag. Its red field was slashed with a diagonal cross of blue, edged in white. Three white stars marched along each of the four arms, a single star in the intersection. This symbol of the attempted secession of the thirteen states seemed part of a past that had eluded her entirely. *My parents never talked about the war. At least, in front of Harmony and me. What a sheltered life we led. I was just a chit of a girl. It all seemed so distant. Stories in the newspapers. Popular songs. But nothing to do with me.*

Thinking on Hollis' reaction last night, she sighed. All the comments, discussions, arguments, remembrances of the war that had been flying about her for nearly a month. All that explosive emotion, stored in a piece of fabric.

She examined the flag. The stars seemed larger on Hollis' flag than the stars on the cloth strips or the one she'd seen in Reuben's photocase.

Inez went to her dressing room and retrieved the two strips of bunting: the one found by the river, the other from Eli's saddlebag. She unfurled them both and draped them on the flag, trying to match up positions.

Aside from a different colored border, the strips matched the design of Hollis' flag. But they seemed from a smaller version, as if someone had sized down Hollis' flag and then cut it into pieces. And given it a different colored border.

Eli's strip fit to one side of the center star. The other piece, its white edging bordering one long side, seemed to belong at the flag's leading edge. Provided one took into account the missing star. *I'll bet this strip belonged to Hiram Holt. And the missing star is the lining in Reuben's photocase. The photocase that holds an image of his father and Eli Carter.*

If all the pieces were the same width.... She measured with her eyes. *It would take seven to make the flag whole.*

A knock at the door broke her reverie.

"Come in."

Hollis and One-Eyed Jack entered, bringing the heavy stale scent of the stable fire with them. Hollis dumped what was left of Inez's tack—her astride saddle and a jangle of stirrups, bridle, and bit—inside the door. Jack added a singed horse blanket. They lingered by the door, as if uncertain of their welcome.

Hollis' clothes were clean but ill-fitting, much too baggy for his snake-like frame—no doubt offerings from one of the various relief societies from around town, or maybe a sympathetic friend. His face was cleaned up from the previous night, but its usual pinched contours were even tighter, due most likely to exhaustion, grief, and anger over the blaze, rather than anything to do with her.

Jack, on the other hand, looked as if he'd been nearly barbecued. The long scraggly hair under his dented derby was considerably shorter on one side. His eyebrows were gone. The coal-black beard as well. Seeing Jack's naked face was nearly as much of a shock to Inez as if he'd strolled into her office in the altogether. His face was reddened and blistered, the single eye blinked, forlorn and bloodshot, the patch still intact over the empty socket of its mate.

Inez nodded at the clean glasses she'd set out on her end table and held up a sealed bottle of Jack Daniels. A mute truce in the ongoing verbal scuffles between herself and the ex-marshal.

Hollis hesitated, as if unconvinced the temporary truce between them wasn't some kind of trick. He finally hobbled forward. His fancy boots, Inez noted, had been saved from the fire, but barely, and looked the worse for wear.

Hollis and Jack each retrieved a glass. Jack also brought one over for Inez. She filled them all, and they drank.

The sensory blast that comes with high-proof alcohol cleared throats and loosened tongues all around.

Hollis moved over to the sofa and raised his half-empty glass in salute. "T' the battle flag of the Army of Northern Virginia."

He then craned his neck to peer at the overlaid patchwork strips. "Hmpf. Where'd you get these? I'm guessin' they're from a cavalry flag."

"One is Eli's," said Inez.

Hollis grunted. "So, how'd you hear 'bout the flag, that brotherhood, an' all?" He teetered back on charred boot heels, eyes half-lidded. Inez was reminded of a snake wavering, trying to decide whether to strike or just slither on by.

"I didn't. Not really. But I've been trying to put together the bits and pieces." She gestured at the remnants. "The longer one is Eli's. I found it...." She stopped, not wanting to unbalance the tenuous peace she'd forged with Hollis by letting him know she'd snooped around. "I found the other by the river. Near where Eli met a man, possibly Hiram Holt from Missouri."

"Hiram Holt?" Hollis frowned.

Inez leaned forward. "What can you tell me?"

He hesitated, pulling on the shortened end of his mustache.

She set the bottle down. "Look, Hollis. This all ties into the Denver and Rio Grande's arrival here in Leadville. And generals from the war. The Rio Grande, as you know, is headed by General Palmer. General Grant's arriving on the Rio Grande train today.

Are there other generals about? I don't know. But something's afoot, and I don't think it's good. I know you're unhappy with the Rio Grande, especially with the arson of your livery. And most likely you're not happy about Grant's visit either. But the war, it all happened long ago. And the train's on its way to town. There's not much time."

He nodded, silent, then said, "Back when Eli and I met, it was near the end of the war. For some time afterward, we were workin' the same outfits. What Eli said once was that there was a brotherhood. A group of men. Missourians, mostly from the same battalion. They'd each made a pledge to kill one of the blue-belly generals that helped destroy the Confederacy. And each of the men took a piece of the flag, vowin' that, when the deeds were done, they'd put the flag back t'gether. Eli told me all this and showed me that there." He gestured with his empty glass toward the strip of flag. "Crazy talk. We must've been tight on some rotgut or other. But at the time, it sounded like a good idea. Get some of the Yanks, like Booth did Lincoln. Like I said, crazy talk. I didn't think any more of it when I sobered up."

Inez held out the bottle. He held out his glass. She filled it again.

He continued. "The group was sharpshooters and snipers that turned into hardcases after the war. But that was years ago." He shook his head. "Eli'd sure had a change of heart by the time I partnered up with him at the livery."

"He married," Inez said. "Lillian."

"Yeah." Hollis looked at her through slitted eyes. Suspicious again. "Didn't know you and Eli were on such friendly speakin' terms."

"I told her," Jack mumbled, looking like he very much wished he had his beard to hide behind.

"Well. Don't make no difference. I never heard Eli talk about it here in Leadville. In fact, he damn near hated hearin' anything about the war."

"Did he mention any names from this group?" Inez looked from Hollis to Jack. "Hiram Holt? Brodie Duncan?"

The two men looked at each other.

Hollis frowned. "All's I know is, a sharpshooter headed it. Some real whingdinger of a shootist. I'd just supposed it all faded away over time. Hell, that's a long time to keep somethin' like that a secret. And to carry through."

"A sharpshooter." Inez turned the glass in her hand. "Hiram Holt was a Rebel sharpshooter. For the Ninth Missouri. He had a Whitworth and was a crack shot, to hear others tell it."

Hollis looked at her as if she'd grown an extra set of arms. "Where'd you come by all that? And who's this Hiram Holt?"

"Maybe the ringleader you spoke of. But he's gone now. Probably dead. His son carries a photocase with a tintype of Hiram and Eli, side-by-side. Rifles in hand. Eli with that Sharps he took from a dead Union soldier. Hiram with a Whitworth. The case had a single star, like those," she gestured at the flag, "in its lining."

"The man. Who brought the Sharps to Eli. Saw him right here." Jack let out a nearly ignitable burp. "That night."

"What night?" Inez was nonplussed. Then she remembered the night of the North/South fight in her saloon. Jack, venturing inside the State Street entrance, staring at the men by the Harrison Avenue door, and stepping back out. "The night of the fight here at the saloon?"

"Yep. Came by the livery." He squinched up his face, apparently calculating, then gave up. "Some time ago."

"So, which one was he?"

"Big fella. Real big. Whupped the lunatic."

Inez blinked, incredulous. "Preston Holt? No. It couldn't be." She then realized Jack's error. "Oh! I'll bet that was Hiram Holt. Preston and Hiram are brothers. I've been told they look alike."

"Saw the other one too."

"What other one?"

"He waited. Outside. When the big fella brought the Sharps. Looked like he didn't want t' been seen. Then, they rode off t'gether."

"What did he look like?"

"Scrawny. Little beard. Specs."

"The professor," she said quietly. Then, "Brodie Duncan."

Jack shrugged. "Dunno the name. Looked like him. Acted like him. Not wanting to be seen."

Inez blew out her cheeks in a loud exhale. *So. The professor, Brodie Duncan, lied. He's part of this whole racket as well. He came out with Hiram and just got a different job with the railroad. One better suited to his talents, no doubt.*

"I can't picture Brodie Duncan as a sharpshooter." She shook her head. "The war doesn't seem to drive him, the way it does the others."

"Well, mebbe they're all gone now, this brotherhood." Hollis put down his glass. "Unless you're wrong, Miz Stannert, and that Duncan fella's one of them."

"Maybe." Inez was quiet a moment. "But consider. If the other flag strips are the same size, there are five more around somewhere. Maybe the men who took those pieces have thrown them out, or folded them away and forgotten them. But maybe not. Maybe those men are still living as if the past fifteen years have never been."

Chapter Fifty-One

Inez felt she hardly had time to eat, blink, or breathe. She moved efficiently behind the bar with Abe, the two of them so used to working around each other that they moved as in a choreographed dance.

But Inez wasn't feeling particularly graceful. She swiped the sweat from her face, glancing out the State Street window. So many pine boughs festooned the outside that Inez thought the saloon must give the appearance of being in a miniature forest.

Out the window, she could just see Sol's ladder, his shoes, and his trousers to the knees as he hammered the last of the nails into the final banner. At the eleventh hour, Inez had agreed that, if material could be found, a banner could also be erected above the State Street door. Sol had dashed off and managed to acquire what Inez suspected was the last available length of banner fabric in Leadville, and had lettered "Welcome, General!" in black paint.

"Who knows?" said Abe. "Maybe he'll stop and quench his thirst, if we look welcomin' enough."

"Well, we certainly have enough Old Crow in stock," said Inez, wiping the bar with a rag already damp from spillage.

The door swung open, and a clump of men entered. Inez looked up, hoping against hope Preston Holt, Reverend Sands, or McMurtrie would appear.

"You expectin' someone, Mrs. Stannert?" Abe loaded five tankards of beer on a tray for a group lucky enough to have snagged a table an hour before and who showed no intentions of quitting their claim.

"I'm hoping to spot Reverend Sands or someone from the Rio Grande." She blew upward, trying to dislodge a sweaty strand of hair that had unfurled from her hairpins and lodged against her forehead.

"Well, don't see any so far, but here comes Doc."

Sure enough, Doc approached the bar with considerable spring in his lopsided gait. He wore a brand new jacket and a well brushed top hat.

"Mrs. Stannert, a brandy, if you please, to celebrate General Grant's impending arrival."

She delivered the drink and leaned over the bar. "Doc. I need to talk to you about Reverend Sands. What he's doing. Those notes you mentioned, that were received by the railroad. Did any of them talk about a plot against—"

Alarmed, Doc held up a hand. "Not here." He looked around, as if expecting to see eyes upon them, then back at her, eyebrows crowding together. "I expected the good reverend to be more discreet in his disclosures to you."

"He told me nothing." That stung more than she would let on. "But I suspect perhaps Elijah Carter was trying to warn—"

He had pulled out his pocketwatch. The snap of the cover springing open was like scissors to her speech. He said quietly, but pointedly, "Thirteen members of the Union Veteran Association took the down train to Canon City to meet General Grant and his party early today. But we...that is, the two of us left here to hold down the fort...received a telegram that the general's train was detained two hours on account of a washout west of Pueblo, which required building a temporary bridge. It was nearly three o'clock when the train finally arrived in Pueblo." He snapped the watch shut. "What's topmost on my mind right now is that our august visitors are not arriving at five, or even six, which is what the crowds out there are expecting. More likely, it'll be toward dusk. Don't worry, Mrs. Stannert, about that other business. All is well. The good Reverend J. B. Sands is a wonder, and I think there's naught to do but wait for the rather delayed arrival of our guests."

"But Doc—"

He guzzled the liquor at a pace that did it no justice, pulled out an enormous handkerchief, white and starched, and patted his mouth dry. "Must run. More communiqués expected. The procession will be heading down to the Boulevard soon, so we're ready to meet our guest whenever he arrives." He hurried out.

Inez exhaled in frustration and scowled at the partially empty glass. "Why do I even bother? Men! Well, perhaps he has sorted it out—"

She picked up the snifter to put it in the dirty-glass tub as another figure moved in to fill the vacuum at the bar. She glanced up, the automatic "What's your pleasure?" dying on her lips.

Delaney sneered at her from across the bar.

Inez gaped, wordless.

"Think you'll lift that ban long enough t' sell me a beer?" He tapped a nickel on the bar. "Everyone else in town is celebrating. Guess I'll be mourning by my lonesome unless you plan to drink with me."

"I'm not selling you anything after what you did last week," she said savagely. "What the hell are you doing here anyway? I heard you were dead!"

"Me?" Delaney seemed to find this hilarious. "Still alive and kicking. Can't say the same's true of your friend Holt, though."

Inez froze. "What are you talking about?"

"Haven't heard?" Delaney didn't sound the least bit sorry. "He's dead."

The universe shrank down until Delaney's eyes—black pools of malice—and his crooked smile filled it.

"You're lying." Her voice seemed to come from far away.

"Why would I lie? He was shot in the back a couple of days ago. Ask anyone working the Rio Grande, they'll tell you the same."

Couple of days ago.

The response she'd formulated to throw into Delaney's smirking face stuck in her throat.

All the questions she'd planned to ask Preston. All the apologies, explanations she'd planned to give, when she saw him again. All died inside her, unspoken.

"Wouldn't you know," he continued in a conversational tone. "The Holt kid's been missing ever since. Bets are, he pulled the trigger. That whole clan was trouble from the word go. Payroll guards, bullshit. Didn't trust none of them. Roamin' around, stickin' their noses where they didn't belong. Piss-poor Missourians to a man. Good riddance."

The brandy dregs struck him straight on, drenching his hat, collar, and jacket.

"Get out!" said Inez. "Now."

Delaney took out his handkerchief and mopped his face, not taking his eyes from Inez.

Abe was suddenly beside her. "Think you heard the lady."

Delaney pushed off from the bar. "Where I'm from, ladies don't wear trousers and hang around with niggers."

Abe seized Inez's arm, guessing correctly that she was ready to throw the snifter at the railroader. "Let him go, Mrs. Stannert. Man just wants to stir things up. Ain't worth the cost of the glassware or a bullet."

Once Delaney was gone, Abe eased his grasp and slid a glass of whiskey in front of her. "Mrs. Stannert, I'm thinkin' you need this."

She still gripped the empty glass. The aromatic fragrance of spilled brandy filled her head. She put the snifter down with extreme care, as if it could shatter more easily than the most fragile of dreams. "I need some air. For just a minute."

She headed for the Harrison Avenue door.

Outside, a surging mass of humanity crushed the streets and walkways. Civic and military organizations marched up and down Harrison, nearly obscured by clouds of dust.

Inez leaned against the plank exterior of the Silver Queen. She closed her eyes, turned her face skyward, and focused on her senses—touch, sound, taste. Anything that could counteract the surge of emotions threatening to engulf her. Heat of the sun on her face. Discordant music from brass bands, all practicing their separate tunes for General Grant's arrival. Shouting of orders. Solid beat of marching feet and hooves. Dust stinging the inner passages of her nose. Thrumming of the boardwalk through the soles of her shoes.

The warmth on her face vanished. She opened her eyes to clouds across the sun.

A familiar voice at her elbow said, "Mrs. Stannert?"

Inez looked over at Terry O'Loughlin, tapping a white envelope against her lower lip.

Terry appeared relieved. "I'm glad I found you here. I have a message for you. And I wasn't certain about the propriety of...." She glanced at the saloon.

Inez pushed away from the wall. "I thought you were keeping Susan company at her studio."

"I was. But she closed the shop when she left with the railroad man."

"Railroad man?" Alarms went off in Inez's mind. "What railroad man?"

The blat of a sour trumpet drew Terry's attention to the street. She looked back at Inez, startled. "What? Oh. It's all right. Susan knew him. She introduced him as 'the professor.' Anyhow, he said there was some new evidence and Mr. Preston Holt wanted her to come down right away and take a look at the place where the accident had been. He said it was very important. I know she didn't want to miss the parade, but he promised to get her back by nightfall. I offered to go too, but the little dogcart he brought would only hold Susan and besides—"

"The professor?" Chills started at the base of Inez's neck and spread over her shoulders and down her arms like a contagion. "He said Preston Holt had questions? Now? Today?"

"Well, yes. Isn't that the Mr. Holt we met at the restaurant?"

"Miss O'Loughlin. Terry." Inez seized her hand. "Preston Holt is dead. He died several days ago."

Terry's mouth fell open. She looked down at the envelope in her hand. "I don't understand. The professor, he asked if I knew you and if I would deliver this." She thrust the envelope at Inez.

Inez seized the envelope and ripped it open so violently that the paper inside almost escaped. She gripped the single page:

Mrs. Stannert,

Heed these words carefully. It's my guess our journey has become clear to you, and we cannot take a chance of you telling others. Your friend is well. But, we travel a dangerous road. It's best for all if you keep your qualms to yourself. When we succeed, and you'll know when we do, your friend will return. If we are intercepted and our journey's cut short, pray for your friend's soul.

The note was unsigned, but Inez knew that tiny, cramped script as well as she knew her own.

Something is about to happen, and he thinks I know what it is. Something that impelled him to take Susan to guarantee my silence. What? What is it?

Her mind raced frantically, searching out connections she'd somehow missed.

What did she know for certain about Brodie Duncan? That his father was from Missouri. His mother from Tennessee. That he was in Tennessee at the war's end, went to Scotland for a time, and returned to Missouri to teach in the same small town where he'd been raised. That he knew the Holts and Eli and Lillian Carter. That he traveled out with Hiram and Reuben to Colorado, and was privy to Rio Grande business through his job. That he'd bought a prospector's kit, but took only the rope, pickaxes, and giant powder.

And she knew his destination, if that much of his story to Susan was true. A big "if," she had to admit. But it made sense that he'd tell Susan the truth of that so she would not raise an alarm on the journey. *But if she becomes suspicious of his motives, what will he do to her? Kill her, no doubt.*

Inez shoved her panic aside and forced herself to picture the view from Disappointment Gulch. The landscape opened before her, in her mind's eye. The main railroad track. The siding and cars. The abandoned charcoal kilns.

The trestle.

Certainty dawned like the white-hot morning sun.

"Oh my God!" Inez said aloud.

He's going to blow up the trestle and the incoming train. The train that's bringing General Grant to Leadville.

She fixed Terry with a hard stare. "I've got to go. Right now. Thank you, Miss O'Loughlin. And please, tell no one about this message. No one!"

Chapter Fifty-Two

Inez spotted the bend that heralded the approach to the gulch and the kilns, and pulled Lucy to a stop. Lucy's sides heaved, the near flat-out run from Malta having taken its toll on her.

Back at the saloon, she'd pulled Abe aside and thrust the crumpled note at him. "From the professor. He obviously doesn't know me very well or he'd never have sent this note to me. I will not sit here obediently, faint and trembling like some hysterical woman, while he rides off with Susan to....You know, I didn't see clearly what he was up to until this note. If he'd just snuck off to do his dirty work and left us alone....Unfortunately, he didn't spell out his plans or even sign the note. So it's going to be hard to convince anyone of the danger, based on what this note says."

She then provided Abe with the briefest of explanations, along with her ultimate destination.

"Damn, Inez. You can't go alone." Abe looked around the crowded bar. "I'll come with you."

"No! The note says he'll kill her if....Abe, I won't chance anything until Susan is safe. After that, I'll find a lawman to deal with him properly. Keep the note. Show it to no one but Reverend Sands, should he come by. But tell the reverend, we must be careful. For Susan's sake."

Inez had dashed upstairs to change into the same dusty men's clothes from the previous week. She grabbed her pocket revolver and, with only a moment's hesitation, the Sharps rifle and its box of linen-jacketed cartridges. *I need something for distance. I doubt very much that, if I'm right, the professor will simply allow me to stroll up and stick my pistol in his back.*

His back.

Preston Holt had been shot in the back.

Tears sprang to her eyes, and she scrubbed them away roughly.

Inez pushed Lucy hard down the oddly vacant road. Travelers and residents along the Arkansas Valley, she thought, most likely were gathered at the stations where Grant's train might stop. Every one of them no doubt hoping to get a glimpse of the great man or shake his hand.

But the folks in Malta and Leadville may not get that chance, if I'm right about the professor and no one stops him.

She clenched her teeth, the grit of dust grinding and drying her mouth, and pushed on. Lucy's hooves pounded in a beat that turned into a chant in her mind: *Brodie Duncan. Brodie Duncan. Brodie Duncan.*

Other thoughts clipped through her mind, making, breaking links, harmonizing or clashing like lines of music, the linkage of one note to the next, one small detail to the next.

The professor had taken the Whitworth rifle from under Preston's bunk—the very rifle Hiram had employed as a Confederate sharpshooter. But remembering the whispered conversation outside the bunk car, she was sure he'd retrieved it for someone else.

Reuben.

Hiram would have taught his son how to shoot, just as Hiram and Preston's father had taught them. A skill passed on from father to son.

And did Hiram also bequeath his hatred of the North to his son?

Inez faltered.

Suppose Reuben is there? That it's not just the professor, but Reuben as well? I must be very careful. The stakes are so high. I must be sure of all the players, before I enter the game.

She remembered again Frisco Flo's comment that Reuben had a girl sweet on him. Inez thought back on the dark-haired, dark-eyed girl who shrank into the shadows when Reuben had entered the door behind her…and she bet she knew who the girl was.

And I'll bet that girl opened the window for him and the professor.

Why had he shot at her from the window? Because she'd thrown him out of the saloon? Because they'd figured out she had been hidden under the bunk when the professor had come for the gun? Or maybe they were afraid Susan had told her something about the deaths on the tracks, something that pointed back to them? And she had been asking lots of questions, circling around them, closing in.

It could be any of those, or some combination.

They probably wanted to get me out of the way.

And the professor had told Preston that Delaney was dead, that Reuben was to blame. A ruse to kill Preston.

He was getting too close. So who pulled the trigger? The professor? Or Reuben?

The part she couldn't figure was why Brodie Duncan was involved. There was something about him that rang true when he'd said, "It's not my war." He'd said not a word about Grant. The only general she'd heard him rail against was Palmer. Was Palmer on the train? The professor, with his position in the Rio Grande, would know. The invisible man—delivering missives, taking notes, walking a step behind the important men.

At the kilns, she stopped, dismounted, and listened. At first, all she heard was Lucy's labored breathing.

Suppose I'm wrong? Suppose he's somewhere else, that Susan is already dead.

Dread, dark as midnight, spread its wings inside her.

Pushing her fears aside, Inez laid a hand on Lucy's lathered coat and strained to listen.

Then she heard them. Men's voices. One shouting, one replying.

Two of them. The professor and Reuben?

She pulled Lucy around the cluster of kilns, looking for a place to tie her, and spied the dogcart and horse. Then, another horse as well.

Inez moved farther up Disappointment Gulch, to the very outskirts of the kiln field, and tried to tie Lucy to a crooked stump behind one of the towering, beehive shaped structures. Lucy snorted and pulled back, rolling her eyes. "Lucy!" she hissed, tugging on the reins. "Now's not the time." Then Inez became aware of the cloying sickly smell of rotting flesh.

In the westering sun, Inez saw the cloud of flies clustered around the mouth of the kiln, crawling through the cracks in the makeshift wood door blocking the entrance.

Holding her breath, expecting the worst, Inez grasped an edge of the door and pulled hard.

The door gave way. The dying sun picked out two misshapen lumps inside, blackened by charcoal dust, flies, and squirming vermin. Inez made out a hand, bloated, cracked, nearly eaten away except for a gold ring.

It was the only detail she gathered before turning away and vomiting on the dirt.

Wiping her mouth on her sleeve, she retrieved Lucy, who had backed away, and led her horse further up the gulch.

She pulled out Eli's Sharps rifle, thinking what pleasure it would give her to use it on the men who killed Eli and Preston, then moved toward the path up the side of the gulch.

Inez toiled up the short hill to the shoulder of the gulch where Susan had originally tied her horse and burro. If she was right, she'd see the professor and Reuben down by the riverbank, preparing the trestle for its destruction.

And I'll be above them, taking aim. Just like they did at Eli Carter.

At the top of the shoulder, she moved forward in a crouch, finally dropping to her belly at the sloping edge. She adjusted her slouch hat to shield her eyes. The sun rested on the peaks of the Sawatch Range across the Arkansas Valley. A bank of towering clouds hovered above, as if waiting for God's hand to push them down and crush the sun's fire against the peaks.

Down in the shadowed ravine of the river, she spotted a single figure, pacing on the bank. Revolver in hand. And a small campfire, smokeless, mostly coals and embers.

She shaded her eyes to be sure.

The professor.

Wearing a dark, military-style greatcoat, far too large for his frame. The greatcoat, she'd wager, off Preston Holt's back. A flash of anger seared her, quick as lightning. In its wake grew a steel cold resolve.

She opened the cartridge tin and set it to one side. The linen-shrouded bullets lined up like soldiers in the tin, waiting for their orders.

She poured the percussion caps into the top of the tin.

Loaded and readied the Sharps. Positioned a nearby flat-topped rock under the rifle barrel. Pulled the hammer back with her hand. Propped herself up on her elbows.

And waited.

The professor stopped pacing, turned his face downstream, cupped his mouth and shouted. "Have ye taken care of the Rebel hussy, soldier? We need to prepare for the coming of the gray coats!"

Inez frowned, perplexed. *Rebel hussy? Gray coats? What is the professor doing, pretending to be a Union soldier?*

Weston Croy emerged around a bend in the streambed, moving slowly, cradling an unidentifiable burden tenderly in his arms.

Weston! Inez almost bolted upright with the shock of seeing him. *Is the professor playing to Weston's madness? But for what purpose?*

"She won't bother us," he said. His voice, so jittery and manic before, now sounded calm, rational. A white cloth around one arm was stained red.

It looks like Addie Croy shot true with her revolver. Pray Heaven that I do the same, if it comes to that.

"Good! We've got to thaw that giant powder out fast, if it's going to be in place before the train arrives. Those Rebel generals'll learn a thing or two about the might of the Union Army and its men when they're standin' at Hell's gates!"

"Yes sir." Weston slowly bent his knees and placed a bundle of long red tubes on the ground.

Giant powder?

The hairs prickled on her neck.

"We can't hurry the thawing, sir. Could be dangerous." Weston sounded all business, which Inez found far more frightening than his crazy talk.

"It'll be even more dangerous if the Confederate train gets through!" shouted the professor. "Ye successfully fired that nest of Rebel sympathizers in town. Now we've got to stop the reinforcements from arriving! Ye've a chance to kill the enemy's generals, man!"

Weston set fire to the livery?

Even as the professor shouted, Inez noticed he was backing away from the unstable dynamite as far as the riverbank and the walls of the ravine would allow.

Weston set two tubes in a fry pan and placed it over the coals. Inez hesitated, wondering if Reuben might be there.

If he is, he must be guarding Susan. But they've said nothing about him. I'll wager he's not part of this, for whatever reason. It's time for me to enter their game and up the stakes.

She lifted her head slightly and shouted, "Duncan! Croy!"

They froze. Their faces, white under their hats, turned upward toward her voice.

Inez continued, "Drop the gun! Put your hands up where I can see them. And stand aside."

The professor screamed in rage, "Damn you! Ye can't stop us. And if you kill us, the lass will never be found!"

"How do I know she's not already dead?"

"The Union army doesn't kill women! When we're done, we'll release her. But if you interfere—"

Inez screamed back, "I thought it was not your war, Brodie Duncan."

"It's *not* the war. It's Palmer, damn his eyes! And what he did to us in Tennessee!"

The last note. The final refrain. The look on Brodie Duncan's face when Doc had refused to pass judgment on Reuben in the bar. She nearly came to her feet in the realization. "You were the boy in Tennessee! The bushwhacker who nearly killed Palmer!"

"I had him! In my sights. Pulled the trigger. And missed! I missed!" He almost cried. "I was no bushwhacker. I was fifteen! We tried stayin' neutral. Left Missouri. Went to Tennessee, my mother's clan. But his cavalry, Palmer's damned cavalry, burned the barn. Took the animals. Even ripped out the fence posts! Left us nothing. In winter! A death sentence. Why, why did they take everything, leave us not even a crust? My mother always said, 'twas not our war. I cared naught for which side won. But I swore, if I ever got another chance at Palmer, my hand would not waver!"

His own voice, rebounding off the rock, seemed to bring him back to the present.

He stopped, looked at Weston.

Weston was motionless, on his knees by the fire.

Is Weston listening to this tirade? Is it getting through?

"You made it your war!" She made sure her words carried. "When you killed Elijah Carter. By the tracks. Or did you kill Hiram Holt? Then, Preston Holt! And you shot at me! You're at the center of a bloodbath!"

"Reuben shot Carter, for killing his own father! I had nothing against the man. I was never part of their little cabal of the flag. 'Twas only for the best, who didn't miss their targets. Me, I was a disgrace in their eyes. But here, they were happy to let me be their eyes and ears, to tell them of Grant's coming and learn of Palmer's bloody ways. Reuben, he'd not listen to me with Hiram gone. He wanted to kill you, and the lass. We didn't know what she saw, what she might remember. And you, we were never sure. What she might have told you in her injury. What you heard and saw. All your questions, gettin' closer to the truth of it. Then Preston and his suspicions. Oh, that was the worst. Reuben said he'd kill his own father's brother, if I'd lure him out. But then, he vanishes, takes off with that young whore. Leaves me to do the killing, which I've no choice but to do, though no stomach for it. And leaves me to fight the final battle!"

Reuben's vanished?

Inez risked a quick glance behind her, then to the side, where the promontory above Susan's ledge jutted out, high above her, cutting off her view to the south.

Eyes. She could feel them everywhere. Watching her.

The professor whirled on Weston, as if only then remembering he was there. "Soldier! The enemy, they're tryin' to confuse us! The men who died, they were secessionists, all! Missouri scum. We're protectin' the Union."

Inez's full attention reverted to the scene below. "Weston Croy, don't believe him! Brodie Duncan is no soldier, he's an impostor! Preston Holt, the man he killed, fought for the Union. Like Reverend Sands, the Leadville minister who tried to help you."

The professor jumped as if she'd scorched him with a branding iron. "Reverend Sands?!" A note of fear braided through his rage.

A bare slice of the sun hovered, spreading along the mountain tops, dyeing their peaks gold, gilding the clouds with the gleam of precious metal. A final ray shot into Inez's eyes, then slid below the range, surrendering to the coming gloom.

The clouds lowered, claiming victory from the light.

A faint flash over the mountains preceded the distant roll of thunder.

A solid plop of rain fell on Inez's gloved hand.

She hastily drew the tin of cartridges and percussion caps closer, to shelter them from the rain. *The linen cloth, the powder within, will they fire wet?*

She tried again. "Weston Croy! General Ulysses S. Grant is on the train you are preparing to destroy!"

The professor swung toward Weston. "Soldier! Do not listen to her. That's a direct order."

Weston remained on his knees. Then, he lifted his face, searching the hillside. He said in wonderment, "Addie? Is that you?"

The professor cursed and aimed his pistol at Weston.

From her vantage point, Inez could see, far down the valley and approaching, a pinpoint of light.

On the sighing of the wind, she heard the faraway whistle of an approaching train.

The professor heard it too.

"Dammit! Men—including engineers—are shot in the Union army for disobeying orders, Private Croy. If this explosive is as unstable as you say, let's use it to our advantage. Tie it to the track! When the train runs over it, we'll be victorious."

Weston removed the fry pan from the fire.

Inez pulled the set trigger. "Stop! Or I'll shoot!"

"Ha!" It was not a laugh so much as a shriek. "Shoot Private Croy, and ye'll blow us all to bits. And if you can shoot me or him from the top of that hill then you're a better shot than that pup Holt, who missed you when he had plenty of time to aim. I'm no gambler, and I say you cannae do it."

She ripped the glove off her right hand with her teeth and set her eye to the sight. *If I stop him, I stop Weston. At least, I pray so.*

A gust of cool wind bearing the scent of rain brushed her cheeks.

Another drop hit her bare hand.

Her finger rested, light as a lover's touch, on the hair-trigger. *Let it end now.*

She heard a scuff of boot on the rocks behind her. Heavy breathing of someone coming up fast.

Her finger tightened.

The boom of the Sharps nearly deafened Inez to the shot from behind her.

Below, the professor clutched his arm with a cry, dropped his gun.

Weston, arms full of unstable dynamite, stumbled.

The flash lit the riverbed, a sun born in a thunder of sound.

A heavy weight fell on her back, knocking the wind from her. A man's body covered her; a hand forced her head to the ground.

Dirt and debris, heaved up from the riverbank by the explosion, fell around her.

Pebbles, dirt, struck her hat, pattering like rain.

Then, silence reigned.

Sound emerged once more, muffled as if through cotton wadding.

The ground trembled again. This time with a rhythmic vibration.

Inez lifted her head.

The engine's headlight, which before had been a prick in the distance, was now a solid lantern, the body of the train snaking behind in the dusk. With a shriek, the train thundered across the trestle bridge, to the west and away to Leadville.

She felt, more than heard, the breathing of the man still resting on her back. One hand holding her arm to the ground. The other, holding a rifle to the side, protecting her, sheltering her from harm.

Then, a fervent voice in her ear: "I thought we'd be blown to kingdom come."

It was Reverend Sands.

Chapter Fifty-Three

Around the bend of the riverbank, Inez and Sands discovered a small cave dug into the side of the steep stony ravine. It held what remained of the cache of giant powder. Susan, blocked by a partially filled box, was in the back.

Susan peered out over the top of the box, her wide frightened eyes visible even in the coming twilight. Working on the theory that the rest of the giant powder might be sensitive, Sands carefully pulled out the box and set it in the dirt to one side. Inez and the reverend helped Susan wiggle out. She was trussed up with the stout rope the professor had bought from Evan's mercantile and gagged to boot.

When they removed the gag, Susan's first words were "Inez! Reverend Sands! Thank heaven it's you. I heard an explosion. Did they blow up the bridge? But I thought I heard the explosion first, and then the train." Her next words were "If I'd put that gun in my pocket like you told me to, Inez, maybe this wouldn't have happened."

"If you had tried to use it, the professor might have overcome his reluctance to doing his own killing and you wouldn't be here to talk about it," Inez answered.

As they searched for a way up the steep bank, Inez explained what had happened.

Susan's teeth were chattering, but she refused the overcoat Sands offered, insisting she would be fine. "It's just I was afraid I'd be stuck here forever or that maybe they'd changed their minds and....Well. I recognized him. The professor. Only by then, it was too late. The closer we came to this place, the more he talked and talked and the more nervous and uneasy I felt. Then, we arrived in the kiln field and he said, 'Wait, I need to move these.' He was referring to a couple of bags in the cart. But his words brought it all back. He was the one who said he needed to move the bodies before blowing up the tracks. I never saw him then, but his voice....Why I didn't remember before, I don't know. Maybe because I wasn't really listening to him when he came to my studio for a portrait. Or maybe returning to this place brought it back." She shivered.

"You must have been frightened," said Inez.

"I didn't want to let on I knew who he was. I thought I'd make a dash for the road and yell for help, once I'd gotten out of the cart. But Weston Croy was here. Waiting. And they had guns. The professor told me if I didn't make trouble, they'd let me go, but if I made so much as made a peep, they'd kill me. There wasn't much choice. Weston bundled me into that little cave and told me if I even wiggled a toe, the powder would explode. He said crazy things. That he didn't want me to die, just wanted me to stay put until they'd destroyed the bridge, killed the Rebel generals, and the engineering unit got away."

"Well, from what the professor said, it's pretty clear that Reuben was the man on the ridge top above you that morning," Inez said. "And Elijah Carter and Hiram Holt were the original men on the tracks. I think Eli wanted to stop Hiram from carrying through on his plans to kill a general—whether Palmer or Grant, or both. I know Eli tried to find Marshal Ayres shortly before he left town, without success. Maybe he was hoping to enlist help from him."

Sands nodded. "Could be. We'll never know, now."

"And then, when Eli's business partner, Bart Hollis, followed him to Malta, Eli drove him away. I suppose he didn't think Hollis would help him stop Hiram."

The three of them straggled up the riverbank, giving a wide berth to the site of the explosion, and passed through the silent kiln field to fetch the horses and the cart.

Inez paused, some distance from the kiln she'd opened earlier, and said in a low voice to Reverend Sands, "I believe Elijah Carter and Hiram Holt are in there."

"Reuben seems to have disappeared." Sands kept his arm firmly around Inez's waist. "He's proved the most elusive of the bunch."

Inez thought of Duncan's remark about Reuben and a young prostitute. "A certain dark-eyed, dark-haired girl at Frisco Flo's might know his whereabouts."

When they reached the cart and animals, Susan said, "If you two ride in front of me, I think I can manage the cart."

They tied the lead of Weston's horse to the back of the cart, crossed the river, and set on the road to Leadville.

"Do you think we're too late to see General Grant?" Susan sounded wistful.

"Maybe not," said Sands. "He's planning a long stop at Malta. I think many of the Rio Grande crew are hoping he'll say a few words and shake some hands. He'll probably oblige."

"I thought you were on that train," said Inez in a low voice.

They rode side by side. Occasionally, his leg brushed hers.

"Change of plans yesterday after a discussion with Snow and Palmer. I took the early train this morning to Leadville. Spoke with Jed Elliston about his source for those Rio Grande articles. Talked with Hollis at some length. Then, talked with Abe. Once I heard where you'd gone and why, I cut my investigations short."

"Did Snow really engage Weston Croy to burn Hollis' livery?"

Sands sighed. "Snow became a tad overzealous in his attempts to secure right-of-way before Grant's arrival. The thought of General Grant being deposited among the tree stumps at the end of Third Street, because he couldn't move the condemnation procedure along faster or get the holdouts to agree to terms, must have been the last straw. I'm not certain how he lit on Weston Croy to further his plan, but it appears Brodie Duncan was the go-between. Needless to say, Palmer is not pleased."

He shifted. "Not that the fire changed much. Hollis said he won't sell. So, the Rio Grande will push through with condemnation. Hollis will lose in any case. The Rio Grande isn't waiting.

They're planning on an extension through the Ten Mile District to Kokomo. They hope to get there within sixty days, barring bad luck. And, as you might have surmised, the Rio Grande road doesn't allow bad luck to interfere with its plans very much."

"What happened to Snow? And Birdie?" She stared straight ahead at the road and tried to make it a neutral question.

"Snow resigned. He's headed back to Philadelphia and civilization, taking his daughter with him." Inez could feel him looking steadily at her as he added, "He decided the far west is too rough for her temperament."

Not enough steel to her spine. Inez suffered the uncharitable thought to die in silence. Instead she asked, "How did you get tangled up in this? You seem on familiar terms with General Palmer."

The silence stretched beyond her words, and she feared he'd not answer.

Finally, he said, "I told you, once, about my sister and her plans to help the Union during the war. Judith's connections in Philadelphia, many of them became my own later. Many of the officers, they didn't know exactly what she was doing, but she was widely respected for her courage. Her resolve. I first met Palmer and others in those days."

The chirps and twilight songs of birds and the rushing of the river sang counterpoint to the creak of cart wheels and the soft clomp of hoofs on the dirt road. A light rain began to fall.

"So, this meeting I heard about in the Board of Trade Saloon, with you, McMurtrie, Snow, Doc...." She couldn't say Preston Holt's name. "I suppose that had to do with all this."

"I suppose I can tell you now since Duncan and Croy are dead. The danger appears to be past." He glanced back at Susan. "Miss Carothers, do you need a blanket?"

"There's one here in the cart."

He nodded. "Malta's ahead. Then it's three miles to Leadville." He then said to Inez, "Palmer received anonymous notes from Leadville. The first said a plot was being hatched against him and the railroad. That the threat came from within his very own organization."

"I'll bet Eli Carter wrote it," said Inez softly.

"Probably. Then, Grant accepted Palmer's invitation to visit Colorado Springs and partake of the Rio Grande's hospitality. Soon after, and before his visit was widely known outside of the Rio Grande inner circle, another note arrived, saying that there was a grave danger to General Grant as well. That last one was dated just the day before the explosion by the siding."

"The explosion that Susan witnessed."

Sands grunted. "At that point, the railroad began to sit up and take serious notice."

"I wonder…with all those expert marksmen, why dynamite supply cars and blow up tracks? Why not just bide their time and wait for the generals to arrive?"

"I believe it was their attempt to create overall havoc for the Rio Grande as well as provide misdirection. Rumors were that those responsible for the sabotage were from a rival railroad—the Santa Fe was an obvious choice, with the South Park being another possibility. There was even talk of citizens, disgruntled with certain Rio Grande actions regarding routes and right-of-way, being responsible. Of course, all those whispers and rumors pointed to the enemy being outside the ranks, not within."

"So why wasn't Grant's visit cancelled?"

"No one wanted to call it off. Not the Rio Grande. Not the Union Veterans Association. Not Grant. And he was told of the possible danger. Remember, no one knew if the notes were bona fide. But they did want someone to…investigate is probably the proper word. Ask questions. Discreetly. And if there were folks causing trouble…." Sands looked away. Inez had no clue as to his expression as he continued, "It was hoped that troublemakers could be persuaded to desist."

He looked back at her. "On one hand, the sharpshooters from Missouri. You know about them. On the other, Brodie Duncan. Snow's clerk, courier, and all-around errand boy. Also from Missouri, with a grudge against Palmer. He was the most difficult piece of the puzzle to work out. I got lucky while in the Springs. A newsman from the *Colorado Springs Gazette* had recognized Duncan in Leadville and had a few things to say about him."

They reached Malta and moved quickly up the main street, which seemed oddly deserted. An inebriated pedestrian said they'd "just missed" Grant.

"The train's heading to Leadville," he said. "You can probably catch the procession. He'll be getting out on the Boulevard, east of the tollgate. A carriage'll take him into town."

"Will we get there in time?" Susan asked anxiously behind them.

"If we keep to a steady pace," Sands assured her.

As they left Malta behind, Inez, who was still pondering Brodie Duncan, said to Sands, "Duncan tried to kill Palmer once before. During the war, Duncan and his mother left Missouri and fled to Tennessee. He was a boy of fifteen when he shot at General Palmer...and missed. He was caught, and Palmer let him go. To think, that act of kindness from so many years ago bore such unexpected fruit. What an unfortunate coincidence that Duncan should have joined forces with those men who were gunning for the old Union generals."

"Not coincidence at all. Like draws like. Men with a common cause always manage to find others like themselves. And Missouri had more than her share of miseries, before, during, and after the war."

"The men from Missouri. They carried their hate, their hopes for vengeance so long." She paused, then spoke past the lump in her throat, "You know about Preston Holt? That he's dead. Duncan shot him in the back."

Sands reached out, took Inez's right hand, and held it fast. "It would take more than one misplaced bullet to kill Preston Holt."

For a moment, it was as if everything in the world had stopped moving. The only thing she felt for certain was the reverend's hand, warm and tight around hers. "But I heard—"

"You heard what was put out and around. What we wanted people to hear. Preston was left for dead but was found before that became the case. He told us about Duncan. About his brother Hiram. And his suspicions about Reuben. It wasn't easy for him. He's always believed in family. Loyalty. Couldn't imagine a better person at my back. Preston's a fighter. The doctors say he'll make it."

He squeezed her hand once. Then let it go.

The three of them—Sands, Inez, and Susan—entered Leadville's city limits.

The rain picked up with the wind.

Inez finally saw the Boulevard, lit with bonfires. Leadville's cavalry companies lined each side of the road in open ranks, ready to receive the general. Behind the cavalry, masses of people seethed, wet hats, cloaks, waterproofs, gleaming in the light of the bonfires. The train rested, its engine panting, at the junction of the Boulevard and the foot of West Third Street. The grand procession, headed by the mayor and city council, and consisting of members of societies both military and civic, waited en masse, on Third.

Susan pulled up beside Inez and stood in the cart, straining her eyes toward the train.

Sands and Inez moved their horses closer together to make room for the people on foot who crowded around them as the reception committee disembarked from the train.

Sands once again reached for her. "About Miss Snow."

She slid her bare hand into his gloved one. "You don't have to say a thing."

She took a deep breath. "I've decided. To get a divorce. I'm not going to keep starting at shadows. Wondering at every turn if Mark will show or if he won't. I refuse to live in the darkness anymore."

Sands raised her hand to his lips. Kissed it.

They both turned eyes toward the train.

A compact, gray figure appeared on the platform, hat in hand. General Ulysses S. Grant.

The crowd surged forward, and roars from a thousand voices rose to envelop him

Author's Note

Working in the shadows of history is, for me, one of the pleasures of writing historical fiction. To that end, real places, people, and events march through *Iron Ties* along with the creations of my overactive imagination.

First, to places. Leadville, Colorado, exists. You can visit it, walk the streets, learn its history, and—who knows?—maybe uncover the traces of an ancestor or two. For an entertaining account of Leadville's history, Edward Blair's *Leadville, Colorado's Magic City* is a good place to start. Two other resources on Leadville and its history are the everything-you-ever-wanted-to-know, two-volume work *History of Leadville and Lake County, Colorado,* by Don and Jean Griswold, and the much harder-to-find gem *A Social History of Leadville, Colorado, during the Boom Days, 1877–1881*, which is Eugene Floyd Irey's Ph.D. thesis from 1951.

The 1880 census claimed about 15,000 souls inhabited this silver mining boom town, a number hotly contested by local press and others, who placed the population closer to 40,000. It is mind-boggling (at least to me) to consider that all these folks and more—because some fair number no doubt were merely "passing through"—came up to this 10,000-foot-high city before the arrival of the train: they took stagecoaches, wagons, or horses, or depended on their own two feet to power them over high mountain passes.

Today, we have it easy. To get to Leadville, hop into your motorized vehicle, head west from Denver on I-70 into the

Rocky Mountains, take the Copper Mountain exit, and follow the signs up over Fremont Pass and down into Leadville. Or, you can take a longer route through South Park and Fairplay, up over Trout Creek Pass, then head north on 24, paralleling the Arkansas River and the route of the long-gone Denver & Rio Grande tracks to Leadville.

If you take this leisurely drive up the Arkansas Valley, you'll see signs for some of the places mentioned in *Iron Ties*, including Granite, Twin Lakes, and Malta. But if you look for Disappointment Gulch, you will look in vain. The terrain that inspired my fictional gulch is right around Granite—an area of craggy outcroppings with the tracks running along the base, separating ridge from river. But no real gulch that matched this geology existed closer to Leadville, hence my disappointment (and poetic license).

As for the rest of this note, I'll give you fair warning: Spoilers lie ahead.

Iron Ties is based on two historical events: the coming of the Denver and Rio Grande railroad to Leadville in the summer of 1880 and the arrival of Civil War general Ulysses S. Grant on the first D&RG train to Leadville, on July 22, 1880. It seems that not all were happy with the arrival of the D&RG and/or Grant. George Elder, a young Leadville lawyer, wrote home in July 1879, "The AT&St Fe RR [Atchison, Topeka and Santa Fe] would have reached Leadville by the Middle of September if it had not been for the interference of the D & R G RR, the latter road has been playing the part of the 'Dog in the Manger'. There is a strong feeling growing against the D & R G RR and its whole course has been a matter of condemnation for months back." The D&RG spent years tussling (in the courts, in the newspapers, and on the ground) with the Santa Fe railroad over right-of-way to Leadville. Fractious encounters with the Denver, South Park, and Pacific also occurred in the mid-1880s.

And then, there was the announcement of Grant's visit, with a plea in one of the local papers for Leadvillites to "set aside politics and welcome our guest." In 1880, the Civil War was not that far removed…a mere 15 years. Thinking on this, I remembered veterans of the Vietnam War discussing how a smell, a sudden sound, a dream, could bring the war flooding back as if it were yesterday. Might this not also be true for those who fought in the Civil War? And what would it mean to those veterans—Union and Confederate—to know that one of the pre-eminent generals from the North would be coming to town?

Little did I know that my decision to plunge into matters of railroads and the Civil War would nearly drown me in mountains of research and reference materials. Many excellent books exist about both topics; I'll mention a few here. Eric T. Dean, Jr.,'s *Shook Over Hell: Post-Traumatic Stress, Vietnam, and the Civil War* provides a thorough look at the psychological after-effects of the Civil War. Tony Horwitz's *Confederates in the Attic* is an interesting "journey" through the current-day South and demonstrates how the Civil War still echoes in the present. From Herman Hattaway's *Shades of Blue and Gray*, and James M. McPherson's *The Most Fearful Ordeal*, I moved to Michael Shaara's *The Killer Angels* and Bell I. Wiley's *The Life of Johnny Reb and the Life of Billy Yank*, and thence to James G. Hollandsworth, Jr.'s *The Louisiana Native Guards* and more…and more….I finally had to remind myself that I was NOT writing a Civil War epic, and move on.

To better understand what happened in Missouri during and after the Civil War and the War's (and the railroads') effects upon those who suffered through those hard times, I found T. J. Stiles' *Jesse James: Last Rebel of the Civil War* and Edward E. Leslie's *The Devil Knows How to Ride: The True Story of William Clarke Quantrill and His Confederate Raiders* very useful.

Roy Marcot's *Civil War Chief of Sharpshooters Hiram Berdan: Military Commander and Firearms Inventor* introduced me to Berdan's Sharpshooters, and the slim volume *The Confederate Whitworth Sharpshooters* by John Anderson Morrow provided insight, as did many other books and people. As an aside, R. L. Wilson's *Silk and Steel* was quite enlightening and might provide food for thought for anyone who believes the "weaker sex" and firearms don't mix. For information on the D&RG

and the building and running of railroads in general, I relied heavily on Robert Athearn's *The Denver and Rio Grande Western Railroad,* Stephen E. Ambrose's *Nothing Like It in the World,* David Hayward Bain's *Empire Express,* and Margaret Coel's *Goin' Railroading.*

Now, to the generals. There is plenty written about Ulysses S. Grant, but what about General William Jackson Palmer? Who was this man, who was raised a Philadelphia Quaker, became a Civil War general, and founded the Rio Grande as well as the city of Colorado Springs in Colorado? The readable *A Builder of the West* by John Fisher gave me the clues I needed. Every life has its shadows, and all I needed was something dark enough to hold a bit of mystery. I found it in an account of an incident that took place at the end of the War, with a young unnamed boy—all of 15—who took a potshot at General Palmer and missed.

Other "real-life" people who walk through these pages include D&RG chief engineer J. A. McMurtrie, and Marshal Cy Ayres. Their treatment in *Iron Ties* is purely fictional. (Although I have to say that what bits I found about McMurtrie indicated that he was a fellow not to be trifled with.)

As for the rest of the story, I took a broad paintbrush to some of the events and situations of the times. There was indeed a big mining strike in May and early June 1880. After the D&RG determined a location for their depot and freight yards, the good Sisters of Charity did indeed receive threats from "lot jumpers" anxious to move in on the lot housing St. Vincent's Hospital and make a killing. And some property owners north of Capitol Hill dug in their heels and refused to sell to the Rio Grande. Laying of track through town stopped, and Grant detrained not at the depot as hoped and planned, but at the foot of Third Street. Leadville did have a thriving charcoal business that suffered due to the coming of the railroads (albeit much later in time than indicated here), and certain transportation businesses—stage lines and haul companies—took hits from the railroad's coming as well.

These were exciting times in Leadville's history, with more excitement yet to come, so stay tuned.

Glossary

blasting cap: A small tube filled with detonating substances; used to detonate high explosives.

card shark: A professional cheater at cards.

cardsharp: One who habitually cheats at cards.

eminent domain: A term applied in law to the sovereign right of a state to appropriate private property to public uses, whether the owner consents or not. (From *Encyclopedia Britannica*, 1911)

fishplate: Metal plate bolted along sides of two rails or beams.

gandy dancer: A laborer in a railroad section gang.

giant powder: Dynamite composed of nitroglycerin and kieselguhr (a siliceous earth used to absorb the nitroglycerin).

percussion cap: A thin metal cap containing an explosive substance, such as fulminate of mercury, that explodes on being struck.

road agent: A highwayman in the mountain districts of North America. (And my favorite definition:) The name applied in the mountains to a ruffian who has given up honest work in the store, in the mine, in the ranch, for the perils and profits of the highway. (From *Dictionary of Phrase and Fable*, 1898)

rolling stock: The wheeled vehicles owned and used by a railroad or motor carrier.